Also by Aharon Appelfeld

Badenheim 1939

The Age of Wonders

The S

TZILI

The Story of a Life

Aharon Appelfeld

Translated by Dalya Bilu

E. P. Dutton, Inc.   *New York*

Published in the United States by E. P. Dutton, Inc.
2 Park Avenue, New York, N.Y. 10016

Library of Congress Cataloging in Publication Data

Appelfeld, Aron.
    Tzili, the story of a life.

    I. Title.
PJ5054.A755T9   1982   892.4'36   82-17770

ISBN: 0-525-24187-6

10 9 8 7 6 5 4 3 2

This novel was first serialized in *Molad*, in Israel, in the spring of 1982.

TZILI

The Story of a Life

TZILI

The Story of a Life

Also by Aharon Appelfeld

Badenheim 1939

The Age of Wonders

1

Perhaps it would be better to leave the story of Tzili Kraus's life untold. Her fate was a cruel and inglorious one, and but for the fact that it actually happened we would never have been able to tell her story. We will tell it in all simplicity, and begin right away by saying: Tzili was not an only child; she had older brothers and sisters. The family was large, poor, and harassed, and Tzili grew up neglected among the abandoned objects in the yard.

Her father was an invalid and her mother busy all day long in their little shop. In the evening, sometimes without even thinking, one of her brothers or sisters would pick her out of the dirt and take her into the house. She was a quiet creature, devoid of charm and almost mute. Tzili would get up early in the morning and go to bed at night like a squirrel, without complaints or tears.

And thus she grew. Most of the summer and autumn she spent out of doors. In winter she snuggled into her pillows. Since she was small and skinny and didn't get in anyone's way, they ignored her existence. Every now and then her mother would remember her and cry: "Tzili, where are you?" "Here." The answer would not be long in coming, and the mother's sudden panic would pass.

When she was seven years old they sewed her a satchel, bought her two copybooks, and sent her to school. It was a country school, built of gray stone and covered with a tiled roof. In this building she studied for five years. Unlike other members of her race, Tzili did not shine at school. She was clumsy and somewhat withdrawn. The big letters on the blackboard made her head spin. At the end of the first term there was no longer any doubt: Tzili was dull-witted. The mother was busy and harassed but she gave vent to her anger nevertheless: "You must work harder. Why don't you work harder?" The sick father, hearing the mother's threats, sighed in his bed: What was to become of them?

Tzili would learn things by heart and immediately forget them again. Even the gentile children knew more than she did. She would get mixed up. A Jewish girl without any brains! They delighted in her misfortune. Tzili would promise herself not to get mixed up, but the moment she stood in front of the blackboard the words vanished and her hands froze.

For hours she sat and studied. But all her efforts didn't help her. In the fourth grade she still hadn't mastered the multiplication table and her hand-writing was vague and confused. Sometimes her mother lost her temper and hit her. The sick father was no gentler than the mother. He would call her and ask: "Why don't you study?"

"I do study."

"Why don't you know anything?"

Tzili would hang her head.

"Why are you bringing this disgrace on your family?" He would grind his teeth.

The father's illness was fatal, but the dull presence of his youngest daughter hurt him more than his wound. Again and again he blamed her laziness, her unwillingness, but never her inability. "If you want to you can." This wasn't a judgment, but a faith. In this faith they were all united, the mother in the shop and her daughters at their books.

Tzili's brothers and sisters all worked with a will. They prepared for external examinations, registered for crash courses, devoured supplementary material. Tzili cooked, washed dishes, and weeded the garden. She was small and thin, and kneeling in the garden she looked like a servant girl.

But all her hard work did not save her from her disgrace. Again and again: "Why don't you know anything? Even the gentile children know more than you do." The riddle of Tzili's failure tortured everyone, but especially the mother. From time to time a deep groan burst from her chest, as if she were mourning a premature death.

In the winter evil rumors were already rife, but only echoes reached the remoter districts. The Kraus family labored like ants. They hoarded food, the daughters memorized dates, the younger son drew clumsy geometric figures on long sheets of paper. The examinations were imminent, and they cast their shadow over everyone. Heavy sighs emerged from the father's darkened room: "Study, children, study. Don't be lazy." The vestiges of a liturgical chant in his voice aroused his daughters' ire.

At home Tzili was sometimes forgotten, but at school, among all the gentile children, she was the butt of constant ridicule and scorn. Strange: she never cried or begged for mercy. Every day she went to her torture chamber and swallowed the dose of insults meted out to her.

Once a week a tutor came from the village to teach her her prayers. The family no longer observed the rituals of the Jewish religion, but her mother for some reason got it into her head that religious study would be good for Tzili, besides putting a little money the old man's way. The tutor came on different days of the week, in the afternoons. He never raised his voice to Tzili. For the first hour he would tell her stories from the Bible and for the second he would read the prayer

4

book with her. At the end of the lesson she would make him a cup of tea. "How is the child progressing?" the mother would ask every now and then. "She's a good girl," the old man would say. He knew that the family did not keep the Sabbath or pray, and he wondered why it had fallen to the lot of this dull child to keep the spark alive. Tzili did her best to please the old man, but as far as reading was concerned her progress left much to be desired. Among her brothers and sisters the old man's visits gave rise to indignation. He wore a white coat and shabby shoes, and his eyes glinted with the skepticism of a man whose scholarship had not helped him in his hour of need. His sons had emigrated to America, and he was left alone in the derelict old house. He knew that he was nothing but a lackey in the service of Tzili's family's hysteria, and that her brothers and sisters could not bear his presence in the house. He swallowed his humiliation quietly, but not without disgust.

At the end of the reading in the prayer book he would ask Tzili, in the traditional, unvarying formula:

"What is man?"

And Tzili would reply: "Dust and ashes."

"And before whom is he destined to stand in judgment?"

"Before the King of Kings, the Holy One blessed be He."

"And what must he do?"

"Pray and observe the commandments of the Torah."

"And where are the commandments of the Torah written?"

"In the Torah."

This set formula, spoken in a kind of lilt, would awaken loud echoes in Tzili's soul, and their reverberations spread throughout her body. Strange: Tzili was not afraid of the old man. His visits filled her with a kind of serenity which remained with her and protected her for many hours afterward. At night she would recite "Hear, O Israel" aloud, as he had instructed her, covering her face.

And thus she grew. But for the old man's visits her life would have been even more wretched. She learned to take up as little space as possible. She even went to the lavatory in secret, so as not to draw attention to herself. The old man, to tell the truth, felt no affection for her. From time to time he grew impatient and scolded her, but she liked listening to his voice and imagined that she heard tenderness in it.

2

When the war broke out they all ran away, leaving Tzili to look after the house. They thought nobody would harm a feeble-minded little girl, and until the storm had spent itself, she could take care of their property for them. Tzili heard their verdict without protest. They left in a panic, without time for second thoughts. "We'll come back for you later," said her brothers as they lifted their father onto the stretcher. And thus they parted from her.

That same night the soldiers invaded the town and destroyed it. A terrible wailing rose into the air. But Tzili, for some reason, escaped unharmed. Perhaps they didn't see her. She lay in the yard, among the barrels in the shed, covered with sacking. She knew that she had to look after the house, but her fear stopped her from doing so. Secretly she hoped for the sound of a familiar voice coming to call her. The air was full of loud screams, barks, and shots. In her fear she repeated the words she had been taught by the old man, over and over again. The mumbled words calmed her and she fell asleep.

She slept for a long time. When she woke it was night and everything was completely still. She poked her head out of the sacking, and the night sky appeared through the cracks in the roof of the shed. She lifted the upper half of her body, propping herself up on her elbows. Her feet were numb with cold. She passed both hands over the round columns of her legs and rubbed them. A pain shot through her feet.

For a long time she lay supporting herself on her elbows, looking at the sky. And while she lay listening, her lips parted and mumbled:

"Before whom is he destined to stand in judgment?"

"Before the King of Kings, the Holy One blessed be He."

The old man had insisted on the proper pronunciation of the words, and it was this insistence she remembered now.

But in the meantime the numbness left her legs, and she kicked away the sacking. She said to herself: "I must get up," and she stood up. The shed was much higher than she was. It was made of rough planks and used to store wood, barrels, an old bathtub, and a few earthenware pots. No one but Tzili paid any attention to this old shed, but for her it was a hiding place. Now she felt a kind of intimacy with the abandoned objects lying in it.

For the first time she found herself under the open night sky. When she was a baby they would close the shutters very early, and later on, when she grew up, they never let her go outside in the dark. For the first time she touched the darkness with her fingers.

She turned right, into the open fields. The sky suddenly grew taller, and she was small next to the standing corn. For a long time she walked without turning her head. Afterward she stopped and listened to the rustle of the leaves. A light breeze blew and the cool darkness assuaged her thirst a little.

On either side stretched crowded cornfields, one plot next to the other, with here and there a fence. Once or twice she stumbled and fell but she immediately rose to her feet again. In the end she hitched her dress up and tucked it into her belt, and this immediately liberated her legs. From now on she walked easily.

For some reason she began to run. A memory invaded her and frightened her. The memory was so dim that after she ran a little way it disappeared. She resumed her previous pace.

Her oldest sister, who was preparing for examinations, was the worst of them all. When she was swotting, she would chase Tzili away without even lifting her head from her books. Tzili loved her sister and the harsh words hurt her. Once her sister had said: "Get out of my sight. I never want to see you again. You make me nervous." Strange: these words rather than any others were the ones that seemed to carve themselves out of the darkness.

The darkness seeped slowly away. A few pale stripes appeared in the sky and turned a deeper pink. Tzili bent over to rub her feet and sat down. Unthinkingly she sank her teeth into a cornstalk. A stream of cool liquid washed her throat.

The light broke above her and poured onto her head. A few solitary animal cries drifted through the valley and a loud chorus of barks immediately rose to join them. She sat and listened. The distant sounds cradled her. Without thinking she fell asleep.

The sun warmed her body and she slept for many hours. When she woke she was bathed in sweat. She picked up her dress and shook off the grains of sand sticking to her skin. The sun caressed her limbs and for the first time she felt the sweet pain of being alone.

And while everything was still quiet and wrapped in shadows a shot pierced the air, followed by a sharp, interrupted scream. She bent down and covered her face. For a long time she did not lift her head. Now it seemed to her that something had happened to her body, in the region of the chest, but it was only a vague, hollow numbness after a day without eating.

The sun sank and Tzili saw her father lying on his bed. The last days at home, the rumors and the panic. Books and copybooks. No one showed any consideration for the feelings of his fellows. The examinations, which were to take place shortly in the distant town, threatened them all, especially her oldest sister. She tore out her hair in despair. Their mother too, in the shop, between one customer and the next, appeared to be repeating dates and formulas to herself. The truth was that she was angry. Only the sick father lay calmly in his bed. As if he had succeeded in steering the household onto the right course. He seemed to have forgotten his illness, perhaps even the dull presence of his youngest daughter. What he had failed to accomplish in his own life his children would accomplish for him: they would study. They would bring diplomas home.

And with these sights before her eyes she fell asleep.

3

When she woke, her memory was empty and weightless. She rose and left the cornfield and made for the outskirts of the forest. As if to spite her, another picture rose before her eyes, it too from the last days at home. Her youngest brother was adamant: he had to have a bicycle—all his friends, even the poorest, had bicycles. All his mother's pleas were in vain. She had no money. And what she had was not enough. Their father needed medicines. Tzili's seventeen-year-old brother shouted so loudly in the shop that strangers came in to quiet him. The mother wept with rage. And the older sister, who did not leave her books for a moment, shrieked: because of her family she would fail her exams. Tzili now remembered with great clarity her sister's white hand waving despairingly, as if she were drowning.

The day passed slowly, and visions of food no longer troubled her. She saw what was before her eyes: a thin forest and the golden calm of summer. All she had endured in the past days lost its terror.

She was borne forward unthinkingly on a stream of light. Even when she washed her face in the river she felt no strangeness. As if it had always been her habit to do so.

And while she was standing there a rustle went through the field. At first she thought it was the rustle of the leaves, but she immediately realized her mistake: her nose picked up the scent of a man. Before she had time to recover she saw, right next to her, a man sitting on a little hillock.

"Who's there?" said the man, without raising his voice.

"Me," said Tzili, her usual reply to this question.

"Who do you belong to?" he asked, in the village way.

When she did not answer right away, the man raised his head and added: "What are you doing here?"

When she saw that the man was blind, she relaxed and said: "I came to see if the corn was ready for the harvesting." She had often heard these words spoken in the shop. Since the same sentence, with slight variations, was repeated every season, it had become part of her memory.

"The corn came up nicely this year," said the blind man, stroking his jacket. "Am I mistaken?"

"No father, you're not mistaken."

"How high is it?"

"As high as a man, or even higher."

"The rains were plentiful," said the blind man, and licked his lips.

His blind face went blank and he fell silent.

"What time is it?"

"Noon, father."

He was wearing a coarse linen jacket and he was barefoot. He sat at his ease. The years of labor were evident in his sturdy shoulders. Now he was looking for a word to say, but the word evaded him. He licked his lips.

"You're Maria's daughter, aren't you?" he said and chuckled.

"Yes," said Tzili, lowering her voice.

"So we're not strangers."

Maria's name was a household word throughout the district. She had many daughters, all bastards. Because they were all good-looking, like their mother, nobody harmed them. Young and old alike availed themselves of their favors. Even the Jews who came for the summer holidays. In Tzili's house Maria's name was never spoken directly.

A number of years before, Tzili's older brother had gotten one of Maria's daughters into trouble. Maria herself had appeared in the shop and created a scene. For days, the family had consulted in whispers, and in the end they had been obliged to hand over a tidy sum. The mother, worn out with work, had refused to forgive her son. She found frequent occasions to refer to his crime. Tzili had not, of course, grasped the details of the

15

affair, but she sensed that it was something dark and sordid, not to be spoken of directly. Later on, their mother forgave her brother, because he began to study and also to excel.

"Sit down," said the blind man. "What's your hurry?"

She approached and seated herself wordlessly by his side. She was used to the blind. They would congregate outside the shop and sit there for hours at a time. Every now and then her mother would emerge and offer them a loaf of bread, and they would munch it noisily. Mostly they would sit in silence, but sometimes they would grow irritable and begin to quarrel. Her father would go out to restore order. Tzili would sit and watch them for hours. Their mute, upraised faces reminded her of people praying.

The blind man seemed to rouse himself. He groped for his satchel, took out a pear and said: "Here, take it."

Tzili took it and immediately sank her teeth into the fruit.

"I have some smoked meat too—will you have some?"

"I will."

He held the thick sandwich out in his big hand. Tzili looked at the big pale hand and took the sandwich. "Maria's daughters are all good-looking girls," he said and snickered. Now that he had straightened the upper half of his body he looked very strong. Even his white hands. "I don't like eating alone. Eating alone depresses me," he confessed. He chewed calmly and carefully, as blind men will, as if they were suspicious even of the food they put in their mouths.

As he ate he said: "They're killing the Jews. The pests. Let them go to America." But he didn't seem particularly concerned. He was more concerned with the coming harvest.

"Why are you so silent?" he said suddenly.

"What's there to say?"

"Maria's daughters are a cunning lot."

Tzili did not yet know that the notorious name of Maria would be her shield from danger. All her senses were concentrated on the thick sandwich the blind man had given her.

Once Maria had been a customer at the shop. She was a handsome, well-dressed woman and she used city words. They said that Maria had a soft spot for Jews, which did not add to her reputation. Her daughters too had inherited this fondness. And when the Jewish vacationers appeared, Maria would have a taste of what it meant to be indulged.

Tzili now remembered nothing but the heavy scent Maria left behind her in the shop. She liked breathing in this scent.

The blind man said casually: "Maria's daughters

love the Jews, may God forgive them." And he snickered to himself again. Then he sat there quietly, as if he were a cow chewing the cud.

Now there was no sound but for the birds and the rustling of the leaves, and they too seemed muted. The blind man abandoned his full face to the sun and seemed about to fall asleep.

Suddenly he asked: "Is there anyone in the field?"

"No."

"And where did you come from?" The full face smiled.

"From the village square."

"And there's no one in the field?" he asked again, as if he wanted to hear the sound of his own voice.

"No one."

Upon hearing Tzili's reply he reached out and put his hand on her shoulder. Tzili's shoulder slumped under the weight of his hand.

"Why are you so skinny?" said the blind man, apparently encountering her narrow shoulder bones. "How old are you?"

"Thirteen."

"And so skinny." He clutched her with his other hand, too, the one he had been leaning on.

Tzili's body recoiled from the violence of the peasant's embrace, and he threw her onto the ground with no more ado.

A scream escaped her lips.

The blind man, apparently taken aback by this reaction, hurried to stop her mouth but his hand missed its aim and fell onto her neck. Her body writhed under the blind man's heavy hands.

"Quiet! What's the matter with you?" He tried to quiet her as if she were a restless animal. Tzili choked. She tried to wriggle out from under the weight.

"What has your mother been feeding you to make you choke like that?"

The blind man loosened his grip, apparently under the impression that Tzili was too stunned to move. With a swift, agile movement she slipped out of his hands.

"Where are you?" he said, spreading out his hands.

Tzili retreated on her hands and knees.

"Where are you?" He groped on the ground. And when there was no reply, he started waving his hands in the air and cursing. His voice, which had sounded soft a moment before, grew hoarse and angry.

For some reason Tzili did not run away. She crawled on all fours to the field. Evening fell and she curled up. The blind man's strong hands were still imprinted on her shoulders, but the pain faded as the darkness deepened.

Later the blind man's son came to take him home. As soon as he heard his son approaching, the blind man began to curse. The son said that one of the shafts had broken on the way and he had had to go back to the village to get another cart. The father was not convinced by this story and he said: "Why couldn't you walk?"

"Sorry, father, I didn't think of it. I didn't have the sense."

"But for the girls you've got sense enough."

"What girls, father?" said the son innocently.

"God damn your soul," said the blind man and spat.

4

By now Tzili's memories of home were blurred. They've all gone, she said blankly to herself. The little food she ate appeased her hunger. She was tired. A kind of hollowness, without even the shadow of a thought, plunged her into a deep sleep.

But her body had no rest that night. It seethed. Painful sensations woke her from time to time. What's happening to me? she asked herself, not without resentment. She feared her body, as if something alien had taken possession of it.

When she woke and rose to her feet it was still night. She felt her feet, and when she found nothing wrong with them she was reassured. She sat and listened attentively to her body. It was a cloudless and windless night. Above the bowed tops of the corn a dull flame gleamed. From below, the stalks looked like tall trees. She was astonished by the stillness.

And while she stood there listening she felt a liquid oozing from her body. She felt her belly, it was tight but dry. Her muscles throbbed rhythmically. "What's happening to me?" she said.

21

When dawn broke she saw that her dress was stained with a number of bright spots of blood. She lifted up her dress. There were a couple of spots on the ground too. "I'm going to die." The words escaped her lips.

A number of years before, her oldest sister had cut her finger on a kitchen knife. And by the time the male nurse came, the floor was covered with dark blood stains. When he finally arrived, he clapped his hands to his head in horror. And ever since they had spoken about Blanca's weak, wounded finger in solicitous tones.

"I'm going to die," she said, and all at once she rose to her feet. The sudden movement alarmed her even more. A chill ran down her spine and she shivered. The thought that soon she would be lying dead became more concrete to her than her own feet. She began to whimper like an animal. She knew that she must not scream, but fear made her reckless. "Mother, mother!" she wailed. She went on screaming for a long time. Her voice grew weaker and weaker and she fell to the ground with her arms spread out, as she imagined her body would lie in death.

When she had composed herself a little, she saw her sister sitting at the table. In the last year she had tortured herself with algebra. They had to bring a tutor from the neighboring town. The tutor turned out to be a harsh, strict man and Blanca was terrified of him. She wept, but no one paid any attention to her tears. The father too, from his sick bed, demanded the impossible of her. And she did it too. Although she did not complete the paper and obtained a low mark, she did not fail. Now Tzili saw her sister as she had never seen her before, struggling with both hands against the Angel of Death.

And as the light rose higher in the sky, Tzili heard the trudge of approaching feet. One of the blind man's daughters was leading her father to his place. He was grumbling. Cursing his wife and daughters. The girl did not reply. Tzili listened intently to the footsteps. When they reached his place on the hillock the girl said: "With your permission, father, I'll go back to the pasture now."

"Go!" He dismissed her, but immediately changed his mind and added: "That's the way you honor your father."

"What shall I do, father?" Her voice trembled.

"Tell your father the latest news in the village."

"They chased the Jews away and they killed them too."

"All of them?" he asked, with a dry kind of curiosity.

"Yes, father."

"And their houses? What happened to their houses?"

"The peasants are looting them," she said, lowering her voice as if she were repeating some scandalous piece of gossip.

"What do you say? Maybe you can find me a winter coat."

"I'll look for one, father."

"Don't forget."

"I won't forget."

Tzili took in this exchange, but not its terrible meaning. She was no longer afraid. She knew that the blind man would not move from his place.

5

Hours of silence came. Her oppression lifted. And after her weeping she felt a sense of release. "It's better now," she whispered, to banish the remnants of the fear still congealed inside her. She lay flat on her back. The late summer sunlight warmed her body from top to toe. The last words left her and the old hunger that had troubled her the day before came back.

When night fell she bandaged her loins with her shawl, and without thinking about where she was going she walked on. The night was clear, and delicate drops of light sparkled on the broad cornfields. The bandage pressing against her felt good, and she walked on. She came across a stream and bent down to cup the water in her hands and drink. Only now did she realize how thirsty she was. She sat calmly and watched the running water. The sights of home dissolved in the cool air. Her fear shrank. From time to time brief words or syllables escaped her lips, but they were only the sighs that come after long weeping.

She slept and woke and slept again and saw her old teacher. The look in his eye was neither kindly nor benign, but appraising, the way he looked at her when she was reading from the prayer book. It was a dispassionate, slightly mocking look. Strange, she tried to explain something to him but the words were muted in her mouth. In the end she succeeded in saying: I am setting out on a long journey. Give me your blessing, teacher. But she didn't really say it, she only imagined saying it. Her intention made no impression on the old man, as if it were just one more of her many mistakes.

Afterward she wandered in the outskirts of the forest. Her food was meager: a few wild cherries, apples, and various kinds of sour little fruits which quenched her thirst. The hunger for bread left her. From time to time she went down to the river and dipped her feet in the water. The cold water brought back memories of the winter, her sick father groaning and asking for another blanket. But these were only fleeting sensations. Day by day her body was detaching itself from home. The wound was fresh but not unhealthy. The seeds of oblivion had already been sown. She did not wash her body. She was afraid of removing the shawl from her loins. The sour smell grew worse.

"You must wash yourself," a voice whispered.

"I'm afraid."

"You must wash yourself," the voice repeated.

In the afternoon, without taking off her dress,

she stepped into the river. The water seeped into her until she felt it burn. And immediately drops of blood rose to the surface of the water and surrounded her. She gazed at them in astonishment. Afterward she lay on the ground.

The water was good for her, but not the fruit. In these early days she did not yet know how to distinguish between red and red, between black and black. She plucked whatever came to hand, blackberries and raspberries, strawberries and cherries. In the evening she had severe pain in her stomach and diarrhea. Her slender legs could not stand up to the pain and they gave way beneath her. "God, God." The words escaped her lips. Her voice disappeared into the lofty greenness. If she had had the strength, she would have crawled into the village and given herself up.

"What are you doing here?"

She was suddenly startled by a peasant's voice.

"I'm ill."

"Who do you belong to?"

"Maria."

The peasant stared at her in disgust, pursed his mouth, and turned away without another word.

6

Autumn was already at its height, and in the evenings the horizon was blue with cold. Tzili would
find shelter for the night in deserted barns and
stables. From time to time she would approach a
farmhouse and ask for a piece of bread. Her
clothes gave off a bad, moldy smell and her face
was covered with a rash of little pimples.

She did not know how repulsive she looked.
She roamed the outskirts of the forest and the
peasants who crossed her path averted their eyes.
When she approached farmhouses to beg for bread
the housewives would chase her away as if she
were a mangy dog. "Here's Maria's daughter," she
would hear them say. Her ugly existence became a
byword and a cautionary tale in the mouths of the
local peasants, but the passing days were kind to
her, molding her in secret, at first deadening and
then quickening her with new life. The sick blood
poured out of her. She learned to walk barefoot, to
bathe in the icy water, to tell the edible berries
from the poisonous ones, to climb the trees. The
sun worked wonders with her. The visions of the
night gradually left her. She saw only what was in

front of her eyes, a tree, a puddle, the autumn leaves changing color.

For hours she would sit and gaze at the empty fields sinking slowly into grayness. In the orchards the leaves turned red. Her life seemed to fall away from her, she coiled in on herself like a cocoon. And at night she fell unconscious onto the straw.

One day she came across a hut on the fringes of the forest. Autumn was drawing to a close. It rained and hailed incessantly, and the frost ate into her bones. But she was no longer afraid of anyone, not even the wild dogs.

A woman opened the door and said: "Who are you?"

"Maria's daughter," said Tzili.

"Maria's daughter! Why are you standing there? Come inside!"

The woman seemed thunderstruck. "Maria's daughter, barefoot in this frost! Take off your clothes. I'll give you a gown."

Tzili took off her mildewed clothes and put on the gown. It was a fancy city gown, flowered and soaked in perfume. After many months of wandering, she had a roof over her head.

"Your mother and I were young together once, in the city. Fate must have brought you to my door."

Tzili looked at her from close up: a woman no longer young, with frizzy hair and prominent cheekbones.

"And what is your mother doing now?"

Tzili hesitated a moment and said: "She's at home."

"My name is Katerina," said the woman. "If you see your mother tell her you saw Katerina. She'll be very glad to hear it. We had a lot of good times together in the city, especially with the Jews."

Tzili trembled.

"The Jews are great lovers. Ours aren't a patch on them, I can tell you that—but we were fools then, we came back to the village to look for husbands. We were young and afraid of our fathers. Jewish lovers are worth their weight in gold. Let me give you some soup," said Katerina and hurried off to fetch a bowl of soup.

After many days of wandering, loneliness, and cold, she took in the hot liquid like a healing balm.

Katerina poured herself a drink and immediately embarked on reminiscences of her bygone days in the city, when she and Maria had queened it with the Jews, at first as chambermaids and later as mistresses. Her voice was full of longing.

"The Jews are gentle. The Jews are generous and kind. They know how to treat a woman properly. Not like our men, who don't know anything except how to beat us up." In the course of the years she had learned a little Yiddish, and she still remembered a few words—the word *dafka*, for instance.

Tzili felt drawn into the charmed circle of Katerina's memories. "Thank you," she said.

"You don't have to thank me, girl," scolded Katerina. "Your mother and I were good friends once. We sat in the same cafés together, made love to the same man."

Katerina poured herself drink after drink. Her high cheekbones stuck out and her eyes peered into the distance with a birdlike sharpness. Suddenly she said: "The Jews, damn them, know how to give a woman what she needs. What does a woman need, after all? A little kindness, money, a box of chocolates every now and then, a bed to lie on. What more does a woman need? And what have I got now? You can see for yourself.

"Your mother and I were fools, stupid fools. What's there to be afraid of? I'm not afraid of hell. My late mother never stopped nagging me: Katerina, why don't you get married? All the other girls are getting married. And I like a fool listened to her. I'll never forgive her. And you." She turned to Tzili with a piercing look. "You don't get married, you hear me? And don't bring any little bastards into the world either. Only the Jews, only the Jews—they're the only ones who'll take you out to cafés, to restaurants, to the cinema. They'll always take you to a clean hotel, only the Jews."

Tzili no longer took in the words. The warmth and the scented gown cradled her: her head dropped and she fell asleep.

7

From the first day Tzili knew what was expected
of her. She swept the floor and washed the dishes,
she hurried to peel the potatoes. No work was too
arduous for her. The months out of doors seemed
to have taught her what it meant to serve others.
She never left a job half done and she never got
mixed up. And whenever it stopped raining she
would take the skinny old cow out to graze.

Katerina lay in her bed wrapped in goat skins,
coughing and sipping tea and vodka by turn. From
time to time she rose and went to stand by the
window. It was a poor house with a dilapidated
stable beside it. And in the yard: a few pieces of
wood, a gaping fence, and a neglected vegetable
patch. These were the houses outside the village
borders, where the lepers and the lunatics, the
horse thieves and the prostitutes lived. For generations one had replaced the other here, without re-
pairing the houses or cultivating the plots. The
passing seasons would knead such places in their
hands until they could not be told apart from
abandoned forest clearings.

In the evening the softness would come back to her voice and she would speak again of the days in the city when she and Maria walked the streets together. What was left of all that now? She was here and they were there. In the city a thousand lights shone—and here she was surrounded by mud, madmen and lepers.

Sometimes she put on one of her old dresses, made up her face, stood by the window, and announced: "Tomorrow I'm leaving. I'm sick of this. I'm only forty. A woman of forty isn't ready for the rubbish dump yet. The Jews will take me as I am. They love me."

Of course, these were hallucinations. Nobody came to take her away. Her cough gave her no rest, and every now and then she would wake the sleeping Tzili and command her: "Make me some tea. I'm dying." At night, when a fit of coughing seized her, her face grew bitter and malign, and no one escaped the rough edge of her tongue, not even the Jews.

Once in a while an old customer appeared and breathed new life into the hut. Katerina would get dressed, make up her face, and douse herself with perfume. She liked the robust peasants, who clutched her round the waist and crushed her body to them. Her old voice would come back to her, very feminine. All of a sudden she would be transformed, laughing and joking, reminiscing

34

about times gone by. And she would reprimand Tzili too, and instruct her: "That's not the way to offer a man a drink. A man likes his vodka first, bread later." Or: "Don't cut the sausage so thin."

But such evenings were few and far between. Katerina would wrap herself in blankets and whimper in a sick voice: "I'm cold. Why don't you make the fire properly? The wood's wet. This wetness is driving me out of my mind."

Tzili learned that Katerina was a bold, hot-tempered woman. Knives and axes had no fears for her. At the sight of an unsheathed knife all her beauty burst forth. With drunks she was gentle, speaking to them in a tender and maternal voice.

Although their houses were far apart, Katerina was at daggers drawn with her neighbors. Once a day the leper would emerge from his house and curse Katerina, yelling at the top of his voice. And when he started walking toward her door, Katerina would rush out to meet him like a mad-dened dog. He was a big peasant, his body pink all over from the disease.

Winter came, and snow. Tzili went far into the forest to gather firewood. When she came back in the evening with a bundle of twigs on her shoul-ders bigger than she was, Katerina was still not satisfied. She would grumble: "I'm cold. Why didn't you bring thicker branches? You're spoiled. You need a good hiding. I took you in like a mother and you're shirking your work. You're like your mother. She only looked out for herself. I'm going to give you a good beating."

Of Katerina's plans for her Tzili had no inkling. Her life was one of labor, oblivion, and uncomprehending delight. She delighted in the hut, the faded feminine objects, and the scents that frequently filled the air. She even delighted in the emaciated cow.

From time to time Katerina gave her significant looks: "Your breasts are growing. But you're still too skinny. You should eat more potatoes. How old are you? At your age I was already on the streets." Or sometimes in a maternal voice: "Why don't you comb your hair? People are coming and your hair's not combed."

Winter deepened and Katerina's cough never left her for an instant. She drank vodka and boiling-hot tea, but the cough would not go away. From night to night it grew harsher. She would wake Tzili up and scold her: "Why don't you bring me a glass of tea? Can't you hear me coughing?" Tzili would tear herself out of her sleep and hasten to get Katerina a glass of tea.

It was a long winter and Katerina never stopped grumbling and cursing her sisters, her father, and all the seekers of her favors who had devoured her body. Her face grew haggard. She could no longer stand on her feet. There were no more visitors. The only ones who still came were drunk or crazy.

At first she tried to pretend, but now it was no longer possible to hide her illness. The men fled from the house. Katerina accompanied their flight with curses. But the worst of her rage she spent on Tzili. From time to time she threw a plate or a pot at her. Tzili absorbed the blows in silence. Once Katerina said to her: "At your age I was already keeping my father."

8

Spring came and Katerina felt better. Tzili made up a bed for her outside the door. Now too she kept up a constant stream of abuse, but to Tzili she spoke mildly: "Why don't you go and wash yourself? There's a mirror in the house. Go and comb your hair." And once she even offered her one of her scented creams. "A girl of your age should perfume her neck."

Tzili worked without a break from morning to night. She ate whatever she could lay her hands on: bread, milk, and vegetables from the garden. Her day was full to overflowing. And at night she fell onto her bed like a sack.

No one came to ask for Katerina's favors any more and her money ran out. Even the male nurse, who pulled out two of her teeth, failed to collect his due. Katerina would stand slumped in the doorway.

One evening she asked Tzili: "Have you ever been to bed with a man?"

"No." Tzili shuddered.

"And don't you feel the need? At your age," said Katerina, with almost maternal tenderness, "I had already known many men. I was even married."

"Did you have any children?" asked Tzili.

"I did, but I gave them away when they were babies."

Tzili asked no more. Katerina's face was angry and bitter. She realized that she shouldn't have asked.

Summer came and there was no end to Katerina's complaints. She would speak of her youth, of her lovers, of the city and of money. Now she hardened her heart toward her Jewish lovers too and abused them roundly. The accusations poured out of her in a vindictive stream, scrambled up with fantasies and wishes. Every now and then she would get up and hurl a plate across the room, and the walls would shake with the clatter and the curses. Tzili's movements grew more and more confined, and the old fear came back to her.

From time to time Katerina would berate her: "At your age I was already keeping my father, and you . . ."

"What do you want me to do, mother?"

"Do you have to ask? I didn't have to ask my father. I went to the city and sent him money every month. A daughter has to look after her parents. I let those guzzlers devour my body."

Tzili's heart was full of foreboding. She guessed

that something bad was going to happen, but she didn't know what. Her happiest hours were the ones she spent in the meadows grazing the cow. The air and light kneaded her limbs with a firm and gentle touch. From time to time she would take off her clothes and bathe in the river.

Katerina watched her with an eagle eye: "Your health is improving every day and I'm being eaten up with illness." Her back was very bent, and without her front teeth her face had a ghoulish, nightmare look.

One evening an old client of Katerina's came to call, a burly middle-aged peasant. Katerina was lying in bed.

"What's the matter with you?" he asked in surprise.

"I'm resting. Can't a woman rest?"

"I just wanted to say hello," he said, retreating to the door.

"Why not stay a while and have a drink?"

"I've already had more than enough."

"Just one little drink."

"Thanks. I just dropped in to say hello."

Suddenly she raised herself on her elbows, smiled and said: "Why don't you take the little lass to bed? You won't be sorry."

The peasant turned his head with a dull, slow movement, like an animal, and an embarrassed smile appeared on his lips.

"She may be small but she's got plenty of flesh

on her bones." Katerina coaxed him. "You can take my word for it."

Tzili was standing in the scullery. The words were quite clear. They sent a shiver down her spine.

"Come here," commanded Katerina. "Show him your thighs."

Tzili stood still.

"Pick up your dress," commanded Katerina.

Tzili picked up her dress.

"You see, I wasn't lying to you."

The peasant dropped his eyes. He examined Tzili's legs. "She's too young," he said.

"Don't be a fool."

Tzili stood holding her dress fearfully in her hands.

"I'll come on Sunday," said the peasant.

"She's got breasts already, can't you see?"

"I'll come on Sunday," repeated the peasant.

"Go then. You're a fool. Any other man would jump at the chance."

"I don't feel like it today. I'll come on Sunday."

But he lingered in the doorway, measuring the little girl with his eyes, and for a moment he seemed about to drag her into the scullery. In the end he recovered himself and repeated: "I'll come on Sunday."

"You fool," said Katerina with an offended air, as if she had offered him a tasty dish and he had refused to eat it. And to Tzili she said: "Don't stand there like a lump of wood."

Tzili dropped her dress.

For a moment longer Katerina surveyed the peasant with her bloodshot eyes. Then she picked up a wooden plate and threw it. The plate hit Tzili and she screamed. "What are you screaming about? At your age I was already keeping my father."

The peasant hesitated no longer. He picked up his heels and ran.

Now Katerina gave her tongue free rein, abusing and cursing everyone, especially Maria. Tzili's fears were concentrated on the sharp knife lying next to the bed. The knife sailed through the air and hit the door. Tzili fled.

9

The night was full and starless. Tzili walked along the paths she now knew by heart. For some reason she kept close to the river. On either side, the cornfields stretched, broad and dark. "I'll go on," she said, without knowing what she was saying.

She had learned many things during the past year: how to launder clothes, wash dishes, offer a man a drink, collect firewood, and pasture a cow, but above all she had learned the virtues of the wind and the water. She knew the north wind and the cold river water. They had kneaded her from within. She had grown taller and her arms had grown strong. The further she walked from Katerina's hut the more closely she felt her presence. As if she were still standing in the scullery. She felt no resentment toward her.

"I'll go on," she said, but her legs refused to move.

She remembered the long, cozy nights at Katerina's. Katerina lying in bed and weaving fantasies about her youth in the city, parties and lovers. Her face calm and a smile on her lips. When she spoke about the Jews her smile narrowed and grew more modest, as if she were revealing some great secret. It seemed then as if she acquiesced in everything, even in the disease devouring her body. Such was life.

Sometimes too she would speak of her beliefs, her fear of God and his Messiah, and at these moments a strange light seemed to touch her face. Her mother and father she could not forgive. And once she even said: "Pardon me for not being able to forgive you."

Tzili felt affection even for the old, used objects Katerina had collected over the years. Gilt powder boxes, bottles of eau de cologne, crumpled silk petticoats and dozens of lipsticks—these objects held an intimate kind of magic.

And she remembered too: "Have you ever been to bed with a man?"

"No."

"And don't you feel the need?"

Katerina's face grew cunning and wanton.

And on one of the last days Katerina asked: "You won't desert me?"

"No," promised Tzili.

"Swear by our Lord Saviour."

"I swear by our Lord Saviour."

Of the extent to which she had been changed by the months with Katerina, Tzili was unaware. Her feet had thickened and she now walked surely

46

over the hard ground. And she had learned something else too: there were men and there were
women and between them there was an eternal
enmity. Women could not survive save by cunning.

Sometimes she said to herself: I'll go back to
Katerina. She'll forgive me. But when she turned
around her legs froze. It was not the knife itself she
feared but the glitter of the blade.

Summer was at its height, and there was no rain.
She lived on the fruit growing wild on the river
banks. Sometimes she approached a farmhouse.

"Who are you?"

"Maria's daughter."

Maria's reputation had reached even these remote farmhouses. At the sound of her name, a look
of loathing appeared on the faces of the farmers'
wives. Sometimes they said in astonishment:
"You're Maria's daughter!" The farmers themselves were less severe: in their youth they had
availed themselves freely of Maria's favors, and in
later years too they had occasionally climbed into
her bed.

And one day, as she stood in a field, the old
memory came back to confront her: her father lying on his sickbed, the sound of his sighs rending
the air, her mother in the shop struggling with the
violent peasants. Blanca as always, under the
shadow of the impending examinations, a pile of
books and papers on her table. And in the middle

of the panic, the bustle, and the hysteria, the clear sound of her father's voice: "Where's Tzili?"

"Here I am."

"Come here. What mark did you get in the arithmetic test?"

"I failed, father."

"You failed again."

"This time Blanca helped me."

"And it didn't do any good. What will become of you?"

"I don't know."

"You must try harder."

Tzili shuddered at the clear vision that came to her in the middle of the field. For a moment she stood looking around her, and then she picked up her feet and began to run. Her panic-stricken flight blurred the vision and she fell spread-eagled onto the ground. The field stretched yellow-gray around her without a soul in sight.

"Katerina," she said, "I'm coming back to you." As soon as the words were out of her mouth she saw the burly peasant in front of her, examining her thighs as she lifted up her skirt. Now she was no longer afraid of him. She was afraid of the ancient sights pressing themselves upon her with a harsh kind of clarity.

10

In the autumn she found shelter with an old couple. They lived in a poor hut far from everything.

"Who are you?" asked the peasant.

"Maria's daughter."

"That whore," said his wife. "I don't want her daughter in the house."

"She'll help us," said the man.

"No bastard is going to bring us salvation," grumbled the wife.

"Quiet, woman." He cut her short.

And thus Tzili found a shelter. Unlike Katerina's place, there were no luxuries here. The hut was composed of one long room containing a stove, a rough wooden table, and two benches. In the corner, a couple of stools. And above the stools a Madonna carved in oak, as simple as the work of a child.

It was a long, gray autumn, and on the monotonous plains everything seemed made of mud and fog. Even the people seemed to be made of the same substance: rough and violent, their tongue that of the pitchfork and cattle prod. The wife would wake her while it was still dark and push her outside with grunts: go milk the cows, go take them to the meadow.

The long hours in the meadows were her own. Her imagination did not soar but the little she possessed warmed her like soft, pure wool. Katerina, of course. In this gray place her former life with Katerina seemed full of interest. Here there were only cows, cows and speechlessness. The man and his wife communicated in grunts. If they ran short of milk or wood for the fire, the wife never asked why but brandished the rope as a sign that something was amiss.

Here for the first time she felt the full strength of her arms. At Katerina's they had grown stronger. Now she lifted the pitchfork easily into the air. The columns of her legs too were full of muscles. She ate whatever she could lay her hands on, heartily. But life was not as simple as she imagined. One night she awoke to the touch of a hand on her leg. To her surprise it was the old man. The old woman climbed out of bed after him shouting: "Adulterer!" And he returned chastised to his bed.

This was all the old woman was waiting for. After that she spoke to Tzili like a stray mongrel dog.

It was the middle of winter and the days darkened. The snow piled up in the doorway and barred their way out. Tzili sat for hours in the stable with the cows. She sensed the thin pipes joining her to these dumb worlds. She did not know what one said to cows, but she felt the warmth emanating from their bodies seeping into her. Sometimes she saw her mother in the shop struggling with hooligans. A woman without fear. In this dark stable everything seemed so remote— was more like a previous incarnation than her own life.

Between one darkness and the next the old woman would beat Tzili. The bastard had to be beaten so that she would know who she was and what she had to do to mend her ways. The woman would beat her fervently, as if she were performing some secret religious duty.

When spring comes I'll run away, Tzili would say to herself on her bed at night. Or: Why did I ever leave Katerina? She was good to me. Now she felt a secret affection for Katerina's hut, as if it were not a miserable cottage but an enchanted palace.

Sometimes she would hear her voice saying, "The Jews are weak, but they're gentle too. A Jew would never strike a woman." This mystery seemed to melt into Tzili's body and flood it with sweetness. At times like these her mind would shrink to next to nothing and she would be given over entirely to sensations. When she heard Katerina's voice she would curl up and listen as if to music.

But the old man could not rest, and every now

and then he would dart out of bed and try to reach her. And once, in his avidity, he bit her leg, but the old woman was too quick for him and dragged him off before he could go any further. "Adulterer!" she cried.

Sometimes he would put on an expression of injured innocence and say: "What harm have I done?"

"Your evil thoughts are driving you out of your mind."

"What have I done?"

"You can still ask!"

"I swear to you . . ." The old man would try to justify himself.

"Don't swear. You'll roast in hell!"

"Me?"

"You, you rascal."

The winter stretched out long and cold, and the grayness changed from one shade to another. There was nowhere to hide. It seemed that the whole universe was about to sink beneath the weight of the black snow. Once the old woman asked her: "How long is it since you saw your mother?"

"Many years."

"It was from her that you learned your wicked ways. Why are you silent? You can tell us. We know your mother only too well. Her and all her scandals. Even I had to watch my old man day and night. Not that it did me any good. Men are born adulterers. They'd find a way to cheat on their wives in hell itself."

Toward the end of winter the old woman lost control of herself. She beat Tzili indiscriminately. "If I don't make her mend her ways, who will?" She beat her devoutly with a wet rope so that the strokes would leave their mark on her back. Tzili screamed with pain, but her screams did not help her. The old woman beat her with extraordinary strength. And once, when the old man tried to intervene, she said: "You'd better shut up or I'll beat you too. You old lecher. God will thank me for it." And the old man, who usually gave back as good as he got, kept quiet. As if he had heard a warning voice from on high.

11

When the snow began to thaw she fled. The old woman guessed that she was about to escape and kept muttering to herself: "As long as she's here I'm going to teach her a lesson she'll never forget. Who knows what she's still capable of?"

Now Tzili was like a prisoner freed from chains. She ran. The heads of the mountains were still capped with snow, but in the black valleys below, the rivers flowed loud and torrential as waterfalls.

Her body was bruised and swollen. In the last days the old woman had whipped her mercilessly. She had whipped her as if it were her solemn duty to do so, until in the end Tzili too felt that she was only getting what she deserved.

But for the mud she would have walked by the riverside. She liked walking on the banks of the river. For some reason she believed that nothing bad would happen to her next to the water, but she was obliged to walk across the bare mountainside, washed by the melted snow. The valleys were full of mud.

She came to the edge of a forest. The fields

spreading below it steamed in the sun. She sat down and fell asleep. When she woke the sun was on the other side of the horizon, low and cold.

She tried to remember. She no longer remembered anything. The long winter had annihilated even the little memory she possessed. Only her feet sensed the earth as they walked. She knew this piece of ground better than her own body. A strange, uncomprehending sorrow suddenly took hold of her.

She took the rags carefully off her feet and then bound them on again. She treated her feet with a curious solemnity. It did not occur to her to ask what would happen when darkness fell. The sun was sinking fast on the horizon. For some reason she remembered that Katerina had once said to her, in a rare moment of peace: "Women are lucky. They don't have to go to war."

Now she felt detached from everyone. She had felt the same thing before, but not in the same way. Sometimes she would imagine that someone was waiting for her, far away on the horizon. And she would feel herself drawn toward it. Now she seemed to understand instinctively that there was no point going on.

As she sat staring into space, a sudden dread descended on her. What is it? she said and rose to her feet. There was no sound but for the gurgle of the water. On the leafless trees in the distance a blue light flickered.

It occurred to her that this was her punishment. The old woman had said that many punishments were in store for her. "There's no salvation for bastards!" she would shriek.

"What have I done wrong?" Tzili once asked uncautiously.

"You were born in sin," said the old woman. "A woman born in sin has to be cleansed, she has to be purified."

"How is that done?" asked Tzili meekly.

"I'll help you," said the old woman.

That night she found shelter in an abandoned shed. It was cold and her body was sore, but she was content, like a lost animal whose neck has been freed from its yoke at last. She slept for hours on the damp straw. And in her dreams she saw Katerina, not the sick Katerina but the young Katerina. She was wearing a transparent dress, sitting by a dressing table, and powdering her face.

12

When she woke it was daylight. Scented vapors rose from the fields. And while she was sitting there a man seemed to come floating up from the depths of the earth. For a moment they measured each other with their eyes. She saw immediately: he was not a peasant. His city suit was faded and his face exhausted.

"Who are you?" he asked in the local dialect. His voice was weak but clear.

"Me?" she asked, startled.

"Where are you from?"

"The village."

This reply confused him. He turned his head slowly to see if anyone was there. There was no one. She smelled the stale odor of his mildewed clothes.

"And what are you doing here?"

She raised herself slightly on her hands and said: "Nothing."

The man made a gesture with his hand as if he was about to turn his back on her. But then he said: "And when are you going back there?"

"Me?"

Now it appeared that the conversation was over. But the man was not satisfied. He stroked his coat. He seemed about forty and his hands were a grayish white, like the hands of someone who had not known the shelter of a man-made roof for a long time.

Tzili rose to her feet. The man's appearance revolted her, but it did not frighten her. His soft flabbiness.

"Haven't you got any bread?" he asked.

"No."

"And no sausage either?"

"No."

"A pity. I would have given you money for them," he said and turned to go. But he changed his mind and said in a clear voice: "Haven't you got any parents?"

This question seemed to startle her. She took a step backward and said in a weak voice: "No."

Her reply appeared to excite the stranger, and he said with a kind of eagerness: "What do you say?" The trace of a crooked smile appeared on his gray-white face.

"So you're one of us."

There was something repulsive about his smile. Her body shrank and she recoiled. As if some loathsome reptile had crossed her path. "Tell me," he pressed her, standing his ground. "You're one of us, aren't you?"

For a moment she wanted to say no and run away, but her legs refused to move.

"So you're one of us," he said and took a few steps toward her. "Don't be afraid. My name's Mark. What's yours?"

He took off his hat, as if he wished to indicate with this gesture not only respect but also submission. His bald head was no different from his face, a pale gray.

"How long have you been here?"

Tzili couldn't open her mouth.

"I've lost everyone. I'd made up my mind to die tonight." Even this sentence, which was spoken with great emotion, did not move her. She stood frozen, as if she were caught up in an incomprehensible nightmare. "And you, where are you from? Have you been wandering for long?" he continued rapidly, in Tzili's mother tongue, a mixture of German and Yiddish, and with the very same accent.

"My name is Tzili," said Tzili.

The man seemed overcome. He sank onto his knees and said: "I'm glad. I'm very glad. Come with me. I have a little bread left."

Evening fell. The fruit trees on the hillside glowed with light. In the forest it was already dark.

"I've been here a month already," said the man, composing himself. "And in all that time I haven't seen a soul. What about you? Do you know anybody?" He spoke quickly, swallowing his words, getting out everything he had stored up in the long, cold days alone. She did not understand much, but one thing she understood: in all the countryside around them there were no Jews left.

"And your parents?" he asked.

Tzili shuddered. "I don't know, I don't know. Why do you ask?"

The stranger fell silent and asked no more.

In his hideout, it transpired, he had some crusts of bread, a few potatoes, and even a little vodka.

"Here," he said, and offered her a piece of bread.

Tzili took the bread and immediately sank her teeth into it.

The stranger looked at her for a long time, and a crooked smile spread over his face. He sat cross-legged on the ground. After a while he said: "I couldn't believe at first that you were Jewish. What did you do to change yourself?"

"Nothing."

"Nothing, what do you say? I will never be able to change. I'm too old to change, and to tell the truth I don't even know if I want to."

Later on he asked: "Why don't you say anything?" Tzili shivered. She was no longer accustomed to the old words, the words from home. She had never possessed an abundance of words, and the months she had spent in the company of the old peasants had cut them off at the roots. This stranger, who had brought the smell of home back to her senses, agitated her more than he frightened her.

When it grew dark he lit a fire. He explained: the entire area was surrounded by swamps. And now with the thawing of the snow it would be inaccessible to their enemies. It was a good thing that the winter was over. There was a practical note now in his voice. The suffering seemed to have vanished from his face, giving way to a businesslike expression. There was no anger or wonder in it.

13

When she woke there was light in the sky and the man was still sitting opposite her, in the same position. "You fell asleep," he said. He rose to his feet and his whole body was exposed: medium height, a worn-out face, and a crumpled suit, very faded at the knees. A few spots of grease. Swollen pockets.

"Ever since I escaped from the camp I haven't been able to sleep. I'm afraid of falling asleep. Are you afraid too?"

"No," said Tzili simply.

"I envy you."

The signs of spring were everywhere. Rivulets of melted snow wound their way down the slopes, dragging gray lumps of ice with them. There was not a soul to be seen, only the sound of the water growing louder and louder until it deafened them with its roar.

He looked at her and said: "If you hadn't told me, I'd never have guessed that you were Jewish. How did you do it?"

"I don't know. I didn't do anything."

"If I don't change they'll get me in the end. Nothing will save me. They won't let anyone escape. I once saw them with my own eyes hunting down a little Jewish child."

"And do they kill everyone?" Tzili asked.

"What do you think?" he said in an unpleasant tone of voice.

His face suddenly lost all its softness and a dry, bitter expression came over his lips. Her uncautious question had apparently angered him.

"And where were you all the time?" he demanded.

"With Katerina."

"A peasant woman?"

"Yes."

He dropped his head and muttered to himself. Apparently in anger, and also perhaps regret. His cheekbones projected, pulling the skin tight.

"And what did you do there?" He went on interrogating her.

"I worked."

"And did she know that you were Jewish?"

"No."

"Strange."

In the afternoon he grew restless and agitated. He ran from tree to tree, beating his head with his fists and reproaching himself: "Why did I run away? Why did I have to run away? I abandoned them all and ran away. God will never forgive me."

Tzili saw him in his despair and said nothing. The old words which had begun to stir in her retreated even further. In the end she said, for some reason: "Why are you crying?"

"I'm not crying. I'm angry with myself."

"Why?"

"Because I'm a criminal."

Tzili was sorry for asking and she said: "Forgive me."

"There's nothing to forgive."

Later on he told her. He had escaped and left his wife and two children behind in the camp. He had tried to drag them too through the narrow aperture he had dug with his bare hands, but they were afraid. She was, his wife.

And while he was talking it began to rain. They found a shelter under the branches. The man forgot his despair for a moment and spread a tattered blanket over the branches. The rain stopped.

"And did you too leave everyone behind?" he asked.

Tzili said nothing.

"Why don't you tell me?"

"Tell you what?"

"How you got away?"

"My parents left me behind to look after the house. They promised to come back. I waited for them."

"And ever since then you've been wandering?"

For some reason he tore off a lump of bread and offered her a piece.

She gnawed it without a word.

"The bread should be heated up. It's wet."

"It doesn't matter."

"Don't you suffer from pains in your stomach?"

"No."

"I suffer terribly from pains in my stomach."

The rain stopped and a blue-green light floated above the horizon. The gurgling of the water had given way to a steady flow. The man washed his face in the rivulet and said: "How good it is. Why don't you wash your face in the water too?"

Tzili took a handful of water and washed her face.

They sat silently by the little stream. Tzili felt that her life had led her to a new destination, it too unknown. The closeness of the man did not excite her, but his questions upset her. Now that he had stopped asking she felt better.

Suddenly he raised his eyes from the water and said: "Why don't you go down to the village and bring us something to eat? We have nothing to eat. The little we had is gone."

"All right, I'll go," she said.

"And you won't forget to come back?"

"I won't forget," she said, blushing.

Immediately he corrected himself and said: "You can buy whatever you want, it doesn't matter, as long as it's something to fill our bellies. I'd go myself, and willingly, but I'd be found out. It's a pity I haven't got any other clothes. You understand."

"I understand," said Tzili submissively.

"I'd go myself if I could," he said again, in a tone which was at once ingratiating and calculating. "You, how shall I put it, you've changed, you've changed for the better. Nobody would ever suspect you. You say your r's exactly like they do. Where do you get it all from?"

"I don't know."

Now there was something frightening in his appearance. As if he had risen from his despair another man, terrifyingly practical.

14

Early in the morning she set out. He stood watching her receding figure for a long time. Once again she was by herself. She knew that the stranger had done something to her, but what? She walked for hours, looking for ways around the melted snow, and in the end she found an open path, paved with stones.

A woman was standing next to one of the huts, and Tzili addressed her in the country dialect: "Have you any bread?"

"What will you give me for it?"

"Money."

"Show me."

Tzili showed her.

"And how much will I give you for it?"

"Two loaves."

The old peasant woman muttered a curse, went inside, and emerged immediately with two loaves in her hands. The transaction was over in a moment.

"Who do you belong to?" she remembered to ask.

"To Maria."

"Maria? *Tfu*." The woman spat. "Get out of my sight."

Tzili clasped the bread in both hands. The bread was still warm, and it was only after she had walked for some distance that the tears gushed out of her eyes. For the first time in many days she saw the face of her mother, a face no longer young. Worn with work and suffering. Her feet froze on the ground, but as in days gone by she knew that she must not stand still, and she continued on her way.

The trees were putting out leaves. Tzili jumped over the puddles without getting wet. She knew the way and weaved between the paths, taking shortcuts and making detours like a creature native to the place. She walked very quickly and arrived before evening fell. Mark was sitting in his place. His tired, hungry eyes had a dull, indifferent look.

"I brought bread," she said.

Mark roused himself: "I thought you were lost." He fell on the bread and tore it to shreds with his teeth, without offering any to Tzili. She observed him for a moment: his eyes seemed to have come alive and all his senses concentrated on chewing.

"Won't you have some too?" he said when he was finished eating.

Tzili stretched out her hand and took a piece of

72

bread. She wasn't hungry. The long walk had tired her into a stupor. Her tears too had dried up. She sat without moving.

Mark passed his right hand over his mouth and said: "A cigarette, if only I had a cigarette."

Tzili made no response.

He went on: "Without cigarettes there's no point in living." Then he dug his nails into the ground and began singing a strange song. Tzili remembered the melody but she couldn't understand the words. Gradually his voice lost its lilt and the song trailed off into a mutter.

The evening was cold and Mark lit a fire. During the long days of his stay here he had learned to make fire from two pieces of flint and a thread of wool which he plucked from his coat. Tzili marveled momentarily at his dexterity. The agitation faded from his face and he asked in a practical tone of voice: "How did you get the bread? Fresh bread?"

Tzili answered him shortly.

"And they didn't suspect you?"

For a long time they sat by the little fire, which gave off a pleasant warmth.

"Why are you so silent?"

Tzili hung her head, and an involuntary smile curved her lips.

The craving for cigarettes did not leave him. The fresh bread had given him back his taste for life, but he lost it again immediately. For hours he sat nibbling blades of grass, chewing them up and spitting them to one side. He had a tense, bitter look. From time to time he cursed himself for being a slave to his addiction. Tzili was worn out and she fell asleep where she sat.

15

When she woke she kept her eyes closed. She felt Mark's eyes on her. She lay without moving. The fire had not gone out, which meant that Mark had not slept all night.

When she finally opened her eyes it was already morning. Mark asked: "Did you sleep?" The sun rose in the sky and the horizons opened out one after the other until the misty plains were revealed in the distance. Here and there they could see a peasant ploughing.

"It's a good place," said Mark. "You can see a long way from here." The agitation had faded from his face, and a kind of complacency that did not suit him had taken its place. Tzili imagined she could see in him one of the Jewish salesmen who used to drop into her mother's shop. Mark asked her: "Did you go to school?"

"Yes."

"A Jewish school?"

"No. There wasn't one. I studied Judaism with an old teacher. The Pentateuch and prayers."

"Funny," he said, "it sounds so far away. As if it never happened. And do you still remember anything?"

"Hear, O Israel."

"And do you recite it?"

"No," she said and hung her head.

"In my family we weren't observant any more," said Mark in a whisper. "Was your family religious?"

"No, I don't think so."

"You said they brought you a teacher of religion."

"It was only for me, because I didn't do well at school. My brothers and sisters were all good at school. They were going to take external examinations."

"Strange," said Mark.

"I had trouble learning."

"What does it matter now?" said Mark. "We're all doomed anyway."

Tzili did not understand the word but she sensed that it held something bad.

After a pause Mark said: "You've changed very nicely, you've done it very cleverly. I can't imagine a change like that taking place in me. Even the forests won't change me now."

"Why?" asked Tzili.

"Because everything about me gives me away— my appearance, from top to toe, my nose, my accent, the way I eat, sit, sleep, everything. Even

76

though I've never had anything to do with what's called Jewish tradition. My late father used to call himself a free man. He was fond of that phrase, I remember, but here in this place I've discovered, looking at the peasants ploughing in the valley, their serenity, that I myself—I won't be able to change anymore. I'm a coward. All the Jews are cowards and I'm no different from them. You understand."

Tzili understood nothing of this outburst, but she felt the pain pouring out of the words and she said: "What do you want to do?"

"What do I want to do? I want to go down to the village and buy myself a packet of tobacco. That's all I want. I have no greater desire. I'm a nervous man and without cigarettes I'm an insect, less than an insect, I'm nothing."

"I'll buy it for you."

"Thank you," said Mark, ashamed. "Forgive me. I have no more money. I'll give you a coat. That's good, isn't it?"

"Yes, that's good," said Tzili. "That's very good."

In the tent of branches he had a haversack full of things. He spread them out now on the ground to dry. His clothes, his wife's and children's clothes. He spread them out slowly, like a merchant displaying his wares on the counter.

Tzili shuddered at the sight of the little garments spotted with food stains. Mark spread them out without any order and they steamed and gave off a stench of mildew and sour-sweet. "We must dry them," said Mark in a businesslike tone. "Otherwise they'll rot." He added: "I'll give you my coat. It's a good coat, pure wool. I bought it a year ago. I hope you'll be able to get me some cigarettes for it. Without cigarettes to smoke I get very nervous."

Strange, his nervousness was not apparent now. He stood next to the steaming clothes, turning them over one by one, as if they were pieces of meat on a fire. Tzili too did not take her eyes off the stained children's clothes shrinking in the sun.

Toward evening he gathered the clothes up carefully and folded them. The coat intended for selling he put aside. "For this, I hope, we'll be able to get some tobacco. It's a good coat, almost new," he muttered to himself.

That night Mark did not light a fire. He sat and sucked soft little twigs. Chewing the twigs seemed to blunt his craving for cigarettes. Tzili sat not far from him, staring into the darkness.

"I wanted to study medicine," Mark recalled, "but my parents didn't have the money to send me to Vienna. I sat for external matriculation exams and my marks weren't anything to write home about, only average. And then I married very young, too young I'd say. Of course, nothing came of my plans to study. A pity."

"What's your wife's name?" asked Tzili.

"Why do you ask?" said Mark in surprise.

"No reason."

"Blanca."

"How strange," said Tzili. "My sister's name is Blanca too."

Mark rose to his feet. Tzili's remark had abruptly stopped the flow of his memories. He put his hands in his trouser pocket, stuck out his chest, and said: "You must go to sleep. Tomorrow you have a long walk in front of you."

The strangeness of his voice frightened Tzili and she immediately got up and went to lie down on the pile of leaves.

16

She slept deeply, without feeling the wind. When she woke a mug of hot herb tea was waiting for her.

"I couldn't sleep," he said.

"Why can't you sleep?"

"I can't fall asleep without a cigarette."

Tzili put the coat into a sack and rose to her feet.

Mark sat in his place next to the fire. His dull eyes were bloodshot from lack of sleep. For some reason he touched the sack and said: "It's a good coat, almost new."

"I'll look after it," said Tzili without thinking, and set off.

I'll bring him cigarettes, he'll be happy if I bring him cigarettes. This thought immediately strengthened her legs. The summer was in full glory, and in the distant, yellow fields she could see the farmers cutting corn. She crossed the mountainside and when she came to the river she picked up her dress and waded across it. Light burst from every direction, bright and clear. She approached the plots of cultivated land without fear, as if she had known them all her life. With every step she felt the looseness of the fertile soil.

"Have you any tobacco?" she asked a peasant woman standing at the doorway of her hut.

"And what will you give me in exchange?"

"I have a coat," said Tzili and held it up with both hands.

"Where did you steal it?"

"I didn't steal it. I got it as a present."

Upon hearing this reply an old crone emerged from the hut and announced in a loud voice: "Leave the whore's little bastard alone." But the younger woman, who liked the look of the coat, said: "And what else do you want for it?"

"Bread and sausage."

Tzili knew how to bargain. And after an exchange of arguments, curses, and accusations, and after the coat had been turned inside out and felt all over, they agreed on two loaves of bread, two joints of meat, and a bundle of tobacco leaves.

"You'll catch it if the owner comes and demands his coat back. We'll kill you," the old crone said threateningly.

Tzili put the bread, meat, and tobacco into her sack and turned to go without saying a word. The old crone showed no signs of satisfaction at the transaction, but the young woman made no attempt to hide her delight in the city coat.

On the way back Tzili sat and paddled in the

water. The sun shone and silence rose from the forest. She sat for an hour without moving from her place and in the end she said to herself: Mark is sad because he has no cigarettes. When he has cigarettes he'll be happy. This thought brought her to her feet and she started to run, taking shortcuts wherever she could.

Toward evening she arrived. Mark bowed his head as if she had brought him news of some great honor, an honor of which he was not unworthy. He took the bundle of tobacco leaves, stroking and sniffing them. Before long he had a cigarette rolled from newspaper. An awkward joy flooded him. In the camp people would fight over a cigarette stub more than over a piece of bread. He spoke of the camp now as if he were about to return to it.

That evening he lit a fire again. They ate and drank herb tea. Mark found a few dry logs and they burned steadily and gave off a pleasant warmth. The wind dropped too, and seemed gentler than before, the shadows it brought from the forest less menacing. Mark was apparently affected by these small changes. Without any warning he suddenly burst into tears.

"What's wrong?"

"I remembered."

"What?"

"Everything that's happened to me in the past year."

Tzili rose to her feet. She wanted to say something but the words would not come. In the end she said: "I'll bring you more tobacco."

"Thank you," he said. "I sit here eating and smoking and they're all over there. Who knows where they are by now." His gray face seemed to grow grayer, a yellow stain spread over his forehead.

"They'll all come back," said Tzili, without knowing what she was saying.

These words calmed him immediately. He asked about the way and the village, and how she had obtained the food and the tobacco, and in general what the peasants were saying.

"They don't say anything," said Tzili quietly.

"And they didn't say anything about the Jews?"

"No."

For a few minutes he sat without moving, wrapped up in himself. His dull, bloodshot eyes slowly closed. And suddenly he dropped to the ground and fell asleep.

17

Every week she went down to the plains to renew their supplies. She was quiet, like a person doing what had to be done without unnecessary words. She would bathe in the river, and when she returned her body gave off a smell of cool water.

She would tell him about her adventures on the plains: a drunken peasant woman had tried to hit her, a peasant had set his dog on her, a passerby had tried to rob her of the clothes she had taken to barter. She spoke simply, as if she were recounting everyday experiences.

And because the weather was fine, and the rains scattered, they would sit for hours by the fire eating, drinking herb tea, listening to the forest and hardly speaking. Mark stopped speaking of the camp and its horrors. He spoke now about the advantages of this high, remote place. And once he said: "The air here is very fresh. Can you feel how fresh it is?" He pronounced the word "fresh" very distinctly, with a secret happiness. Sometimes he used words that Tzili did not understand.

Once Tzili asked what the words "out of this world" meant.

"Don't you understand?"

"No."

"It's very simple: out of this world—out of the ordinary, very nice."

"From God?" she puzzled.

"Not necessarily."

But it wasn't always like this. Sometimes a suppressed rage welled up in him. "What happened to you? Why are you so late?" When he saw the supplies, he recovered his spirits. In the end he would ask her pardon. She, for her part, was no longer afraid of him.

Day by day he changed. He would sit for hours looking at the wild flowers growing in all the colors of the rainbow. Sometimes he would pluck a flower and whisper: "How lovely, how modest." Even the weeds moved him. And once he said, as if talking to himself: "In Jewish families there's never any time. Everyone's in a hurry, everyone's in a panic. What for?" There was a kind of music in his voice, a melancholy music.

The days went by one after the other and nothing happened to arouse their suspicions. On the contrary, the silence deepened. The corn was cut in one field after the other and the fruit was gathered in the orchards, and Mark, for some reason, decided to dig a bunker, in case of trouble.

This thought came to him suddenly one afternoon, and he immediately set out to survey the terrain. Straight away he found a suitable place, next to a little mound covered with a tangle of thorns. In his haversack he had a simple kitchen knife. This domestic article, dull with use, fired the desire for activity in him. He set to work to make a spade. The hard, concentrated work changed his face; he stopped talking, as if he had found a purpose for his transitory life, a purpose in which he drowned himself completely.

Every week Tzili went down to the plains and brought back not only bread and sausages but also vodka, in exchange for the clothes which Mark gave her with an abstracted expression on his face. His outbursts did not cease, but they were only momentary flare-ups, few and far between. Activity, on the whole, made him agreeable.

Once he said to her: "My late father's love for the German language knew no bounds. He had a special fondness for irregular verbs. He knew them all. And with me he was very strict about the correct pronunciation. The German lessons with my father were like a nightmare. I always got mixed up and in his fanaticism he never overlooked my mistakes. He made me write them down over and over again. My mother knew German well but not perfectly, and my father would lose his temper and correct her in front of other people. A mistake in grammar would drive him out of his mind. In the provinces people are more fanatical about the German language than in the city."

"What are the provinces?" asked Tzili.

"Don't you know? Places without gymnasiums, without theaters." Suddenly he burst out laughing. "If my father knew what the products of his culture were up to now he would say, 'Impossible, impossible.'"

"Why impossible?" said Tzili.

"Because it's a word he used a lot."

After many days of slow, stubborn carving, Mark had a spade, a strong spade. The carved instrument brightened his eyes, and he couldn't stop touching it. He was in good spirits and he told her stories about all the peculiar tutors his father hired to teach him mathematics and Latin. Young Jewish vagabonds, for the most part, who had not completed their university degrees, who ended up by getting some girl, usually not Jewish, into trouble, and had to be sent packing in a hurry. Mark told these stories slowly, imitating his teachers' gestures and describing their various weaknesses, their fondness for alcohol, and so on. This language was easier for Tzili to understand. Sometimes she would ask him questions and he would reply in detail.

And then he started digging. He worked for hours at a stretch. Every now and then it started raining and the digging was disrupted. Mark would grow angry, but his anger did not last long. The backbreaking work gave him the look of a simple laborer. Tzili stopped asking questions and Mark stopped telling stories.

After a week of work the bunker was ready, dug firmly into the earth. And it was just what was needed for the cold autumn season, a shelter for the cold nights. Mark was sure that the Germans would never reach them, but it was better to be careful, just in case. Tzili noticed that Mark often used the word *careful* now. It was a word he had hardly ever used before.

He put the finishing touches to the bunker without excitement. A quiet happiness spread over his face and hands. Now she saw that his cheeks were tanned and his arms, which had seemed so weak and flabby, were full and firm. He looked like a laboring man who knew how to enjoy his labors.

What will happen when we've sold all the clothes? the thought crossed Tzili's mind. This thought did not appear to trouble Mark. He was so pleased with the bunker, he kept repeating: "It's a good bunker, a comfortable bunker. It will stand up well to the rain."

18

After this the days grew cold and cloudy and Mark drank a lot of vodka. The tan faded suddenly from his face. He would sit silently, and sometimes he would talk to himself, as if Tzili weren't there. On her return from the plains he would ask: "What did you bring?" If she had brought vodka he would say nothing. If she hadn't he would say: "Why didn't you bring vodka?"

At night the words would well up in him and come out in long, clumsy, half-swallowed sentences. Tzili could not understand, but she sensed: Mark was now living in another world, a world which was full of people. Day after day he sat and drank. His face grew lean. There was a kind of strength in this leanness. His days became confused with his nights. Sometimes he would fall asleep in the middle of the day and sometimes he would sit up until late at night. Once he turned to her in the middle of the night and said: "What are you doing here?"

"Nothing."

"Why don't you go down to the village and bring supplies? Our supplies are running out."

"It's night."

"In that case," he said, "we'll wait for the dawn."

He's sad, he's drunk, she would murmur to herself. If I bring him tobacco and vodka he'll feel better. She no longer dared to return without vodka. Sometimes she would sleep in the forest because she was afraid to come back without vodka.

At that time Mark said many strange and confused things. Tzili would sit at a distance and watch him. Alien hands seemed to be clutching at him and kneading him. Sometimes he would lie in his vomit like a hired hand on a drunken spree. His old face, the face of a healthy working man, was wiped away.

And once in his drunkenness he cried: "If only I'd studied medicine I wouldn't be here. I'd be in America." In his haversack, it transpired, were a couple of books which he had once used to prepare for the entrance exams to Vienna University. And once, when it seemed to her that he was calmer, he suddenly burst out in a loud cry: "Commerce has driven the Jews out of their minds. You can cheat people for one year, even for one hundred years, but not for two thousand years!" In his drunkenness he would shout, make speeches, tear sentences to shreds and piece them together again.

Tzili sensed that he was struggling with people who were far away and strangers to her, but nevertheless—she was afraid. His lean cheeks were full of strength. On her return from the plains she would hear his voice from a long way off, rending the silence.

And again, just when she thought that his agitation had died down, he fell on her without any warning: "Why didn't you learn French?"

"We didn't learn French at school, we learned German."

"Barbarous. Why didn't they teach you French? And it's not as if you know German either. What you speak is jargon. It drives me out of my mind. There's no culture without language. If only people learned languages at school the world would be a different place. Do you promise me that you'll learn French?"

"I promise."

Afterward it began to rain and Mark dragged himself to the bunker. A rough wind was blowing. Mark's words went on echoing in the air for a long time. And Tzili, without knowing what she was doing, went up to the bunker and called softly: "It's me, Tzili. Don't worry. Tomorrow I'll bring you vodka and sausage."

19

After this the autumn weather grew finer and a cold, clear sun shone on their temporary shelter. Mark's troubled spirit seemed to lighten too and he stopped cursing. He didn't stop drinking, but his drinking no longer put him in a rage. Now he would often say: "There was something I wanted to say, but it's slipped my mind." A weak smile would break through the clouds, darkening his face. Far-off, forgotten things continued to trouble him, but not in the same shocking way. Now he would speak softly of the need to study languages, acquire a liberal profession, escape from the provinces, but he no longer scolded Tzili.

He would speak of the approaching winter as a frontier beyond which lay life and hope. And Tzili sensed that Mark was now absorbed in listening to himself. Every now and then he would conclude aloud: "There's still hope. There's still hope."

And once he questioned her about her religious studies. Tzili's life at home now felt so remote and scattered that it didn't seem to belong to her. On the way to the plains she would wonder about Maria, whose name she had so unthinkingly adopted. The more she thought about her, the clearer her features grew. A tall, proud woman, she gave her body to anyone who wanted it, but not without getting a good price. And when her daughters grew up, they too adopted their mother's gestures, they too were bold.

She didn't tell him about Maria, just as she didn't tell him about Katerina. Her femininity blossomed within her, blind and sweet. Outwardly too she changed. The pimples didn't disappear from her face, but her limbs were full of strength. She walked easily, even when she had a heavy sack to carry.

"How old are you?" Mark had once asked her in the days of his drunkenness. Afterward he didn't ask again. Now he would beg her pardon for his drunken behavior; his face recovered its former mildness. Tzili's happiness knew no bounds. Mark had recovered and he would never shout at her again. For some reason she believed that the new drink, which the peasants called slivovitz, was responsible for this change.

It seemed to Tzili that the happy days of the summer were about to return, but she was wrong. Mark now craved a woman. This secret he was keeping even from himself. He would urge Tzili to go down to the plains even before it was necessary. Her blooming presence was driving him wild.

And while Tzili was busy pondering ways and means of getting hold of the new, calming drink, Mark suddenly said: "I love you."

Tzili's mouth fell open. His voice was familiar, but very different. She was surprised, but not altogether. The last few nights had been cold and they had both slept in the bunker. They had sat together until late at night, with a warm, dark intimacy between them.

Mark stretched out his arms and clasped her round the waist. Tzili's body shrank from his hands. "You don't love me," he mumbled. The tighter he held her, the more her body shrank. But he was determined, and he slid her dress up with nimble fingers. "No," she managed to murmur. But it was already too late.

Afterward he sat by her side and stroked her body. Strange words came tumbling out of his mouth. For some reason he began talking again about the advantages of the place, the beautiful marshes, the forests, and the fresh air. The words were external, and they brushed past her naked body like a cold wind.

From now on they stayed in the bunker. The rain poured down, but for the time being they were sheltered against it. Mark drank all the time, but never to excess. His happiness was a drunken happiness, and he wanted to cut it up into little pieces and make it last. From time to time he ventured out to confirm what he already knew—that outside it was cold, dark, and damp.

"Tell me about yourself. Why don't you tell me?" he would press her. The truth was that he only wanted to hear her voice. He showered many words on her during their days together in the bunker. His heart overflowed. Tzili, for her part, accepted her happiness quietly. Secretly she was glad that Mark loved her.

Their supplies ran short. Tzili put off going out from day to day. She liked it in this new darkness. She learned to drink the insidious drug, and the more she drank the more slothful her body became. "I'd go myself, but the peasants would betray me." Mark would excuse himself. And in the meantime the rain and cold hemmed them in. They snuggled up together and their small happiness knew no bounds.

Distant sights, hungry malevolent shadows invaded the bunker in dense crowds. Tzili did not know the bitter, emaciated people. Mark went outside and cut branches with his kitchen knife to block up the openings, hurling curses in all directions. For a moment or two it seemed that he had succeeded in chasing them off. But the harder the rain fell the more bitter the struggle became, and from day to day the shadows prevailed. In vain

Tzili tried to calm him. His happiness was being attacked from every quarter. Tzili too seemed affected by the same secret poison.

"Enough," he announced, "I'm going down."

"No, I'll go," said Tzili.

The dark, rainy plains now drew Mark to them. "I have to go on a tour of inspection," he announced. It was no longer a caprice but a spell. The plains drew him like a magnet.

20

But in the meantime they put off the decision from day to day. They learned to go short and to share this frugality too. He would drink only once a day and smoke only twice, half a cigarette. The slight tremor came back to his fingers, like a man deprived of alcohol. But for the many shadows besieging their temporary shelter, their small happiness would have been complete.

From time to time, when the shadows deepened, he would go outside and shout: "Come inside, please. We have a wonderful bunker. It's a pity we haven't got any food. Otherwise we'd hold a banquet for you." These announcements would calm them, but not for long.

Afterward he said: "There's nothing else for it, we'll have to go down. Death isn't as terrible as it seems. A man, after all, is not an insect. All you have to do is overcome your fear." These words did not encourage Tzili. The dark, muddy plains became more frightening from day to day. Now it seemed that not only the peasants lay in wait for her there but also her father, her mother, and her sisters.

And reality stole upon them unawares. Wetness began to seep through the walls of the bunker. At first only a slight dampness, but later real wetness. Mark worked without a pause to stop up the cracks. The work distracted him from the multitude of shadows lying in wait outside. From time to time he brandished his spade as if he were chasing away a troublesome flock of birds.

One evening, as they were lying in the darkness, snuggling up to each other for warmth, the storm broke in and a torrent of water flooded the bunker. Mark was sure that the multitudes of shadows waiting in the trees to trap him were to blame. He rushed outside, shouting at the top of his voice: "Criminals."

Now they stood next to the trees, looking down at the gray slopes shivering in the rain. And just when it seemed that the steady, penetrating drizzle would never stop, the clouds vanished and a round sun appeared in the sky.

"I knew it," said Mark.

If only Tzili had said, "I'll go down," he might have let her go. Perhaps he would have gone with her. But she didn't say anything. She was afraid of the plains. And since she was silent, Mark said: "I'm going down."

In the meantime they made a little fire and drank herb tea. Mark was very excited. He spoke in lofty, dramatic words about the need to change, to adapt to local conditions, and not to be afraid. Fear corrupts human dignity, he said. The resolution he had had while building the bunker came back to his face. Now he was even more resolute, determined to go down to the plains and not to be afraid.

"Don't go," said Tzili.

"I must go down. Inspection of the terrain has become imperative—if only from the point of view of general security needs. Who knows what the villagers have got up their sleeves? They may be getting ready for a surprise attack. I can't allow them to take us by surprise."

Tzili could not understand what he was talking about, but the lofty, resolute words, which at first had given her a sense of security, began to hurt her, and the more he talked the more they stung. He spoke of reassessment and reappraisal, of diversion and camouflage. Tzili understood none of his many words, but this she understood: he was talking of another world.

"Don't go." She clung to him.

"You have to understand," he said in a gentle voice. "Once you conquer your fear everything looks different. I'm happy now that I've conquered my fear. All my life fear has tortured me shamefully, you understand, shamefully. Now I'm a free man."

Afterward they sat together for a long time. But

although Tzili now said, "I'll go down. They know me, they won't hurt me," Mark had made up his mind: "This time I'm going down." And he went down.

21

Mark receded rapidly and in a few minutes he was gone. She sat still and felt the silence deepening around her. The sky changed color and a shudder passed over the mountainside.

Tzili rose to her feet and went into the bunker. It was dark and warm inside the bunker. The haversack lay to one side. For the past few days Mark had refused to go into the bunker. "A man is not a mole. This lying about is shameful." He used the word *shameful* often, pronouncing it in a foreign accent, apparently German.

The daylight hours crept slowly by, and Tzili concentrated her thoughts on Mark's progress across the mountainside. She imagined him going up and down the same paths that she herself had taken. She saw him pass by the hut where she had bartered a garment for a sausage. She saw it all so clearly that she felt as if she herself were there with him.

In the afternoon she lit a fire and said: "I'll make Mark some herb tea. He likes herb tea."

Mark was late.

"Don't worry, he'll come back," a voice from home said in her ear. But when twilight fell and Mark did not return anxiety began dripping into her soul. She went down to the river and washed the mugs. The cold water banished the anxiety for a moment. For some reason she spread a cloth on the ground.

Darkness fell. The days she had spent with Mark had blunted her fear of the night. Now she was alone again. Mark's voice came to her and she heard: "A man is not an insect. Death isn't as terrible as it seems." Now these words were accompanied by the music of a military band. Like in her childhood, on the Day of Independence, when the army held parades and the bugles played. The military voice gave her back a kind of confidence.

Mark was late.

Now she felt that the domestic smells that had enveloped the place were fading away. Fresh, cold air blew in their place. It occurred to her that if she took the clothes out of the haversack and spread them around, the homely smells would come back to fill the air, and perhaps Mark would sense them. Immediately she took the haversack out of the bunker and spread the clothes on the ground. The brightly colored clothes, all damp and crumpled, gave off a confined, moldy smell.

He's lost, he must be lost. She clung to this sentence like an anchor. She fell to her knees by the clothes. They were children's clothes, small and shrunken with the damp, spotted with food stains and a little torn.

Afterward she turned aside to listen. Apart from an occasional rustle or murmur there was nothing to be heard. From the distant huts scattered between the swamps, isolated barks reached her ears.

After midnight a thin drizzle began to fall and she put the things back into the bunker. This small activity revived an old scene in her memory. She remembered the first days, before the bunker, when she had brought him the tobacco. The way he had rolled the shredded leaves in a piece of newspaper, the way he had recovered his looks, his smile, and the light on his face.

The rain stopped but the wind grew stronger, bending the trees with broad, sweeping movements. Tzili went into the bunker. It was warm and full of the smell of tobacco. She breathed in the smell.

She sat in the dark and for some reason she thought about Mark's wife. Mark seldom spoke of her. Once she had even sensed a note of resentment against her. She imagined her as a tall, thin woman sheltering her children under her coat. Strange, she felt a kind of kinship with her.

22

The next day Mark still did not return. She stood on the edge of the plateau exposed to the wind. The downward slope drew her too. The slope was not steep and it glittered with puddles of water. Now she felt that something had been taken from her, something that belonged to her youth. She covered her face in shame.

For hours she sat and practiced the words, so that she would be ready for him when he came. "Where were you Mark? I was very worried. Here is some herb tea for you. You must be thirsty." She did not prepare many words, and the few she did prepare, she repeated over and over again in a voice which had a formal ring in her ears. Repeating the words put her to sleep. She would wake up in alarm and go to the bunker. The walls of the bunker had collapsed, the flimsy roof had caved in, and the floor was covered by a spreading gray puddle. There was an alien spirit in it, but it was the only place she could go to. Everywhere else was even more alien.

The days dragged out long and heavy. Tzili did

not stir. And once a voice burst out from within her: "Mark." The voice slid down the mountainside, echoing as it went. No one answered.

Overnight the winds changed and the winter winds came, thin and sharp as knives. The fire burned but it did not warm her. Low, dark clouds covered the somber sky. She prayed often. This was the prayer which she repeated over and over: "God, bring Mark back. If you bring Mark back to me, I'll go down to the plains and I won't be lazy."

How many days had Mark been gone? At first she kept track, but then she lost count. Sometimes she saw Mark struggling with the peasants and hurling pointed sticks at them, like the ones he had made for the walls of the bunker. Sometimes he looked tired and crushed. Like the first time she had seen him, pale and gray. Man is not an insect, she remembered and made an effort to get up and stand erect.

For days she had had nothing to eat. Here and there she still found a few withered wild apples, but for the most part she now lived off roots. The roots were sweet and juicy. "I'll go on," she said, but she didn't move. For hours she sat and gazed at the mountainside sloping down to the plains, the two marshes, the shelter, and the haversack. Sometimes she took out the clothes and spread them on the ground, but Mark did not respond to her call.

The moment she decided to leave she would

imagine that she heard footsteps approaching. A little longer, she would say to herself. Death is not as terrible as it seems.

Sometimes the cold would envelop her in sweetness. She would close her eyes and curl up tightly and wait for a hand to come and take her away. But none came. Winter winds tore across the hillside, cruel and cutting. "I'll go on," she said, and lifted the haversack onto her shoulders. The haversack was soaked through and heavy, with every step she felt that the burden was too heavy to bear.

"Did you see a man pass by?" she asked a peasant woman standing at the doorway of her hut.

"There's no man here. They've all been conscripted. Who do you belong to?"

"Maria."

"Which Maria?"

And when she did not reply the peasant woman understood which Maria she meant, snickered aloud, and said: "Be off with you, wretch! Get out of my sight."

One by one Tzili gave the little garments away in exchange for bread. "If I meet Mark I'll tell him that I was hungry. He won't be angry." The haversack on her back grew more burdensome from day to day but she didn't take it off. The damp warmth stuck to her back. She went from tree to tree. She believed that next to one of the trees she would find him.

23

It began to snow and she was obliged to look for work. The long tramp had weakened her. Overnight she lost her freedom and became a serf.

At this time the Germans were on the retreat, but here it was the middle of winter and the snow fell without a break. The peasants drove her mercilessly. She cleaned the cow shed, milked the cows, peeled potatoes, washed dishes, brought firewood from the forest. At night the peasant's wife would mutter: "You know who your mother is. You must pay for your sins. Your mother has corrupted whole villages. If you follow in her footsteps I'll beat you black and blue."

Sometimes she went out at night and lay down in the snow. For some reason the snow refused to absorb her. She would return to her sufferings, meek and submissive. One evening on her way back from the forest she heard a voice. "Tzili," called the voice.

"I'm Tzili," said Tzili. "Who are you?"

"I'm Mark," said the voice. "Have you forgotten me?"

"No," said Tzili, frightened. "I'm waiting for you. Where are you?"

"Not far," said the voice, "but I can't come out of hiding. Death is not as terrible as it seems. All you have to do is conquer your fear."

She woke up. Her feet were frozen.

From then on Mark appeared often. He would surprise her at every turn, especially his voice. It seemed to her that he was hovering nearby, unchanged but thinner and unable to emerge from his hiding place. And once she heard quite clearly: "Don't be afraid. The transition is easy in the end." These apparitions filled her with a kind of warmth. And at night, when the stick or the rope fell on her back, she would say to herself, "Never mind. Mark will come to rescue you in the spring."

And in the middle of the hard, grim winter she sensed that her belly had changed and was slightly swollen. At first it seemed an insignificant change. But it did not take long for her to understand: Mark was inside her. This discovery frightened her. She remembered the time when her sister Yetty fell in love with a young officer from Moravia, and everyone became angry with her. Not because she had fallen in love with a gentile but because the intimate relations between them were likely to get her into trouble. And indeed, in the end it came out that the officer was an immoral drunkard, and but for the fact that his regiment was transferred the affair would certainly have ended badly. It remained as a wound in her sister's heart, and at home it came up among other unfortunate affairs in whispers, in veiled words. And Tzili, it transpired, although she was very young at the time, had known how to put the pieces together and make a picture, albeit incomplete.

There was no more possibility of doubt: she was pregnant. The peasant woman for whom she slaved soon noticed that something was amiss. "Pregnant," she hissed. "I knew what you were the minute I set eyes on you."

Tzili herself, when the first fear had passed, suddenly felt a new strength in her body. She worked till late at night, no work was too hard for them to burden her with, but she did not weaken. She drew strength from the air, from the fresh milk, and from the hope that one day she would be able to tell Mark that she was bearing his child. The complications, of course, were beyond her grasp.

And in the meantime the peasant woman beat her constantly. She was old but strong, and she beat Tzili religiously. Not in anger but in righteousness. Ever since her discovery that Tzili was pregnant her blows had grown more violent, as if she wanted to tear the embryo from her belly.

Heaven and hell merged into one. When she went to graze the cow or gather wood in the forest she felt Mark close by her side, even closer than in the days when they had slept together in the bunker. She spoke to him simply, as if she were chatting to a companion while she worked. The work did not stop her from hearing his voice. His words too were clear and simple. "I'll come in the spring," he said. "In the spring the war will end and everyone will return."

Once she dared to ask him: "Won't your wife be angry with me?"

"My wife," said Mark, "is a very forgiving woman."

"As for me," said Tzili, "I love your children as if they were my own."

"In that case," said Mark in a practical tone of voice, "all we have to do is wait for the war to end."

But at night when she returned to the hut reality showed itself in all its nakedness. The peasant's wife beat her as if she were a rebellious animal, in a passion of rage and fury. At first Tzili screamed and bit her lips. Later she stopped screaming. She absorbed the blows with her eyes closed, as if she knew that this was her lot in life.

One night she snatched the rope from the woman and said: "No, you won't. I'm not an animal. I'm a woman." The peasant's wife, apparently startled by Tzili's resolution, stood rooted to the spot, but she immediately recovered, snatched the rope from Tzili's hand, and began to beat her with her fists.

It was the height of winter and there was nowhere to escape to. She worked, and the work strengthened her. The thought that Mark would come for her in the spring was no longer a hope but a certainty.

Once the peasant's wife asked her: "Who made you pregnant?"

"A man."

"What man?"

"A good man."

"And what will you do with the baby when it's born?"

"I'll bring it up."

"And who will provide for you?"

"I'll work, but not for you." The words came out of her mouth directly and quietly.

The peasant's wife ranted and raved.

The next day she said to Tzili: "Take your things and get out of my sight. I never want to see you again."

Tzili took up the haversack and left.

24

Once more she had won her freedom. At that time the great battlefronts were collapsing, and the first refugees were groping their way across the broad fields of snow. Against the vast whiteness they looked like swarms of insects. Tzili was drawn toward them as if she realized that her fate was no different from theirs.

Strange, precisely now, at the hour of her new-found freedom, Mark stopped speaking to her. "Where are you and why don't you speak to me?" she would ask in despair. Nothing stirred in the silence, and but for her own voice no other voice was heard.

In one of the bunkers she came across three men. They were wrapped from top to toe in heavy, tattered coats. Their bloodshot eyes peeped through their rags, alert and sardonic.

"Who are you?"

"My name is Tzili."

"So you're one of us. Where have you left every-one?"

"I," said Tzili, "have lost everyone."

"In that case why don't you come with us? What have you got in that haversack?"

"Clothes."

"And haven't you got any bread?" one of them said in an unpleasant voice.

"Who are you?" she asked.

"Can't you see? We're partisans. Haven't you got any bread in that haversack?"

"No I haven't," she said and turned to go.

"Where are you going?"

"I'm going to Mark."

"We know the whole area. There's no one here. You'd better stay with us. We'll keep you amused."

"I," said Tzili opening her coat, "am a pregnant woman."

"Leave the haversack with us. We'll look after it for you."

"The haversack isn't mine. It belongs to Mark. He left it in my care."

"Don't boast. You should learn to be more modest."

"I'm not afraid. Death is not as terrible as it seems."

"Cheeky brat," said the man and rose to his feet. Tzili stared at him.

"Where did you learn that?" said the man, taking a step backward.

Tzili stood still. A strength not hers was in her eyes.

"Go then, bitch," said the man and went back to the bunker.

From then on the snow stretched before her white and empty. Tzili felt a kind of warmth spreading through her. She walked along a row of trees, which now seemed rootless, stuck into the snow like pegs.

From time to time a harassed survivor appeared, asked the way, and disappeared again. Tzili knew that her fate was no different from the survivors, but she kept away from them as if they were brothers who might say: "We told you so."

And while she was walking without knowing where her feet would lead her, the walls of snow began to shudder. It was the month of March and new winds invaded the landscape. On the mountain slopes the first stripes of brown earth appeared. Not long afterward the brown stripes widened.

And suddenly she saw what she had not seen before: the mountain, undistinguished and not particularly lofty, the mountain where she and Mark had spent the summer, and not far from where she was standing the foot of the slope, and next to it the valley leading to Katerina's house. As if the whole world had narrowed down to a piece of land which she could feel with her hands.

She stood for a moment as if she were trying to absorb all these painful places into her body. She herself felt no pain.

And while she was standing there sunk into herself a refugee approached her and he said: "Jewish girl, where are you from?"

"From here."

"And you weren't in the camps?"

"No."

"I lost everyone. What shall I do?"

"In the spring they'll all come back. I'm sure of it."

"How do you know?"

"I'm quite sure. You can believe me." There was strength in her voice. And the man stood rooted to the spot.

"Thank you," he said, as if he had been given a great gift.

"Don't mention it," said Tzili, as she had been taught to say at home.

Without asking for further details, the man vanished as abruptly as he had appeared.

Evening drew near and the last rays of the sun fell golden on the hillside. "I lived here and now I'm leaving," said Tzili, and she felt a slight twinge in her chest. The embryo throbbed gently in her belly. Her vision narrowed even further. Now she could picture to herself the paths lying underneath the carpet of snow. There was no resentment in her heart, only longing, longing for the earth on which she stood. Everything beyond this little corner of the world seemed alien and remote to her.

For days she had not tasted food. She would sit for hours sucking the snow. The melted snow assuaged her hunger. The liquids refreshed her. Now she felt a faint anxiety.

And while she was standing transfixed by what she saw, Mark rose up before her.

"Mark," the word burst from her throat.

Mark seemed surprised. He stood still. And then he asked: "Why are you going to the refugees? Don't you know how bad they are?"

"I was looking for you."

"You won't find me there. I keep as far away as possible from them."

"Where are you?"

"Setting sail."

"Where to?"

All at once a flock of birds rose into the air and crossed the darkening horizon, and Tzili understood that he had only called her in order to take his leave.

She put the haversack down on the snow. Her eyes opened and she said: "My search was in vain." It was her own voice which had come back to her.

"So you're abandoning me to the refugees, those

bad, wicked people." A voice that had been locked up inside her broke out and rose into the air. "I'm asking you a question. Answer me. If you don't want me, tell me. I'm not complaining. I love you anyway. I'll make you herb tea if you like. The mountain is unoccupied. It's waiting for us. There's no one there; we can go back to it. It's a good mountain, you said so yourself. I'll go to the village and bring back supplies, I won't be lazy. You can believe me. Don't you believe me?"

After this she sat for hours next to the haversack. She woke up and fell asleep again, and when she finally rose to her feet brown vapors were already rising from the valleys. Here and there a peasant stretched himself as if after a long sleep. There were no refugees to be seen.

"So you're abandoning me," the old anger flickered up in her again. It wasn't really anger, but only a weak echo of anger. She was with herself as if after a long hunger. She narrowed her eyes and stroked her belly, and then she said to herself: "Mark's probably not allowed to leave, for the time being. Later on, they'll let him go. He's not his own boss, after all."

The snow thawed and the first convoys of refugees poured down the hillsides. Strange, thought Tzili, the war's over and I didn't know. Mark must have known before me; he must be happy now. Suddenly she felt that her life was moving toward some other destination, where the colors were different. She heard the voices of the refugees, and the sound was so familiar that it hurt her.

She thought that she would go to the high mountain where she had first met Mark. She set her steps in that direction but the road was covered with mud and she gave up. Later, she said to herself.

Afterward the commotion died down and the lips of the land could be heard quietly sucking all over the plains. The liquids were being absorbed into the earth.

"Thank you, Maria," said Tzili. "Thanks to you I'm still alive. But for you I would already be in another world. Thanks to you I'm still here. Isn't it strange that thanks to you I'm still here? I'm grateful to you, Maria." Tzili was surprised by the words that came out of her mouth.

She let the memory of Maria flow over her for a moment, and as she did so she saw her figure emerge from the mist and stand solidly before her eyes. A tall, strong woman dressed with simple elegance. When she came into her mother's shop she filled it with the breath of city streets, cafés, and theaters. She never hid her opinions. She would often say that she was fond of the Jews, although not the religious ones. Those she had always hated, but the freethinking Jews who lived in the city were men after her own heart. They knew what civilization meant; they knew how to get the most out of life in the city. Of course, her appearances would always be accompanied by a certain fear, because of her connections with the provincial officials, the tax collectors, the police, and the hospitals. And when her daughters grew up, the circle of her acquaintances was enlarged. Not without scandals, of course.

And when Tzili's brother got one of her daughters into trouble, Maria's tone changed. She threatened them brutally, and in the end she extorted a tidy sum. Tzili remembered this episode too, but she felt no resentment. A proud woman, she concluded to herself.

Katerina, with whom she had spent two whole seasons, had often used this combination of words—"a proud woman." Katerina too, Tzili now remembered with affection.

And while Tzili was standing there in a kind of trance, the refugees streamed toward her in a hungry swarm. She wanted to run for her life, but it was too late. They surrounded her on all sides: "Who are you?"

"I'm from here." At last she found the words.

"And where were you during the war?"

"Here."

"Can't you see?" One of the refugees interrupted. "She's afraid."

"And you weren't in any of the camps?"

"No."

"And no one gave you away?"

"Can't you see?" The same man intervened again. "She doesn't look Jewish. She looks healthy."

"A miracle," said the questioner and turned aside.

The news spread from one to the other but it made no impression on the refugees.

Later on Tzili asked: "Did you see Mark?"

"What's his last name?" asked a woman.

Tzili hung her head. She did not know.

The cold spring sun exposed them like moles. A motley crew of men, women, and children. The cold light showed up their ragged clothes. The convoy turned south and Tzili went with them. No one asked, "Where are you from?" or "Where are you going?" From time to time a supply-laden cart appeared and the people swarmed over it like ants. The familiar words from home now sounded wild and foreign to her. The refugees did not appear contented with anything. They argued, laughed, and fought, and at night they fell to the ground like sacks.

"What am I doing here?" Tzili asked herself. "I prefer the mountains and the rivers. Mark himself told me not to go with them. If I go too far, who knows if I'll ever find him?"

From here she could still see the mountain where Mark had revealed himself to her, illuminated in the cold evening light. Now the bunker was ruined and the wind blew through it. Her voice broke with longing. No memory stirred in her, only a thin stream of longing flowing out of her toward the distant mountaintop. The calm of evening fell upon the deserted ranges and she fell asleep.

25

They made their way southward. The peasants stood by the roadside displaying their wares: bread, vodka, and smoked meat. But the refugees walked past without buying or bartering. Suffering had made them indifferent. But Tzili was hungry. She sold a garment and received bread and smoked meat in exchange. "Look," said one of the survivors, "she's eating."

Now she saw them from close up: thin, speechless, and withdrawn. The terror had not yet faded from their faces.

The sun sank in the sky and the crust of the earth dried up. The first ploughmen appeared on the mountainsides next to the plains. There were no clouds to darken the sky, only the trees, and the quietness.

They moved slowly through the landscape, looking around them as they walked. They slept a lot. Hardly a word was spoken. A kind of secret veiled their faces. Tzili feared this secret more than the dark nights in the forest.

A convoy of prisoners was led past in chains. From time to time a soldier fired a shot into the air and the prisoners all bent their heads at once. No one looked at them. The survivors were sunk into themselves.

A man came up to Tzili and asked: "Where are you from?" It wasn't the man himself who asked the question, but something inside him, as in a nightmare.

Tzili felt as if her eyes had been opened. She heard words which she had not heard for years, and they lapped against her ears with their whispers. "If I meet my mother, what will I say to her?" She did not know what everyone else already knew: apart from this handful of survivors, there were no Jews left.

The sun opened out. The people unbuttoned their damp clothes and sprawled on the river bank and slept. The long, damp years of the war steamed out of their moldy bodies. Even at night the smell did not disappear. Only Tzili did not sleep. The way the people slept filled her with wonder. A warm breeze touched them gently in their deep sleep. Are they happy? Tzili asked herself. They slept in a heap, defenseless bodies suddenly abandoned by danger.

The next day too no one woke up. "What do they do in their sleep?" she asked without knowing what she was asking. "I'll go on," she said. "No one will notice my absence. I'll work for the peasants like I did before. If I work hard they'll give me bread. What more do I need?" Her thoughts flowed as of their own accord. All the years of the war, in the forest and on the roads, even when she and Mark were together, she had not thought. Now the thoughts seemed to come floating up to the surface of her mind.

For a moment she thought of getting up and leaving the sleeping people and returning to the mountain where she had first met Mark. The mountain itself had disappeared from view, but she could still see the swamps below it. They shone like two polished mirrors. Her longings were deep and charged with heavy feelings. They drew her like a magnet, but as soon as she rose to her feet she felt that her body had lost its lightness. Not only her belly was swollen but also her legs. The light, strong columns which had borne her like the wind were no longer what they had been.

Now she knew that she would never go back to that enchanted mountain; everything that had happened there would remain buried inside her. She would wander far and wide, but she would never see the mountain again. Her fate would be the fate of these refugees sleeping beside her.

She wanted to weep but the tears remained locked inside her. She sat without moving and felt the sleep of the refugees invading her body. And soon she too was deep in sleep.

26

Their sleep lasted a number of days. From time to time one of them opened his eyes and stretched his arms as if he were trying to wake up. All in vain. He too, like everyone else, was stuck to the ground.

Tzili opened the haversack and spread the clothes out to dry. Two long dresses, a petticoat, children's trousers, the kitchen knife which Mark had used to make the bunker, and two books—this is what was left.

From the size of the garments Tzili understood that Mark's wife was a tall, slender woman and the children were about five years old, thin like their mother. And she noticed too that the dresses buttoned up to the neck, which meant that Mark's wife was from a traditional family. The petticoat was plain, without any flowers. There were two yellow stains on it, apparently from the damp.

She sat looking at the inanimate objects as if she were trying to make them speak. From time to time she stroked them. The silence all around, as in the wake of every war, was profound.

Whenever she felt hunger gnawing at her stomach she would take a garment from the haversack and offer it in exchange for food. At first she had asked Mark to forgive her, although then too, she had not given the matter too much thought. Later she had stopped asking. She was often hungry and she bartered one garment after the other. The haversack had emptied fast, and now this was all that was left.

These things I won't sell, she said to herself, although she knew that the first time she felt hungry she would have to sell them. She would often feel a voracious greed for food, a greed she could not overcome. Mark will understand, she said to herself, it's not my fault.

She sat and listened to the pulsing of the embryo inside her. It floated quietly in her womb, and from time to time it kicked. It's alive, she told herself, and she was glad.

The next day spring burst forth in a profusion of flowers. And the sleepers awoke. It was not an easy awakening. For hours they went on lying, stuck to the ground. Not as many as they had seemed at first—about thirty people all told.

In the afternoon, as the heat of the sun increased, a few of them rose to their feet. In the light of the sun they looked thin and somewhat transparent. Someone approached her and said: "Where are you from?" He spoke in German Jewish. He looked like Mark, only taller and younger.

"From here," said Tzili.

"I don't understand," said the man. "You weren't born here, were you?"

"Yes," said Tzili.

"And what did you speak at home?"

"We tried to speak German."

"That's funny, so did we," said the stranger, opening his eyes wide. "My grandmother and grandfather still spoke Yiddish. I liked the way they talked."

Tzili had never seen her grandfather. This grandfather, her father's father, a rabbi in a remote village in the Carpathian mountains, had lived to a ripe old age and had never forgiven his son for abandoning the faith of his fathers. His name was never mentioned at home. Her mother's parents had died young.

"Where are we going?" the man asked.

"I don't know."

"I have to get there soon. My engineering studies were interrupted in the middle. I've missed enough already. If I don't arrive in time I may be too late to register. A person starts a course of study and all of a sudden a war comes and messes everything up."

"Where were you during the war?" asked Tzili.

"Why do you ask? With everyone else, of course. Can't you see?" he said and stretched out

135

his arm. There was a number there, tattooed in dark blue on his skin. "But I don't want to talk about it. If I start talking about it, I'll never stop. I've made up my mind that from now on I'm starting my life again. And for me that means studying. Completing my studies, to be precise."

This logic astounded Tzili. Now she saw: the man spoke quietly enough, but his right hand waved jerkily as he spoke and fell abruptly to his side, as if it had been cut off in midair.

He added: "I've always been an outstanding student. My average was ninety. And that's no joke. Of course, it made the others jealous. But what of it? I was only doing what I was supposed to do. I like engineering. I've always liked it."

Tzili was enchanted by his eloquence. It was a long time since she had heard such an uninterrupted flow of words. It was the way Blanca and Yetty and her brothers used to talk. Exams, exams always around the corner. Now the words momentarily warmed her frozen memory.

After a pause he said: "There were two exams I didn't take, through no fault of my own. I won't let them get away with it. It wasn't my fault."

"Never mind," said Tzili, for some reason.

"I won't let them get away with it. It wasn't my fault."

And for a moment it seemed that they were sitting, not in an open field in the spring after the war, but in a salon where coffee and cheesecake were being served. The hostess asks: "Who else wants coffee?" A student on vacation speaks of his achievements. Tzili now remembered her own home, her sister Blanca, sulkily hunching her shoulder, her books piled on the table.

The man rose to his feet and said: "I'm not hanging around here. I haven't got any time to waste. These people are sleeping as if time lasts forever."

"They're tired," said Tzili.

"I don't accept that," said the man, with a peculiar gravity. "There's a limit to what a person can afford to miss. I've made up my mind to finish. I'm not going to leave my studies broken off in the middle. I have to get there in time. If I arrive in time I'll be able to register for the second semester."

Tzili asked no more. His eloquence stunned her. And as he spoke, scene after scene of a drama not unfamiliar to her unfolded before her eyes: a race whose demanding pace had not been softened even by the years of war.

He looked around him and said: "I'm going. There's nothing for me to do here."

Tzili remembered that Mark too had stood on the mountainside and announced firmly that he was going. If she had said to him then, "Don't go," perhaps he would not have gone.

"Mark," she said.

The man turned his head and said, "My name isn't Mark. My name's Max, Max Engelbaum. Remember it."

"Don't go," said Tzili.

"Thank you," said the man, "but I haven't any time to waste. I have no intention of spending my time sleeping. And in general, if you understand me, I don't want to spend any more time in the company of these people." He made a funny little half bow, like a clerk rising from his desk, and abruptly said: "Adieu."

Tzili noticed that he walked away the way people had walked toward the railway station in former days, with brisk, purposeful steps which from a distance looked slightly ridiculous.

"Adieu," he called again, as if he were about to step onto the carriage stair.

The awakening lasted a number of days. It was a slow, wordless awakening. The refugees sat on the banks of the river and gazed at the water. The water was very clear now and a kind of radiance shone on its surface. No one went down to bathe. From time to time a word or phrase rose into the air. They were struggling with the coils of their sleep, which were still lying on the ground.

Tzili felt that she had come a very long way. And if she stayed with these people she would go even further away. Where was Mark? Was he too following her, or was he perhaps still waiting, imprisoned in the same place? Perhaps he did not know that the war was over.

And while she was sitting and staring, a woman came up to her and said: "You need milk."

"I have none," said Tzili apologetically.

"You need milk, I said." The woman was no longer young. Her face was haggard and there was a kind of fury in the set of her mouth.

"I'll see to it," said Tzili, in order to appease the woman's wrath.

"Do it straight away. A pregnant woman needs milk. It's as necessary to her as the air she breathes, and you sit here doing nothing."

Tzili said no more. When she did not respond, the woman grew angry and said: "A woman should look after her body. A woman is not an insect. And by the way, where's the bastard who did this to you?"

"His name is Mark," said Tzili softly.

"In that case, let him take care of it."

"He's not here."

"Where is he?"

Tzili sat looking at her without resentment. No one interfered. They were sitting sunk into themselves. The woman turned away and went to sit on the river bank.

That night cool spring winds blew, bringing with them shadows from the mountains. Quiet shadows that clung soundlessly to the trees but that nevertheless caused a commotion. At first people tried to chase them away as if they were birds, but for some reason the shadows clung to the trees and refused to go.

And as if to spite them, the night was very bright, and they could see the shadows clearly, breathing fearfully.

"Go away, leave us alone!" The shouts arose from every side. And when the shadows refused to go, people began to beat them.

The shadows did not react. Their stubborn resistance infuriated the people and they cast off all restraint.

All night long the battle lasted. Bodies and shadows fought each other in silence, violently. The only sound was the thud of their blows.

When day broke the shadows fled.

The survivors were not happy. A kind of sadness darkened their daylight hours. Tzili did not stir from her corner. She too was affected by the sadness. Now she understood what she had not understood before: everything was gone, gone forever. She would remain alone, alone forever. Even the fetus inside her, because it was inside her, would be as lonely as she. No one would ever ask again: "Where were you and what happened to you?" And if someone did ask, she would not reply. She loved Mark now more than ever, but she loved his wife and children too.

The woman who had grown angry with her before on account of the milk now sat wrapped up in herself. A kind of tenderness shone from her eyes, as if she were, not a woman who had lost herself and all she possessed, but a woman with children, whose love for her children was too much for her to bear.

27

Spring was now at its height, its light was everywhere. Some of the people could not bear the silence and left. The rest sat on the ground and played cards. The old madness, buried for years, broke out: cards and gambling. All at once they shook off their damp, rotting rags and put on carefree expressions, laughing and teasing each other. Tzili did not yet know that a new way of life was unconsciously coming into being here.

The holiday atmosphere reminded Tzili of her parents. When she was still small they had spent their summer vacations in a pension on the banks of the Danube. Her parents were short of money, but they had spared no effort in order to be in the company, if only for two weeks, of speakers of correct German. As if to spite them, however, most of the people there spoke Yiddish. This annoyed her father greatly, and he said: "You can't get away from them. They creep in everywhere." Afterward he fell ill, and they stayed at home and spent their money on doctors and medicine.

No one spoke of the war anymore. The card

games devoured their time. A few of them went to buy supplies, but as soon as they got back they joined enthusiastically in the game. Every now and then someone would remember to say: "What will become of us?" But the question was not serious. It was only part of the game. "What's wrong with staying right here? We've got plenty of coffee, cigarettes—we can stay here for the rest of our lives"—someone would nevertheless take the trouble to reply.

Not far from where they sat the troops passed by, a vigorous army liberated from the siege, invading the countryside on fresh young horses. They all admired the Russians, the volunteers and the partisans, but it was not an admiration which entailed a desire for action. "Let the soldiers fight, let them avenge us."

Tzili was with herself and the tiny fetus in her womb. Words which Mark had spoken to her on the mountain rang in her ears. Scenes from the mountain days passed before her eyes like vivid, ritual tableaus. Mark no longer appeared to her. For hours she sat and waited for him to reveal himself. He's dead—the thought flashed through her mind and immediately disappeared.

One evening a few more Jewish survivors appeared, bringing a new commotion. And one of them, a youthful-looking man, spoke of the coming salvation. He spoke of the cleansing of sins, the purification of the soul. He spoke eloquently, in a pleasant voice. His appearance was not ravaged. Thin, but not horrifyingly thin. Some of them recognized him and remembered him from the camp as a quiet young man, working and suffering in silence. They had never imagined that he had so much to say.

Tzili liked the look of him and she drew near to hear him speak. He spoke patiently, imploringly, without raising his voice. As if he were speaking of things that were self-evident. And for a moment it seemed that he was not speaking, but singing.

The people were absorbed in their card game, and the young man's eloquence disturbed them. At first they asked him to leave them alone and go somewhere else. The young man begged their pardon and said that he had only come to tell them what he himself had been told. And if what he had been told was true, he could not be silent.

It was obvious that he was a well-brought-up young man. He spoke politely in a correct German Jewish, and wished no one any harm. But his apologies were to no avail. They ordered him to leave, or at any rate to shut up. The young man seemed about to depart, but something inside him, something compulsive, stopped him, and he stood his ground and went on talking. One of the card players, who had been losing and was in a bad mood, stood up and hit him.

To everyone's surprise, the young man burst out crying.

It was more like wailing than crying. The whole night long he sat and wailed. Through his wailing the history of his life emerged. He was an architect. Like his father and forefathers, he was remote from Jewish affairs, busy trying to set up an independent studio. The war took him completely by surprise. In the camp something had happened to him. His workmate in the forced labor gang, something of a Jewish scholar although not a believer, had taught him a little Bible, Mishna, and the Sayings of the Fathers. After the war he had begun to hear voices, clear, unconfused voices, and one evening the cry had burst from his throat: "Jews repent, return to your Father in Heaven."

From then on he never stopped talking, explaining, and calling on the Jews to repent. And when people refused to listen or hit him, he fell to the ground and wept.

The next day one of the card players found a way to get rid of him. He approached the young man and said to him in his own language, in a whisper: "Why waste your time on these stubborn Jews? Down below, not far from here, there are plenty of survivors, gentle people like you. They're waiting for someone to come and show them the way. You'll do it. You're just the right person. Believe me."

Strange, these words had an immediate effect. He rose to his feet and asked the way, and without another word he set out.

Tzili felt sorry for the young man who had been led astray. She covered her face with her hands. The others too seemed unhappy. They returned to their card playing as if it were not a game, but an urgent duty.

28

After this the weather was fine and mild, without wind or rain. The grass grew thick and wild and the people sat about drinking coffee and playing cards. There were no quarrels, and for a while it seemed as if things would go on like this forever.

From time to time peasant women would appear, spread out their wares on flowered cloths, and offer the survivors apples, smoked meat, and black bread. The survivors bartered clothes for food. Some of them had gold coins too, old watches, and all kinds of trinkets they had kept with them through the years of the war. They gave these things away for food without haggling about their worth.

Tzili too sold a dress. In exchange she received a joint of smoked meat, two loaves of fresh bread, and a piece of cheese. She remembered the woman's anger and asked for milk, but they had no milk. Tzili sat on the ground and ate heartily.

Apart from the card game nobody took any interest in anything. The woman who had scolded

Tzili for not providing herself with milk played avidly. Tzili sat and watched them for hours at a time. Their faces reminded her of people from home, but nevertheless they looked like strangers. Perhaps because of the smell, the wet rot of years which clung to them still.

And while they were all absorbed in their eager game, a sudden fear fell on Tzili. What would she do if they all came back? What would she say, and how would she explain? She would say that she loved Mark. She now feared the questions she would be asked more than she feared the strangers. She curled up and closed her eyes. The fear which came from far away invaded her sleep too. She saw her mother looking at her through a very narrow slit. Her face was blurred but her question was clear: Who was this seducer, who was this Mark?

And Tzili's fears were not in vain. One evening everything exploded. One of the card players, a quiet man with the face of a clerk, gentle-mannered and seemingly content, suddenly threw his cards down and said: "What am I doing here?"

At first this sentence seemed part of the game, annoyance at some little loss, a provocative remark. The game went on for some time longer, without anyone sensing the dynamite about to explode.

Suddenly the man rose to his feet and said: "What am I doing here?"

"What do you mean, what are you doing here?" they said. "You're playing cards."

"I'm a murderer," he said, not in anger, but with a kind of quiet deliberation, as if the scream in his throat had turned, within a short space of time, to a clear admission of guilt.

"Don't talk like that," they said.

"You know it better than I do," he said. "You'll be my witnesses when the time comes."

"Of course we'll be your witnesses. Of course we will."

"You'll say that Zigi Baum is a murderer."

"That you can't expect of us."

"I, for one, don't intend hiding anything."

This exchange, proceeding without anger, in a matter-of-fact tone, turned gradually into a menacing confrontation.

"You won't tell the truth, then?"

"Of course we'll tell the truth."

"A man abandons his wife and children, his father and his mother. What is he if not a murderer?" He raised his head and a smile broke out on his face. Now he looked like a man who had done what had to be done and was about to take up his practical duties again. He took off his coat, sat down on the ground, and looked around him. He showed no signs of agitation.

For a moment it seemed as if he were about to ask a question. All eyes were on him. He bowed his head. They averted their eyes.

"It's not a big thing to ask, I think," he said to himself. "I didn't want to ask you to do it, I don't know if I should have asked you. The day of judgment will come in the end. If not in this world then in the next. I can't imagine life without justice."

He did not seem confused. There was a straightforward kind of matter of factness in his look. As if he wanted to bring a certain matter up for discussion, a matter which had become a little complicated, but not to such an extent that it could not be discussed with people who were close to him.

He took his tobacco out of his pocket, rolled himself a cigarette, lit it and inhaled the smoke.

Everyone breathed a sigh of relief. He said: "This is good tobacco. It's got the right degree of moisture. You remember how we used to fight over cigarette stubs? We lost our human image. Pardon me—do you say human image or divine image?"

"Neither," said a voice from behind.

This remark was apparently not to his liking. He clamped his teeth on the cigarette and passed his hand over his hair. Now you could see how old he was: not more than thirty-five. His cheeks were slightly lined, his nose was straight, and his ears were set close to his head. There was a concentrated look in his eyes.

"How much do I owe?" he asked one of the others. "I lost, I think."

"It's all written down. You'll pay us back later."

"I don't like being in debt. How much do I owe?"

There was no response. He inhaled and blew the smoke out downward. "Strange," he said. "The war is over. I never imagined it would end like this."

Darkness fell and the tension relaxed. Zigi looked slightly ashamed of the scandal he had caused.

And while they were all sitting there, Zigi rose to his feet, stretched his arms, and raised his knees as if he were about to run a race. In the camp too he had been in the habit of taking short runs, in order to warm himself up. They had saved him then from depression.

Now it seemed as if he were about to take a run, as in the old days. One, two, he said, and set out. He ran six full rounds, and on the seventh he rose into the air and with a broad, slow movement cast himself into the water.

For a moment they all stood rooted to the spot. Then they all rushed together to the single hurricane lamp and stood waving it in the air. "Zigi, Zigi," they cried. A few of them jumped into the river.

All night long they labored in the icy water.

Some of them swam far out, but they did not find Zigi.

And when morning broke the river was smooth and placid. A greenish-blue light shone on its surface. No one spoke. They spread their clothes out to dry and the old moldy smell, which seemed to have gone away, rose once more into the air.

Afterward they lit a fire and sat down to eat. Their hunger was voracious. The loaves of bread disappeared one after the other.

Tzili forgot herself for a moment. Zigi's athletic run went on flashing past her eyes, with great rapidity. It seemed to her that he would soon rise from the river, shake the water off his body, and announce: "The river's fine for swimming."

In the afternoon the place suddenly seemed confined and threatening, the light oppressive. The peasant women came and spread their wares on their flowered cloths, but no one bought anything. The women sat and looked at them with watchful eyes. One of them asked: "Why aren't you buying today? We have bread and smoked meat. Fresh milk too."

"Let's go," someone said, and immediately they all stood up. Tzili too raised her heavy body from the ground. No one asked: "Where to?" A dumb wonder stared from their faces, as after enduring grief. Tzili was glad that the haversack was empty, and now she had nothing but her own body to carry.

29

They walked along the riverside, toward the south. The sun shone on the green fields. Now it seemed that Zigi Baum was floating on the current, his arms outspread. Every now and then his image was reflected on the surface of the water. No one stopped to gaze at this shining reflection. The current widened as it approached the dam, a mighty torrent of water.

Later on a few people turned off to the right. They turned off together, without asking any questions or saying good-by. Tzili watched them walk away. They showed no signs of anger or of happiness. They went on walking at the same pace— for some reason, in another direction.

Tzili, it appeared, was already in the sixth month of her pregnancy. Her belly was taut and heavy but her legs, despite the difficulties of the road, walked without stumbling. When the refugees stopped to rest, they ate in silence. The strange disappearance of Zigi Baum had infected them with a subtle terror, unlike anything they had experienced before.

Tzili was happy. Not a happiness which had any outward manifestations: the fetus stirring inside her gave her an appetite and a lust for life. Not so the others: death clung even to their clothes. They tried to shake it off by walking.

From time to time they quickened their pace and Tzili fell behind. They were as absorbed in themselves now as they had been before in their card game. No one asked: "Where is she?" but nevertheless Tzili felt that their closeness to her was stronger than their distraction.

She no longer thought much about Mark. As if he had set out on a long journey from which it would take a long time to return. He appeared to her now as a tiny figure on the distant horizon, beyond the reach of her voice. She still loved him, but with a different kind of love. A love which had no real taste. From time to time a kind of awe descended on her and she knew: it was Mark, watching her—not uncritically—from afar.

She would say: Mark is inside me, but she didn't really feel it. The fetus was now hers, a secret which no one but she could touch.

Once, when they had stopped to rest, a woman asked her: "Isn't it hard for you?"

"No," said Tzili simply.

"And do you want the baby?"

"Yes."

The woman was surprised by Tzili's reply. She looked at her as if she were some stupid, senseless creature. Then she was sorry and her expression changed to one of wonder and pity: "How will you bring it up?"

"I'll keep it with me all the time," said Tzili simply.

Tzili too wanted to ask: "Where are you from?" But she had learned not to ask. On their last halt a quarrel had broken out between two women as a result of a tactless question. People were very tense and questions brought their repressed anger seething to the surface.

"How old are you?" asked the woman.

"Fifteen."

"So young." Wonder softened the woman's face.

Tzili offered her a piece of bread and she said, "Thank you."

"I," said the woman, "have lost my children. It seems to me that I did everything I could, but they were lost anyway. The oldest was nine and the youngest seven. And I am alive, as you see, even eating. Me they didn't harm. I must be made of iron."

A pain shot through Tzili's diaphragm and she closed her eyes.

"Don't you feel well?" asked the woman.

"It'll pass," said Tzili.

"Give me your mug and I'll fetch you some water."

When the woman returned Tzili was already sitting calmly on the ground. The woman raised the cup to Tzili's mouth and Tzili drank. The woman now wanted more than anything to help Tzili, but she did not know how. Tzili, in spite of everything, had more food than she did.

Straight after this night fell and the woman sank to the ground and slept. She shrank to the size of a child of six. Tzili wanted to cover the woman with her tattered coat, but she immediately suppressed this impulse. She did not want to frighten her.

The others were awake but passive. The isolated words which fluttered in the air were as inward as a conversation between two lovers, no longer young.

The night was warm and fine and Tzili remembered the little yard at home, where she had spent so many hours. Every now and then her mother would call, "Tzili," and Tzili would reply, "Here I am." Of her entire childhood, only this was left. All the rest was shrouded in a heavy mist. She was seized by longing for the little yard. As if it were the misty edge of the Garden of Eden.

"I have to eat." She banished the vision and immediately put her hand into the haversack and tore off a piece of bread. The bread was dry. A few gains of coal were embedded in its bottom crust. She liked the taste of the bread. Afterward she ate a little smoked meat. With every bite she felt her hunger dulled.

30

The summer took them by surprise, hot and broad, filling them with a will to live. The paths all flowed together into green creeks, bordered by tall trees. Refugees streamed from all directions, and for some reason the sight recalled summer holidays, youth movements, seasonal vacations, all kinds of forgotten youthful pleasures. Words from the old lexicon floated in the air. Only their clothes, like an eternal disgrace, went on steaming.

Tzili sat still, this happiness made her anxious. Soon it would give way to screams, pain, and despair.

That night they made a fire, sang and danced, and drank. And as after every catastrophe: embraces, couplings, and despondency in their wake. Tall women with the traces of an old elegance still clinging to them lay sunbathing shamelessly next to the lake.

"What does it matter—there's no point in living anymore anyway," a woman who had apparently run wild all night confessed. She was strong and healthy, fit to bring many more children into the world.

"And you won't go to Palestine?" asked her friend.

"No," said the woman decisively.

"Why not?"

"I want to go to hell."

From this conversation Tzili absorbed the word "Palestine." Once when her sister Yetty had become involved with the Moravian officer, there had been talk of sending her to Palestine. At first Yetty had refused, but then she changed her mind and wanted to go. But by then they didn't have the money to send her. Now Tzili thought often of her sister Yetty. Where was she now?

Tzili's fears were not in vain. The calamities came thick and fast: one woman threw herself into the lake and another swallowed poison. The marvelous oblivion was gone in an instant and the same healthy woman, the one who had refused to go to Palestine, announced: "Death will follow us all our lives, wherever we go. There'll be no more peace for us."

In the afternoon the body was recovered from the lake and the funerals took place one after the other. One of the men, who had the look of a public official even in his rags, spoke at length about the great obligations which were now facing them all. He spoke about memory, the long memory of the Jewish people, the eternal life of the tribe, and the historic necessity of the return to the motherland. Many wept.

After the funeral there was a big argument and the words of the official were heard again. It appeared that the woman who had taken poison had taken it because of a broken promise: someone who wanted to sleep with her had promised to marry her, and the next day he had changed his mind. The woman, who in all the years of suffering had kept the poison hidden in the lining of her coat without using it, had used it now. And something else: before taking the poison the woman had announced her intention of taking it, but no one had believed her.

Now there was nothing left but to say: Because of one night in bed a person commits suicide? So what if he slept with her? So what if he promised her? What do we have left but for the little pleasures of life? Do we have to give those up too?

Tzili took in the words with her eyes shut. She understood the words now, but she did not justify any of them in her heart. She sensed only one thing: the grief which had washed through her too had now become empty and pointless.

31

Now they streamed with the sun toward the sea. And at night they grilled silver fish, fresh from the river, on glowing coals. The nights were warm and clear, bringing to mind a life in which pleasures were real.

There was no lack of quarrels in this mixture. The summer sun worked its magic. As if the years in the camps had vanished without a trace. A forgetfulness which was not without humor. Like, for example, the woman who performed night after night, singing, reciting, and exposing her thighs. No one reminded her of her sins in the labor camp. She was now their carnival queen.

Now too there were those who could not stand the merriment and left. There was no lack of prosecutors, accusers, stirrers up of the past, and spoilsports. At this time too, the first visionaries appeared: short, ardent men who spoke about the salvation of the soul with extraordinary passion. You couldn't get away from them. But the desire to forget was stronger than all these. They ate and drank until late at night.

"What are you doing here?" A man would accost her from time to time, but on seeing that she was pregnant he would withdraw at once and leave her alone.

Tzili was very weak now. The long march had worn her out. From time to time a pain would pierce her and afterward she would feel giddy. Her legs swelled up too, but she bit her lips and said nothing. She was proud that her legs bore her and her baby. For some reason she believed that if her legs were healthy no harm would befall her.

And her life narrowed down to little worries. She forgot everyone and if she remembered them it was casually and absentmindedly. She was with herself, or rather with her body, which kept her occupied day and night. Sometimes someone offered her a piece of fish or bread. When she was very hungry she would stretch out her hand and beg. She wasn't ashamed to beg.

Without anyone noticing, the green creeks turned into a green plain dotted with little lakes. The landscape was so lovely that it hurt, but people were so obsessed with their merrymaking that they took no notice of the change. After a night of drinking they would sleep.

The convoy proceeded slowly and at a ragged pace. Sometimes a sudden panic took hold of them and made them run. Tzili limped after them with the last of her strength. They traipsed from place to place as if they were at the mercy of their changing moods. At this time fate presented Tzili with a moment of peace. Everything was full of joy—the light and the water and her body bearing her baby within it—but not for long.

During one of the panic flights she felt she could not go on. She tried to get up but immediately collapsed again. But for the fat woman, the one who sang and recited and bared her thighs—but for her and the fact that she noticed Tzili's absence and immediately cried: "We've left the child behind"—they would have gone on without her. At first no one paid any attention to her cry, but she was determined to be heard. She called out again, with a kind of authority, like a woman used to raising her voice, and the convoy drew to a halt.

No one knew what to do. During the years of the war they had learned to run and to stop for no one. The fat woman made them stop. "Man is not an insect. This time no one will shirk his duty." A sudden shame covered their faces.

There was no doctor among them, but there was a man who had been a merchant in peacetime and claimed that he had once taken a course in first aid, and he said: "We'll have to carry her on a stretcher." Strange: the words did their work at once. One of them went to fetch wood and another rope, and the skinny merchant, who never opened his mouth, knelt down and with movements that were almost prayerful he joined and he knotted. And they produced a sheet too, and a ragged blanket, and even some pins and some hooks. By nightfall the merchant could survey his handiwork and say: "She'll be quite comfortable on this."

And the next day when the stretcher bearers lifted the stretcher onto their shoulders and set out at the head of the convoy, a mighty song burst from their throats. A rousing sound, like pent up water bursting from a dam. "We are the torch bearers," roared the stretcher bearers, and everyone else joined in.

They carried the stretcher along the creeks and sang. The summer, the glorious summer, turned every corner golden. Tzili herself closed her eyes and tried to make the giddiness go away. The merchant urged the stretcher bearers on: "Run, boys, run. The child needs a doctor." All his anxieties gathered together in his face. And when they stopped he would sit next to her and feed her. He bought whatever he could lay his hands on, but to Tzili he gave only milk products and fruit. Tzili had lost her appetite.

"Thank you," said Tzili.

"There's no reason to thank me."

"Why not?"

"What else have I got to do?" His eyes opened and in the white of the left eye a yellow stain glittered. His despair was naked.

"You're helping me."

"What of it?"

And Tzili stopped thanking him.

At night he would fold his legs and sleep at her side. And Tzili was suddenly freed of the burden of her survival. The stretcher bearers took turns carrying her from place to place. There was not a village or a town to be seen, only here and there a house, here and there a farmer.

"Where are you from?" asked Tzili.

The merchant told her, unwillingly and without going into detail, but he did tell her about Palestine. In his youth he had wanted to go to Palestine. He had spent some time on a Zionist training farm, and he even had a certificate, but his late father had fallen ill and his illness had lasted for years. After that he had married and had children.

There was nothing captivating in the way he spoke. It was evident that he wanted to cut things short in everything concerning himself, like a merchant who put his trust in practical affairs and knew that they took precedence over emotions. Tzili asked no further. He himself left the stretcher only to fetch milk for her. Tzili drank the milk in spite of herself, so that he would not worry.

He never asked: "Where are you from?" or "What happened to you?" He would sit by her side as dumb as an animal. His face was ageless. Sometimes he looked old and clumsy and sometimes as agile as a man of thirty.

Once Tzili tried to get off the stretcher. He scolded her roundly. On no account was she to get off the stretcher until she saw a doctor. He knew that this was so from the first aid course.

And the fat woman who had saved Tzili started entertaining them again at night. She would sing and recite and expose her fat thighs. The merchant raised Tzili's head and she saw everything. She felt no affection for any of them, but they were carrying her, taking turns to carry her, from place to place. Between one pain and the next she wanted to say a kind word to the merchant, but she was afraid of offending him. He for his part walked by her side like a man doing his duty, without any exaggeration. Tzili grew accustomed to him, as if he were an irritating brother.

And thus they reached Zagreb. Zagreb was in turmoil. In the yard of the Joint Distribution Committee people were distributing biscuits, canned goods, and colored socks from America. In the courtyard they all mingled freely: visionaries, merchants, moneychangers, and sick people. No one knew what to do in the strange, half-ruined city. Someone shouted loudly: "If you want to get to Palestine, you'd better go to Naples. Here they're nothing but a bunch of money-grubbing profiteers and crooks."

The stretcher bearers put the stretcher down in a shady corner and said: "From now on somebody else can take over." The merchant was alarmed by this announcement and he implored them: "You've done great things, why not carry on?" But they no longer took any notice of him. The sight of the city had apparently confused them. Suddenly they looked tall and ungainly. In vain the merchant pleaded with them. They stood their ground: "From now on it's not our job." The merchant stood helplessly in the middle of the courtyard. There was no doctor present, and the officials of the Joint Committee were busy defending themselves from the survivors, who assailed their caged counters with great force.

If only the merchant had said, "I can't go on anymore," it would have been easier for Tzili. His desperate scurrying about hurt her. But he did not abandon her. He kept on charging into the crowd and asking: "Is there a doctor here? Is there a doctor here?"

People came and went and in the big courtyard, enclosed in a wall of medium height, men and women slept by day and by night. Every now and then an official would emerge and threaten the sleepers or the people besieging the doors. The official's neat appearance recalled other days, but not his voice.

And there was a visionary there too, thin and vacant-faced, who wandered through the crowds muttering: "Repent, repent." People would throw him a coin on condition that he shut up. And he would accept the condition, but not for long.

Pain assailed Tzili from every quarter. Her feet were frozen. The merchant ran from place to place, drugged with the little mission he had taken upon himself. No one came to his aid. When night fell, he put his head between his knees and wept.

In the end a military ambulance came and took her away. The merchant begged them: "Take me, take me too. The child has no one in the whole world." The driver ignored his despairing cries and drove away.

Tzili's pains were very bad, and the sight of the imploring merchant running after the ambulance made them worse. She wanted to scream, but she didn't have the strength.

32

It was a makeshift hospital housed in an army barracks partitioned with blankets. Soldiers and partisans, women and children, lay crowded together. Screams rose from every side. Tzili was placed on a big bed, apparently requisitioned from one of the bombed houses.

For days she had not heard the throbbing of the fetus. Now it seemed to her that it was stirring again. The nurse sponged her down with a warm, wet cloth and asked: "Where are you from?" And Tzili told her. The broad, placid face of the gentile nurse brought her a sudden serenity. It was evident that the young nurse came from a good home. She did her work quietly, without superfluous gestures.

Tzili asked wonderingly: "Where are you from?" "From here," said the nurse. A disinterested light shone from her blue eyes. The nurse told her that every day more soldiers and refugees were brought to the hospital. There were no beds and no doctors. The few doctors there were torn between the hospitals scattered throughout the ruined city.

Later Tzili fell asleep. She slept deeply. She saw Mark and he looked like the merchant who had taken care of her. Tzili told him that she had been obliged to sell all the clothes in the haversack and in the commotion she had lost the haversack too. Perhaps it was with the merchant. "The merchant?" asked Mark in surprise. "Who is this merchant?" Tzili was alarmed by Mark's astonished face. She told him, at length, of all that had happened to her since leaving the mountain. Mark bowed his head and said: "It's not my business anymore." There was a note of criticism in his voice. Tzili made haste to appease him. Her voice choked and she woke up.

The next day the doctor came and examined her. He spoke German. Tzili answered his hurried questions quietly. He told the nurse that she had to be taken to the surgical ward that same night. Tzili saw the morning light darken next to the window. The bars reminded her of home.

They took her to the surgical ward while it was still light. There was a queue and the gentile nurse, who spoke to her in broken German mixed with Slavic words, held her hand. From her Tzili learned that the fetus inside her was dead, and that soon it would be removed from her womb. The anesthetist was a short man wearing a Balaklava hat. Tzili screamed once and that was all.

Then it was night. A long night, carved out of stone, which lasted for three days. Several times they tried to wake her. Medics and soldiers rushed frantically about carrying stretchers. Tzili wandered in a dark stone tunnel, strangers and acquaintances passing before her eyes, clear and unblurred. I'm going back, she said to herself and clung tightly to the wooden handle.

When she woke the nurse was standing beside her. Tzili asked, for some reason, if the merchant too had been hurt. The nurse told her that the operation had not taken long, the doctors were satisfied, and now she must rest. She held a spoon to her mouth.

"Was I good?" asked Tzili.

"You were very good."

"Why did I scream?" she wondered.

"You didn't scream, you didn't make a sound."

In the evening the nurse told her that she had not stirred from the hospital for a whole week. Every day they brought more soldiers and refugees, some of them badly hurt, and she could not leave. Her fiancé was probably angry with her. Her round face looked worried.

"He'll take you back," said Tzili.

"He's not an easy man," confessed the nurse.

"Tell him that you love him."

"He wants to sleep with me," the nurse whispered in her ear.

Tzili laughed. The thin gruel and the conversation distracted her from her pain. Her mind was empty of thought or sorrow. And the pain too grew duller. All she wanted was to sleep. Sleep drew her like a magnet.

33

She fell asleep again. In the meantime the soldiers and refugees crammed the hut until there was no room to move. The medics pushed the beds together and they moved Tzili's bed into the doorway. She slept. Someone strange and far away ordered her not to dream, and she obeyed him and stopped dreaming. She floated on the surface of a vacant sleep for a few days, and when she woke her memory was emptier than ever.

The hut stretched lengthwise before her, full of men, women, and children. The torn partitions no longer hid anything. "Don't shout," grumbled the medics, "it won't do you any good." They were tired of the commotion and of the suffering. The nurses were more tolerant, and at night they would cuddle with the medics or the ambulant patients.

Tzili lay awake. Of all her scattered life it seemed to her that nothing was left. Even her body was no longer hers. A jumble of sounds and shapes flowed into her without touching her.

"Are you back from your leave?" she remembered to ask the nurse.

"I quarreled with my fiancé."

"Why?"

"He's jealous of me. He hit me. I swore never to see him again." Her big peasant hands expressed more than her face.

"And you, did you love him?" she asked Tzili without looking at her.

"Who?"

"Your fiancé."

"Yes," said Tzili, quickly.

"With Jews, perhaps, it's different."

Bitter lines had appeared overnight on her peasant's face. Tzili now felt a kind of solidarity with this country girl whose fiancé had beaten her with his hard fists.

At night the hut was full of screams. One of the medics attacked a refugee and called him a Jewish crook. A sudden dread ran through Tzili's body.

The next day, when she stood up, she realized for the first time that she had lost her sense of balance too. She stood leaning against the wall, and for a moment it seemed to her that she would never again be able to stand upright without support.

"Haven't you seen a haversack anywhere?" she asked one of the medics.

"There's disinfection here. We burn everything."

Women who were no longer young stood next to the lavatories and smeared creams on their faces. They spoke to each other in whispers and laughed provocatively. The years of suffering had bowed their bodies but had not destroyed their will to live. One of the women sat on a bench and massaged her swollen legs with pulling, clutching movements.

Later the medics brought in a lot of new patients. They reclassified the patients and put the ones who were getting better out in the yard.

They put Tzili's bed out too. All the gentile nurses' pleading was in vain.

The next day officials from the Joint Committee came to the yard and distributed dresses and shoes and flowered petticoats. There was a rush on the boxes, and the officials who had come to give things to the women had to beat them off instead. Tzili received a red dress, a petticoat, and a pair of high-heeled shoes. A heavy smell of perfume still clung to the crumpled goods.

"What are you fighting for?" an official asked accusingly.

"For a pretty dress," one of the women answered boldly.

"You people were in the camps weren't you? From you we expect something different," said someone in an American accent.

Later the gentile nurse came and spoke encouragingly to Tzili. "You must be strong and hold your head high. Don't give yourself away and don't show any feelings. What happened to you could have happened to anyone. You have to forget. It's not a tragedy. You're young and pretty. Don't think about the past. Think about the future. And don't get married."

She spoke to her like a loyal friend, or an older sister. Tzili felt the external words spoken by the gentile nurse strengthening her. She wanted to thank her and she didn't know how. She gave her the petticoat she had just received from the Joint Committee. The nurse took it and put it into the big pocket in her apron.

Early in the morning they chased everyone out of the yard.

34

Now everyone streamed to the beach. Fishermen stood by little booths and sold grilled fish. The smell of the fires spread a homely cheerfulness around. Before the war the place had evidently been a jolly seaside promenade. A few traces of the old life still clung to the peeling walls.

Beyond the walls lay the beach, white and spotted with oil stains, here and there an old signpost, a few shacks and boats. Tzili was weak and hungry. There was no familiar face to which she could turn, only strange refugees with swollen packs on their backs and hunger and urgency on their faces. They streamed over the sand to the sea.

Tzili sat down and watched. The old desire to watch came back to her. At night the people lit fires and sang rousing Zionist songs. No one knew how long they would be there. They had food. Tzili too went down to the sea and sat among the refugees. The wound in her stomach was apparently healing. The pain was bad but not unendurable.

"These fish are excellent."

"Fish is good for you."

"I'm going up to buy another one."

These sentences for some reason penetrated into Tzili's head, and she marveled at them.

Somewhere a quarrel broke out. A hefty man shouted at the top of his voice: "No one's going to kill me anymore." Somewhere else people were dancing the hora. One of the refugees sitting next to Tzili remarked: "Palestine's not the place for me."

"Why not?" his friend asked him teasingly.

"I'm tired."

"But you're still strong."

"Yes, but there's no more faith in me."

"And what are you going to do instead?"

"I don't know."

Someone lit an oil lamp and illuminated the darkness. The voice of the refugee died down.

And while Tzili sat watching a fat woman approached her and said: "Aren't you Tzili?"

"Yes," she said. "My name is Tzili."

It was the fat woman who had entertained them on their way to Zagreb, singing and reciting and baring her fleshy thighs.

"I'm glad you're here. They've all abandoned me," she said and lowered her heavy body to the ground. "With all the pretty shiksas here, what do they need me for?"

"And where are you going to go?" said Tzili carefully.

"What choice do I have?" The woman's reply was not slow in coming.

For a moment they sat together in silence.

"And you?" asked the woman.

Tzili told her. The fat woman stared at her, devouring every detail. All the great troubles inhabiting her great body seemed to make way for a moment for Tzili's secret.

"I too have nobody left in the world. At first I didn't understand, now I understand. There's the world, and there's Linda. And Linda has nobody in the whole wide world."

One of the officials got onto a box. He spoke in grand, thunderous words. As if he had a loudspeaker stuck to his mouth. He spoke of Palestine, land of liberty.

"Where can a person buy a grilled fish?" said Linda. "I'm going to buy a grilled fish. The hunger's driving me out of my mind. I'll be right back. Don't you leave me too."

Tzili was captivated for a moment by the speaker's voice. He thundered about the need for renewal and dedication. No one interrupted him. It was evident that the words had been pent up in him for a long time. Now their hour had come.

Linda brought two grilled fish. "Linda has to eat. Linda's hungry." She spoke about herself in the third person. She held a fish in a cardboard wrapper out to Tzili.

Tzili tasted and said: "It tastes good."

"Before the war I was a cabaret singer. My parents disapproved of my way of life," Linda suddenly confessed.

"They've forgiven you," said Tzili.

"No one forgives Linda. Linda doesn't forgive herself."

"In Palestine everything will be different," said Tzili, repeating the speaker's words.

Linda chewed the fish and said nothing.

Tzili felt a warm intimacy with this fat woman who spoke about herself in the third person.

All night the speakers spoke. Loud words flooded the dark beach. A thin man spoke of the agonies of rebirth in Palestine. Linda did not find these voices to her taste. In the end she could no longer restrain herself and she called out: "We've had enough words. No more words." And when the speaker took no notice of her threats she went and stood next to the box and announced: "This is fat Linda here. Don't anyone dare come near this box. I'm declaring a cease-words. It's time for silence now." She went back and sat down. No one reacted. People were tired, they huddled in their coats. After a few moments she said to herself: "Phooey. This rebirth makes me sick."

That same night they were taken aboard the

ship. It was a small ship with a bare mast and a chimney. Two projectors illuminated the shore.

"What I'd like now," said Tzili for some reason, "is a pear."

"Linda hasn't got a pear. What a pity that Linda hasn't got a pear."

"I feel ashamed," said Tzili.

"Why do you feel ashamed?"

"Because that's what came into my head."

"I have every respect for such little wishes. Linda herself is all one little wish."

For the time being the sight was not an inspiring one. People climbed over ropes and tarpaulins. Someone shouted: "There's a queue here, no one will get in without waiting in the queue."

The crush was bad and Tzili felt that pain was about to engulf her again. Linda no longer waited for favors and in a thunderous voice she cried: "Make way for the girl. The girl has undergone an operation." No one moved. Linda shouted again, and when no one paid any attention she spread out her arms and swept a couple of young men from their places on a bench.

"Now, in the name of justice, she'll sit down. Her name is Tzili."

Later on, when the commotion had died down and some of the people had gone down to the cabins below and a wind began to blow on the deck, Tzili said: "Thank you."

"What for?"

"For finding me a place."

"Don't thank me. It's your place."

Afterward shouts were heard from below. People were apparently beating the informers and collaborators in the dark, and the latter were screaming at the tops of their voices. Up on the deck, too, there was no peace. In vain the officials tried to restore order.

Between one scream and the next Linda told Tzili what had happened to her during the war. She had a lover, a gentile estate owner who had hidden her in his granaries. She moved from one granary to another. At first she had a wonderful time, she was very happy. But later she came to realize that her lover was a goy in every sense of the word, drunk and violent. She was forced to flee, and in the end she fled to a camp. She didn't like the Jews, but she liked them better than the gentiles. Jews were sloppy but not cruel. She was in the camp for a full year. She learned Yiddish there, and every night she performed for the inmates. She had no regrets. There was a kind of cruel honesty in her brown eyes.

The little ship strained its engines to cross the stormy sea. Up on the deck they did not feel it rock. Most of the day the passengers slept in the striped coats they had been given by the Joint Committee. From time to time the ship sounded its horn.

Linda managed to get hold of a bottle of brandy at last, and her joy knew no bounds. She hugged the bottle and spoke to it in Hungarian. She started drinking right away, and when her heart was glad with brandy she began to sing. The songs she sang were old Hungarian lullabies.

THE REFERENCE SHELF   VOLUME 37 NUMBER 5

AMERICAN
LABOR TODAY

EDITED BY
HERBERT L. MARX, JR.

THE H. W. WILSON COMPANY
NEW YORK   1965

THE REFERENCE SHELF

The books in this series contain reprints of articles, excerpts from books, and addresses on current issues and social trends in the United States and other countries. There are six separately bound numbers in each volume, all of which are generally published in the same calendar year. One number is a collection of recent speeches; each of the others is devoted to a single subject and gives background information and discussion from various points of view, concluding with a comprehensive bibliography.

Subscribers to the current volume receive the books as issued. The subscription rate is $12 ($15 foreign) for a volume of six numbers. Single numbers are $3 each.

PREFACE

This Labor Day [1965] finds more of the country's workers en-joying higher wages and broader comprehensive benefits than ever be-fore. . . . [But] automation and the changes it is bringing in the labor force remain inadequately resolved problems for most unions. Techno-logical innovation is imperative if the economy is to keep moving forward and providing ever higher living standards for America, but the solutions for the human problems of change remain spotty.

Total union membership is shrinking both absolutely and as a percentage of the labor force, according to an authoritative new study by Leo Troy for the National Bureau of Economic Research. Union leadership also finds itself under challenge. Nine of the twenty-seven AFL-CIO vice presidents no longer head their own unions. When the Federation marks its tenth anniversary at San Francisco in December [1965], it will have to decide how to infuse more vitality into its high command. The record this Labor Day shows how far American labor has come—and how many problems it still has to solve.[1]

The excerpt reprinted above serves as a fitting introduction to AMERICAN LABOR TODAY. Not many years ago, the subject of unionism itself was a controversial one. This is no longer gen-erally true, although there is no lack of criticism of certain aspects of unionism and certain unions themselves. Not so long ago, it was assumed that unions would continue to grow in their control of the American workforce and correspondingly in their economic influence. Today, American unions appear to have reached a plateau of growth and influence.

Against such a background, this volume reviews American labor three decades after labor's Magna Carta—the Wagner Act of 1935—and one decade after the formation of the American Federation of Labor—Congress of Industrial Organizations, which brought together the formerly rival AFL and CIO.

The first section of this volume is an overview of labor's stance in today's prosperous economic world. The second section deals with a new and fascinating chapter in labor union development —the steady rise of membership independence within unions.

[1] From "Labor's Unsolved Problems," editorial. New York *Times*. p 14. S. 6, '65.
© 1965 by The New York Times Company. Reprinted by permission.

3

Section III deals with the many facets, some quite new, of collective bargaining. Here, more than in the recruitment of new members or in other areas, unions (together with management) have shown the greatest ingenuity and adaptability.

Section IV summarizes recent developments in labor law and in proposed legislation, including "right-to-work" laws; the Landrum-Griffin Act of 1959 to promote union democracy; antitrust measures; and compulsory arbitration of labor disputes.

In Section V, American labor's role in the world today is examined. In the final section, diverse views are expressed on the pros and cons of unionism, with some suggestions for the future.

The editor expresses sincere appreciation to the organizations, publications, and authors who have granted permission to include the materials which make up this volume.

HERBERT L. MARX, JR.

September 1965

A NOTE TO THE READER

The subject of this volume has been dealt with in two earlier Reference Shelf books: *The American Labor Movement,* by Walter M. Daniels (Volume 30, Number 3), published in 1958; and *American Labor Unions: Organization, Aims, and Power,* by Herbert L. Marx, Jr. (Volume 21, Number 5), published in 1950. The reader is referred to these volumes for additional background material.

CONTENTS

I. WHERE LABOR STANDS TODAY

EDITOR'S INTRODUCTION

Ever changing in direction and emphasis, but not necessarily growing in size or strength—that is a fair over-all description of the organized labor movement today. This section is designed to reflect this changing panorama of American labor in the 1960's.

The first selection gives a brief review of union history over the past eighty years and summarizes union activities today. Following this, Professor Joel Seidman looks at the current sources of union strength and weakness, and John Pomfret highlights the leadership crisis in the movement.

There follows a sharp contrast between two venerable trade unions—the Amalgamated Clothing Workers, which has survived and prospered as it has been able to adapt to new conditions, and the Brotherhood of Locomotive Firemen and Enginemen, victim both of modern railroad techniques and a strong though understandable resistance to change. No single union can be said to be typical of all others, but the progress and the problems of the clothing workers and the railroad firemen are reflected to some degree in many other unions.

New directions in union organization are spotlighted in the final two selections. The description of the opportunity (largely unmet) for union organization in the South is by a professional organizer for the Teamsters' union; as a sidelight, he indicates some of the reasons for the steady growth in membership of this strong union, while many others are static or diminish in size. The selection of Stanley Elam on union organization among teachers points up one aspect of the drive to bring the increasing number of white-collar and professional employees into the ranks of the organized.

LABOR UNIONS SINCE 1885 [1]

The American labor movement as it has grown and evolved has been fashioned by the character, spirit, and aspirations common to the workers of the United States. American unions have rarely expressed either utopian or revolutionary aims. They have usually been animated by the same philosophy that guided Samuel Gompers, leader of the AFL until his death in 1924. Gompers sought to have unions recognized by employers as representatives of their employees; and he constantly tried to convince the public at large that unions should be accepted as "an integral social element" seeking labor's advancement in a manner consistent with general reform and progress and with "a better life for all."

These concepts and aims are likewise emphasized in the AFL-CIO [American Federation of Labor-Congress of Industrial Organizations] constitution. The first aim set forth is the securing of "improved wages, hours, and working conditions." The Federation should encourage unorganized workers to form "unions of their own choosing." All workers, "without regard to race, creed, color, national origin, or ancestry," should "share equally in the benefits of union organization." Participation in the nation's political affairs is strongly favored, but unions should not come under the control of any political party. Workers are encouraged "to exercise their full rights and responsibilities of citizenship." International interests are recognized in the constitution's commitment to promote "the cause of peace and freedom" and "to aid, assist, and cooperate with free and democratic labor movements throughout the world." Finally, the constitution declared the Federation's intent to seek the fulfillment of the hopes and aspirations of workers "through democratic processes within the framework of our constitutional government and consistent with our institutions and traditions."

Unions have won acceptance, both nationally and in most local communities. This recognition is evident in the day-to-day relationships between workers, their local union officials, and

[1] From *Brief History of the American Labor Movement.* United States. Department of Labor. Bureau of Labor Statistics. Supt. of Docs. Washington, D.C. 20402 '64. p 66-73.

employers. It is at this basic level of job relations that the democratic processes of collective bargaining and union-management joint action to settle disputes and work together are best demonstrated. At the local and community level, many unions have formed special committees or groups to participate in community activities. Increasing numbers of union members are elected or appointed to local government organizations, such as school boards, city councils, and libraries, as well as to many other civic enterprises.

Unions have always encouraged labor's participation in national affairs and have sought to strengthen labor's influence on national policy. Historically, they took an active part in bringing about the establishment of the Department of Labor in 1913. They strongly supported changes in public policy for dealing with economic crises and modern industrial and social needs. During World War I, World War II, and the Korean emergency, many union officials served on public agencies. More recently, unions and their leaders have participated on various government boards or commissions. Trade union representatives serve on advisory committees to various agencies of Federal and state governments, are elected to public office, and appointed to posts of responsibility.

Collateral Union Activities

Next in importance to the collective bargaining function of unions . . . is the constant desire to organize the unorganized workers within their jurisdiction. Historically, of course, this was the principal and most challenging union objective. It was in this area that many hard-fought struggles occurred. Decades ago, unions and employers became locked in bitter and occasionally bloody disputes, as, for example, the railroad uprisings of 1877; the Homestead steel strike of 1892; and the conflicts in the anthracite and bituminous coal fields in the early 1900's. In later years, widespread conflicts were avoided, the most serious occurring during the organized campaigns of the Steel Workers Organizing Committee in 1937 when a number of workers lost their lives and many others were injured.

Today, violent clashes of union organizers or strikers and company guards or strikebreakers are rare, although occasionally a tense struggle is precipitated by an obdurate employer or overly militant or undisciplined unionists. Organizing activity, however, is still vital to union health and growth, especially in an expanding or a rapidly changing economy. Unions have found special need for organizing activities when employers or industries are shifting to new localities which have unorganized segments of workers in establishments that are competing with unionized plants with higher wages and labor standards.

Among the traditional functions of unions is the maintenance of mutual benefit funds. Public social security programs and the supplemental or fringe benefit clauses of collective agreements have reduced the earlier importance of the fraternal benefit functions based on member contributions. Some unions, however, especially among the older craft unions, continue to provide a program of sickness, death, unemployment, old-age, disability, and other benefits. Recently, more and more unions have developed programs to enrich the lives of their older, retired members. In some instances, these programs have included recreational and cultural facilities and the construction of homes or even planned communities.

Educational facilities for their members are provided by many national unions. Certain craft unions support trade schools to help members develop or improve their skills. Educational programs conducted as part of regular union meetings or in special classes or "institutes" have a more general purpose. Some educational work is aimed at training officials in handling union work; accounting methods, for example, for treasurers; or techniques of handling shop grievances for shop stewards who represent the workers in a particular factory or establishment. Classes are provided also for the study of parliamentary law, public speaking, and American government and democracy. Some of the larger unions maintain extensive training schools that provide formal teaching and field work for candidates for official union positions. Many universities and colleges now provide special facilities and scholarships, often in cooperation with unions. The number of such programs has increased greatly in recent years, thus attesting to the importance the union movement attaches to educational activities.

Most unions publish newspapers or journals. These range in size from leaflets to full-size magazines containing, in addition to union news, special departments and articles on national and international issues. Unions also publish a wide variety of pamphlets and special reports. These, and their radio and television programs, are often designed to inform the public, as well as members, of union activities and objectives.

Closely associated with union educational and publications programs are the research activities, which have also expanded greatly in the last two decades. Most of the larger unions now have research departments, although some engage independent specialists to prepare economic briefs and other needed data. The AFL-CIO also maintains a research organization. The status of research and educational work in the national and international unions and the state branches was indicated broadly by a study made in 1962. Among the 181 unions reporting to the Bureau of Labor Statistics, 101 unions stated that they had research directors and 89 had education directors.

The growth of research and educational facilities reflects the increasing use of factual data on wages, employment, prices, and profits in collective bargaining and in public relations. The increased union testimony and appearances before public agencies, and also the widespread use of arbitration, emphasized the need for accurate data and for clear analysis for meeting both management scrutiny and public evaluation of economic issues of interest to unions.

Other types of professional employees frequently found on the staffs of national unions include lawyers, accountants, editors, and others. Occasionally, specialists in such fields as public relations and insurance or health programs are employed.

Foreign Affairs

The long-standing union interest in world affairs was intensified by World War II and postwar problems. Unions were particularly active in programs for rehabilitating war-torn countries and for reinforcing resistance, especially among workers, to the inroads of communism.

The CIO, late in 1945, joined with labor organizations of fifty-four countries, including the Soviet Union, to form the World Federation of Trade Unions (WFTU). The AFL refused to join on the ground that the Soviet unions were state-dominated, not free unions. It soon became apparent that the Communist unions were determined to make use of the WFTU as a tool of the Communist governments. In 1949, therefore, the CIO and other non-Communist unions withdrew from the WFTU.

Shortly thereafter, the AFL and the CIO agreed to joint participation in a new organization, and on December 7, 1949, the International Confederation of Free Trade Unions (ICFTU) was formed by delegates from fifty-one countries representing unions with nearly 50 million members. By the time of the AFL-CIO merger, unions of seventy-six countries, with about 54.5 million members, were represented in the ICFTU. American unions also joined with the labor movement in Latin American countries in the Inter-American Regional Organization of Workers (ORIT) as part of the ICFTU. Steps were taken to support democratic union movements in critical areas such as Southeast Asia and Africa. Union opposition to communism continued unabated.

The American labor movement has taken an active part in the International Labor Organization (ILO) since 1934, when the United States became a member. Since the merger, the AFL-CIO has continued this activity. The ILO is a worldwide organization —now affiliated with the United Nations—with 108 member states. Each country has tripartite representation in the ILO, sending delegates from government and national organizations of workers and employers to its annual meetings. The ILO seeks to raise labor standards and improve working conditions by means of recommendations and conventions subject to ratification by each country; by technical guidance and assistance for increasing productivity, especially in underdeveloped countries; and by the spread of information and mutual understanding on labor-management problems. Established under the Versailles Treaty after

World War I, the ILO had Samuel Gompers, then president of the AFL, as one of its founders.

Representatives of the labor movement in the United States also have participated in the conduct of labor affairs in the United States Government's Agency for International Development and its predecessor agencies. This agency provides funds and technical assistance to countries throughout the world that need help to strengthen their economy and their way of life. Individuals from union ranks also serve as labor advisers or attachés to American embassies in a number of countries. In this role, they interpret the labor movement in this country to government officials and workers abroad as well as acquaint United States officials of significant developments in the country in which they are stationed. [See "U.S. Labor Abroad," in Section V, below.]

Changes Since 1885

In 1885, seventy years before the merging of the AFL and the CIO, the labor movement, though small and torn by dissension, was on the eve of formal organization of the AFL. The status of unions and the conditions of workers have undergone remarkable improvement since then.

As a rule, workers in 1885 had a work schedule of ten hours a day. The six-day week was prevalent except for workers in employment requiring continuous operation. Many such workers had a seven-day schedule. In 1885, premium pay for overtime, paid vacations and holidays, and income upon retirement were almost unknown. . . . [Today] these supplementary benefits . . . [are] customary and departures from the prevailing forty-hour, five-day weekly work schedules found in manufacturing industries . . . [are] generally in the direction of shorter working time. Even in trade and service industries, in which hours for appreciable proportions of employees exceeded forty a week, the tendency toward shorter working time . . . [is] apparent.

Valid comparisons of wages require consideration of price changes over the years. Although prices have risen substantially, real wages or the purchasing power of the worker's income have increased even more since the mid-1880's. Taking into account the highly complex changes that have occurred in the nation's economic and social life between 1885 and 1963, the general level of wages in 1963 in terms of buying power was over three times as great as in 1885. In addition, fringe benefits which today are common were virtually nonexistent when Samuel Gompers first embarked on his efforts to build an enduring labor movement in the United States.

Throughout the period, union members shared the generally prevalent American preference for self-help—individually and by association with their fellow workers. Nevertheless, as bearers of the brunt of competitive wage cutting, sweatshop conditions, depression and unemployment, with other workers, they led the way in support of corrective measures which needed the helping hand of government. Policies such as limitations on child labor, protection of women and children as workers, the public regulation of workplaces for maintenance of safety and sanitation, tax reforms, and enforcement of employers' liability for accidents and industrial diseases gradually were adopted by the states or by the Federal Government. In those early measures, as in the more recent adoption of social security, legal minimum wages, and laws safeguarding basic rights and collective bargaining privileges, labor's influence and labor's gains have been conspicuous.

For the most part, however, the Government's role in times of peace normally remains supplemental—to establish the basic rules and to set minimum standards in the field of wages and labor-management relations. Workers continue to rely upon their initiative and skills as individuals and upon their group activities and collective strength to resolve their problems and to forge ahead. It is primarily through such efforts that unions have grown and gained acceptance by employers and the public as an integral and important part of the country's economic and social structure.

LABOR UNIONS TODAY AND TOMORROW [2]

A decade has passed since the merger of the AFL and CIO ended twenty years of division in the ranks of the American labor movement, bringing with it the promise of an end to raiding, the hope that competing unions would voluntarily merge, the expectation that vast organizational drives would be launched, and the granting of increased power to the Federation to stamp out communism and corruption, protect the rights of members, and end racial discrimination. . . .

Union Effectiveness

How is the effectiveness of unionism to be measured? Among the many possible devices would be the volume of union membership, along with its direction and rate of change; the volume of fresh organizing effort, and the success attending it; the loyalty of the membership; the volume and success of collective bargaining; and the influence of the labor movement on government policy and in the community at large.

The Bureau of Labor Statistics, which periodically reports on the membership of national and international unions based in the United States, shows that the peak membership, excluding the approximately one million members who live in Canada, occurred in 1956, when 17,490,000 were enrolled. After that time, except for a moderate gain from 1958 to 1959, the number slipped steadily until 1961, when the figure stood at 16,303,000. The year of 1962 . . . witnessed a recovery to 16,586,000 due in large part to an increase in unionism in the Federal service. To these figures must be added 450,000 workers who belong to unaffiliated local unions. . . . [In 1964] the AFL-CIO reported that its membership growth was continuing, with the first half of 1964 showing a net gain of 274,000 over the corresponding period of 1963.

[2] From "Sources for Future Growth and Decline in American Trade Unions," address delivered at the December 1964 meeting of the Industrial Relations Research Association by Joel Seidman, professor of industrial relations, Graduate School of Business, University of Chicago. *Proceedings of the Seventeenth Annual Meeting.* Industrial Relations Research Association. University of Wisconsin. Madison. '65. p 98-103. Reprinted by permission.

In terms proportionate to the labor force, the slippage is even greater, from 24.8 per cent in 1956 to 22.2 per cent in 1962. In percentage terms, relative to the civilian labor force, the American labor movement reached its peak in 1953, at 25.2 per cent, while its losses have been counterbalanced roughly by its gains since 1945. For almost two decades, relative to the civilian labor force, the expansion of American union membership has been arrested, and for the last decade the trend has been downward.

If one looks at the success of first organizing efforts, as evidenced by results of NLRB [National Labor Relations Board] elections, one sees a steady slippage in the past dozen years. The unions won 72 per cent of the 6,866 elections conducted in 1952, receiving 75 per cent of the vote cast, and did approximately as well the following year, when 77 per cent of the votes favored unions and 71 per cent of the elections were won by them. From 1954 through 1959, however, union victories ranged between 61 and 67 per cent; and in 1960 the percentage dropped to 59 and in the following year to 56. For . . . [1962 and 1963] it has stood again at 59. The percentage of pro-union votes has followed a roughly parallel course, dropping from 70 per cent or higher in the 1952-55 period to between 60 and 65 per cent in each of the five following years and to 59 per cent in 1961. The record for 1962 and 1963 showed a moderate improvement, to 62 and 61 per cent, respectively.

While it is harder to appraise the attitudes of those who are already members, since payment of monthly dues is usually assured by a security clause and since attendance at meetings is but a poor indicator of degree of support, it seems clear that disaffection, where it has occurred, has not often gone to the point of desiring elimination of the union. The provisions of the Taft-Hartley Act for decertification of the bargaining agency provide the most authoritative evidence on this point. The number of such elections is small—fewer than 160 in each year before 1959 and ranging from 216 to 285 in each year since. Yet these figures are to be compared to the 2,500 to 5,000 new certifications won by unions in each recent year, on top of the tens of thousands of certifications made earlier. The bargaining units in which de-

certification has been sought have tended to be small ones, moreover, with an average of only 69 valid ballots cast in each election, though approximately 90 per cent of the eligibles have voted.
Though two thirds of the elections have resulted in decertifica-
tions, just over half of the votes have been cast in favor of continued union representation. Surely the conclusion must be that
workers, once they experience union representation, overwhelmingly wish it continued, with a relatively small number of exceptions found, primarily in very small units. . . .

Far from being under attack for failing to advance wages sufficiently, unions have rather been criticized for raising wages too
rapidly, with resulting pressure on the level of prices. The study
. . . by Albert Rees of patterns of wages, prices, and productivity
showed that average money earnings in manufacturing, together
with employer's wage supplements such as social security and
welfare payments, had risen from 44.1 cents per hour in 1933,
which might be taken roughly as the year in which collective
bargaining began in most manufacturing industries and revived
in others, to $2.24 in 1957. Translated into real wages in 1957
dollars, the increase was from 95.9 cents in 1933 to $2.24 in 1957,
. . . 234 per cent [of the 1933 figure]. Meanwhile the output per
man-hour in manufacturing rose by 187 per cent. While other
factors played a part, it seems likely that unions were largely responsible for this tendency of real wages to rise faster than productivity. The . . . [1964] automobile settlement, in which the wage
cost was estimated to rise from 4.5 to 4.7 per cent annually. despite
the appeals of the Council of Economic Advisers and other high
Administration figures to remain within the 3.2 per cent average
productivity rise of recent years, is continued evidence of a like
policy and like effectiveness.

If one turns to fringe benefits, one discerns no lack either of
ingenuity or of determination in the development of a host of
benefits, ranging from health and welfare funds to supplementary
unemployment benefits, and from sabbatical vacations to plans
for sharing in profits or in savings of costs. Emphasis has shifted
in recent years from increases in monetary wages to the achievement of the greatest possible job or income security. The growing

use of study committees for noncrisis bargaining is evidence that new techniques are developing within the framework of collective bargaining. . . . [See Section III, below.]

If the passage of legislation is the key test, labor influence has been relatively weak at the national level, as is shown by the passage of the Taft-Hartley Act, bitterly opposed by the entire labor movement, and the inclusion in the Labor-Management Reporting and Disclosure Act of many provisions thought unwise by most labor leaders. At the state level, labor's legislative strength in many of the industrialized states is offset by its weakness in the less urbanized states of the southern, southwestern, and western portions of the country, as is evidenced by the passage in many of these states of right-to-work laws over the vigorous opposition of the labor movement. [See " 'Right-to-Work' Law Background," in Section IV, below.] The public disposition, as shown by the legislation referred to above, is to reform unionism and curtail its power rather than to seek its elimination.

On the other hand, much of the legislation in which the labor movement has a strong interest, from retraining programs or housing to help for depressed areas, is likely to be passed, along with minimum wage amendments, Social Security law changes, and other measures. The list of issues pending in Congress and in the state legislatures on which the labor movement exerts some influence is very long indeed, embracing a large percentage of the social and economic problems confronting the country. With regard to most of these issues, however, labor represents but one political force among many that seek to influence legislative action.

This raises the question whether labor's political strength could be more effectively deployed by a change in its basic strategy, which is to operate as a pressure group within the Democratic party. Labor leaders such as Walter Reuther have talked in past years about the possible formation of a labor party; and still another pattern of action is provided in New York by the Liberal party, made up of the needle trades unionists and others, whose 250,000 to 400,000 votes often play a balance-of-power role in that state. In assessing the relative effectiveness of these forms of political action, one must remember that unions represent a minority group whose percentage has shrunk in recent years, and whose members, while predominantly Democratic, represent other political views as well. It is highly questionable whether any other political policy would advance union legislative aims more than labor's operation as a pressure group within the Democratic party has done.

Factors Beyond Union Control

This assessment of union effectiveness reveals both strengths and weaknesses. To what extent are the elements of weakness due to forces beyond union control, and to what extent to failures or inadequacies within the labor movement itself? . . .

Probably the most fundamental factor is technological advance, with automation as the extreme case, that is eroding the base of union membership in a wide variety of industries. While the advancing technology affects white-collar as well as blue-collar workers, for the union movement the effect on blue-collar workers is the more important. Unions in steel, automobiles, railroading, coal mining, meat packing, and many other industries have lost membership, not because of any decline of worker interest in unionism, but because of reductions in the number of blue-collar workers employed in their industries. While other types of work will in turn be needed as the direct or indirect results of automation, most of these workers, because of skill, working conditions, or physical location, are not likely to respond to the appeals of unionism as readily as those who are being displaced.

Automation affects the bargaining power of unions in still other ways. Automatic equipment in industries such as oil refineries and telephone communication makes it possible for companies, with the aid of supervisors and others outside the bargaining units, to maintain production or service despite strikes by union members. Union bargaining strength is also affected adversely by unemployment, which has been fluctuating between 5 and 5.5 per cent of the labor force, and which can be traced, among other causes, to technological innovation and to insufficient demand.

Year by year the number of white-collar workers has been growing, until they outnumber the blue-collar workers in the economy; and white-collar workers, for psychological and other reasons, are more difficult to interest in unions, despite some measure of union success in white-collar, technical, and professional areas. Unionism is powerful in the entertainment industry, and has achieved varying degrees of success among newspaper writers, sales people, clerical workers, government employees, and other groups of white-collar workers. Teachers are now winning bargaining rights in many areas [see "Teachers and Labor Unions," in this section, below], and Federal employees are joining unions in response to President Kennedy's executive order of 1962. Yet not more than 2.5 million white-collar workers are union members, out of a potential white-collar membership of perhaps 20 million or even more.

Another long-range trend is the growing proportion of women in the labor force, now at about one third. Women have helped to build unions, as in the garment trades, in telephones, and in teaching. Yet it remains true that women are more difficult to organize than men, because of a primary orientation toward family and homemaking rather than the workplace.

To the labor movement's problems caused by impersonal factors such as automation and shifts in the composition of the labor force must be added changes in the policy of management and of government. Personnel practices of nonunion firms have improved enormously with the expansion of unionism, partly because unions drew attention to the human relations aspects of production and partly because of an effort to forestall unionization. Many nonunion establishments follow the practice of matching union gains in their industries. Along with generous compensation policies go training of the supervisory staff in human relations problems and provision of some system of handling whatever grievances may arise. Workers employed in establishments following such policies simply do not have the dissatisfactions that led to the ready pro-union attitudes in years past.

Management has an advantage in many nonunion establishments for still other reasons. Early union drives concentrated on large plants and on the major centers of each industry, leaving small and scattered plants, many of them in small towns or in the more remote centers of the country, in the nonunion column. Even if these plants presented no other problems, they would be relatively difficult and expensive to organize. But small plants, in addition, permit a closer relationship between management and employees. The special problems of organizing in the South, and in predominantly rural areas, complicate the problems facing unions, and afford management a better opportunity to defeat organizing efforts. [See "Union Organization in the South," in this section, below.]

Government policy has also intensified some of the problems confronting labor, notably by permitting employers far greater latitude in communications with workers during pre-election campaigns than was once thought proper. While in part the question concerns the constitutionally guaranteed right of speech, in part it involves the determination of the proper boundary line between the right to speak and the right not to listen, and between the right to speak and the obligation not to coerce. The captive audience issue, like the prediction that unionization might cause the plant to lose business and therefore reduce employment, or even shut down, are in an area where a relatively minor shift in government policy can have a substantial impact on the ability of management to resist an organizing drive. Federal restrictions on organizational picketing and secondary boycotts have also hampered union organizing efforts, though there is a widespread feeling, which many students of industrial relations share, that the use of such tactics should properly be banned by public policy.

Factors Under Union Control

Yet the evidence suggests that unions have also contributed to the difficulties that confront them, by outmoded structure, by inadequate organizing efforts, and by faulty internal practices. At a time when established skills are rapidly being made obsolete by technological advance, and when many corporations are crossing industry lines in order to diversify their products, the number of very small national unions remains very large. . . . [The Bureau of Labor Statistics'] *Directory of National and International Labor Unions in the United States, 1963* lists 181 organizations, only 44 of which have memberships in excess of 100,000. Of the remainder, 27 are credited with between 50,000 and 100,000, 26 are between 25,000 and 50,000, and 80 are under 25,000, the remaining four having returned no membership figures. The 80 with membership below 25,000 each included 14 with fewer than 1,000 each. Though some small unions have substantial bargaining power—as witness the Air Line Pilots, with 16,650 members— for the most part this proliferation of small national unions makes little sense in relationship to the organizing and collective bargaining problems of today.

The BLS *Directory* lists 36 unions in transportation; 22 in Federal, state, and local government; 20 in metals, machinery, and equipment; 16 in clothing, textiles, and leather products; 16 in contract construction; 13 in food, beverages, and tobacco; 11 in printing and publishing; and 10 in stone, clay, and glass. Merging of unions into broad industry groupings such as these would eliminate a large percentage of jurisdictional disputes, release funds and energies for organizing efforts, and greatly simplify the structure of collective bargaining.

Still another structural problem that calls for reexamination concerns the relationship between the national unions and the Federation. The AFL-CIO, though armed with more power than the AFL had ever possessed, is less centralized than was the CIO, for reasons peculiar to the history of each federation. Yet it would be strange if the growth of a complex society and an integrated economy did not also call for more power in the hands of the labor Federation. Few would argue that the AFL-CIO has made vigorous use of the powers conferred upon it at the time of the merger with respect to such areas as organizing, ethical practices, and civil rights. The vast drives that were confidently expected, as in the white-collar field and in the South, were never launched, primarily because the national unions could not resolve their jurisdictional claims; after a brave start in the area of ethical practices, the Federation has been content, with the passage of the Reporting and Disclosure Act, to leave policing to the Federal Government; and with regard to civil rights the Federation, while seeking to persuade, has made little attempt to use its authority.

The above comments are not meant to suggest that union organizing efforts have either been entirely lacking or entirely ineffective. The AFL-CIO reports that its affiliates, in the first eight years after the merger, organized establishments with some 2 million employees, though the net membership gain was small and in percentage terms there was a decline. After long delays and many hesitations a coordinated organizing drive was finally launched in the Los Angeles area, which brought in 46,000 members in a two-year period. Similar coordinated organizing drives are under way elsewhere, as in the Baltimore-Washington area.

Shortcomings in union internal practices have been so widely publicized by congressional investigations and commented upon by so many private investigators, including some who were deeply sympathetic to organized labor, that there is no need to rehearse this evidence here. It is enough to say that corruption has led to the expulsion of several unions, including the powerful Teamsters, from the AFL-CIO; that a New York-New Jersey governmental agency has been created to police various aspects of New York harbor operations; and that the Labor-Management Reporting and Disclosure Act of 1959 has sought both to prevent improper financial practices and to assure observance of reasonable standards of union democracy. [See "The Landrum-Griffin Act of 1959," in Section IV, below.]

Federal regulation, while improving current behavior and offering some assurance against a return to past abuses, cannot eradicate the image of unionism, widely disseminated by the congressional hearings, as permeated with corrupt and dictatorial practices. If the spontaneous enthusiasm of blue-collar workers in the 1930's for unionism is tempered today, this is surely one of the contributing factors, as it is also an obstacle to the recruitment of white-collar and professional workers. Nor is the public image of unionism helped by such factors as the high salaries of many national union heads, the widespread refusal to admit the legitimacy of internal political organization, or the general failure to set up impartial systems of judicial review in disciplinary cases. Public review boards established by such unions as the UAW [United Automobile, Aerospace and Agricultural Implement Workers] and the Upholsterers go a long way to restore confidence in the impartiality of union justice. [See "UAW Public Review Board," in section IV, below.]

Still another area of internal union practice involves the treatment of minorities, particularly Negroes and Puerto Ricans. While the industrial unions, on the whole, have dealt fairly with such minorities, some of the craft unions have treated them as second-class citizens or even barred them from membership. Conflicts between Negro organizations and craft unions over admission of minority group members to apprenticeship programs have caused some loss of union enthusiasm among Negroes. [See "Union Organization in the South," in this section, below.]

Prospects for the Future

Is the labor movement likely to gain in membership and bargaining effectiveness in the years ahead, or continue the . . . [long-term] decline in numbers, at least relative to the labor force, and be forced into a more and more defensive posture in collective bargaining? Or, to put the issue into more policy-oriented terms, are there changes that the labor movement should make in order to increase its effectiveness? Some changes in three important areas—national union structure, relations between the national unions and the Federation, and internal union practices —would seem warranted.

Yet there is no assurance that changes in these areas would cause either rapid membership growth or increased collective bargaining effectiveness. The economic, social, and legal framework within which the labor movement operates handicaps unionism in a number of important respects, as we have seen. In collective bargaining, the main business of the labor movement, the record seems much more impressive. There are many who would criticize union bargaining policy for too much emphasis upon outmoded rules or for resisting technological advance too strongly; but this is a criticism, not of weakness, but of the use to which strength is put. Probably the most disturbing factor, from the point of view of the labor movement's prospects for membership growth, is that its strength is largely concentrated in the declining sectors of the economy, whether these are identified by the nature of the work, the type of industry, or the geographical area.

Yet union growth, throughout its history in this country, has tended to come in spurts, associated with such factors as reviving prosperity, war, resentment against poor personnel practices, or the passage of favorable labor legislation. At times in the past the labor movement has seemed to hold far less promise than it does today, only to become revitalized by an influx of new members. It would be rash to try to predict the time or the extent of the next upsurge; but it would be equally rash, in view of labor history, to assert that we have seen tne last of the great membership advances of the American labor movement.

NEED FOR IMAGINATIVE LEADERSHIP [3]

The ignominious fall of James B. Carey at the age of fifty-three illustrates one aspect of a problem that American unions have never solved: How to develop new leaders and provide for their orderly elevation to high posts.

. . . [Until early 1965] Mr. Carey was the president of the International Union of Electrical Workers, a member of the Executive Council of the American Federation of Labor and Congress of Industrial Organizations and secretary-treasurer of the Federation's Industrial Union Department. Today [because of his election defeat as IUE president by Paul Jennings] he has no power or influence and no foreseeable future in the union movement he has served for thirty-two years.

[3] From "Labor and Its Leaders," by John D. Pomfret, Washington staff correspondent. New York *Times.* p 39. Ap. 8, '65. © 1965 by The New York Times Company. Reprinted by permission.

This is characteristic of the end of a union leader's career whether it comes by defeat, retirement or resignation. The loss of power and prestige is enormous.

That is one reason why union leaders cling so tenaciously to their posts, often into old age. This propensity has created one of the major obstacles to the development of new leadership.

There are others.

Most unions are oligarchies. Power rests in the hands of the president and a few loyal supporters.

But they cannot act entirely without restraint. The trappings of democracy are there—conventions, provision for regular elections and so on. Conventions are usually ceremonial and elections are rarely contested, but they provide the means by which union leaders can be deposed.

Consequently, union leaders function in a political atmosphere. It is, however, a political atmosphere with a difference. Instead of trying to defeat the opposition that is inevitably going to be there, as in the case of most public elective offices, union leaders concentrate on preventing it from springing up in the first place. . . . Few unions have developed ways of encouraging new talent to develop and find its way to the top—a phenomenon that is commonplace and systematic among major corporations.

In addition, unions draw their leaders from a relatively small pool. With only rare exceptions, they come from the ranks of the workers the union represents. Going outside to search for new talent—bringing in a promising man from another union or a college campus—is virtually unheard of.

Nor do most unions make any provision for training new leaders—a subject to which many companies devote a good deal of attention.

The would-be national union leader is expected to battle his way up through a variety of subordinate elective offices—shop steward, local union officer, district leader. At every step of the way he must take care not to antagonize the top leader, who usually is in a position to arrange for his defeat. Some men have little appetite for this kind of struggle and go elsewhere to find an outlet for their talents.

The concentration of union power poses a major problem. A national union president customarily makes all the important policy decisions for his organization. He casts a big shadow. Subordinate union leaders have much less relative authority than, for example, a corporation vice president. Talented men who might be content with a lesser post that carried real authority seldom can find this authority short of the top job in a national union.

The personal nature of union power makes it difficult to have a debate over union policy without having it appear to be an attack on the leader. What in other institutions would be considered normal disagreement over policy has a tendency within unions either not to occur at all or to be transformed into an all-out struggle for power.

Some union officials are concerned about the failure of unions to find ways of developing talented leaders, but they are not optimistic about the prospect for change. A failure to develop new techniques, however, could prove costly.

The unions confront some formidable problems. At the bargaining table, they must deal with technological change. On the organizing front, they must seek to enlist the millions of white-collar workers who are largely unorganized and who, with each year that passes, account for a larger proportion of the work force.

Although these challenges do not seem so dramatic as those of the 1930's, most union leaders would agree that the need for imaginative leadership is as great now as it ever was.

HALF-CENTURY OF A MODEL UNION—I [4]

The day after Christmas . . . [1914] 134 disillusioned members of the United Garment Workers Union gathered in Webster Hall . . . [New York City] to form what they hoped would be a more perfect union of workers in the garment trades.

To indicate its character as a union of all the workers in the industry, they named it the Amalgamated Clothing Workers of America.

[4] From "Born of Strife 50 Years Ago, Amalgamated Union Prospers," by Foster Hailey, staff correspondent. New York *Times.* p 47. D. 27, '64. © 1964 by The New York Times Company. Reprinted by permission.

The group, representing about 40,000 workers on men's clothing in New York, Chicago, Baltimore, Montreal and several East Coast and Canadian towns, was largely without funds, and the Baltimore garment workers were on strike.

. . . [In May 1964] at the Amalgamated's biennial and anniversary convention, the delegates represented almost 400,000 members in forty-one states, Canada and Puerto Rico. Its 6,000 members in Mississippi represent the largest organized union group there. . . .

The union today is the principal owner of two banks, . . . two insurance companies, . . . four cooperative housing projects, . . . an employer-financed pension fund with $124 million in the bank, numerous health and dental clinics and direct union assets of several million dollars. [See the following selection, "The Business Story."]

Although founded by immigrants from Europe, largely Jews and Italians who were Socialists or whose fathers were, there now are probably more Republicans than Socialists in the union. It has consistently followed the democratic principles of its first president, the late Sidney Hillman, of whom it was said that "he put his faith in the gospel according to Hart Schaffner & Marx instead of Karl."

The reference to Hart Schaffner & Marx, the Chicago clothing manufacturer, is an apt one. For it was in the bitter strike of the winter of 1910-11 in Chicago, which had begun with a walkout of fourteen women pants makers at the Hart Schaffner & Marx plant, that the Amalgamated had its genesis.

Two strikers were killed and scores injured before the strike, which developed into an industrywide walkout in Chicago, was settled. The strikers found the United Garment Workers of little aid, since its members were largely the more highly skilled, highly paid with little interest in the lower-paid workers.

The settlement itself put its stamp on the union. The strike was ended by an appeal to reason, by the appeal of social worker Jane Addams to Joseph Schaffner to go down to his factory and see the conditions under which many of his workers toiled for as little as $2 for a sixty-hour week. And all issues were settled by arbitration.

The Amalgamated in its fifty-year history has called few strikes and no major one since 1921. Yet its workers are among the highest paid among the needle trades and the best protected by health and insurance and retirement programs.

The history of the Amalgamated parallels that of Sidney Hillman, the Lithuanian immigrant who was its leader for thirty-two years and who became a controversial political figure during the New Deal days and particularly the last presidential campaign of Franklin D. Roosevelt in 1944.

At the Democratic convention that summer, some of the Roosevelt lieutenants reportedly were told to "clear it with Sidney" before making a final decision on who would be chosen as the vice presidential candidate. . . .

Mr. Hillman had become a prominent political figure long before that, however. He had helped found Labor's Non-Partisan League, had helped frame the National Industrial Recovery Act in 1933 and served on the board of the National Recovery Administration.

As World War II neared, he served on the National Defense Advisory Commission and was co-chairman for several months of the Office of Production Management. In 1943, he was the first chairman of the Congress of Industrial Organizations' Political Action Committee. . . .

Mr. Hillman . . . [was] a leader of the 1910-11 strike. The leader of the fourteen women who walked out, incidentally, was a young woman named Bessie Abramowitz, who became Mrs. Hillman in 1916 and still is active in the union.

When the strike ended he became a full-time union business agent. In 1914, he was elected president of the new Amalgamated.

The union grew steadily under his leadership. Beginning with a paid membership of 25,000 in 1914, that total had grown to 100,000 by 1918, to 175,000 by 1929 and then to its present 385,000 to 390,000.

Two of Mr. Hillman's associates of those early days in Chicago were Jacob S. Potofsky, who succeeded to the presidency on Mr. Hillman's death in 1946, and Frank Rosenblum, secretary-treasurer.

A third member of the one-time big four of the Amalgamated is Hyman Blumberg, executive vice president. He is the only one who did not begin his union activities in Chicago.

From the very beginning of the Amalgamated Mr. Hillman and his colleagues recognized the interdependence of employer and employees and the union struggled always to organize the whole industry so that the man with the union shop could not be undercut by nonunion competitors.

Although Amalgamated has 97 per cent of the workers in its field, there still are approximately 75,000 unorganized workers in the cotton-garment industry, Mr. Potofsky has estimated. The union hopes to bring them all into the fold.

Although the basic membership of the Amalgamated still is among the workers on men's clothing, it has expanded in recent years into the laundry and dry cleaning fields and among retail clerks.

The parent United Garment Workers Union still is in existence as a craft union of the more highly skilled workers, but its membership is not large and it does not play a prominent part in the men's clothing trade.

HALF-CENTURY OF A MODEL UNION—II
(THE BUSINESS STORY) [5]

In 1914 . . . [the Amalgamated Clothing Workers Union] was struggling to get a foothold in the clothing industry, where wages were low and the work-week was long.

Now . . . this union counts its membership at 385,000, owns banks and insurance companies, puts up the money to build housing projects, and has come to be known as one of the big businesses of the labor movement.

[5] From "When a Big Union Gets into Big Business." *U. S. News & World Report.* 56:91-3. My. 18, '64. Reprinted from *U. S. News & World Report,* published at Washington.

This is the rags-to-riches story of the Amalgamated Clothing Workers of America. . . .

In 1914, a clothing worker was making about $1 a day, and the union had to scratch for rent money. Today, the average wage in the men's clothing industry is more than $15 a day, plus "fringes," and the international union lists assets in the hundreds of millions.

The union's business enterprises are varied, and are designed primarily to help members. Yet a good deal of the union's business is done with the public. This is true particularly of its banking operations.

The union owns and operates two banks, one in New York, one in Chicago. Their combined assets are estimated at $164 million.

The two banks emphasize service to Amalgamated's members and to other workers, union and nonunion. But deposits are accepted from, and loans are made to, the general public.

The Amalgamated Trust & Savings Bank of Chicago was established in 1922, the New York bank a year later.

Occasionally one of the banks will make a loan to a company with which the union has a contract, if the firm is in financial trouble. Generally the banks do not make such loans, however—they try to avoid "conflict of interest."

Maxwell Brandwen, managing director of the Amalgamated Bank of New York, put it this way: "We will make a loan in a situation where a firm cannot raise the money elsewhere, when otherwise it will have to close down and throw our members out of work."

Aside from personal loans, the banks at times make loans to unions whose members are striking—the money to be passed out to strikers for food. A big function of the banks is financing of housing developments.

The union is in the insurance business in a big way, too, mainly as a service to its members. This undertaking was begun when the union checked on the cost of providing life and health insurance for members and decided it could cut administrative costs by establishing its own firms to handle the employer-financed insurance programs.

The companies do not sell insurance to individuals, but specialize in death and health benefits.

In 1962 and 1963, the union reports, more than $40 million was paid out in insurance claims.

Reserves of the union's two insurance companies total $66 million.

The Clothing Workers Union was a pioneer in the insurance field. A dozen years before a Federal system of unemployment benefits was set up under the New Deal, the union had its own plan for layoff benefits.

The insurance fund for this program, jointly financed by members and employers, was switched into the life and health insurance plan after state unemployment benefits became available.

The union now is building its fourth housing development, in the New York area. When it is completed, the union estimates the total investment in land and buildings will come to about $60 million.

The first of the union's housing developments was begun in 1926 as a low-cost cooperative development in New York. All developments sponsored by the union are open to all workers, whether union members or not.

The union provides all sorts of other services to its members. Pensions are arranged for retired workers, financed by employer contributions. Nearly $36 million in pensions was distributed in the last two years.

Health clinics have been set up in many cities where the union operates. Services vary, but as a rule include medical care at a clinic, diagnostic, laboratory and X-ray examinations, physical therapy and rehabilitation.

DEATH OF A UNION [6]

Can a union be killed?

If so, the Brotherhood of Locomotive Firemen and Enginemen should be on its way out. . . . [In 1964] it was in effect sentenced to execution, when a national arbitration board created by Congress gave railroads the right eventually to eliminate the jobs of nearly all the union's members (mostly firemen who, on diesel locomotives, have no fires to tend). . . . [In one year] its membership . . . dropped 20 per cent to forty thousand, indicating that its final agony might already have begun.

But at union headquarters . . . President H. E. Gilbert pledges: "We're not only going to survive, we're going to grow stronger." Nor can his statement be dismissed—for the union would appear, at minimum, to be able to create considerable turmoil while fighting to stay alive. An attack it already has launched on the arbitration award, and the way railroads are applying it, conceivably could tie up in a long dispute carrier attempts to cut costs by dropping assertedly unneeded workers.

In any event, the outcome will indicate something of considerable importance to all American labor relations. For only the arbitration award, and the special law that led to it, make the Firemen's case unique. Otherwise, that case is an extreme example of a trend troubling many other unions: the tendency of advancing technology to wipe out certain types of jobs.

If the Firemen Brotherhood dies, its demise will prove that this tendency can destroy whole unions—even long-established and once-mighty ones (the Brotherhood was founded . . . [in 1874] and in the heyday of the steam locomotive, in 1928, it boasted 120,000 members). But if the Brotherhood can survive, despite the odds against it, some labor specialists might be tempted to conclude that labor unions are immortal, possessing a life almost independent of the usefulness of the crafts they represent.

[6] From an article by James R. Macdonald, staff reporter. *Wall Street Journal.* p 1+. Mr. 1, '65. Reprinted by permission.

Right now, the odds against this seem extremely long. The Firemen, in close alliance with other rail unions, fought for five years against a batch of railroad demands to stop "featherbedding"; the rails' demand for the right to wipe out firemen's jobs was perhaps the key one. Hours before a nationwide rail strike was to begin in 1963, Congress passed a special law setting up an extraordinary board to make a binding arbitration award. The award, taking effect . . . March 31, [1964] gave railroads the right ultimately to fire, or switch into other jobs, or retire without replacing, 90 per cent of the firemen on freight and switching-yard diesels.

The effect has been striking. Since dismissals already have started, and no new firemen are being hired, the union has been losing not only members but dues income. In [the first] eleven months under the award its general fund has dropped over $330,000, to about $1 million currently.

The arbitration ruling also has put steam in a drive to repeal the "full-crew" laws that once protected railroad jobs in fourteen states, so that the award can be applied there. Already Mississippi, California, Arizona and North Dakota have repealed their full-crew laws, and similar statutes are under attack in all ten states where they still apply.

In fighting such moves, the Brotherhood appears to have lost the support of some of its one-time labor allies. The Brotherhood of Locomotive Engineers, for instance, has pulled out of joint efforts to block repeal of the full-crew laws. Grand Chief Engineer Perry Heath flatly declares there's no sense "fighting a lost cause to save the Firemen."

Indeed, the Engineers seem to be trying to hasten the Firemen's demise by raiding the union of the few members it could hope to keep if the arbitration award is fully carried out. Both unions legally can represent both firemen and engineers. So the Engineers Brotherhood is urging Firemen members to switch unions—or, as they put it, to "get into the engine service organization with a future."

Still, the Firemen are drafting strategy for survival. The key element: an attempt to get the arbitration award scrapped, or at least softened, so that fewer firemen's jobs will be wiped out, and those more slowly. The union won't accept the award "as the final solution," says Mr. Gilbert. . . .

The Brotherhood gets a chance to attack the award itself [soon]. The special law creating the arbitration panel specified that any award was to last two years. Meanwhile the roads and the union were supposed to study jointly the effects of eliminating firemen's jobs and then negotiate a permanent agreement to replace the award.

The two years are up March 31, 1966—but . . . [in the first year] there has been no joint study, no negotiation, and seemingly no disposition on either side to get any going. So what happens if the award runs out with things still in that state, as seems highly likely? That plunges the dispute into a legal no man's land, with few if any precedents for guideposts, since the special law setting up an arbitration panel to make an award binding for two years created a unique situation.

The Firemen contend that, in the absence of either a binding award or a negotiated agreement, the old contract, requiring a fireman on every engine, will come back into effect. Then, says Mr. Gilbert, the union can demand not only that all elimination of firemen's jobs be stopped, but that all the firemen already dismissed be rehired, with replacement of those transferred or retired. The railroads contend that the terms of the arbitration award continue until a new agreement replaces them—so that they could go on eliminating firemen's jobs. Impartial legal experts say the situation is so unusual it's impossible to determine now who is right, and believe the issue may have to be settled by the courts—opening the way, perhaps, for a long series of verdicts, injunctions, and appeals such as occurred before the arbitration award went into effect.

Outside the union, few people find it conceivable that such a legal battle, drawn out as it might be, would end in a complete overturning of the arbitration award, since that was mandated by Congress and presumably expressed the national will. Even Mr. Gilbert admits "I don't have my head in the sand and I realize no one can ignore what has already happened." The

Brotherhood's real hope, many management and outside experts think, is ultimately to force the railroads into a negotiated agreement that would preserve at least some firemen's jobs and thus preserve the union.

To drum up public support for such an agreement, the Firemen already have launched a publicity campaign. In newspaper ads, the union has pointed to what it contends is an increase in railroad accidents since the roads have been removing firemen. The ads have been careful not to charge all of the increase directly to the absence of firemen. But "we do make it clear that the accident rate is definitely on the increase and that the only change in railroad operations has been removal of the firemen," says William Loftus, public relations director of the Brotherhood. The union has long contended that a fireman with no fires to tend performs a useful—indeed vital—service as a lookout for the engineer.

This campaign has hardly fired the railroads with enthusiasm for a negotiated contract that would preserve firemen's jobs. The National Railway Labor Conference, rail management's bargaining unit, denounces the ads as "so misleading that they can only be taken as a deliberate attempt to deceive the public." It charges the union is including in its "accident" statistics incidents as trivial as employees reporting cinders in their eyes. Mr. Gilbert concedes the union's accident figures aren't all on major wrecks, but contends rail managements have been concealing some accidents so that the union's figures, far from being inflated, aren't even complete.

Be that as it may, the Firemen face some severe obstacles in shooting for an eventual negotiated agreement. The ultimate weapon of a union seeking such an agreement is, of course, the strike—but rail managements would be unlikely to be impressed by a strike of firemen they are anxious to get rid of anyway. If other unions joined, of course, it would be a different story—but it was precisely the threat of such a nationwide rail strike that led to the Firemen's current predicament, by prompting Congress to pass the law setting up the arbitration panel.

Moreover, there is at least some question whether other rail unions would back the Firemen in a strike, since some of their leaders regard the Brotherhood's battle as a "lost cause." The only precedent is a chilling one for the Firemen. In May 1958 the Firemen faced somewhat the same situation in Canada that they now do in the United States: A Royal Commission recommended firemen's jobs be eliminated by attrition, with some immediate dismissals; the Canadian Pacific threatened to put the recommendation into effect when it couldn't reach a negotiated agreement with the union; and the Firemen struck.

The outcome: The Engineers Brotherhood told its Canadian members that it was up to them individually whether or not to cross the Firemen's picket lines—but that under Dominion law they could be liable for a fine and possible imprisonment if they did not. Many engineers did cross the picket lines, keeping locomotives running and vastly weakening the Firemen's strike. The strike broke in three days when the Canadian government threatened to pass the Royal Commission recommendations as a law, and firemen's jobs are slowly being eliminated on all Canadian freight and yard diesels.

The Firemen's chances of avoiding such a situation in the United States would hardly seem to be helped by the furious battle now raging between them and the Engineers Brotherhood. . . . Engineers and Firemen are busily accusing each other of having started the raids back and forth between the two unions, and both are boasting of big gains. So far, however, the contest seems to be a standoff. In the most important test to date, the Firemen tried in a bargaining election to take over the rival union's contract for engineers on the Illinois Central Railroad, but were swamped in the vote.

Merger overtures have been no more successful; the Firemen have been proposing a merger of the two unions for fifteen years, but the Engineers consistently have refused. "A merger of the two engine service organizations is the only real solution—but given the present leadership of the Engineers, I see no immediate hope of that being accomplished, barring a massive rank-and-file revolt within the Engineers," says the Firemen's Mr. Gilbert. He makes no secret of the fact that he is trying to provoke such a revolt, but so far there are no signs of one starting.

Whatever comes of these efforts, some Firemen Brotherhood jobs and salaries are threatened even if the union itself survives. To keep the fight for life going with dues-paying membership shrinking drastically, Mr. Gilbert is pushing cost-cutting proposals that promise considerable pain.

The union now has a complex structure of 900 locals, grouped into 270 "general committees"—usually one for each railroad, but two or more for some big roads—each headed by a general chairman. About half the general chairmen spend full time on union business, and thus draw salaries ranging from $6,000 to $12,000 a year. At the Cleveland Grand Lodge 14 salaried Brotherhood vice presidents, and six alternate vice presidents who are paid for specific jobs, account for much of a headquarters payroll of $305,000 a year.

Mr. Gilbert is pushing a consolidation program to cut the number of locals to 700, and the number of general committees and general chairmen to 200; he estimates each move would save about $100,000 a year. At the 1963 Brotherhood convention he also proposed to drop four international vice presidents, cutting the Grand Lodge payroll by $40,000 to $60,000 a year. Delegates at that convention—perhaps with an anxious thought to the future security of their own jobs, as well as the jobs of the firemen they represent—voted him down, but Mr. Gilbert says he intends to renew the proposal at the next convention in 1967.

UNION ORGANIZATION IN THE SOUTH [7]

Remarks about the reasons for plants moving South—accessibility to new markets, reduction of transportation costs, cheaper labor, lower taxes, evasion of collective bargaining obligations—are true.

[7] From "The Process of Unionization in the South," address by Tony Zivalich, organizer, Truck Drivers and Helpers, Local 728 (Georgia), International Brotherhood of Teamsters. *Labor Law Journal.* 15:468-73. Jl. '64. Reprinted by permission. (The address was delivered at the 1964 spring meeting of the Industrial Relations Research Association, Gatlinburg, Tennessee.)

In addition, . . . the South is an area where many northern companies are experimenting with their latest automated equipment. There are several advantages to this approach. Most areas in the South are anxious to have an industry move in. If an automated plant lives up to its expectations, the company has another lever when bargaining with the union representing the employees in its home plant; and also, it eliminates, for practical purposes, the possibility of some snoopy reporter doing a series of articles about how company A, with its new highly automated plant will soon lay off x number of people who have become unnecessary in its new operation. In the distribution field, it is not unusual for a company to build a huge warehouse, with tow lines, electronic tabulating, king-size tow motors, palletizers, and employ only ten men, whereas in older warehouses one hundred fifty men might handle the same amount of goods. . . .

At nearly every labor convention, a delegate from Iowa or Michigan makes a committee report to the convention over the loss of membership in various local unions because of the southern exodus and how this has sapped their bargaining power, etc. The delegates are indignant, motions are made to back up resolutions, and the convention report has several pages of the . . . theme "we are going to organize the South immediately." X number of dollars are allocated for this purpose.

But, very little happens. The South is still unorganized. The situation gets worse. Numerically, the unions have less of a percentage of the entire work force organized. Even though the Teamsters are the most successful in organizing, including the South, not enough, in my opinion, is being done. . . .

Will the South be organized? Probably not to the degree that is desired.

Can it be organized? Yes! First of all, there's a real need. In Georgia, 13.7 per cent of eligible workers are in unions. The need to have a voice in your affairs is a universal need. Paternalism has to go. Even in primitive countries people are tired of being *told* when to go to work, when to go to bed, what to do. . . .

Secondly, there is an economic need. When a man leaves the farm and moves to the factory, his earnings seem like big money.

His wife takes a job. They get a place to rent. His wife gets pregnant. Soon two or three children have to be fed, clothed and sheltered. The wife no longer works. Soon the illusion vanishes. Fifty or sixty dollars a week isn't enough to raise a family decently. . . . When the first garnishment hits him, he becomes aware of his economic needs. Although these needs are present, the unions haven't been able to convince the majority of workers of the solution to these needs.

Union organizing is nothing but the selling of intangibles. If you ask a union organizer what he is selling, he can't tell you; that's how intangible it is.

Seriously, in organizing you must be able to communicate to a worker the idea that he, collectively with his fellow workers, can better his economic life if they assume the responsibility of exercising their right to organize. This is basically what unions are about.

The notion that an organizer can go into a campaign and tell the workers, "I can get you 28 cents an hour, and we can do this, and we can do that if you vote the union in," is utter nonsense. An organizer with this approach will fall flat on his face in a short period of time.

If an organizer promised 28 cents an hour, and was successful in getting a 26 cents an hour increase, the people, particularly in the South, would go to their graves believing that the organizer received 1 cent of the difference, the employer 1 cent, and that they were shortchanged.

In addition, there is sufficient evidence to warrant the conclusion that the South can be organized. As examples, the . . . [AFL-CIO Industrial Union Department] with their saturation campaign in South Carolina have done a very good job. They have organized some plants that three years ago people thought couldn't be organized. . . . Mike Bothello and the textile organizers have organized some mills in northern Georgia which were considered impossible. John Marler and the Lithographers have doubled their membership in Atlanta in the last four years. The Retail Clerks and the Meatcutters have considerable increases in their membership the last three years.

And to be subjective, twelve years ago my own Local [728 of the Teamsters] had 1500 members. Five years ago it had 5,000 members. Today it has over 9,000 members. In the last five years, the largest group organized had slightly less than 300 people. If 50 people are in a shop which we organize, it is considered a fair-sized plant. Most times the unit will be 15 to 20 workers.

Basing a conclusion on these facts, it is plain that the South can be organized. . . .

Our organizing is now a booming business. We haven't made a house call in three years. Not that we don't believe in house calls, but there isn't the time for individual organizing. If people are desirous of organization, they call us. We arrange for a meeting, usually at the hall. (Actually we have an edge over other unions. Our drivers go in and out of every plant. They are our best salesmen. Most drivers are the best paid working people in the community. People approach the drivers and the drivers refer them to us.)

When the group comes to the hall, we check the company, number of workers eligible, type of work, etc. We always ask "Why pick the Teamsters?" . . . The first reason given is the strength of the Teamsters. Expecting "ideals" to be the motivating factor for attraction to any union would leave one disappointed. If at this meeting we find that this is a machine shop, and we feel the Machinists can do a better job, we refer them to the Machinists and make the connection. The same with Bakery Workers, Lithographers, Meatcutters, and other unions that we get along with, and we get along with most of them. Sometimes, the workers object to this because of an unpleasant experience in the past, or an unsuccessful campaign by another union, or because their minds are made up. If this is the case, we say "O. K. If we engage in a campaign and are successful and you care to switch allegiance later to another International, we'll arrange it." We mean this.

The Teamsters have enough organizing to do in our own theoretical jurisdiction. Those fifty-eight warehouses that have been built in Atlanta in the last four years aren't all organized yet. (Our actual jurisdiction is anyone unorganized.)

Assuming that these workers wish to be organized by us, we then proceed to the business at hand. We evaluate, from questioning them, their enthusiasm and whether or not an election could be won if the campaign is undertaken. . . . From talking to just a few men, organizers are expected to have the complete picture of the plant, its employees, the physical layout and working conditions.

Once we determine an election can be won, we do some research. The ultimate criterion is to analyze whether or not we could win a strike against the particular company. Elections are much easier to win than strikes down South. We must be reasonably certain that once an election is won we have the economic leverage at our disposal to put us on an equal footing with the employer. In theory, once an election is won and the union becomes certified, the Federal law compels the employer to "bargain in good faith." Our experience shows that most companies are advised by their attorneys that as long as they agree to meet in negotiations, this passes the minimum requirements of "bargaining in good faith." If our analysis indicates difficulty in our ability to force a fair settlement, we will so advise the men and explain the risks involved.

Our organization doesn't believe in going through with an election just to have an election. On occasion, if the boss has bought off some of the key men, we will withdraw our petition and tentatively arrange with the men to make another attempt in six months. In this manner, it becomes very expensive for an employer to have us looking down his throat twice a year.

The power structure and the reaction to the Teamsters varies throughout Georgia. In general, it is fair to say that the Chambers of Commerce are anti-union. The Georgia Chamber of Commerce was good enough to distribute to their membership a booklet titled "Preventive Unionitis." . . . On the one hand they issue statements recommending that their member companies, particularly restaurants, hotels and the like, shift gears with the times and integrate their establishments. On the other hand, they remind the companies to utilize the race question in their booklet by advising their readers to be sure to point out to their unorganized employees that the unions are and have been supporters of Negro rights, especially in the recent controversial school issue.

It is safe to say that the establishments hate unions with a passion, the Teamsters with a purple passion, and probably Labor Board agents as representatives of the Federal Government with a triple purple passion.

For example, the Butchers held an election in Monroe, Georgia, which is a quiet town with elms, dogwood trees, very little industry and no unions. The day of the election every city policeman and county patrolman was on hand to greet the Board Agent and the union observers. The psychological impact on the workers was predictable enough—shades of the Gestapo. Usually in the smaller towns, organizing campaigns result in front page editorials of the local papers where the union is epitomized as an agent of the devil. It's common knowledge that various ministers will be recruited to warn the wives and members of the inherent evils that unions bring about. In numerous cases, the bankers counsel with the most active union-minded worker to remind him of the precariousness of his financial position and the choke-hold that could be utilized against him. Race-baiting is a part of nearly every campaign. . . . On occasion, the White Citizens Councils feel they have something at stake and attempt to intervene, but they are easily disposed of.

Our only weapon against this type of reaction is to forewarn the people of its inevitability and then ride it out. The same thing actually goes on in many rural areas of the North, only it's a little more sophisticated.

The reasons that the Teamsters are relatively successful in the South are easily stated. First, we have plenty of free advertising. No matter how deep in the hills you go, everyone knows Jim Hoffa and the Teamsters. I tell a story and it's true. A number of people were asked why they contacted us for organization. Some replied they never heard of any other unions. Others said they couldn't think of any other union, and some even said that they dialed information, asked the number of the union, and the operator . . . referred them to us.

Secondly, and although seemingly a paradox, it is quite true. Our union does not equivocate or pussyfoot on the race question. On the job and at the hall all members are union brothers. There are no ifs, ands or buts. We don't need and we don't want anyone in our organization who cannot see the necessity and the logic of our position. It would be lovely if I could state that none of our members has bigotry in their hearts, but it would be a lie. However, I can say that the leadership of the International and our Local tolerates no nonsense on this issue. It is our sincere hope, of course, that by working together on the job and at the union meetings, all workers will get to know each other as individuals. Our experience shows that this is paramount, or you really don't have a union. Many examples can be given to confirm this.

Thirdly, we work harder than most unions. Maybe it's a reaction to our notoriety or maybe it's because there is so much pressure on us that the weak sisters have fallen by the wayside, but the Teamsters hustle.

What is needed to do an effective job of organizing the South?

This is all, in my personal opinion:

1. Money.

2. More trained organizers. (Not apprentices, porkchoppers [paid "drones"], or political refugees.)

3. Assignment to a particular area. (Workers want you to be a member of the community.)

4. Development of "native clergy." Too many times potentially good organizers are not recruited by their respective internationals. I believe there is plenty of talent in the ranks of labor's southern membership. Men should be recruited, trained in other parts of the country with some old-timers, and assigned as organizers in their home areas. In addition, they should remain apolitical of local union politics and be paid the same wages as organizers in the North.

5. More trained technicians, economists, public relations men, and a closer alliance with the academic world to keep abreast of the latest developments.

6. Closer cooperation of all unions in any struggle with any employer by any union. Any other course is contrary to the principles of trade unionism.

7. A definite push by all international unions to compel, if necessary, their southern locals to cooperate with organizations promoting civil liberties and civil rights. . . .

8. A divorce from the archaic practice of automatically endorsing any Democratic nominee for any political office. It's about time the unions weren't beholden to one party. This has minimized any bargaining power we have had to put pressure for legislation to meet social needs.

9. Plain work—*hard* work.

Will it be done? I said probably not, but it's a wonderful challenge, and the climate is beautiful.

Possibly because of being in the Bible Belt for so long, I will close by saying "the harvest is ripe, the laborers are few."

TEACHERS AND LABOR UNIONS [8]

In the fall of 1961, education's organizational David met Goliath in the opening skirmish of what has grown to be a noisy battle for the loyalties of American teachers. David won the first round. The occasion was an election among New York City teachers to select an agent to bargain with the Board of Education. The United Federation of Teachers, an affiliate of the 60,000-member American Federation of Teachers (AFL-CIO), beat the hastily organized Teachers Bargaining Organization, supported by the 714,000-member National Education Association.

The UFT went on to win, in three years, salary increases amounting to about $1,500 per teacher, plus many other concessions which bite into board of education policy-making preroga-

[8] From "Union or Guild? Organizing the Teachers," by Stanley Elam, editor, *Phi Delta Kappan*, official journal of the professional education fraternity. *Nation*. 198:651-3. Je. 29, '64. Reprinted by permission.

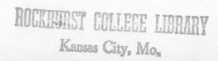

tives. These include reductions in instructional load, increases in specialized services and guarantees against overlarge classes. Such gains have made the UFT the leading spirit among AFT affiliates and in the teacher union movement.

Since 1961, the AFT has increased its membership by nearly 70 per cent . . . while the NEA has gained about 25 per cent and will fail to reach its "Million or More by '64" goal set in 1960. The NEA claims its affiliates have established formal "professional negotiation" agreements in sixty-five cities located in thirteen states; it has requests pending before fourteen other boards. The AFT locals have fewer written acknowledgments of formal relationships, but many of those they do have are in major metropolitan areas.

To the outsider, the AFT-NEA battle looks like little more than another jurisdictional wrangle between competing unions. To the board of education member it is more evidence of the bad judgment and poor taste of which he has long suspected teachers. To the school administrator, by-passed and ignored, it has really frightening implications. What is happening to his traditional role as boss man?

But to many public school teachers, these developments are the most hopeful sign in generations that education can achieve its long-term goals of status and welfare. Making less than one fourth as much (under $6,000 per year) as the average self-employed physician, publicly regarded as only slightly less grubby than social workers, and viewed by themselves as more nearly mice than men, teachers still have a long way to go, despite real gains in recent years. Like other minority groups, they are speeding up now that the goal is in sight.

Of the alternative paths to this utopia the NEA lays claim to the "professional" route, and the word has an undeniable appeal to teachers. The AFT leadership continues to profess disdain for the NEA brand of professionalism and asserts pride in the union way. Observers who try to view the NEA-AFT rivalry objectively, however, can detect little operational difference between the NEA's program of "professional negotiations" backed by "sanctions" and the AFT program of "collective bargaining" backed by the strike threat. (Both the NEA and the AFT officially renounce the strike as an instrument of policy—after all, it is illegal for public employees in several states—but both have used it in some form.) The verbal conflict has done little more than add some colorful new phrases to drab pedagogical language, with the AFT winning the phrase-making contest. To the AFT, NEA activities constitute "collective begging." NEA efforts to secure legislative provision of duty-free lunch periods are styled "right-to-eat" laws. The AFT newspaper recently characterized the 1963 National School Boards Association convention, where union trespass on board domain was deplored, as being "redolent of the medieval divine right of kings."

There was a time when AFT claims that the NEA is a company union had considerable substance, because administrators—hired by boards to secure, evaluate and fire teachers—were admitted to local associations. That was before the city-by-city struggle for bargaining rights began. Now it seems likely, although there are no good statistics on the point, that the membership of NEA affiliates which exclude administrators is greater than the total membership of AFT affiliates. One of the ironies of the recent bargaining election in Milwaukee—noted by the AFT for its humor but apparently not for its threat—lay in the fact that to come under the new Wisconsin law authorizing such elections for public employees, the Milwaukee Teachers Association (NEA) had to get itself declared a union. Some observers say NEA affiliates are now acting more like unions than the unions themselves, but their terminology must never be contaminated.

The Milwaukee election, won by the NEA after a wicked battle, may turn out to be the most significant of the recent series, in which the AFT won only four out of eleven (there is one stalemate) but got representation rights for nearly 11,000 teachers, including 10,000 in Detroit, to the NEA's total of 7,000. Milwaukee is significant because it proved the wealthy AFL-CIO Industrial Union Department to be relatively ineffective in influencing teachers. The IUD poured money and men (including

Walter Reuther) into the campaign, but only about 200 teachers switched to the union camp.

Milwaukee suggests that the NEA can, if it continues to accelerate its current program, eliminate the AFT except in the largest cities where unionism is a way of life. There is little doubt that the NEA means to do just that. In Allan West, brought from Utah to head its new "Urban Project," it has a hard-driving and coolly calculating organizer. After the Milwaukee victory he was made head of the NEA field services. Literature pouring from NEA presses includes compilations of sample board-teacher agreements, guidelines for professional negotiations. Seminars and workshops are being held throughout the country. The AFT build-up, even with IUD money, does not as yet match this effort.

The truth is that labor affiliation may, after all, prove to be the AFT's vulnerable spot. A few years ago the interests of organized labor and the AFT seemed to coincide. Affiliation was attractive to the teachers because they were weak; not until recently did AFT membership include more than 5 per cent of the nation's certified teachers. Affiliation was attractive to leaders of organized labor because the blue-collar worker pool is diminishing with automation. The teaching profession seemed the ideal opening into the white-collar field. After the New York UFT victory proved that at least some teachers were ready for tough-minded union methods, Walter Reuther and James Carey became advocates of this strategy.

But New York teachers and schools are not typical. The most important deterrent to membership in the AFT remains the reluctance of teachers to become identified with blue-collar workers. Mostly, teachers come from what the sociologists call upwardly mobile families. They are almost morbidly white-collar-conscious and the NEA works on that bias. Most NEA leaders come from antiunion small cities and towns. They argue that union affiliation limits the independence of the AFT and they have a point. If administrative membership causes conflict of interest in the NEA, labor affiliation may be as embarrassing to the AFT. For example, in the Indiana tax battle last year, the AFL-CIO brought suit to declare a new sales tax unconstitutional. The resulting delay cost the state $39 million which might have been spent for education.

Moreover, the AFT bureaucracy fails to realize that recent victories are quite likely to be empty. The Chicago-based leaders are the prisoners of their own slogans. To them, the NEA remains a company union. They continue to call their affiliates locals, not associations. They copy AFL-CIO strategy even while the AFL-CIO is reconsidering its own methods. At one time the AFT boasted such intellectual leaders as John Dewey, John Childs and George Counts. Today it fails to make a place in the organization for Myron Lieberman, its best theoretician. . . . Lieberman's 1960 book, *The Future of Public Education,* was a landmark in the analysis of teacher organizations, but it questioned the need and the appropriateness of labor affiliation and probably cost the author the AFT presidency in 1962. . . .

Because there are so many unanswered questions and because the battle lines are so fluid, no one can say with certainty whether the NEA or the AFT will emerge the eventual winner in the accelerating rivalry. One thing seems certain: teachers are breaking the master-servant pattern that once characterized their relations with boards of education. The new relationship is already being crystallized into law; for example, Wisconsin has set up an employee relations board with authority to supervise elections and decide questions in dispute.

A constellation of forces is likely to encourage these developments. The reduction in number of school districts from over 120,000 in 1941 to fewer than 40,000 today has destroyed forever the unequal bargaining of the individual teacher with the board and superintendent. The teacher shortage that has existed since 1950 has combined with the population explosion and the tax squeeze to encourage growth of strong teacher blocs. A higher proportion of ambitious young men with families to support has come into teaching in recent years; they are much harder to satisfy than are second-income women teachers. It is this group at the secondary school level that gives the union movement much of its vigor.

The only foreseeable adverse factor is a surplus of teachers, predicted by the Labor Department for the last half of the 1960's. But by then teacher organizations may be so powerful that they can successfully turn their attention to control over entry into teaching. That will mark the day when the word professional has the same meaning for education that it now has for law, medicine and plumbing.

II.   THE UNION MEMBER SPEAKS UP

EDITOR'S INTRODUCTION

The most startling and significant change during the 1960's in the American labor movement has been the new attitude of the individual union member towards his labor union. This section is devoted to an examination of this recent upheaval; indeed, it would not have been possible to prepare such a section even a decade ago.

The change can be summarized in this manner: as unions grew in strength and influence, the ordinary worker looked to his union as his protector and champion in dealing with "the boss." Today, many, many union members, while still maintaining varying attitudes toward management, have come to look on the union as a third party, to be dealt with at arm's length.

Professor Ivar Berg and Thomas R. Brooks examine this "revolt" in the first two articles in this section. Sidney Lens then examines the natural consequence of the union's becoming part of an "establishment": even the paid and supposedly dedicated union staff members have decided it is time to organize themselves to bargain with the "boss" (in this case, the union). Finally, Barry Goldwater offers his views on the union member as a person, rather than simply as a number on a seniority list or a figure on a picket line.

RISING MEMBERSHIP INDEPENDENCE [1]

Not since wartime, when workers walked out on wildcat strikes in defiance of their union leaders, has the press become as excited . . . over the rash of "revolts" by workers against labor officials. The excitement was of two sorts, one could notice, de-

[1] From "The Nice Kind of Union Democracy," by Ivar Berg, assistant professor of social science and business, Columbia University. *Columbia University Forum.* 5:18-23. Spring '62. Reprinted from the *Columbia University Forum* by permission of the publisher Columbia University, Copyright © 1962.

pending upon the leaders in question. That is how the press conveniently, if unintentionally, began to clarify a remarkable, and remarkably distasteful, view of "union democracy" that is gaining a good deal of currency in this country.

In the summer of 1961, members of Local 72 of the United Auto Workers, who are employed by the American Motors company's huge Kenosha, Wisconsin, plant, rejected a daring new profit-sharing agreement extolled by Walter Reuther and by the unorthodox Mr. [George] Romney [then president of American Motors]. (The workers ratified it in a second vote held some weeks later.) In New York, striking cement truck drivers thrice voted down settlements commended to them by Teamster boss Jimmy Hoffa, even as milk deliverers in Cincinnati voted themselves out of the Teamsters Union altogether. Meanwhile, players in the New York Philharmonic struck to dramatize their demand to participate in contract negotiations between their local union and managers of the symphony. Lastly, companywide negotiations between United Auto Workers leaders and General Motors representatives were complicated by walkouts, while similar negotiations between the Ford Motor Company and the UAW were upset when local after local struck to force consideration of such luxuries as the right to an unhurried trip to the toilet.

Now when human discontent in a union serves to slow down our four-wheeled economy, when it inhibits the nourishing flow of cement or when it offends patrons of the fine arts with picket signs, indignation is supposed to be justified. Increasingly we are given to see by a number of editorialists that the private interests of intractable union members are trivial compared with the interests of the defenseless public; equally clear is the obligation of unions to confine disputes affecting the public to disputes with employers and to keep these, in turn, to a minimum. Unions are to have a sense of "public responsibility" and come to negotiations with demands to which employers may confidently address themselves; when agreement is reached between negotiating teams, there is to be no costly interference with the public's convenience brought on by recalcitrant members. Above all, it has now become a part of the conventional wisdom that "strikes are extremely costly, and the fewer we have the better." . . .

But then there is the principle of union democracy to be considered. Thus, when milk deliverers in Cincinnati voted themselves out of the Teamsters this past summer, there was no little joy in the press. Dissident drivers were interviewed and their actions reported as hopeful signs that even Hoffa could not violate minimum democratic requirements forever without paying a price. Yet when some of Walter Reuther's striking auto workers voted down a hard-won settlement at Kenosha, a number of newspapers inveighed against prolongation of a strike that seriously and needlessly hampered the manufacture and sales of The Automobile.

Democracy and a healthy economy, we are informed, have major social value. Both must be served—and they were by the milk deliverers but were not by the auto workers. This was, at least, one of the implications of the typical press treatment accorded the refusal of the Kenosha local of the United Auto Workers to ratify the settlement reached between negotiators for the national union and American Motors; it was also the inference to be drawn from press reports of union locals that continued to strike after the national union had reached agreement with the Ford Motor Company at about the same time. . . .

When democratic structure is made complex by multiple layers of organization—districts, boards, "representative" legislative bodies and the like—then the notion of a majority is, commensurately, no longer as simple as it would be under conditions of direct or town hall democracy. Our newspapers (urban) are quick to point this up when they assess the extent to which urban majorities become minorities in the halls of state legislators. They recognize, too, that the Negro majority in some southern states becomes part of a Negro minority as against the white majority in the Federal Congress. Deplored, these results are nevertheless understood by the press. But when the same problems recur in a labor-management setting, then it is economic practice and not democratic theory which inspires the solution.

If a new vote was to be suggested, why should it be for the local that voted *down* the contract? One good answer is that it is convenient for embarrassed union leaders, for disappointed managers who seek to get production lines rolling, and for fair-weather liberals who will apparently buy democracy only when it comes in an economy-size package. It must have come as a shock to all three groups when the president of one of the locals that had *approved* the settlement announced that if the Kenosha vote was to be rerun, then he wanted a new election at *his* local on the ground that the turnout *there* had been unrepresentative. . . .

A final pair of cases, less remote, perhaps, than cement trucking, symphonies and auto factories, will illustrate our ambivalence. Last year, for a forty-eight-hour period, suburban New Yorkers did not have to search their shrubbery for the morning paper; it wasn't there. Nor could they catch the 7:45 to Grand Central Station; there was none. On the first televised newscasts our suburbanites witnessed interviews with rail conductors who had been ordered by their union chiefs to respect picket lines thrown up around Grand Central by striking tugboat crewmen. Some of the railroad men complained before the cameras that they had not chosen, but had been ordered, to respect the picket line and expressed sympathy for stranded commuters, some of whom had democratically traveled on subways for the first time in their lives, according to one announcer. Viewers were informed, on the same news broadcast, that a strike of the Newspaper Deliverers Union against New York publishers had been settled but that deliveries would not begin for forty-eight hours. This very democratic union has a constitutional requirement that members be permitted two full days to study any agreement before they vote on its ratification.

The commuters were thus confronted with a pair of deprivations—one stemming *from* democracy and the other stemming from *lack* of democracy in unions.

Mention of the news deliverers calls to mind that this union is alleged by some labor observers to be one of the most corrupt. When popular discussions of unions appear in the press and on television they tend to focus on union democracy, union corruption and strikes. Lack of the first is generally taken to be a cause of the second; but rarely, as we have seen, is the first "blamed" for the occurrence of the third. Since we find democracy praiseworthy but strikes deplorable, we hesitate to consider any relationship between the two. Similarly, since corruption, by definition, is bad and democracy, by postulation, is good, we deny, *a priori,* any association between democracy and corruption. . . .

If democracy is worth fighting for, worth dying for, then, it may be suggested, it is at least occasionally worth paying for.

THE RANK-AND-FILE REVOLT [2]

Angry, frustrated and haggard from lack of sleep, Thomas W. ("Teddy") Gleason, president of the 60,000-member International Longshoremen's Association, slumped behind his desk in a downtown Manhattan office one gray morning . . . [in January 1965] mulling over a chain of disasters. Only a few days before, he had jubilantly initialed an unprecedented four-year contract with the New York Shipping Association that would mean an eighty-cent-an-hour package increase for 24,000 New York dockworkers. And since New York's contract traditionally sets the pattern for settlements in other ports, it was hardly surprising that Gleason buoyantly predicted an early national settlement. After all, as the ILA leader saw it, the contract was "the greatest in the history of the union."

The union's members thought otherwise. New York longshoremen rejected the contract, sparking a strike that closed every port from Maine to Texas. With that, the power of Teddy Gleason eroded by the hour. He watched impotently as Assistant Secretary of Labor James J. Reynolds and David A. Stowe, a Department of Labor consultant on waterfront problems, ignoring him, set out from Washington to parley with local union leaders in each strikebound port. He swallowed his pride and sent an

[2] From "Labor: The Rank-and-File Revolt," by Thomas R. Brooks, contributing editor. *Dun's Review and Modern Industry.* 85:34-5+. Mr. '65. Reprinted by special permission from *Dun's Review and Modern Industry,* March 1965. Copyright 1965, Dun & Bradstreet Publications Corp.

urgent call for help to his friend, President George Meany of the AFL-CIO, but Meany merely sent a public relations man who drafted a four-page explanatory leaflet on the details of the rejected contract. The final indignity came when Gleason had to spend ten hours licking stamps, stuffing envelopes and trudging three blocks to the local post office with the mail. Asked what had happened, Gleason could only mumble: "It was a misunderstanding."

It was the understatement of the year. For Gleason, like many a union leader these days, is feeling the full force of a wave of resentment that is sweeping through the rank and file of the American labor movement. In some cases the rebellion takes the form of a demand for local autonomy in bargaining. In others, it is a planned series of unauthorized strikes that embarrass and discredit the national union. There are cases where workers either break away to form their own independent organization or invite another unon to stage a "raid." By the time the revolt has run its course, many union presidents and their policies will be overthrown, and the present methods of collective bargaining will be altogether changed.

A decade or more in the making, this surge of discontent has already toppled the administrations of three unions—the Textile Workers, the United Federation of Teachers and the State, County and Municipal Employees union. On the West Coast, 20,000 paper mill workers left their international union, made an alliance with the International Brotherhood of Teamsters, then proceeded to call their first strike in thirty years. Disgruntled members of the United Mine Workers of America have already skirmished with President William A. Boyle, the hand-picked successor of old fire-eater John L. Lewis, and are regrouping for another battle. Even the strike of the New York welfare workers was sparked by a splinter group of militants who broke away from the parent union. As if all this were not enough, the Teamsters, although outlawed by the AFL-CIO, has taken advantage of this feuding to mount successful recruiting campaigns among the disenchanted and the unorganized.

Why has the labor movement foundered precisely at the time when its political influence has seemingly reached an all-time high? Why are blue-collar workers, the backbone of labor, becoming more and more cynical about unions? And why are embattled union leaders, most of whom rose from the ranks in the tough organizing days of the thirties, the current targets of this rank-and-file revolt?

The answer, in a fashionable word, is alienation. No longer can union members identify themselves with a distant, and often authoritarian, figure. To Detroit auto workers, bored and weary with the daily grind of a monotonous task, the lofty generalizations of Walter Reuther about such topics as the problem of recreation for the elderly seem ludicrous. The endless stream of hortatory leaflets and booklets, urging union members to concern themselves with the broad issues of national and international politics, contrast sharply with the crude maneuverings of intraunion political squabbling. More important, grievances on matters apart from wages are either ignored or lost in the limbo of union bureaucracy.

The explosive content of the rank-and-file rebellion is high indeed. A rebellious streak within the United Automobile Workers, for example, shut down General Motors Corporation for thirty days and Ford Motor Company for twenty-eight days . . . [in 1964]. The issue: local working conditions. The walkouts took place despite a favorable national agreement wrapped in a sixty-cent package, enclosing, among other gains, pensions of nearly $400 a month and inducements for early retirement. Significantly, in the year preceding . . . [the 1964] auto talks, there had been an almost complete turnover in the leadership of UAW locals at GM plants. "The strike," a UAW official concedes, "was another expression of the rank-and-file dissatisfaction with the leadership and its inability to correct plant conditions."

Some spokesmen for labor attribute the grass-roots rebellion to the protection afforded dissidents by the Landrum-Griffin Act, which, among other things, attempted to check the power vested in union officials. [See "The Landrum-Griffin Act of 1959, in Section IV, below.] But it is much more than that. For along with the disenchantment of the workers, there is increasing evidence that most major unions are split by struggles between the incumbent administration and local leaders, who are using the militancy of the rank and file to propel themselves to power.

The waterfront strike is a good example. ILA President Gleason's first proposal to the industry was a one-year contract that would postpone such controversial issues as the size of the work gang and flexibility in work assignments. Immediately, Gleason's rival, smooth, articulate Anthony Scotto, who heads Brooklyn local 1814, seized his opportunity. Along with other local presidents he devised a formula for a four-year contract that would allow employers to whittle down the work gangs from twenty to seventeen men, but this bitter pill was sweetened by an annual wage guarantee and a provision for stable employment. Although reluctant, Gleason agreed to go along with this plan, principally because he was assured that the New York members would approve the contract.

When the contract was rejected, Gleason, as the union's top officer, had to accept responsibility for the ensuing national strike. His power and prestige diminished, he watched helplessly as local leaders in other ports demanded the right to negotiate their own contracts rather than follow the New York formula. The attitude of the dissidents was best expressed by Willie C. Wells, president of the ILA's Houston local. Said Wells: "We have been getting pushed around for a long time by the international union to go back to work after the locals in the East settle. The men are going to be rough about it this time, and we are going to stay out until we can get enough to help us catch up with the conditions in the East."

This interrelationship between the struggle for power and the discontent of the rank and file is also clearly evident within the United Steelworkers of America. The roots of the present steel union difficulties go back to 1957 when an unknown millworker, Donald C. Rarick, rolled up a surprising vote of 223,516 to President David J. McDonald's winning total of 404,172. At that time, the thirty-eight district directors of the USW stood behind

McDonald, even though many of them had been hostile to the president. This coalition quelled the Rarick rebellion, without, however, dampening the growing dissatisfaction of the rank and file.

While the silver-haired, ruddy-faced McDonald has won praise from management and the public for his labor statesmanship, steelworkers are stinting in their praise of his achievements. "We've been without a raise for four years now," a husky Indiana steel roller said in explaining his opposition to McDonald. Some steelworkers, too, are critical of McDonald's alleged "high living." When gossip columnists linked his name with Zsa Zsa Gabor, McDonald explained that "We were merely introduced" when he sat at a nearby table in a New York restaurant. "I believe, as John L. Lewis and Philip Murray taught me," says McDonald, "that you travel first class."

Possibly the union members do not resent the high life as much as they do McDonald's absence from the union hall. "Abe [I.W.] Abel has attended about every affair my district has had for the past several years," says William J. Hart, director of a 36,000-member Pittsburgh-area district. "We've invited McDonald, but we haven't been able to get him here for any of them."

Steelworkers are also suspicious of what they call "the secrecy" of the Human Relations Committee. [See "Year-Round Bargaining," in Section III, below.] "The committee," charged Walter J. Burke, Milwaukee District 32 director and an anti-McDonald contender for the USW secretary-treasurership, during the election contest, "has usurped the prerogatives of the negotiating committees." . . . [The result: Abel was elected to the USW presidency in February 1965, sending McDonald into retirement.—Ed.]

For steel management, it made little difference who won. . . . Once battle lines were drawn, both sides became ultramilitant in the effort to win supporters. The difficulties of the winner would lie not so much in securing a raise in wages as in settling local plant working conditions. So, for the first time in years, a national settlement in steel is no guarantee of labor peace.

Leadership fights, such as those in the USW, tend to obscure the real significance of the current rank-and-file rebellion within the unions. Its genesis is in the factory, and its lasting impact is likely to be on the methods of collective bargaining. In the past, the growth of giant corporations made the formation of strong national unions almost inevitable; the national agreement was a consequence. It was useful to corporate management as a means of manpower discipline, while for union members it was a device to equalize wages and work standards. However, in recent years corporations have been decentralizing while labor management has not.

The rank-and-file rebellion, turning as it does on local plant work issues, runs counter to the centralizing tendency of the standard national labor relations contract. UAW local unions, for example, used their right to strike as leverage against both corporate management and the national leaders of the UAW. In effect, during the [1964] negotiations . . . they told UAW President Walter P. Reuther and Louis G. Seaton, GM vice president in charge of personnel, that a national agreement would not preclude their right to settle local plant problems.

It is true that union members are divided over the issue. Some believe that plant problems cannot be solved on a plant-by-plant basis. Striking just one plant, they say, does not bring to bear the power of a companywide or industrywide strike. Others, however, believe they can solve local problems if freed from the restraint imposed by the national union.

This conflict, too, can divide union leadership. For example, General Electric Company and the International Union of Electrical, Radio and Machine Workers have a national agreement that permits "local understandings." GE also encourages its local management to make its own decisions. . . . GE management in Lynn, Massachusetts and IUE Local 201 have been battling over wage-job classification issues. . . . [In January 1965] the union brought the issue to a management study team in New York. But the management group backed its own local people in Lynn. Then Local 201 called a strike, protesting the imposition of the new job rates, claiming that they would lead to a wage cut.

But in Schenectady, Local 301 of the same international union accepted a wage cut for a group of its members. As a result, the local, under the leadership of Leo E. Jandreau, its business agent, . . . [was] battling IUE President James B. Carey over a "local understanding" that the Schenectady IUE members feel saved their jobs, but which Carey has termed a "sellout." [Carey subsequently was defeated in a bitter election battle for the IUE presidency.—Ed.]

Whatever the outcome of such specific local situations, it is clear that there has been a decided shift in the locus of decision-making. No longer can the leadership of a national union impose its will on the rank and file. Even more important, the power structure within the unions must be reconstructed, even to the extent of granting autonomy to local unions at the bargaining table.

Does this mean an end to the national agreement? By no means. It does indicate that national agreements may become more like an umbrella shading a variety of "local understandings" or local agreements, rather than a master plan imposing uniform conditions throughout. The settling of wages and benefits will continue to be spelled out in national agreements. But local agreements will include an ever-widening range of plant job problems. After all, as the ILA strike has shown, such issues have already taken precedence over wages.

UNIONS WITHIN UNIONS [3]

The measure of labor's decline . . . is evidenced, subtly but poignantly, by the increasing trend of the staffs of large unions to organize unions of their own. In the past, dissent in the house of labor translated itself into a vibrant factionalism, with stridency of debate and bitterness of feeling, but withal, clarification of purpose and involvement of the membership. Today's frustration is translated into the formation of unions by secondary union officials against the primary ones. It is a subconscious exposition

[3] From "The Decline of Labor," by Sidney Lens, long-time trade unionist and labor commentator. *Commonweal.* 80:391-4. Je. 19, '64. Reprinted by permission.

of the fact that under present circumstances there are no new fields to plow.

. . . [Recently] the international representatives working for Region 3 of the United Auto Workers—Indiana and Kentucky— signed application cards for a union of their own, and as symptom of their concern plunked down $25 each to finance their efforts. Like ordinary workers in the shop these representatives were expressing a fear for their personal security. Younger men were being recruited to the staff of the UAW and there was increasing anxiety that, as automation chipped away at UAW's membership, layoffs of staff might take place without regard to length of service. Except for one or two men the Region 3 representatives were unanimous. Soon their efforts were being emulated from coast to coast, and at Solidarity House in Detroit, the UAW's national headquarters, a near-100 per cent was enrolled despite pleas by President Walter Reuther to a meeting of these men and women that they could resolve their problems by other methods. In New York and California the staff ranks were similarly solid. A majority of the 720 nonelected officials joined the ranks quickly and like their fellow-staffers in the AFL-CIO itself, the oil union, electrical union, chemical union, rubber workers, ladies' garment union, newspaper guild, teachers' organization, papermakers, and airline pilots, they demanded recognition and collective bargaining rights.

Reuther's reaction was calm and statesmanlike. He sidetracked the effort by forming an elaborate Staff Council of International Representatives to handle grievances. In each regional office and each division of the UAW Grievance Representatives and Alternate Grievance Representatives were to be elected to handle complaints. The method enacted was eminently fair. First stage in the grievance machinery would be a discussion with the regional director or department head; second stage would involve a reduction of the problem to writing and the eliciting of a written reply; third stage would be a meeting between a Staff Appeal Panel and a committee of the International Union's executive board. If after all this there were still no resolution, an impartial outside umpire would hear the evidence and issue a final and binding decision.

The UAW leaned over backward to make the plan painless. Costs of the arbitration and costs of travel by staff appeal members and the forty-one-man committee that would meet with national leadership twice a year were to be borne by the International Union. To reassure the representatives that the program was meaningful Reuther promised he would recommend its incorporation into the UAW's constitution.

The issue of job security, however, was not and could not be resolved. Reuther correctly made it clear that the UAW could not guarantee seniority privileges to its staff because in doing so it would be depriving the rank and file of some of its rights. Unions, he pointed out, are "political." One faction can replace another in a convention election. It would be unfair to an incoming group to saddle it with the staff men who belonged to its rival. Everyone now working for UAW is a member of the "Reuther caucus" and pays $10 a month to finance its work. A rival caucus could hardly be expected to work through "Reutherites." Reuther promised that insofar as possible the regional leaders and department heads would consider length of service in making assignments and laying off reps [representatives—the term used for union staff members who work with local unions], but it could not be bound by it.

The only basis in his plan for challenging a layoff is where there has been "personal discrimination." The Council of International Representatives can discuss wages, conditions, and other problems, but it cannot guarantee jobs based on seniority, nor can it, in an emergency, go out on strike. In essence, these limitations exist also in the other unions where a staff group has been granted collective bargaining rights.

Most of the labor leaders who have been confronted with this problem of staff organization have accepted it with grace. James B. Carey of the International Union of Electrical Workers (IUE) recognized the staff union without a second's hesitation. In a few instances, however, bitter feelings have been engendered. George Meany at first refused to deal with the Field Representatives' Federation formed shortly after the AFL and CIO merged. He gave in only when the National Labor Relations Board announced that organizers must be treated like other types of employees, subject to NLRB jurisdiction, and ordered an election. Since then he has worked with FRF in a fair and equitable manner.

The one labor leader who has balked is David Dubinsky, President of the International Ladies' Garment Workers' Union (ILGWU). When his 250 staff members established the Federation of Union Representatives (FOUR), he showered bombast on them, fired one or two and reassigned others to their disadvantage. He refused categorically to bargain. FOUR's members were for the most part young men who had been given training in the union's highly publicized training institute. They were idealistic and included many young Socialists or ex-Socialists. Dubinsky was fearful they might become another power center in his union, and because they were close to the rank and file might stir up factional strife in the future. He was willing to adjust wages—which in some cases were as low as $65 a week—and evolve a health and welfare program, but he would not tolerate a separate power entity in his organization. He fought FOUR vigorously, even after FOUR had won an election called by the NLRB. The issue is now in the courts.

To the public, particularly the antilabor segment, there is a wry, almost humorous touch to the unionizing of the unionizers. The labor brass, it feels, is getting a taste of its own medicine. "How do they like it when their own subordinates organize? They try to subvert unionism just as if they were industrial employers. Yet they insist on union shops for the general worker." Dubinsky's resistance, especially, became a *cause célèbre* for a while and was used as an argument by employers when they berated unionism. Reuther's Council is being called by some a "company union."

None of this, in my opinion, is justified. There is merit to Reuther's rationale that the relationship between an international rep and the parent union is not comparable to that between factory employer and employee. The rep is himself a union member, pledged to carry out the purposes of his organization. He cannot be permitted to go out on strike while the General Motors workers, for instance, are themselves on the picket line. Though he may have a divergence of interests with the policymakers in his union, he cannot have a divergence with the union itself. To allow him to strike would rob the union membership of part of its right to strike; to grant him full seniority rights would take away from the membership some of its prerogatives.

But while all this is true, the conflict between secondary and primary leadership in a dozen unions and in the AFL-CIO itself is an ominous sign. The staffs, like typical employees, are organizing *against* something and against someone. They must have good and sufficient cause to be doing it. It is not a prank or an effort at forming a professional society; it is a reflection of something that has gone wrong in the house of labor.

Thousands of secondary union leaders once—not too long ago —had a measure of power of their own. As shop committeemen or local union presidents they expressed their own judgments and fought for their own principles. Their support in the rank and file gave them a base of power with which they could pressure even the top leadership. But as members of the staff they have lost this role. They are today only slightly more independent than bank employees, simply a link in the chain of communications between fifteen or twenty national leaders and the rank and file for whom they formerly spoke. They are enmeshed in an institutional operation just as if they were junior executives of Bell Telephone.

I know at least fifty staff members of former CIO unions, by way of example, who are opposed to labor being aligned with the Democrats and who favor a labor party. Yet none of them can argue their position publicly, nor can they round up rank and file support for such views without being fired. Some are forced to work in Democratic party campaigns even though they are at political loggerheads with the candidates for whom they are working. Many staff people disagree totally with the AFL-CIO position on the arms race, or with that of the UAW, which is milder. Not a few have deep misgivings about specific collective bargaining proposals (such as Reuther's profit-sharing plan), or with the degree of union militancy on unemployment or automation. But in dealings with the locals they service, they must be silent. They must act like good soldiers "carrying out policy."

Theoretically UAW staff members are part of the "Reuther caucus," but even here their wings are clipped. The area of decision has narrowed, with the decline of factionalism, with long-term contracts, and centralized national bargaining, to a dozen or so men at the top of the union pyramid. To quarrel with a decision of that pyramid is not quite so dangerous as to quarrel with a boss in a factory, but it is of the same genre. A regional director can show his displeasure at a recalcitrant by making tough assignments; a representative who likes to stay close to home may be assigned to an organizing drive three hundred miles away; a representative who prefers arbitration work, which normally has a regular nine to five schedule, may be assigned to organizing work, which calls for leafleting at 6 A.M. and making house calls to prospective unionists during the evening. The labor unions have become institutionalized, and though the higher officials may be called, as C. Wright Mills called them, the new men of power, the secondary leaders, who once possessed important prerogatives at the lower levels, now are politically disfranchised within their unions. . . .

The sad fact is that labor today is involved in no great causes. Its power elite on the Executive Council of the AFL-CIO were unwilling, with a few exceptions, to even endorse the great civil rights demonstration . . . [in August 1963]. They are not only cautious on the matter of disarmament, but the Meany faction at least is as rabid as the Pentagon for continuing the arms race. The few words that are spoken at each convention against unemployment are automatic salaams just for the record. There is no flare of militancy. Indeed a new school of apologists has arisen within labor circles and in the universities to explain this is the way things should be in a "mature" movement.

Perhaps. But these theorists might ponder why union officials insist on unionizing. At bottom this is not just a quest for personal security, but a groping for idealism, for causes, for a new insurgent impulse.

THE UNION MEMBER AS A PERSON [4]

During the past quarter of a century, America has become a society of competing pressure groups. The feeling has become almost universal that the individual, by himself and unorganized, is virtually helpless to achieve what are, at bottom, individual goals—economic well-being generally, a rising standard of living, improved education, cultural development, and dignified human treatment in social and economic relationships. . . .

It cannot be emphasized strongly enough that these pressure group organizations often serve to aggrandize their own leaders and bureaucracy as well, sometimes at the expense of the membership. And, what is more important, all of these pressure group organizations, even when functioning properly, serve only a part of the individual's needs. In an ominous development, however, many of these organizations increasingly act as though they were empowered to serve the total man, the individual member in all his manifold aspects.

To take the most obvious contemporary example, the labor unions would now speak and act for the individual union member, not merely in his capacity as an employee facing management, but in his capacity as a citizen. Thus, in the name of its members, who in many cases have not been consulted, the union leadership takes official positions on issues ranging from the minimum wage to UN action in the Congo, and endorses and supports, with money contributed from the hard-earned wages of its members, favored political candidates for public office ranging from city alderman to the presidency itself.

It is instructive to note, parenthetically, that some labor unions, aiming at the "total man," set up vacation resorts (at reduced rates), publish newspapers, establish schools, engage in cultural activities (like hiring professional choral groups), and thereby seek, also, to mold their members along predetermined cultural, intellectual, and ideological lines. In all this totalistic organizational activity, the individual is often submerged,

[4] From an article by Barry Goldwater, 1964 Republican candidate for President of the United States and former Senator from Arizona. *University of Detroit Law Journal.* 40:179-88. D. '62. Reprinted by permission.

swamped, and treated as a manipulable statistic. It may happen, as it almost always does, that the same individual is at once a worker, a member of a minority or religious group, a war veteran, a parent of school-age children, a member of a political party, of a fraternal order, or of a cooperative, and, of course, he is always a consumer. Yet, some of "his" organizations tend more and more to speak for him as a "total man," crushing his individuality and diversity through the organization's power and voice.

Even where the organization restricts its activities to more narrow (and hence more legitimate) channels, the individual members are frequently opposed to large portions of the program. But they typically lack the time, the energy, the resources, or the courage (sometimes it takes heroic audacity), to "buck the machine"—to oppose the organization's leadership and bureaucracy. . . .

Labor unions enjoy many special privileges and immunities under Federal law. By far the most important of these is the exclusive right to represent all the employees in the unit for purposes of collective bargaining, even if the union has been selected as bargaining agent by only a narrow majority, which in many circumstances under our existing law, in fact, constitutes only a minority. Under the law, those employees who do not wish to join, as well as those whom the union for whatever reason excludes from membership, can neither bargain for themselves nor select any person or agency other than the union so designated to bargain for them. They are, in reality, the involuntary principals of agents imposed upon them by law. In granting unions this right, the Government, in effect, has bestowed upon them the power of government itself. Although this provision of law has a certain usefulness in the area of collective bargaining, it results in a most serious injustice to those employees who wish to join the union but are excluded by the union itself. They have no voice in helping to determine the union's bargaining demands and policies, are not permitted to do their own bargaining, and are compelled to accept and work under the terms and conditions of the agreements between the union and the employer, even if they find such terms and conditions highly unsatisfactory.

Moreover, in certain industries there is a widespread practice whereby employers recruit their labor force through the local unions in the particular area. This is particularly true in those industries where the most highly skilled, and consequently the most highly paid, employees are needed to perform the work. It is precisely in these industries where union membership exclusionary policies are most widely and persistently applied. As a result, untold numbers of completely qualified workers, who for one reason or another are denied admission to union membership, are excluded not only from many jobs, but particularly from the most highly paid jobs as well. Therefore, no union should be permitted to enjoy the unique and precious privilege of exclusive representation in collective bargaining if it arbitrarily excludes from membership those qualified workers who wish to join the union.

The right of an American citizen to express his political preferences, and to give his support to the candidates and party of his choice is the fundamental political right on which our democratic society is based. Any interference with this right must be viewed with the greatest alarm. One of the most vicious forms of such interference is to exert economic coercion on a citizen in order to compel his support for a particular political party, candidate, or program by threatening him with the loss of his livelihood if he withholds such support.

Thus, to take a hypothetical example, if an employer compelled his employees to contribute to a particular candidate or party as a condition of holding his job, the American public would be shocked beyond measure. An outraged public opinion would quickly compel such an employer to desist from this exercise in political blackmail. Fortunately, instances of this type are so rare as, for all practical purposes, to be nonexistent.

Yet, there is one important and substantial area of American life in which precisely this form of political blackmail is wellnigh universal. Today, the vast majority of labor unions operate under collective bargaining agreements which require employees to join the union and pay periodic dues and initiation fees as a condition of holding their jobs. Regardless of to what use the money an employee must pay to the union is put, no matter how objectionable he finds such use to be, if he refuses for that reason to pay his dues, the union can, and usually does, force the employer to fire him under the union-shop contract.

Every union today is using substantial portions of the funds collected from membership dues and initiation fees in behalf of specific candidates, parties, and political programs. The overwhelming majority of these unions has compulsory union-membership contracts. Nevertheless, many employees who favor rival candidates, parties, and platforms are compelled to contribute their money to support candidates, parties, and political programs they bitterly oppose, or lose their jobs. This widespread practice constitutes the most nakedly brazen form of political coercion which exists in our society, and around which the labor elements have succeeded in erecting an "iron curtain" of public misinformation and consequent apathy. As a result of this conspiracy of silence and the sentimental belief that a union is always the underdog in its dealings with an employer, a belief assiduously cultivated by union leaders and their allies, unions have been able to destroy the fundamental civil rights of an untold number of their members, who are truly the underdogs in their relations with their union leaders. It is necessary, therefore, to correct this intolerable injustice by proposing and supporting measures which will restore to all of our citizens their basic human and constitutional rights to express and support their political preferences completely free from any form of restraint, interference, or coercion.

Labor disputes, increasingly, are erupting into violence. More and more, strikers and picket lines use force and intimidation to prevent employees, who so desire, from working and other individuals from entering upon their own property and operating their own establishments. In certain sections of the country where much of this type of unlawful violence occurs, the police and the public authorities make little or no attempt to enforce the law by preventing the violence or by protecting those who wish to exercise their legal and constitutional rights. Again, the sentimental myth of the union as underdog has been so arduously propagated, by those who are most vociferous in demanding obedience to the law in other areas, that the public has been completely misled and brainwashed into dangerous apathy.

It is essential to arouse the public to demand the elimination of this dangerous threat to our liberties and to the democratic structure of our society. It would be preferable to leave this problem to solution on the state and local level where traditionally it belongs, but there are two factors which make this impracticable and thus require Federal law and the exercise of Federal power in order to attain an effective cure for this malignant social evil.

First, labor unions have attained their present size and strength, and hence their ability to defy the law, as a result of a series of special benefits, rights, privileges, and immunities bestowed upon them by Federal statutes, and enjoyed by no other type of private organization or institution in our society. To enumerate a few of these:

1. unions are immune from taxation; [5]
2. unions are practically immune under the antitrust laws; [6]
3. unions are immune, in many situations, against the issuance of injunctions by Federal courts; [7]
4. unions can compel employees to join unions in order to hold their jobs; [8]
5. unions can use funds, which their members have been compelled to contribute in order to hold their jobs, to finance political programs and candidates which some of these members strongly oppose; [9]
6. unions have been given the absolute right to deny workers admission to union membership, and, in practical effect, are able to deny many workers access to jobs in general and to the higher-paying jobs in particular; [10]

[5] INT. REV. CODE of 1954, § 501 (c) (5).

[6] United States v. Hutcheson, 312 U.S. 219 (1940).

[7] Norris-La Guardia Act, 47 Stat. 70 (1932), 29 U.S.C. § 101-15 (1958).

[8] National Labor Relations Act (Wagner Act) § 8(3), 49 Stat. 452 (1935), as amended 61 Stat. 140 (1947), 29 U.S.C. §158 (a) (3) (1958).

[9] Ibid.

[10] NLRA § 8(b) (1) (A), added by 61 Stat. 141 (1947), 29 U.S.C. § 158(b) (1) (A) (1958).

7. unions have the exclusive right to act as collective bargaining agents even for those workers who either do not wish to join the union or who are excluded from membership in it, even arbitrarily; [11]

8. unions have the right, in some situations, to invade the privacy of workers, even against their will, thus depriving them of a legal right enjoyed by all other individuals in our society;

9. and finally, and of the greatest significance, the granting of these rights by Federal law has resulted in the exclusion of the states from many of the areas covered by these Federal laws, and the states may not lawfully act in these areas. This is known as the doctrine of Federal preemption. [12]

Second, labor disputes involving unlawful picket-line violence, as well as sabotage, threats, assaults on workers both at their homes and at their places of work, vandalism, destruction of property, even bombings, have occurred in many parts of the country. But local and state law enforcement against these illegal activities has been most lax in the industrial North, particularly in the giant urban centers in some of the states in that section of the country.

It must be clearly understood that when a strike occurs which is not caused by any unlawful act of the employer, but is merely a result of his refusal to grant the union's demands, the struck employer has not only a legal, but a constitutional right to continue to operate his plant and to have free access to his property; and any of his workers whom he invites to do so, have both a legal and constitutional right to refuse to join the strike and to enter his property, and continue working. This fundamental right which has existed from the beginning of our Republic was completely affirmed by the Supreme Court of the United States in a case [13] arising more than twenty years ago under the Wagner

---

[11] NLRA § 9(a), 49 Stat. 453 (1935), as amended, 29 U.S.C. § 159(a) (1958).

[12] See, e.g., the following cases for a discussion of the doctrine of Federal preemption in the field of labor law: Westinghouse Salaried Employees v. Westinghouse Elec. Corp., 348 U.S. 437 (1954); Textile Workers v. Lincoln Mills, 353 U.S. 448 (1956).

[13] NLRB v. Mackay Radio & Tel. Co., 304 U.S. 333 (1938).

Act, organized labor's favorite piece of legislation. Not one jot or tittle of this legal doctrine and the basic right which it protects have ever been whittled away by any subsequent judicial decision. It is the law of the land today and every public official in the United States has both a legal and moral duty to honor it and, where the nature of his office so requires, to enforce it. Where this right is violated through threats, intimidation, coercion, or violence, it is the constitutional obligation of state and local officials to prevent such violence, protect the victims of it, and punish the perpetrators, not only because such misconduct constitutes a breach of state or local law but because all law enforcement officials in the United States, on every level of government, are sworn to obey and enforce the Federal Constitution.

In 1959, Congress adopted the Landrum-Griffin Act by overwhelming margins, and it was signed into law by President Eisenhower. In so doing, our Government for the first time recognized the need for Federal regulation of labor unions in order to eliminate corruption and crime, and to protect rank-and-file union members against the tyranny, possible and sometimes actual, of their own labor leaders. However, the bill of rights provisions in the Landrum-Griffin Act which protect rank-and-file members in the exercise of their rights as union members need strengthening. And they need it precisely in that area where the Congress seriously weakened these safeguards by compelling the union member to bring a private suit to enforce his rights instead of requiring an appropriate Federal official or agency to bring such suit in his behalf, as was originally provided by the proposal offered by Senator McClellan, the chairman of the Senate's Labor Racketeering Committee.

The Landrum-Griffin Act, therefore, should be amended to remedy this serious defect by giving the rank-and-file union member the aid and support of the Federal Government in seeking to vindicate his legal rights which have been violated by his union or its leaders.

Free and voluntary collective bargaining is the surest guarantee of the preservation of a genuinely democratic society based primarily on an economic system of free enterprise. An indispensable element of free collective bargaining is the right of employees, acting in concert, to withhold their labor in their effort to induce employers to grant them favorable terms and conditions of employment. This right to strike, subject to certain necessary limitations in the public interest, also constitutes a basic civil liberty. And even though strikes sometimes inflict some economic hardship on the public, a democratic society must be willing to pay that price and insist upon the preservation of the right.

There is, however, another aspect of the right to strike which our public officials, and the public itself, have hitherto largely ignored. Although strikes may sometimes inconvenience the public, they always impose hardship on the strikers and their families. The loss of wages resulting from even a short-lived strike can mean economic disaster for the striking employee and his dependents. Thus, no strike should be embarked upon unless the decision to do so reflects unquestionably the will of the employees themselves, the very people who are sure to suffer hardship because of the strike.

It is true that many union constitutions require a favorable strike vote by a majority of the union members actually voting before the union officers are authorized to call a strike. However, there is no law requiring that such a vote be taken. As a result, many strikes are called by union leaders without adequate consultation with their membership; others are begun on the basis of votes taken by a show of hands in an open union meeting where those who do not favor a strike fear to indicate their opposition. In these situations, as usual, "the Forgotten American" is ignored, and no effort made to determine his wishes.

In reaching a decision of such momentous import to all the wage earners in the struck establishment, certain minimum safeguards should be established by law to guarantee that the decision truly reflects the real wishes of an actual majority of the employees in the establishment. Only by such legislation can the American people be certain that the principles of personal responsibility and individual obligation which, as pointed out above, are essential to the preservation of a free, democratic, and moral society, are being effectively preserved. What is needed is legislation on the subject of strike votes based on the following simple requirements: (1) a strike shall be unlawful unless notice of intention to strike is given to all those concerned at least thirty days prior to the actual commencement of the strike; and (2) at any time after such notice has been given, and prior to the termination of the strike, a petition may be filed by an employee with the National Labor Relations Board, asking the Board to conduct an election by secret ballot among the employees in the establishment to be struck, on the question of whether they favor a strike or its continuation. If such a petition is supported by 30 per cent of said employees, the Board shall conduct such an election and the strike or its continuation shall be lawful only if a majority, so voting, cast their ballots in favor thereof.

This procedure has ample precedent in the existing law governing representation, decertification, and de-authorization elections presently conducted by the Board, and the Board's own administrative requirements and procedures in connection with such elections. These are all based on the principle that such elections will be held upon a showing that a substantial minority of the employees involved (never in any case more than 30 per cent) want such election to be held. The principle is eminently sound and should be extended to the important matter of the strike vote.

III. COLLECTIVE BARGAINING IN THE 1960'S

EDITOR'S INTRODUCTION

Collective bargaining, when everything is said and done, is what unions are all about. The union, holding the proxy of the workers, faces management to win new gains and reinforce old victories. On success or failure at the collective bargaining table rests the future of the union leaders and indeed of the union itself.

Despite scoffers, skeptics, and criers of doom, collective bargaining continues to work. It does so notwithstanding the growing ineffectiveness of strikes (see "Declining Role of the Strike" in this section); new and more widely effective minimum wage laws which reduce the union's role in winning subsistence wages; and management's increasing acceptance of responsibility in its treatment of workers. Every day, new and improved collective bargaining agreements (or labor contracts, as they are more commonly called) are consummated as a result of lengthy and wordy struggles between union and management. This is true even if the final stages of bargaining take place literally in the White House, as was the case in the 1965 negotiations in the steel industry.

The fact that collective bargaining is taking on new shapes and forms is the significant point emphasized in this section. For general background on how collective bargaining works, William E. Simkin, director of the Federal Mediation and Conciliation Service, tells the story of labor-management accommodation in the sophisticated aerospace industry. The next four selections detail the new techniques being widely adopted in the 1960's as modern means of effective collective bargaining. Finally, there is the story of the novel "no strike" strike agreement between the Upholsterers' union and the Dunbar Furniture Company, perhaps an indication of still another new technique in the fascinating development of labor-management relations.

WHEN COLLECTIVE BARGAINING WORKS [1]

Too many of the Monday morning quarterbacks on the trends in labor relations have been talking direly that free collective bargaining is in danger as an institution because a narrow sector in the labor-management field seemed to collapse in chaos . . . . I am referring to the newspaper strikes and the longshore stoppage.

Too little consideration has been given by these same prophets of doom to the substantial successes in collective bargaining that are everywhere around us and have come to be accepted as commonplace. An excellent example is what happened in the aerospace industry. That experience is worth reviewing.

It was back in February 1962 that the Federal Mediation and Conciliation Service, well ahead of the contract expiration dates, began deploying forces and planning how this agency's mediation team could be most useful in assisting nearly two dozen major aerospace producers, as well as numerous supplier firms, and two key labor unions—the International Association of Machinists and the United Auto Workers—in negotiating new labor contracts.

At the outset, the Honorable Arthur J. Goldberg, then Secretary of Labor, . . . frankly told both unions that the Government had a serious concern in the aerospace bargaining and that any prolonged work stoppage clearly involving the public interest would be intolerable.

From then on, the FMCS, the Labor Department both under Mr. Goldberg and his successor, Secretary W. Willard Wirtz, and the White House closely cooperated in settlement efforts. Mediators were carefully assigned to assist in the various sets of company-union negotiations under the Washington direction of myself and Walter A. Maggiolo, the FMCS Director of Mediation Activities, who was specially designated aerospace coordinator for the duration.

[1] From "Aerospace Bargaining: Collective Bargaining *Does* Work," by William E. Simkin. director, Federal Mediation and Conciliation Service. *Labor Law Journal.* 14:834-8. O. '63.

The major scene of negotiations was on the West Coast, where most of the aerospace production is concentrated. And by May 15, 1963, when the Boeing Company agreement was formally ratified by the Machinists Union membership—thereby successfully climaxing the round of aerospace contracts—our battery of mediators had conducted some eight hundred separate peace meetings with the companies and unions concerned.

Over this fifteen-month period it took practically every technique known to the mediator's art (and it is as much an art in the labor relations field as diplomacy is in international relations) to keep the bargaining on the beam and prevent a number of strike threats from materializing.

But it also proved necessary, when the strike peril became most severe, for President Kennedy on three occasions to invoke the national emergency terms of the Taft-Hartley law in order to appoint boards of inquiry and obtain court injunctions. This was done in the cases of Republic Aviation, Lockheed and finally Boeing.

On two other occasions the President, on the recommendation of the FMCS, appointed presidential boards to examine dispute issues and suggest settlement terms. One such board, headed by Professor George W. Taylor of the University of Pennsylvania, submitted recommendations in disputes involving the North American, Lockheed, Convair (General Dynamics), Ryan and Aerojet General aerospace firms. The second board, chaired by Saul Wallen, well-known Boston arbitrator, submitted a report dealing with the Boeing Company bargaining.

It should be mentioned that while the recommendations of these boards were a tremendous help, their advice was not followed precisely in any single case nor did they deal with all issues involved, thereby leaving a wide field for normal mediation.

Some may say that any industry situation in which the President is required to appoint three Taft-Hartley boards and name two other *ad hoc* boards is one that does not exactly reflect a high degree of bargaining success. There is no denying that it would have been preferable if such Government action could have been avoided.

The point, in my mind, is however that by using one device or another, by employment of the array of tools available to the Government, critical stoppages were avoided. There was one bad strike, only one, and it came early in our aerospace experience. It ran for seventy-eight days in mid-1962 at the Republic Aviation Corporation's plant on Long Island. But this was a special case, complicated by contract issues arising out of an announced cutback in jet fighter plane orders at the plant, and did not involve the more critical missile work at stake in most of the rest of the aerospace labor disputes.

A principal issue in controversy at the big West Coast aerospace producers—such as Douglas, Boeing, North American, Lockheed and Convair—was union security. The Machinists and Auto Workers wanted the union shop so as to require all workers to become union members. The firms were stoutly resisting. As in most labor issues there was a good deal of merit to the arguments put forth by both sides.

The rapid advance and frequent change in aerospace technology has meant wide fluctuations in the industry's employment, seriously affecting union membership. Thus the labor organizations have a problem keeping the work force organized to the extent they consider necessary to do the job of bargaining and servicing the day-to-day problems of the employees. At some firms the labor turnover was so extensive that a substantial organizing job was necessary just to keep even.

On the other hand, most of the aerospace firms contended that for them to enter into arrangements such as the union shop or other so-called union security agreements would make union membership compulsory for a very substantial number of employees who had *not* been organized voluntarily.

This was the main dilemma, although in addition to the union shop demand there were in every case a large number of extremely controversial issues involved, such as wages, pay inequities, insurance, pensions and severance pay.

Early in the game, the Douglas Aircraft Company reached a negotiated settlement with the IAM and UAW with the aid of the FMCS after extended negotiations. On the union security question, the agreement included the agency shop, a lesser form of union security permitting workers to remain nonunion so long as they pay the equivalent of regular union dues as a service fee.

Normally a voluntary settlement at such a large company as Douglas would have established a pattern for the rest of the industry. It came just one week ahead of contract expiration deadlines with a number of other large California aerospace producers. These firms were, however, unwilling to accept the agency shop portion of the Douglas settlement and it was only the Douglas pay rates that turned out to be pattern-setting.

With strikes threatening at the Lockheed, North American, Convair and Ryan aerospace firms President Kennedy obtained a sixty-day truce and appointed Dr. Taylor's board to suggest settlement terms. That board ultimately recommended that the union shop issue be decided by secret ballot requiring a two-thirds vote of the employees involved. Such polls were held at North American, Convair and Ryan, and in each case resulted in failure to produce the required two-thirds assent, although there was more than a simple majority approval in all three. This meant the firms would continue their prior maintenance of membership provisions without the union shop.

Lockheed refused to put the matter to a vote and, ultimately, a negotiated compromise was reached with the aid of our mediators on the eve of the expiration of an eighty-day Taft-Hartley law injunction. In lieu of the union shop or agency shop Lockheed agreed to "cooperation" provisions, in which the company will give each new employee a letter urging that he seriously consider joining the union and will help arrange an extensive union steward training program. High-level labor-management committees were established to discuss mutual problems during the life of the contract.

The dispute between the Machinists and the Boeing Company was the final tough hurdle to clear in the aerospace bargaining. Even after the guidance given both sides by the presidential board headed by Mr. Wallen the disputants remained solidly deadlocked on the union shop and many other issues.

Substantial progress was made in negotiations under FMCS auspices after the Wallen Board report, but not enough to avoid a possible Boeing strike and the President invoked the Taft-Hartley emergency provisions. During the ensuing eighty-day injunction period negotiations continued, and on the very day the court injunction was due to expire the parties came to a tentative agreement at meetings in Washington with FMCS mediators.

This resolved the union security issue in still a different way. It was agreed all new workers must become union members except for those who formally declared in writing, during a ten-day "escape" period between the thirtieth and fortieth day following their employment, that they wanted to remain nonmembers. The Boeing agreement was first rejected by the Boeing workers but, after some clarifications were reached between the parties, the workers reconsidered at the President's request, and the agreement was thereupon ratified by a better than 3 to 1 vote.

Thus, the aerospace negotiations were touch-and-go all the way. But they were all eventually resolved peaceably. The whole experience is a case history showing how disputes in vital industries can be handled through collective bargaining provided responsibility and restraint is exercised by the parties. All the aerospace agreements were ultimately arrived at voluntarily with only limited intervention by the Government.

NEW DIRECTIONS IN BARGAINING [2]

Joint study groups and human relations committees created by unions and employers have stirred interest as a new development in collective bargaining. As an innovation to meet changing problems, this approach reflects a vitality and flexibility in collective bargaining. But also because of this very newness and the magnitude of the problems involved, the new approaches still must meet the hard test of experience.

[2] From article in *AFL-CIO American Federationist.* 70:18-21. N. '63. Reprinted by permission.

Nevertheless, the joint study approach is far enough along to consider several questions: Why do they come into being? What are their functions and powers? How are they working out?

First of all, the approach is not new. One of the most successful joint labor-management committees dates back to the 1920's. But the idea of the joint study approach has been spreading rapidly since 1959. These committees now function in the steel, meat-packing, auto, rubber, electrical manufacturing, construction and machinery industries. Other industries are exploring the idea.

If there is anything common to the various joint study groups, it is that they are created as a pragmatic response to real and urgent problems.

In many cases, automation and technological change confront negotiators with problems so complex and overwhelming as to be almost unsolvable under the usual bargaining pressures and procedures. In such situations, it becomes logical to remove such formidable problems from the atmosphere of deadlines and refer them to joint committees. Away from the tension of negotiations, union and employer representatives can freely discuss and better define these long-term problems and shape possible solutions.

But if the joint approach is evidence of a common interest on the part of the union and the employer, it also represents a recognition that conflicts of interest exist.

To the employer, automation promises sharply reduced costs, greater operation efficiency and rising profits. And he would wish to introduce cost-cutting techniques as rapidly as possible.

To the workers and their union, however, automation in some cases has proven devastating. In general, it threatens production standards and job security. The worker's concern is over layoffs, plant closings, changes in job content, loss of skill, loss of income, reduced opportunities and even the permanent loss of his job.

However, both the union and the employer usually recognize the limitations of the joint study groups. They are aware it is not a cure-all nor will it create miracles overnight.

It is obvious that the high-level unemployment . . . [during 1957-63] has been defeating the best efforts of labor and management to stabilize employment. Government policies have failed so far to create the kind of economic growth which would expand job opportunities—a vital prerequisite to ease the harsh impact of change on individuals [although unemployment has diminished considerably since 1963]. Effective solutions to the basic problems thus would seem to be beyond the capabilities of individual unions and employers.

Put in this perspective, there are basic problems which must be met by legislation and national policies and there are other problems which may be within the influence of joint study groups.

The joint study groups vary greatly in their functions and powers and in their effectiveness. Because of this diversity, an examination of a few of the major study groups, with some amount of experience behind them, may be more fruitful than any attempt to generalize.

The Kaiser Steel Plan

The Kaiser Steel Company and the Steelworkers established a tripartite committee in 1960 whose function was to determine how the benefits of technological change would be shared. The company and the union were also anxious to seek a new method of approaching their problems, a way that would avoid the rigidity of contract deadlines as well as frozen positions. . . . [See "The Kaiser Plan," in this section, below.]

American Motors—UAW Contract

The 1961 contract between American Motors and the Auto Workers provided for a joint committee known as the American Motors-UAW Conference. The six-man committee is composed of three union representatives and three company representatives.

The Conference was set up by the parties to discuss "their philosophies, needs and common responsibilities to the community," away from the bargaining table. The Conference has no collective bargaining responsibilities with respect to either contract negotiations or administration. Its purpose is to improve communication and understanding. It is concerned with questions of community facilities, including housing, education, health facilities and recreation.

The 1961 contract also provided for the American Motors Progress Sharing Plan which is essentially a profit-sharing arrangement. It is funded by a 15 per cent allocation from profits, after a return of 10 per cent has been set aside for the stockholders. One third of the employees' amount is used to purchase company stock for the workers. The other two thirds of the employees' share is used primarily for the pension, insurance and supplemental unemployment benefit program, as provided in the contract. The fund is managed by a board of trustees, equally representative of labor and management.

During the first year's experience, an average of 7.3 shares were set aside in trust for each employee. This benefit had a current market value of $129.

Steel: The Human Relations Committee

The Human Relations Committee was created by the Steelworkers and eleven major companies in basic steel in the aftermath of the 116-day strike in 1959. The postwar period had counted many strikes in the industry. With the 1959 strike, both sides recognized the need to explore fresh approaches.

The purpose of the committee was to examine jointly, away from the pressures of contract deadlines, serious problems which held potential for disputes. The agreed-on ground rules were that issues would be mutually chosen, no record would be kept and opinions could be freely expressed.

On the ten-member committee are four members representing the eleven companies and six representatives of the Steelworkers. These top members, who ordinarily would be found on each side's bargaining team, in turn supervise the work of technicians assigned to specific subcommittees.

Subcommittees of the parent group normally run from eight to ten members, usually with a half and half representation. These subcommittees study a wide variety of jointly-selected problems: seniority; grievance procedure and arbitration; economic guides; medical care; job classification; incentives; training needs; income and job security; contracting-out; overtime; supervisors doing bargaining unit work; scheduling and duration of vacations; subsidiaries.

One of the notable contributions of the Human Relations Committee was the sabbatical or extended vacation plan. This plan entitled workers in the top half of the seniority roster a thirteen-weeks' vacation every five years.

Four "experimental" provisions written into the contract deal specifically with the use of outside contractors on maintenance repair and installation work; the use of supervisors on work normally done by steelworkers; preserving the scope of the bargaining unit where certain jobs are combined; and the scheduling of overtime when laid-off employees might be recalled temporarily. . . . [See "Year-Round Bargaining," in this section, below.]

Armour Automation Committee

Plant closings and the resulting layoffs of workers led the Packinghouse Workers and the Meatcutters to establish an automation committee with the Armour Company in 1959.

The committee was tripartite, composed of four representatives of the company, two from each of the unions, an impartial chairman and an impartial executive director.

The committee was to study the problems resulting from the company's modernization program and to recommend solutions. Decentralizing production, closing old plants, introducing new techniques and equipment meant major readjustments for the company and the workers.

Financing of the committee was by a company contribution of one cent for each hundred pounds of total tonnage shipped from plants covered by agreements with the two unions, until a total fund of $500,000 had been accumulated.

The original emphasis was on research rather than providing employee benefits as such. In its initial phase, the fund was used for four major purposes: (1) joint discussion meetings; (2) research study; (3) pilot retraining program and (4) pilot transfer program.

A pilot retraining program was undertaken after the closing of one of the company's plants in Oklahoma City. It had been hoped the program would enable the laid-off workers to secure jobs. However, only 12 per cent of the displaced workers were retrained. Further, these discharged workers had serious difficulties finding jobs because of high unemployment in the area. Even when those who were retrained did find new jobs, they received less pay than they had earned under their Armour contract.

Based on the studies and findings of the automation committee, the parties incorporated a number of specific changes in the 1961 contracts. The new features included: advance notice; transfer of seniority rights; relocation costs; technological adjustment pay; improved severance pay and early retirement at age fifty-five at one and a half times full retirement pay.

The company must give ninety days' advance notice of the closing of a department or plant and must guarantee ninety days of work or equivalent wages from the date of the shutdown notice. . . .

Joint Committees in the Rubber Industry

Complicated questions raised in the 1963 negotiations led the Rubber Workers to provide for joint study committees in their new contracts with the four major rubber producers—Goodyear, Goodrich, Firestone and U.S. Rubber. These committees vary slightly from company to company, but in general they are given broad functions.

The joint study committees are to "study, explore and make recommendations to the parties during the term of the agreement concerning labor relations problems referred to the committee by the parties." They are not restricted to any specific areas, but will be free to investigate all types of problems and questions of concern to the company and the union. They are to develop approaches and possible solutions to problems.

The committees have no authority to bargain for the parties on any issue or to determine disposition of any grievances. The authority is limited to discussion, exploration and study of the subjects referred to it by the parties. Recommendations to the parties are on a confidential basis.

Auto Workers' Committees

In the automobile and agricultural implement industries, the UAW has established joint study committees with each major firm. These committees . . . [began] to function over a year in advance of the 1964 negotiation of new contracts.

The joint committees are to study matters that may later become subject to bargaining. However, the committees have no bargaining authority nor are they concerned with the determination of policy matters. The committees will make no recommendations.

The subjects for study and the schedule of meetings are set by mutual agreement. The subjects and the proceedings of the committees are to be kept confidential. This is to ensure that the discussions of the committees do not become indicators or determinators for collective bargaining. The statements of the parties in the joint study committees cannot be cited as part of any bargaining demand or position of the other party.

The committees are made up of company and union representatives. There are no outside parties as members. Committees and subcommittees have an equal number of company and union representatives.

Council on Industrial Relations

One of the oldest joint committees is the Council on Industrial Relations set up in 1920 by the National Electrical Contractors' Association and the International Brotherhood of Electrical Workers. The Council is a national device for the settling of local grievance or contract disputes after deadlocks develop.

The Council is composed of six representatives of the Contractors' Association and six members of the Brotherhood. Members meet quarterly in various sections of the country and hear the cases brought before them.

The Council operates much like a court, with the parties submitting briefs and presenting arguments. The Council never has had to send a dispute back to the parties without a unanimous decision although, in about one per cent of the 960 cases decided, a four-man executive committee had to make the decision. Never in the forty-three years of the Council's existence has a decision been violated.

The Council covers about 95 per cent of the electrical construction industry. The Council plan does not include the local unions and contractor chapters in New York City and Chicago.

At first the disputes involved interpretations of existing contracts, but now the Council resolves deadlocked contract negotiations as well, deciding what such agreements may contain. Disputes that cannot be settled by negotiations must be submitted to the Council. Strikes and lockouts are barred.

Foundation on Automation

Another type of joint labor-management cooperation is the American Foundation on Automation and Employment, Inc., with John Snyder, Jr., President of U.S. Industries, and A. J. Hayes, President of the Machinists, as co-chairmen. This foundation was established in February 1962 by the union and the manufacturer of automated equipment.

The Foundation is concerned with broad social problems brought on by automation rather than internal labor relations problems between the IAM and U.S. Industries. Its purpose is to "tell the truth about automation" in terms of its impact upon human beings.

It is financed entirely by the company through a levy on every automated machine it sells or leases to another company in the United States. The Foundation is managed jointly by the company and the Machinists. The fund is administered by a nine-member board of trustees—one each from the company and union and seven public members drawn from government, labor and other fields.

Conferences evaluate, discuss and inform the general public of possible solutions to problems of automation. This joint venture is bringing local union officers into contact with Federal Government manpower and training experts as well as college researchers for the purpose of developing solutions to the problems of radical technological changes.

An international conference is being planned in conjunction with the International Labor Organization for an international study of the implications of automation. Further meetings will be concerned with training and retraining needs of workers, as well as with apprenticeship programs.

THE KAISER PLAN [3]

Much of the ferment underlying current labor-management relations can be traced directly to the basic conflict between American industry's drive to attain maximum operating efficiency and organized labor's concern with job security. The inability of both sides to break the ideological bonds of the past has aggravated the situation and has produced unpleasant consequences for the public in the field of transportation—air, sea and rail—in the steel and aerospace industries and in the protracted newspaper strike in New York.

American labor is no longer an oppressed force fighting for recognition and an end to exploitation; American industry is no longer in the hands of the "public-be-damned" type of capitalist who regarded unionism as a form of insidious subversion. Yet the current distemper in labor-management relations reveals a retrogressive tendency, a callous disregard for the general welfare and an irrational refusal to face today's economic realities.

For years, big business and big labor—with big government looking over their shoulders—have opened their contractual negotiations with solemn declarations affirming their awareness of their responsibilities to the public. In the heat of collective bargaining, however, the public interest invariably has been the first to be shunted aside in pursuit of the negotiators' own objectives. The result in many cases has been government intervention, with inevitable cries of "Federal coercion" when pressure is applied to make one or both of the combatants get back to the realization that the public's stake in a settlement transcends their own interests. In the light of these trends, it is refreshing—

[3] From "Breakthrough at Kaiser," by Lawrence T. King, California journalist. Commonweal. 78:11-12. Mr. 29, '63. Reprinted by permission.

and encouraging—to know that there are elements in American labor and industry anxious to forget the shibboleths of the past and get down to the actualities posed by the challenge of automation.

. . . [In December 1963] workers of the Kaiser Steel Corporation's vast complex at Fontana, California, were invited to a meeting at the nearby San Bernardino County fairgrounds to hear for the first time the results of a three-year study by a nine-man commission—representing the Corporation, the United Steelworkers Union and the public—on the problems of increased production, automation and job security. The stage for this unprecedented meeting was set in the bitter steel strike of 1959. At that time Edgar Kaiser broke the solid front of the steel industry by offering to sign a contract with the Steelworkers if the union would agree to the establishment of a tripartite commission that would come up with a "long-range plan for equitable sharing between stockholders, the employees and the public of the fruits of the company's progress."

Many union . . . [theorists] were wary of such a study—their approach had hardened into a philosophy of "make-work" projects, shorter work weeks, longer vacations and earlier retirements. But they readily conceded that acceptance of the proposal was a small price to pay for a contract that would settle the basic issues of wages and work rules. Furthermore, they had been assured that the commission would be empowered only to make recommendations which could be accepted or rejected by a vote of the union membership.

Three years later, when the Fontana workers gathered to hear the details of the commission's study, there was still some doubt as to their reaction to this innovation in labor-management cooperation. Of Kaiser's seven thousand Fontana workers, only about a thousand bothered to attend the meeting. They heard the plan outlined by Kaiser, David McDonald, [then] president of the Steelworkers and Dr. George W. Taylor of the University of Pennsylvania, the public representative on the panel.

By the time the meeting was over, it was evident that the panel had succeeded in dispelling all doubts. In fact, newsmen covering the event reported an "enthusiastic reception" and pre-dicted the Kaiser plan—as it has come to be called—would win acceptance. They proved to be correct. Two months later, it was submitted to a vote; it was approved overwhelmingly. On March 1 [1964] the plan went into effect for a four-year period.

Basically, the plan will give Kaiser employees almost one third of all savings on the cost of producing steel. The savings—whether they be the result of better materials, improved techno-logical processes or the efforts of the workers themselves—will be distributed across the board to all workers, not on an individ-ual basis. This figure was agreed on because labor accounts for one third of all Kaiser production costs.

Under the new concept, the union agreed to give up the individual and work crew incentives, long a vaunted part of its contract. Since these incentives benefited only forty per cent of the Fontana work force, it was clearly a matter of giving up a good thing for a better one. The new incentives for cutting costs and raising productivity will benefit everyone. Part of any savings that might accrue will be used to improve fringe benefits; the rest will go into pay increases.

The most noteworthy feature of the new plan is its far-sighted approach to job security through creation of an employment pool, which will provide a guaranteed wage to any worker replaced by automation while he is undergoing retraining for other plant duties. In addition, employees forced into a shorter work week by fluctuations in steel demand will be paid their full salaries; those reassigned to lower job classifications will continue to get their former pay, and those whose advancement opportunities are curtailed by elimination of job categories by automation will be advanced to the higher pay scale anyway.

If this sounds like a worker's security paradise, there is one element of uncertainty that looms large in the new arrangement: workers laid off because of a decline in the corporation's steel orders will be cut off from these benefits. In short, the corpora-tion and the union have not been able to repeal the economic law of the competitive market; the size of the work force will continue to be governed by consumer demand. For the individual worker, of course, this entails no additional risk, since the work force of any private industry or business is always contingent upon the employer's ability to sell its goods or services.

Inherent in the commission's recommendation, however, is the conviction that industry has an obligation to use its productive capacity to the fullest. By giving the workers a generous share of cost savings, the plan envisions the creation of a real community of interests which will be able to draw upon the knowledge and skills of the entire work force to push technological development to a point where the corporation's products can compete successfully with foreign imports. The long-range projection looks confidently for new, cheaper and better quality products, increasing demand, expansion of plant facilities and generation of new jobs.

The important point about the Kaiser plan is that it is the most intensive effort yet made by a major American industry to do something concrete about the problem of automation. Coming at a time when many industries still look on automation only in terms of cutting labor costs and increasing profits and when many labor unions feel that it is something to be resisted because it threatens the jobs of its members, the Kaiser plan is a reaffirmation of the belief that technological advances can be utilized to benefit all parties concerned. The agreement provides evidence, in the words of Labor Secretary W. Willard Wirtz, that "by serving mutual interest, individual interests can be served."

At the Fontana workers' meeting, Dr. Taylor, who headed the team of public consultants which smoothed out the plan's initial rough spots, stressed the point that success of the proposals was completely dependent upon increased productivity. He also emphasized that the motivating force behind the commission's recommendations was the principle that "technological advances should not be secured without regard for human values."

In his presentation, David McDonald acknowledged that implementation of the plan would not automatically solve all labor-management differences, that bilateral agreement still would be required on the application of work rules and that there still exists the possibility of future work stoppages, but "for reasons other than economic." He left no doubt, however, about his enthusiasm for the commission's work, which he termed "a great step forward toward the achievement of industrial peace."

For his part, Kaiser assured his audience that basic wage patterns still will be set in "Big Steel" negotiations. "If your share of the cost of savings doesn't come up to the level prevailing in the industry," he said, "the company will certainly live up to its contractual obligations to make up the difference. There will be no economic loss for you . . . but this plan offers more. It offers great opportunities."

Kaiser's enthusiasm has not been shared by his colleagues of Big Steel in Pittsburgh, according to press reports. "The union can gain, but not lose," said one executive. "It looks to me like a one-sided affair," another commented. "I think this is something you're going to have to look at for eight or nine years before you know how it will work," a third executive was quoted as saying. . . .

The problem of automation continues to cast a heavy shadow over the entire steel industry. The big question remains: Can Big Steel afford to wait "eight or nine years" before coming to grips with it?

YEAR-ROUND BARGAINING [4]

What is a human relations committee? Essentially it's a name, people, a procedure, and an atmosphere. It's an effort to convert [collective] bargaining from what you might call "trial by combat" into an endless succession of public and private maneuvers. It is a private approach to problem solving in which there is an opportunity to apply reason and fact in continuous discussion away from the pressure of deadlines and without the continuous barrage of public propaganda which usually surrounds approaches to bargaining.

Its origin was in the disastrous experience which we shared with the Steelworkers in 1959 and 1960. I don't know if anybody ever learns much out of a strike except the simple fact that a strike

[4] From an article by R. Heath Larry, administrative vice president—personnel services, United States Steel Corporation. In *Personnel Job in a Changing World*, edited by Jerome W. Blood. American Management Association. New York. '64. p 101-5. Reprinted by permission.

doesn't settle much, but that's a great deal of learning. We did learn that much in 1959 and 1960. We also learned that we were going to have to find a different way, and we began to try to find it. We set up a human relations committee co-chaired by R. Conrad Cooper, executive vice president of personnel services for U.S. Steel, and David McDonald, [then] president of the Steelworkers. . . .

At the outset we did not, in setting ourselves up, involve ourselves with a third party. That decision wasn't reached out of a belief on either side that the public had no interest in the outcome of our endeavors but out of a belief that if we progressed in our relationship as we hoped we could, we would come as near to a fair accommodation of public interest as any third party actions or recommendations would. The decision not to have a third party was made not out of any disrespect for many of the well-known third parties, so-called neutrals who could be brought to mind, but out of a respect for our obligation to ourselves and to the institution of collective bargaining. We felt that if we could establish the necessary degree of understanding, mutual confidence, and respect on our own, it was clearly our responsibility to try.

We have now had two successful negotiations without a strike or even a threat of one. . . . [This was written prior to the 1965 negotiations, during which I. W. Abel replaced McDonald as Steelworkers president. Abel's enthusiasm for year-round bargaining remains to be demonstrated. The 1965 settlement came only after pressure from President Johnson brought the negotiators from the brink of a strike to a peaceful settlement.—Ed.]

There are essentially four ingredients necessary to the successful accomplishment of continuous discussion like this. The first two are almost inseparable. The first is a will, an attitude, a desire. The second is a mechanism or a procedure. The third is a competent staff, and the fourth is some flexibility in points of time. You can have the best mechanism in the world, and without the proper desire to make it work the mechanism is useless. By the same token, you can have the best attitude and the best will in the world, and if you don't have a mechanism through which to funnel the desire and the effort, the will is useless. We have them both.

The will. The first ingredient came from various sources. It couldn't help but come in some measure from the cataclysmic experiences of 1959 and 1960. It could not be entirely disassociated from some of the potential results in external areas which came about as a result of that experience.

There was also increasing evidence that unless something were done somewhere the Government was going to do something, although it wasn't very clear what. It could have been in the direction of compulsory arbitration, it could have been in the direction of restructuring the parties involved, or it could have been something else. But there was a concern as to future Government involvement, and while perhaps at one time the unions were less concerned over Government involvement than they are now, more and more they have come to the belief that the proper avenue is not that one because they may be gobbled up in the process. Their desire to preserve free collective bargaining is of itself a motivating desire to make collective bargaining operate more effectively than before.

The third possible source of the desire to cooperate this way is just simply a growing maturity. People do grow older and wiser from their experiences, and they begin to appreciate the necessity of giving due regard to the economic necessities of life. In an earlier time they might not have felt the necessity to do this. There grows an increasing belief that conflict is of itself not essential to progress and in fact may preclude it.

But whatever the basis for the origin of a real, sincere desire on the part of both the top management of the steel industry and the officers of the steel union, the will and the desire are the ultimate foundation for progress. If they die, disappear, or diminish at some point, the whole mechanism will serve very little purpose. I was much disturbed by a speech which suggested that we ought to require by law continuous year-round discussions. I can think of nothing more fruitless than telling two people who are mad at each other to get in a room to try to kiss and make up. It just won't happen that way. The motivation has got to come from within and not from law.

The procedure. This was the most difficult area of all as we began to work. After all, we had had twenty-five years of really slugging it out with each other; we had twenty-five years of experience in which every time somebody split an infinitive or dropped a hint he was forever bound to whatever he had said, and there was no retraction from position. It was publicized and there you stayed. When these subcommittees were organized, it wasn't easy to get what you called "objective discussion" going. Tradition is pretty hard to overcome quickly.

But little by little we have evolved a few ground rules, one of which is that we aren't going to do anything in the way of researching, reaching conclusions, putting out reports, making minutes, or anything else unless we do it by mutual agreement. That doesn't mean we agree on everything. I wouldn't want anybody to conclude that because we engage in this kind of thing, the institutional robes of both parties have been chucked off and the origins of differences of view, different conceptions of fact, different philosophies have gone. However, if you take a couple of rough objects and rub them together long enough, their edges will tend to smooth down. That's what's going on in our upper tier.

We decided that no matter what it was, whether it was research into fact or a determination to use a particular approach in studying the circumstances relating to a problem, we would do it by agreement. This kept both parties from having a free hunting license. It was frustrating to both of us from time to time, but a little experience proved that we weren't going to make real progress unless we worked that way.

The second thing we concluded was that there could be no record and no publication. Whatever we said could have no relevance either to future formal bargaining or to the grievance and arbitration settlements between the parties which had to go on because if it did we would be back in the old framework again, with everybody afraid to open his mouth for fear that he would prejudice some future position. This was the hardest thing to do because tradition had taught us that we would be tripped up by our mistakes or misstatements.

But we moved along with that concept, found its utility, and added another procedural understanding: that anybody can say today that his firm conviction of the right answer or the fact is thus and so and ten minutes, a half hour, a day, or a month later deny that he ever said it, if that is his desire, without being accused of bad faith.

Often in the course of some of our efforts to evolve recommendations concerning changes in our seniority program, our supplementary unemployment benefits programs, or our extended vacation programs, the union was on this side, the company on the other, and a month later it was just the opposite. It happened time and time again that both of us found out that the things we absolutely knew to be true had no foundation. We would finally decide on something which was often quite different from what either of us thought to be the right and the only sure answer to start with.

A competent staff. The third requisite is staff, staff for the union as well as staff for the company. In this respect the Steelworkers are quite fortunate because they have, probably not as many as they wish they had, but a sizable group of very sophisticated, very well-educated, very sound people. That doesn't mean I always find myself in total agreement with them or they with me, but it does mean that when we are attempting to engage in a disposition of something in the process of reasoning and in the process of understanding the surrounding circumstances and the facts, we're talking to somebody that can respond on the same basis; and all of us have had occasional instances where experience has not justified that kind of observation.

Flexibility of time. We originally had fallen into the pattern of a three-year agreement with a fixed termination date. When the date came, you were through. If you didn't have the job done, that was all, at least so it seemed, because the tradition was that way. We began to move away from that toward a flexible reopening date. Someone described it as an "Ivory Soap" termination: it floats. It doesn't have to be observed on the dates that the notice can be given. That's all to the good. In 1963 we knew we were making progress. We also knew we would be totally unable to make the progress which we needed to make by the time the notice could first be served. But in an atmosphere in which we were both conscious of some progress being made, it became wholly unnecessary to serve the notice.

It is essential when someone attempts to engage in an off-the-record slow-moving way with complex problems, bringing some intelligence and experience to them, that they untether themselves from absolute deadlines in terms of an agreement.

THE USE OF "INFORMED NEUTRALS" [5]

Informed neutrals may play an even greater role in future difficult labor negotiations—to reinforce the voluntary bargaining process. That's an inevitable conclusion from the mediation success of Dr. George W. Taylor and Theodore W. Kheel in the . . . [1964] "insoluble" railroad work rules dispute.

Today's bargaining is characterized by employer efforts to break away from previous contract and job patterns—and by union efforts to preserve the patterns. The railroad rules battle was just one of many current and potential fights involving economic efficiency and job security. Conflicts are likely to increase as automation spreads.

To many in the Administration, the rail dispute was an acid test of bargaining. On Capitol Hill it was watched closely by advocates of compulsory arbitration in transportation and other "emergency" disputes, and by those anxious to broaden existing laws to put the government deeper into bargaining.

The settlement on the rail rules issues shored up bargaining. It undermined—for now—arguments for compulsory arbitration. [See selection on compulsory arbitration in Section IV, below.] And it gave important new support to those who argue that the President doesn't need more power for dealing with deadlocked public interest disputes.

Moreover, the settlement, helped along by two of the country's most expert neutrals, demonstrated again the value of skilled presidential mediators in resolving intractable bargaining problems.

[5] From " 'Informed Neutrals' Score a Triumph." *Business Week.* p 43-4+. My. 9, '64. Reprinted from the May 9, 1964 issue of *Business Week* by special permission. Copyrighted © 1964 by McGraw-Hill, Inc.

No new fields were opened when President Johnson sent Taylor, of the Wharton School of the University of Pennsylvania, and Kheel, New York attorney, as a rescue team into the deadlocked rail negotiations. Presidents often have used informed neutrals in one way or another to clear away labor troubles.

This time, the President's decision to entrust the country's critical dispute to a team of neutrals skilled in labor relations was particularly significant. The alternative was compulsory arbitration directed by Congress. And the men picked, Taylor and Kheel, are firmly opposed to deeper involvement of government in collective bargaining or to any resort to Congress for settling labor problems. . . .

The issues in the dispute appeared insoluble. The parties had engaged in little purposeful bargaining over more than four years. Federal mediators hadn't found the two sides cooperative. The dispute appeared headed toward a strike showdown when President Johnson persuaded the parties to agree to a fifteen-day truce in mid-April [1964].

At Labor Secretary W. Willard Wirtz' suggestion, the President telephoned Taylor in Philadelphia to ask his aid as a "negotiator" in a final intensive effort to get the parties to settle their dispute by bargaining. The President chose Kheel, who had worked with him closely in the past on civil rights matters, as the second man of his team of "new negotiators"—Johnson meant mediators— charged with performing a miracle.

To both men a presidential summons of "I need you in my office at 9:30 tomorrow morning" was impressive, but nothing new. Each had been called at other times by other Presidents for similar labor emergencies. Within hours, both were headed for Washington.

A form of professional mediation was under way, utilizing a team widely known and respected as informed neutrals in today's subtly changing collective bargaining.

Technically, neither Taylor nor Kheel can be described as a "professional mediator" because neither earns a living in the mediation field. But using a test of background and skill, both are about as professional as professionals can be. They are typical of a not very large group of men who can be drafted, on occasion, to reinforce bargaining when regular props fail. . . .

Both Taylor and Kheel are imaginative. They are practical theorists, able to see everyday problems with a short and long perspective. Taylor is credited with working out the maintenance-of-membership alternative to the union shop. [Under maintenance-of-membership, workers are not required to join a union, but if they do join, they must maintain membership for the life of the collective bargaining agreement.—Ed.] Kheel has cut through the inconsequentials to devise formulas for settling the really critical issues in many disputes.

In the railroad dispute, the two special mediators took five days to learn not only the facts of the dispute but also enough about the industry to give the facts a proper background.

Only after that, Taylor and Kheel got down to the job of mediating the dispute. In the steel dispute of 1959-60, Taylor had decided that "goldfish bowl" mediation was called for—there was a point in focusing public attention on the frozen position of the two sides. In the rail dispute, the two men decided that secret mediation would be better—the parties had to be turned from propaganda to specific consideration of their opposed positions.

The issues were rough and the opposed sides were tough-minded. But, on both sides of the table, bargaining professionalism smoothed the way for the adoption of procedures and resulted in disciplined and in time meaningful talks. For example: The parties agreed that in intensive, possibly round-the-clock bargaining some complex issues should be dealt with only when negotiators were fresh, during the day, while others could be handled in the late, weary hours of continuing talks.

The mediators' first problem was to clear out the inconsequentials and to get talk into an area of costs and money values of concessions. To Kheel, every bargaining issue can be and should be brought to this point of cash considerations: What price is management willing to pay for broadened rights and rules changes—and what cost does the union set on contract revisions?

The rail dispute was on its way to a settlement when principles —rights on management's side, job security on the unions' side— began to be discussed in money terms. Dollars in costs can be compromised. Principles defy formula settlements. . . .

Taylor and Kheel . . . [succeeded] because they entered the dispute with the President's strong backing, with new energy and ideas, and respect from both sides as highly competent professionals.

The railroad dispute was a particularly tough one and the long-delayed settlement demonstrated not only the power of the President in a tough labor dispute, but also the potentials in the use of informed neutrals when bargaining becomes stalled.

Mediation, unlike the quasi-judicial arbitration process, has considerable flexibility. The mediators can use every opportunity to narrow differences by any device whatever. And "informed neutrals" are able to bring a fresh, outside viewpoint into the dispute.

Mediators ordinarily recommend terms of a settlement, to be accepted or rejected by the parties, only if both sides request recommendations.

This is the basic difference between mediation and arbitration: The former is reinforced bargaining, with the parties retaining their full freedom of choice and action, the latter is an imposed settlement.

However, there is an element of flexibility even here. Taylor set a precedent in the steel dispute of 1959-60 by a form of super-mediation with recommendations. And Taylor and Kheel gave the parties a single copy of handwritten settlement proposals—with assurances that it would be destroyed if the parties rejected the suggestions. The proposals turned out to be the basis of the final agreement.

These procedures, in skilled hands, have sufficient flexibility to reinforce bargaining with a minimum of infringement on voluntarism. There's no doubt that President Johnson likes the mediation idea now: It worked.

DECLINING ROLE OF THE STRIKE [6]

Strikes are declining in importance as a commonplace weapon in collective bargaining. Big walkouts still occur. . . . But today's trend is away from drop-of-the-hat bargaining strikes and picketing. . . .

According to the Federal Mediation and Conciliation Service, there is a strong and continuing trend "toward a more mature, deliberate, careful consideration and solution of mutual problems by management and labor. There is more reliance on reason and economic justification than . . . on resorting to the naked economic force of strikes."

Generally, 1960 is cited as "a turning point" in labor-management relations. In that year, former Labor Secretary James P. Mitchell reported that man-days lost because of strikes had been cut in half since 1953 and the number of strikes reduced sharply because of "the new sense of responsibility . . . asserted by labor and management."

The massive steel strike of 1959-60, a 119-day shutdown, was, according to Mitchell, a "summit clash" and "a huge object lesson" that labor and management in major industries must pull together in bargaining—"not only because they may want to but also because they have to," Mitchell said.

In . . . [1960-62] work-time lost due to strikes . . . [was] at post-World War II low levels. . . . [In 1963] out of 100,000 contracts negotiated, fewer than 1,500 work stoppages of at least one day's duration occurred in bargaining disputes. Work stoppages for all causes numbered only 3,362, as compared with an annual average of 4,400 in the postwar decade that ended in the mid-1950's.

In 1963, only 941,000 workers were involved in strikes, in contrast to 4.6 million in 1946. Strikes were generally smaller than in the 1950's; only seven involved 10,000 or more workers, only eleven between 5,000 and 10,000. Although they lasted longer (23 days instead of the average 20 in the 1950's) the 16.1

[6] From "The Strike Wanes as a Weapon." *Business Week.* p 43-4. O. 10, '64. Reprinted from the October 10, 1964 issue of *Business Week* by special permission. Copyrighted © 1964 by McGraw-Hill, Inc.

million man-days lost was only 0.13 per cent of total working time—or, according to the Labor Department, "for every 10,000 workers . . . there were only 13 idled due to a work stoppage."

A Labor Department spokesman commented recently that "contemporary strike losses result in far less loss of productive work time than the well-known coffee break," fifteen minutes a day, and only half the lost time caused by industrial accidents. Its cost, based on average hourly earnings in manufacturing, can be estimated at about one third of a billion dollars in wages. . . .

However, Federal mediators have worried eyes on labor's rank-and-file with its potential for forcing bargaining deadlocks—and strikes. To FMCS officials, this is "a significant new factor that has come up in GM, dock, and Detroit and other newspaper strikes—a refusal of rank-and-file and local officials to go along with settlements reached by international officers." [See "The Rank-and-File Revolt," in Section II, above.]

The determination of local unions to set their own contract terms without regard to the views of international officers makes settlement attempts much tougher, the mediators say. Tentative agreements may be reached . . . only to be turned down at local levels. . . .

According to mediators, part of the explanation for local insurgency lies in the locals' determination to protect job rights while international union negotiators—facing the broader pressures and facts of automation—are more willing to take a "responsible" line in attempting to solve new and complex problems.

For instance, ILA [International Longshoremen's Association] officers showed some willingness to negotiate contracts that would reduce work-gangs under some circumstances, while militant locals continued adamant against any cut in twenty-man crews.

Another part of the explanation can be found in increased infighting in unions, which has caused competition between local leaders—in many unions, there has been a big turnover in their ranks in local elections this year—or between local and international officers. . . .

So far, however, worries about locals make only a small dark cloud on a wide, bright horizon. The better labor peace record of recent years, according to FMCS, is a result of factors that still apply—"growing sophistication on the part of all concerned, a realization that both sides have much in common to gain as well as lose, and an expanding awareness and respect for the public and national interest."

Bargaining today is, by and large, more professional—hence more "sophisticated." The parties are ordinarily better prepared. Negotiations are being given more time—bargaining is started earlier or contracts are extended—in an effort to avoid the hazards of "crisis bargaining." And there is a growing awareness of the alternatives to deadlocks and strikes—including greater utilization of mediation, arbitration of some particularly vexing issues, and joint studies and other devices for working out of impasses.

Channels of communication between employers and unions are better and more flexible now. In many bargaining relationships, matters that once would have grown into major negotiating issues are resolved—informally—in continuing "bargaining" while management and labor have flexible positions. What the steel industry and union are doing in their Human Relations Committee, on a formal basis, others are beginning to do without contractual machinery.

"It's not called bargaining, but it's the same thing," a mediator said in a report on such a situation. "There's a rough spot in the contract and they get together and work it out." FMCS has instructed all field personnel to encourage this form of between-bargaining relationship.

Unions are more responsive to alternatives to striking for other reasons than just the "maturity" or "responsibility" credited to them: High unemployment has made them wary of strikes. They have lost membership ground because of the shift in employment patterns from more militant blue-collar to white-collar workers. And industry's increased automation now makes strikes a risk because operations may be continued using supervisory and other nonstriking personnel.

But both sides are probably made more settlement-conscious by two hard facts:

Strike impasses today, with balanced labor and management power, can lead to heavy economic losses—nobody can really afford big strikes on the old careless basis.

They bring the Government into bargaining to an extent welcomed by few in labor or management.

In some disputes, of course, the issues genuinely mean so much to both sides that they choose a test of strength—fully aware of its dangers—rather than give ground. This, after all, is what strikes are for in free collective bargaining. But it grows less likely each year that negotiators will drift into a strike, or risk it for frivolous reasons.

THE "NO STRIKE" STRIKE [7]

Imagine this kind of a labor dispute:

The union calls a strike against the company. But it doesn't set up any picket lines. Instead it instructs the "striking" workers to show up for their jobs as usual, and continue production with no slowdowns.

However, the workers draw only half their usual pay; the rest is deposited in a local bank. The company makes matching deposits out of its treasury. If the "strike" is settled quickly, all deposits are returned. But if it drags on, workers and company lose some or even all of the money, which is then donated to community projects.

This scenario isn't in the least fanciful. It has been written into an experimental agreement . . . signed . . . by an AFL-CIO union and a furniture company in the country town of Berne, Indiana, and will be followed for the first twelve weeks of the next "strike," if there is one, against the company. The idea is twofold. First, to provide a way for labor and management to fight out a contract dispute without hurting the company's customers, the community, or the public generally. Second—by hurting themselves financially, as in a conventional strike—to put pressure on the union and the company to settle their differences quickly.

[7] From "Working 'Strikers,'" article by Kenneth G. Slocum, staff reporter. *Wall Street Journal.* p 1+. My. 20, '64. Reprinted by permission.

As far as experts in the United States Labor Department in Washington know, no such "strike-work" program has been tried in the United States before. And it's getting its start in an extremely small way. The contract . . . covers only 210 production and maintenance workers of the Upholsterers' International Union of North America. They work for Dunbar Furniture Corporation of Berne, which . . . [in 1963] rang up sales of $3.5 million.

But the impact of the plan could be much wider. Before long, it could spread in the furniture industry, which comprises some three thousand manufacturers turning out goods worth $5 billion a year at retail. "Several other companies already have indicated an interest in the plan," says John Snow, executive vice president of the National Association of Furniture Manufacturers, which actively assisted Dunbar in working out the experimental agreement.

Mr. Snow and others hope the plan will win followers outside the furniture industry, too. And at minimum it seems certain to be watched carefully by union, management and Government experts throughout the country as the latest and most radical in a series of new bargaining approaches designed to allow labor and management to settle contract differences while avoiding the devastating impact of strikes on the national economy. . . .

Dunbar Furniture's "strike-work" agreement is . . . separate from the company's regular three-year contract . . . and goes into effect if the union calls a "strike," or management serves notice of a "lockout," when that pact expires.

In that case, the agreement provides that production will continue as usual for twelve weeks. It not only bans actual strikes, lockouts or slowdowns during that period, but forbids either side from filing lawsuits against the other or receiving financial help from any outside source.

Meanwhile, half the workers' wages and matching funds from the company are to be deposited in a special fund in the First Bank of Berne, a town of 2,700. If the "strike" is settled within six weeks, workers and company will get all the money back. If it's settled during the following three weeks 75 per cent of the money will be returned; if it's settled in the next two weeks a 50 per cent refund will be made. Settlement in the twelfth week will bring a 25 per cent refund.

If the dispute drags on longer, the union can start an actual strike, or Dunbar can begin a real lockout. If no such action is taken by the end of the thirteenth week, the old contract is automatically renewed for a year. But in any case, workers and company can no longer get back any of the deposits; they're supposed to agree on some project "for the good of the community" to which the fund is to be donated. If they can't agree on such a project, the money goes automatically to the Berne Ministerial Association, to use as it sees fit for the good of the community.

Supporters of the plan think it will accomplish several objectives. It will "take the public out of the middle, and remove much of the suffering involved in strikes" for innocent bystanders, says Harold D. Sprunger . . . president of Dunbar.

Also, the negotiators emphasize, the plan will give both sides an accurate count, down to the penny, of how much they themselves are losing from the strike—and how much they stand to save if they can agree, quickly. Some observers imply this might put more pressure on the two sides to settle than an actual strike would.

"Many workers and company officials don't really regard costs of a strike as losses, under the attitude that you can't lose what you never had," comments Mr. Snow of the Furniture Association. "Here the losses are real and undeniable."

Sal B. Hoffmann, president of the Upholsterers' International, points out what he considers an even greater prospective benefit. "Furniture is a toughly competitive, cut-throat business, and dealer customers cut off from one supplier are quick to switch to another," he says. "For years we found that we won strikes but (the company) lost customers"—and union members consequently lost jobs when production was resumed. "We believe the place to hurt the employer is in the pocketbook," he adds. "When we can do that and not lose jobs, then we are better off than if we conducted an actual strike."

Dunbar's President Sprunger quickly seconds this view of the impact of actual strikes. After the Upholsterers struck Dunbar for six weeks in 1959, he recalls, the company worked overtime to fill orders that had backed up during the walkout—but only briefly. "Then employment dropped 20 per cent because we had lost regular customers and found difficulty getting them back," he says.

It's not only in furniture, of course, that strikes have such effects. The steel industry has often wailed that it was the 116-day mill strike of 1959 that opened American doors wide to an invasion of imported foreign steel. Industry executives have estimated that invasion by now has wiped out the jobs of fifty thousand steel workers.

Despite these prospective benefits, Dunbar and the Upholsterers didn't have an easy time working out the agreement. The strike-worn plan was first proposed in 1960 by the late Lynn W. Beman, a Chicago labor relations consultant who was then a consultant to the Furniture Association. But company and union haggled over it for four years before finally deciding to give it a try.

The union's President Hoffmann, while backing the plan vigorously now, indicates he had to overcome many doubts of his own about curtailing the chief weapon of any union—the strike—and also had to argue long and hard with fellow union leaders before signing. "Some union men who have lived all their lives by the strike want to know how in the devil we can win a war without a gun," he says.

The plan might seem to be more favorable to the company, since it provides no assurance the union will ever win a wage increase if it seeks one. In theory at least, the company might want a straight extension of an existing contract, and would get one automatically if it just sat still through the twelve weeks of the strike-work program—unless the union could nerve itself to call an actual strike after its members already had suffered through twelve weeks at half-pay.

But Dunbar President Sprunger indicates the company too had its doubts. In negotiating sessions, he says, company officials "found it relatively easy to shoot the plan full of holes" but eventually decided to take it because of "the possibility of preserving customer relationships and employee jobs."

Mr. Sprunger points out that company bank deposits during the twelve-week strike-work period would have the same effect as a 50 per cent increase in labor costs. Taking that much money out of working capital while the company was still producing and had all its normal operating expenses would immediately turn any profit it might be making into a heavy prospective loss, he says. For this reason, company and union negotiators insist the pressure on the two sides to settle should be about equal.

The town of Berne has a big stake in success of the agreement, too. Dunbar is its second biggest employer, and its payroll accounts for 13 per cent of Berne's total payroll income. "Berne still remembers the effect of the last Dunbar strike" says Leslie B. Lehman, vice president of the First Bank of Berne, in lauding the agreement.

IV. EVER-CHANGING LABOR LAW

EDITOR'S INTRODUCTION

The field of labor law is a complex one, imprecise and laden with emotion. Labor law has almost always responded to the mood of the moment: the Wagner Act (1935), specifically endorsing and protecting collective bargaining; the Taft-Hartley Act (1947), reacting from this lopsided endorsement and protection; the Landrum-Griffin Act (1959), applying to all unions yet aiming at evildoers in a minority of unions; and the proposed legislation to repeal the "right-to-work" section of the Taft-Hartley Act.

As a result, much has been left to the courts and to agencies such as the National Labor Relations Board. Without specific, axiomatic legislative guides, both courts and agencies are able to "follow the election returns"; an Eisenhower-appointed NLRB rules one way on an issue; a Kennedy NLRB rules the opposite way; and perhaps a Johnson NLRB finds still another path—all without contradicting the hazy and imprecise labor-management relations laws.

In this section, no attempt is made to trace these sometimes tortuous findings of courts and agencies which are so important in the labor-management field. Instead, several significant developments are highlighted. The first selection explains the change in right-to-work legislation which was before Congress in 1965. Professor Benjamin Aaron then discusses the intricacies of the Landrum-Griffin Act of 1959, still being tested and developed through court interpretation. Connected with this is the study of the Auto Workers' Public Review Board, which seeks to control abuses of union democracy internally, as the Landrum-Griffin Act tries to do from the outside.

Over the years, there has been much discussion concerning the possible application to unions of antitrust legislation, historically applied solely to corporations. James C. Millstone surveys this question and gives an account of recent court rulings.

There is, finally, a review of a recurring legislative topic: Should there be a law to make the arbitration (final and binding settlement) of labor disputes compulsory rather than voluntary? It should be emphasized that this discussion relates to the arbitration of labor disputes resulting from the breakdown of collective bargaining over a new or revised labor agreement. Arbitration of differences arising during the term of a labor agreement (grievance arbitration) is a widely accepted practice and is not included in the current pro-and-con discussions of compulsory arbitration.

"RIGHT-TO-WORK" BACKGROUND [1]

The [congressional] debate over "right-to-work" laws goes back many years. In the 1930's, organized labor won two important concessions that enabled it to acquire muscle and money, and ultimately to improve working conditions. The first concession was the outlawing of the "yellow dog" contract. Under such a contract, a workingman, when he accepted employment, agreed *not* to join a union. The outlawing of such agreements, which led to the growth of strong and responsible unions, has been generally accepted as beneficial to industry, the worker, and the nation.

The second concession won by labor was the closed shop. Under a closed-shop contract, an employer agreed to hire only persons who were *already* members of a union. This, too, increased the unions' strength, but it also raised a serious philosophical question: despite management's past sins, was it really proper for others to dictate whom an employer could hire? In 1947, in passing the Taft-Hartley Act, Congress decreed that the answer should be No. That act permitted the union shop. Under a union-shop contract, the employer may hire anybody he wants but the new employee must then join the union, usually within thirty days after he starts on the job.

There were those who wanted to go even further. Senator Robert A. Taft argued that he could not "imagine any greater limitation on the right of contract than an act which says that A, an

[1] From "'Right to Work': A Hard One for LBJ," by Leonard Baker, Washington correspondent, *Newsday,* Garden City, N.Y. *The Reporter.* 32:23-5. Ja. 14, '65. Reprinted by permission. Copyright 1965 by The Reporter Magazine Company.

employee, a free American citizen, cannot even go to his employer and make a contract with his employer about the terms of his employment," while "the employer must deal with someone elected by a majority of the employees, against whom employee A may have voted." Taft was claiming that it was improper for any worker to be compelled to abide by union rules. A logical extension of his argument would have been a Federal law providing that no man may be compelled to join a union as a condition of his employment.

Congress was unwilling to take that step in 1947, but it did approve 14B, a single sentence of forty-four words reading: "Nothing in this act shall be construed as authorizing the execution or application of agreements requiring membership in a labor organization as a condition of employment in any state or territory in which such execution or application is prohibited by state or territorial law." This in effect means that when a state passes a right-to-work law, an employee of a firm within that state may not be compelled to join a union although a majority of his fellow employees may have voted to be represented by the union.

The Taft-Hartley proposal finally became law on June 23, 1947, when Congress overrode President Truman's veto. But during the preceding five months, there had been a flurry of activity in the various state legislatures to adopt laws forbidding compulsory union membership. Between January 21 and June 10, right-to-work laws were passed in Virginia, Arkansas, Tennessee, South Dakota, North Dakota, North Carolina, Arizona, Georgia, Texas, Iowa, and Nebraska. Earlier legislation in Florida was interpreted as right-to-work in a 1950 court decision. Between 1951 and 1963, eight more states passed such laws: Nevada, Alabama, South Carolina, Mississippi, Utah, Indiana, Kansas, and Wyoming. With the exception of Indiana, right-to-work laws have generally been defeated in industrial states, but it is scarcely a dead issue. [The law was repealed in Indiana in 1965.—Ed.]

Organized labor would like to end the whole thing once and for all by repealing Section 14B. Labor resents the effort, time, and money that have been spent in local fights across the nation. "We could be getting minimum-wage legislation or safety laws through the state legislatures if we didn't have to be always fighting this thing," said one official of the AFL-CIO. Questioned about an estimate that $12 million had been poured into the dispute, he answered: "The national organization has spent less than one sixth of that. But there's no way of knowing what the locals, the international unions, and the regional and state conferences spent. Any figure anyone would give would just be a guess. But both sides have put in millions of dollars."

Those who favor the repeal of 14B argue that permitting a man to be a "free rider," to enjoy all the benefits gained from the union efforts without making any contribution to the union, is grossly unfair to the man's fellow workers who do belong to the union. The opposition to repeal, as outlined in Chamber of Commerce and National Association of Manufacturers printed material, relies heavily on the contention that no man should be compelled to join any organization or support any organization against his will. "No majority, whether it be a slim 50.1 per cent or whopping 99.9 per cent, should be able to compel the minority by a popular vote to join or support the majority—whether in a church, a club, or any private organization. The same principle applies to a union," declares a Chamber of Commerce pamphlet entitled "Exposed, Union Myths About Right to Work."

While the philosophical arguments by both sides are pertinent, they are not the main issue. The main issue is the power of organized labor as a national institution. It is already waning appreciably as the American economy provides fewer jobs for the laborer, common or skilled, and more jobs for the manager and supervisor who traditionally do not belong to unions. Labor is further weakened as industry, becoming more mobile, moves to states having right-to-work laws. In fact, such laws are often passed with the deliberate intention of luring industry away from the high-priced northeastern and middle western labor markets. An argument both for and against "right-to-work," depending on where you sit, is that in states where the law is in force the average per capita annual income is $384 less than the national average.

THE LANDRUM-GRIFFIN ACT OF 1959 [2]

The most recent phase of governmental regulation of the relations between unions and their members began ten years after the passage of the Taft-Hartley Act. In 1957 a Select Committee of the United States Senate, popularly known as the McClellan Committee, commenced an investigation into improper activities in the labor-management field. The investigation, which took the form of highly publicized hearings, lasted for two years and concentrated largely upon alleged union racketeering and corruption. The prime target of the Committee was the powerful Teamsters' Union, although others were also investigated. The Committee's revelations gave support to those who believed that the rights of union members needed additional statutory protection. Others saw an opportunity, by exploiting the unfavorable publicity and lowered prestige suffered by unions, to reduce the economic and political power of organized labor by further restrictive legislation covering such traditional union activities as strikes, boycotts, and picketing. The combined pressures from these two groups, whose basic purposes were quite different, led to the adoption in 1959 of the Labor-Management Reporting and Disclosure Act (LMRDA), commonly known as the Landrum-Griffin Act or the Labor Reform Act.

The LMRDA consists of seven major parts, or "titles." The first six titles relate principally to the administration of internal union affairs, although several reporting and disclosure requirements are also applicable to employers and consultants. . . .

Title I provides that no member of a labor organization may be "fined, suspended, expelled, or otherwise disciplined except for non-payment of dues," unless he has been "(A) served with written specific charges; (B) given a reasonable time to prepare his defense; [and] (C) afforded a full and fair hearing." Closely related to the provision dealing with improper disciplinary action is one forbidding any union to limit the rights of its members to sue the organization or its officers or to institute a proceeding

[2] From "Internal Relations Between Unions and Their Members: United States Report," by Benjamin Aaron, professor of law and director of the Institute of Industrial Relations, University of California, Los Angeles. *Rutgers Law Review*. 18:279-303. Winter '64. Reprinted by permission.

against them before any administrative agency. The same protection is extended to the right of a union member to appear as a witness in any judicial, administrative, or legislative proceeding, to petition any legislature, and to communicate with any legislator. These prohibitions are qualified, however, by a proviso that any member "may be required to exhaust reasonable hearing procedures [but not to exceed a four-month lapse of time]" within the union, before instituting legal or administrative proceedings against the organization or its officers. A third provision expressly preserves "the rights and remedies of any member of a labor organization under any state or Federal law or before any court or other tribunal, or under the constitution and bylaws of any labor organization."

The foregoing substantive and procedural rules represent an attempt to achieve an equitable balance between the union's right to enforce reasonable rules by appropriate disciplinary measures and the member's right to exercise the rights of citizenship and to obtain judicial or administrative relief for any wrongs he has suffered at the hands of the union. The section on disciplinary procedure simply expresses in general terms a body of common law developed by the state courts over many years in an effort to secure for union members the guarantees of notice, full hearing, and an unbiased tribunal. The last of these rights was and remains, even under the LMRDA, the most difficult to establish. The organizational structure of unions, with but few exceptions, does not provide for an independent judiciary. [For an outstanding exception, see "UAW Public Review Board," in this section, below.] Indeed, the disciplinary procedure is usually in the control of those in power. Hence, there is a built-in bias in most disciplinary proceedings which is sometimes impossible to remedy by the process of judicial review. By including the requirement of procedural exhaustion, but limiting it to a four-month period, the LMRDA has, hopefully, brought some order into the chaos created by the innumerable exceptions introduced by common-law decisions. Also, by expressly reserving existing rights, the LMRDA has insured that individual union members will continue to receive protection granted by some state courts in those areas not specifically covered by the Federal statute. Among the most important of the rights not mentioned in the LMRDA but protected under some state court rulings is that of participating in outside political activities contrary to the position taken by the union. . . .

Among the equal rights of membership protected by Title I are the rights "to nominate candidates [and] to vote in elections or referendums of the labor organization." These rights may be enforced by a civil action brought by the complaining member in a Federal district court "for such relief (including injunctions) as may be appropriate." Title IV establishes a series of broad regulations covering nomination of candidates and the conduct of union elections. National unions, except federations such as the AFL-CIO, must elect officers at least every five years; locals, at least every three years; and intermediate bodies, such as joint boards or councils, every four years. In local elections the only authorized method of voting is by secret ballot among members in good standing. National unions may elect officers by that method or at a convention of delegates chosen by secret ballot; corresponding procedures are available to members of intermediate bodies. In any union election held by secret ballot, all members must have at least fifteen days written notice; each member in good standing is entitled to one vote. Elections must conform to the union's constitution and bylaws, insofar as they do not conflict with the statutory requirements. . . .

In addition to nominating and voting in union elections, union members are guaranteed other rights of participation in the affairs of their organizations by Title I. These include the right to participate in union meetings and the right of freedom of speech and assembly. Although the common law enforced such of these rights as were guaranteed by union constitutions and bylaws, the LMRDA has added specific safeguards not generally available until its enactment. . . .

Title I also establishes required procedures for increasing the rates of union dues and initiation fees and for levying special assessments upon the membership. The procedures are extremely detailed; the basic principles established are that fees may be raised and assessments levied only at a meeting of which due notice has been given, and only by at least a majority vote and usually by secret ballot. . . .

Title II of the LMRDA specifies in elaborate detail a wide range of information which must be regularly reported to the Department of Labor by unions, their officers and employees, and by employers and their agents. Violators are subject to both criminal and civil penalties. These provisions reflect the popular belief that a requirement of detailed public disclosure, under pain of serious punishment, is a strong deterrent to illegal behavior; they also reflect the conviction that internal union democracy will be strengthened if the membership is apprised of the details of transactions by union officers. . . .

The provisions of Title V, which are closely related to the reporting and disclosure requirements of Title II, are designed to provide additional protection for unions and their members against dishonest or unworthy officers or representatives. They constitute a determination by Congress as to the minimum ethical and legal standards by which the behavior of union leaders must be measured. The basic provision of Title V declares that union officers and representatives occupy positions of trust and are therefore under a duty, "taking into account the special problems and functions of a labor organization," to manage, spend, and invest union funds and property in accordance with standards generally applicable to trustees. It is clear from the legislative history of Title V, however, that Congress did not intend by this provision to indicate for what purposes a union should expend its money. . . .

The LMRDA has been in effect for only . . . [a few] years, and it is still too soon to make any but the most tentative judgments as to long-range effects of Title I. The number of suits filed by union members against their organizations and officers, although much greater than those arising under any other title of the statute, remains far less than had been generally anticipated. Most courts have shown no special antagonism to unions and, until recently, have tended to construe the rights created by the statute quite narrowly. . . . [Recently] however, there has been a noticeable trend toward a broader interpretation of individual rights of free speech and criticism within the union.

Still, there is little evidence that the LMRDA has awakened a more lively interest on the part of the rank-and-file in the conduct of internal union affairs; apathy continues to be the prevailing mood among the membership of most unions. On the other hand, there has been a very pronounced and encouraging trend within many unions to review their disciplinary procedures and, where necessary, to amend their constitutions and bylaws in order to bring them into conformity with the LMRDA. A recent study reported, for example, that of 70 unions surveyed, 55, covering over 9 million members, had amended one or more of their constitutional provisions relating to disciplining officers or members since the passage of the LMRDA.

For the reasons previously mentioned, the provisions of Titles I and IV relating to the conduct of union elections, as well as to the rights of union members to be candidates and to vote, have not proved as effective as some observers hoped and anticipated. Pre-election remedies have been almost uniformly denied, and post-election remedies, at least from the standpoint of the individual employee, have been rather disappointing. On the positive side, officials of the Department of Labor have reported that the mere probability of a challenge of the election by the Secretary has prompted unions to improve their procedures and to show greater concern for the individual rights protected by law.

There is no way of telling whether the reporting and disclosure requirements of Title II have achieved the purpose for which they were intended. The sheer volume of the reports filed under the new law has made any systematic analysis of their contents impossible. Thus, it seems unlikely that the hope that these documents, which are public information, would be extensively referred to by individual union members or by scholars for research purposes, will be realized. Yet, there remains strong reason to believe that the requirement that union officers disclose the details of any transactions involving possible conflicts of interest will operate as a major deterrent to wrongdoing. That some union officers had violated their trust and had profited personally at the union's expense was established by the findings of the McClellan Committee and has been reaffirmed by the number of convictions of union officers for embezzlement of union funds since the passage of the LMRDA.

Many observers, however, share the concern of unions over the extent of the Secretary of Labor's investigatory powers. The fear is that these powers could become the instrument of governmental oppression of unions rather than simply a means of protecting union members against the dishonesty of their officers. The time may come when additional safeguards against abuse of governmental power are felt to be necessary or desirable; but it seems unlikely that the principle of reporting and disclosure by unions and their officers will be abandoned in the foreseeable future.

It is difficult to overestimate the importance of the provisions in Title V which spell out the fiduciary responsibilities of union officers and employees. The action by Congress in this regard ended, for all practical purposes, an informal debate that had been going on within the American labor movement for some time as to how high a standard of personal accountability should be applied to union leaders. In adopting the fiduciary standard of strict accountability for union officers, representatives, and employees, Congress took a long step in the direction of converting the status of unions from ordinary voluntary organizations to quasi-public utilities. One may safely predict that whatever amendments to the LMRDA may subsequently be enacted, there will be no retreat from the declaration that union officers, representatives, and employees occupy positions of high trust and strict accountability. It is difficult to see how this legislative standard can have any but a beneficial effect on the conduct of internal union affairs.

There can be no doubt that the LMRDA has tended strongly to prevent the imposition of trusteeships for the purposes of looting local union treasuries or maintaining a crude type of political dictatorship. It is less likely that the more subtle uses of trusteeships to preserve the parent organization's dominance over rebellious locals have been seriously affected; indeed, there is no general agreement that they should be. Unions have their own internal problems of federalism. The organization of collective bargaining in the United States requires, in most instances, a strong parent union to give leadership and economic and technical support to the subordinate bodies. The unavoidable price of this leadership and support is a sacrifice of a certain amount of local autonomy, and there is no general agreement as to how much of a sacrifice is necessary or desirable.

UAW PUBLIC REVIEW BOARD [3]

The problem of insuring the protection of basic democratic rights of trade union members has received considerable attention in the United States in recent years. Public attention was first focused on the subject by disclosures of corrupt practices and abuses of the rights of union members in connection with the administration of health and welfare funds in reports issued by the United States Senate Committee on Labor and Public Welfare in 1953 and 1954. At the same time investigations by the New York Crime Commission into the affairs of the International Longshoremen's Association revealed widespread corrupt practices. The revelations produced by both investigations received considerable publicity in the nation's daily newspapers. Then, in 1957, the Senate created a Select Committee on Improper Practices in the Labor or Management Field (McClellan Committee) to investigate more fully the alleged corrupt and undemocratic practices in labor unions and industrial concerns. The investigations of this Committee, fully dramatized in the press, radio, and television, revealed rather extensive corruption and racketeering in a relatively small number of AFL-CIO unions.

As was inevitable, the rank-and-file members of these unions were the principal victims of their leaders' moral turpitude. The funds which were misappropriated either belonged to them in the form of welfare or pension funds or had been contributed by them in the form of dues; the "sweetheart" or collusive contracts usually meant diminished wage returns and inferior fringe benefits; the undemocratic practices coupled in certain instances with racketeer control made it impossible for the rank and file to oust corrupt

[3] From "UAW Public Review Board Report," by David Y. Klein, executive director, Public Review Board, United Automobile, Aerospace and Agricultural Implement Workers of America. *Rutgers Law Review.* 18:304-42. Winter '64. Reprinted by permission.

leadership. The general public, partly as a result of undiscriminating newspaper reporting and partly because of a natural cynicism, tended to attribute to all labor unions the shortcomings of a comparative few.

Various results followed the disclosures. The labor movement, or that is to say the federations of trade union organizations, acted swiftly to divorce themselves from their wayward brethren. Practices which had long been condoned, and which would be condoned again when the furor had subsided, became grounds for expulsion. The International Longshoremen's Association was expelled in 1953 by the AFL Convention. A year later the Retail, Wholesale and Department Store Union was threatened with expulsion by the CIO. Resultant reforms, however, made the implementation of the threat unnecessary. In 1957, following more McClellan Committee revelations, further removals were in order by the joint AFL-CIO Federation which had merged in 1955. Out went the Bakery Workers, the Laundry Workers, and even the unrepentant Teamsters' Union which, with its 1.4 million members, constituted the Federation's largest affiliate. Last-minute promises of reform spared other unions a similar fate. Expulsion from the AFL-CIO has not proved an effective means to bring about reform in corrupt or undemocratic unions. With perhaps one exception, expelled unions do not appear to have been much damaged by their severance. Indeed, the Teamsters' Union has even managed to prosper and grow despite the fact that it does not officially take part in the mutual aid and protection arrangements formulated by AFL-CIO affiliates. Reforms have not resulted either. The leadership in power at the time of expulsion has, for the most part, been able to retain its position. Thus, the practices which led to expulsion presumably continue, albeit less overtly.

A second result of the public disclosure that all in labor's house was not entirely in order, was the declaration of principle in the constitution of the merged AFL and CIO that ethical standards and a machinery for enforcement of these standards should be observed by the affiliate members. Six ethical practices codes covering a wide range of union activity were later adopted by the AFL-CIO Executive Council. These codes, which set out in general terms norms of conduct for AFL-CIO unions, were adopted by the AFL-CIO Executive Council during 1956-57. Enforcement was delegated to the drafting committee which has authority to investigate and to make recommendations to the Executive Council of the AFL-CIO.

Perhaps because banishment has not proven an effective means of combating corruption, enforcement of the ethical practices codes in the AFL-CIO has largely ceased. Expulsion after all is the maximum penalty which the AFL-CIO can impose on an international affiliate; its effectiveness, however, is to a large measure dependent upon whether post-expulsion pressures such as raiding and the chartering of rival unions are applied, and upon how vigorously such policies are pursued. Experience has unfortunately shown that since public attention has been diverted from internal union practices the impetus for such continuing reform has largely waned.

A third result, and the one which is of principal concern here, has been the efforts at self-discipline that have been initiated by some American unions through the adoption of systems of impartial public review of the conduct of internal affairs. By surrendering a portion of their authority to private citizens unconnected with the organization, these unions hoped to reduce effectively the possibility of the occurrence of unfair or improper practices within their internal structures, and, at the same time, to repair in some measure the tattered public image of the labor movement. These experiments in self-discipline have been limited, however, to a mere handful of American unions, and, with one exception, even these have been exceedingly circumspect in surrendering authority to their independent review agencies. The first American trade union to adopt a system of impartial public review was the Upholsterers' International Union of North America, AFL-CIO (UIU). This union of comparatively small membership (55,000) has limited the jurisdiction of its review board to matters involving union discipline. As might be expected under these circumstances, the case experience of the UIU review board has been extremely limited. As of July 1963, it had considered only two appeals.

At its 1960 Constitutional Convention, the United Packinghouse Workers of America, AFL-CIO (UPWA), adopted a resolution approving the action of the Union's Executive Board establishing a Public Review Advisory Commission consisting of five public members not otherwise affiliated with the union to review the "good faith" of any executive board action relating to a complaint of a violation of the AFL-CIO ethical practices codes. The Commission has yet to hear its first case. Most recently, in April 1963, the American Federation of Teachers chartered a new union designed to enlist teachers at the college and the university level. The union, known as the United Federation of College Teachers, has provided in its constitution for final and binding authority to be given to a Public Review Board on all matters of demotion, suspension and expulsion of members. As of the time of the writing of this paper the union had yet to form its review board.

The only union of substantial size to adopt the impartial review system has been the UAW [United Automobile, Aerospace and Agricultural Implement Workers of America]. In 1957, while the findings of the McClellan Committee were making headlines in the nation's daily newspapers, this union of some million and a half workers established at its constitutional convention a Public Review Board (PRB) which was to have unprecedented authority over the union's conduct of its affairs. . . .

In establishing its public review agency the UAW went much further than merely seeking to control corrupt practices. The institution is designed to assure that the basic democratic rights of UAW members will be fully protected; it is in this area of union activity that the PRB has functioned exclusively. The jurisdictional authority of the Board is divided in the auto workers' constitution into roughly two segments. First, the Board has jurisdiction "to deal with matters related to alleged violation of any AFL-CIO ethical practices codes and any additional ethical practices codes that may be adopted by the international union." Second, the Board has been granted jurisdiction over appeals arising under designated procedures set forth in the union's constitution. Two general limitations, however, have been placed on the scope of its review. In appeals which relate to the processing of shop grievances, the PRB has no jurisdiction unless the appellant has alleged that the grievance was improperly handled because of fraud, discrimination or collusion with management. Also, it is prohibited from reviewing an official bargaining policy of the international union. But apart from these exclusions, virtually any subject of dispute can be brought to the PRB for review. The UAW constitution provides that any member of any local union or unit of an amalgamated local union, that is, a subordinate body, may challenge "any action, decision or penalty of that body" by submitting his challenge to "the appropriate body of such local union or unit." Any member who is dissatisfied with the membership's decision with respect to his challenge of the local action, decision, or penalty may appeal. Furthermore, the very defeat by a local general membership of any motion constitutes local action. Thus, it is possible for a member to introduce into the appeal procedure almost any issue merely by raising it before the general membership of his local union in the form of a motion; thereafter, should it be defeated, he may institute an appeal to the appropriate appellate authority.

As the final step in the appeal procedure, a member has a choice of appealing to the UAW constitutional convention which meets biannually, or to the PRB. The decisions of either authority are final and binding on all parties. Decisions of the PRB are not reviewable by the convention and vice versa. Cases which are dismissed by the Board for lack of jurisdiction may be appealed to the convention which, as the body exercising sovereign authority within the union, is empowered to review any and all appeals.

The PRB consists of seven members who are appointed for terms of office between constitutional conventions. Appointments are made by the international president with the approval of the International Executive Board (IEB) and ratification by the constitutional convention. . . . The operation of the PRB is financed by the international union from its general operating fund. . . .

The Public Review Board functions exclusively as an appellate body. A typical case presented to the Board would normally be processed in the following manner: A member aggrieved by an act of his local would, by motion, protest that act to the local membership at its regular monthly meeting. If he should fail to obtain the desired redress here, he may then appeal to the International Executive Board. At this level he would normally be afforded a full-dress hearing before an International Executive Board Appeal Committee with the opportunity to present witnesses on his own behalf, to question those who oppose his position, and to make whatever legal arguments he believes relevant to his case. A verbatim transcript is made of this proceeding. If, after receiving the decision of the IEB, he is still dissatisfied, he may then appeal either to the Public Review Board or to the constitutional convention. . . .

A lesser, but nevertheless significant, function of the Board is to act as a sort of complaint agency. Members with problems concerning their union are encouraged to discuss these problems with the Board's staff, either in person, by telephone, or by mail. Approximately one hundred such inquiries are received by the Board every year. Each is given individual attention and an attempt is made to advise each member of the means available for the solution of his difficulty. Sometimes this will take the form of advising the member of the means whereby he may submit a formal appeal to the union's procedure; on other occasions where it appears that the member's quarrel is really with his employer rather than with his union, the member will be referred to the grievance procedure provided for under his contract. Finally, in those few cases which appear to warrant it, a problem may be referred directly to the office of the international president for investigation. Resort to this latter procedure is undertaken only when it appears that the problem presented is one which is susceptible to resolution by administrative act.

If of no other value, the complaint procedure seems to have a beneficial effect merely in allowing a member to discuss at length with a sympathetic audience problems which to him may seem of the greatest magnitude. The PRB, removed as it is from the mainstream of everyday commerce, is perhaps sometimes in a better position to provide constructive advice to a member than would be his shop steward, committeeman, or even his local president, all of whom are confronted daily with numerous instances of similar problems. . . .

Grievance processing appeals have occurred with far greater frequency than any other type. This single subject has accounted for approximately one-third of all appeals received by the PRB. Grievances, of course, arise out of the work situation. They may concern a variety of subject matters, such as discharge, employer discipline, seniority, wage rates, hours, working conditions, and the like. When an employee feels his rights under the collective bargaining agreement have been violated, his recourse is to the grievance procedure. The union, however, in its role as collective bargaining agent has the responsibility of determining which grievances merit processing and which should be withdrawn for lack of merit or because their pursuance would not be in accord with the current collective bargaining policy of the institution. . . .

In areas of internal union activity, the Board has played a quite different role. A word should be said, however, about the cases which the Board has not been called upon to review, for, in a way they are perhaps equally significant as those which it has considered. While, as has been earlier indicated, the moving forces in the creation of the Board were the revelations of the McClellan Committee, the PRB to date has not received a single appeal which concerned claims of racketeering, corruption, or financial malpractice. This is not to say that there have been no cases of this nature occurring within the UAW in the first six years of the Board's existence; instances of financial abuses have come to the attention of the union authorities during this period. The significant fact, however, is that it has never been necessary for a member of the UAW to take a case of this nature to the PRB to achieve redress.

Certainly the most significant impact which the PRB has had upon the international union in its relationship with its members has been in the area of procedural due process. The insistence by the Board that the union adhere literally to the provisions of its constitution has brought about a most fundamental change by the union in its approach to appeals submitted by members.

It has also resulted in the criticism, however, that the PRB is overtechnical and that it neglects the substance of problems in favor of demanding technical adherence to constitutional procedures. . . .

Trusteeships, the McClellan Committee found, have often been employed by an international union to gain control over a dissenting local or to perpetuate the power of the international officers in control. Within the UAW, however, the device is used relatively infrequently; thus, only four appeals involving this subject have been presented to the PRB. The constitution gives the International Executive Board authority to impose trusteeships where necessary to prevent financial malpractices, assure performance of collective bargaining obligations, restore democratic practices, or to assure the carrying out of the "legitimate objectives" of the union. The PRB has confined its role in reviewing these actions to determining whether the trusteeship was imposed for a reason allowable under the constitution. Using this test of jurisdiction, the phrase "legitimate objectives" has been the subject of considerable contention. In . . . [a] recent case involving a trusteeship, the PRB ruled that a local union in the process of dissolution might properly be brought under international control despite the fact that no evidence of improper practices on the part of any local official had been presented. It was there declared a "legitimate objective" of the union to employ a trusteeship to prevent any *possible* misuse of local funds. . . .

In the final analysis the ability of a labor organization to function as a democratic institution is dependent upon its capability to protect the rights of its members. Unions which can not do this run the risk that control of the institution may some day be wrested from the hands of a defenseless membership by an autocratic leadership. The rank and file of labor organizations discovering themselves in this predicament will find it necessary to enlist the aid of government to rescue them from their plight. Resultant restrictions on the freedom of union activity will, however, affect all unions alike. The question arises . . . by what means labor can most effectively police itself and rid itself of undesirable regulation at the hands of the courts under the

LMRDA. The author believes that machinery for the effective implementation of self-discipline lies within the framework of the AFL-CIO labor federation to which almost all American unions belong. It is within the power of this body, acting through its members, to adopt for all its members a system of impartial review. This could be done through the establishment of regional boards or perhaps even a full-time board with investigatory agents. The mechanics of the system, however, are unimportant; it is the adoption of the principle which is of the greatest moment. The cost in terms of loss of sovereignty will be small in comparison to the long-term benefits in the form of freedom from government restriction which would accrue.

EFFECT OF ANTITRUST LAWS [4]

The Supreme Court has severely altered the relationship of unions to antitrust laws in two recent cases that [former] Justice Arthur J. Goldberg called the most important in the labor field in nearly thirty years.

The decisions sent a wave of panic through union leaders at the outset because they seemed to indicate that accepted contract procedures might violate antitrust laws and subject unions to heavy damage claims.

But . . . since the court spoke, the fears of immediate repercussions have dwindled. Labor lawyers are advising unions to bide their time and see how the new edicts work out in practice.

Analysis by lawyers has led them to conclude that employers will be at least as hard hit as unions and may suffer even more. They have concluded also that the real victim of the decisions is neither unions nor industry, but the collective bargaining system.

Labor lawyers seem agreed that collective bargaining will go on but that discussions will be less free and frank and that, consequently, a tendency toward increased labor strife is a distinct possibility.

[4] From "Antitrust Laws and the Unions," by James C. Millstone, Washington correspondent. *St. Louis Post-Dispatch.* p 1 C+. Je. 27, '65. Reprinted by permission.

Stripped to barest essentials, the new ground broken in the court decisions is this:

In *United Mine Workers v. James M. Pennington,* the court held that a wage agreement between a union and an employer or group of employers, which includes an understanding that the union will seek the same terms from other employers in the industry, may violate antitrust laws.

Until now, labor negotiators believed they could bargain without restrictions on matters involving wages, hours and working conditions. The court action establishes the negative, that negotiators enjoy no absolute immunity from antitrust violations, even when the topic of discussion is wages.

In *Meat Cutters v. Jewel Tea Co.,* a case in which the court could not muster a majority behind any opinion, one segment of the court held that an agreement between a union and a single employer which has an effect on competition may violate antitrust laws if the subject matter is not related to wages, hours or working conditions.

Until now, union lawyers believed a labor organization could violate antitrust laws only when becoming a party to a prior existing combination of employers in restraint of trade.

Labor lawyers note that the court did not spell out what evidence would constitute proof that such agreements had been made nor did it hold that the existence of them was a law violation per se. These matters were left for determination by judges and juries and, eventually, no doubt, by the high court's own elaboration.

The *Pennington* case is by far the more important of the two. Labor lawyers, backed by Justice Goldberg's hard-hitting dissent, say the decision strikes at a widely used bargaining system that has been instrumental in fostering labor peace in recent years. That is the method of pattern bargaining, whereby a union negotiates with an industry leader first in order to reach an agreement that can be applied to all other employers in the industry. The method is used in the automobile, steel, rubber and shipbuilding industries, among others.

The decision also could endanger agreements with multi-employer groups if the contracts were made with an understanding that the same terms would be imposed on employers who were not members of the group.

Multi-employer contracts cover most workers in such industries as clothing manufacturing, coal mining, building construction, trucking and longshoring.

The court action added a new, unsettling chapter to a long and often ambiguous history of labor's relationship to antitrust laws. Congress and the courts have striven since the passage of the Sherman antimonopoly act in 1890 to define that role.

When the courts applied antimonopoly provisions to labor unions, Congress in 1914 passed what became known as the labor exemption to the Sherman act, stating that, "the labor of a human being is not a commodity or article of commerce . . . nor shall such organizations, or the members thereof, be held or construed to be illegal combinations or conspiracies in the restraint of trade under the antitrust laws."

However, the Supreme Court continued to apply antitrust laws to union activity, prompting Congress to attempt to narrow the role of the judiciary. The Wagner Act of 1935 made wages, hours and working conditions mandatory subjects of collective bargaining.

Since then, the court has generally reversed its previous tendency to subject labor to antitrust actions and has shown a more lenient attitude.

In that period, industrywide negotiating has become popular in many fields, and it has become a common practice for both sides to seek a uniform wage scale to apply throughout an industry. This system now appears to be threatened by the latest court decisions.

Justice Byron R. White delivered the court's 6-3 opinion in the *Pennington* case, holding:

> There are limits to what a union or an employer may offer or extract in the name of wages. . . . We think a union forfeits its exemption from the antitrust laws when it is clearly shown that it has agreed with one set of employers to impose a certain wage scale on other bargaining units.

Justice Goldberg's dissent was joined by the court's two most conservative members, Justices John M. Harlan and Potter Stewart. Goldberg's main argument was that negotiations on subjects required under the Wagner Act should be totally exempt from regulation under antitrust laws. . . .

Goldberg's dissent warned that the court decision "will bar a basic element of collective bargaining from the conference room."

Plainly and simply [he wrote] the court would subject both unions and employers to antitrust sanctions, criminal as well as civil, if in collective bargaining they concluded a wage agreement and, as part of the agreement, the union has undertaken to use its best efforts to have this wage accepted by other employers in the industry.

He argued that unions have a right to try for uniform standards in an industry, and that employers have a right to know when making an agreement that their competitors will not be able to operate with lower standards.

The purpose of unions is to eliminate substandard wages, Goldberg said. He said that the philosophy of Congress over the years clearly has been to repudiate "the view that labor is a commodity and thus there should be competition to see who can supply it at the cheapest price."

Labor lawyers see several possible implications in the *Pennington* and *Jewel Tea* decisions. One is that unions may be subjected to numerous antitrust suits that will be decided by judges and juries some of whom may be hostile to unions generally. The UMW faces $50 million in suits pending disposition of the *Pennington* case.

Some lawyers think unions on occasion will be inclined to settle some suits out of court, even though the suits may lack merit, so as not to take a chance on being hit with the treble damages provided under the Sherman Act.

Labor lawyers are confident that litigation stemming from the *Pennington* decision will find its way back to the Supreme Court in coming years and that the ruling will be clarified and softened. In the meantime, unions are being advised to prepare themselves to fight lawsuits.

The suits probably will not be filed by industry but by marginal employers and independent operators. The big companies usually are involved in industrywide agreements and pattern-settling and thus will be as liable to antitrust suits as unions if an agreement between the unions and one or more big companies affecting the entire industry can be proved.

Thus both sides will be anxious to avoid an appearance of conspiracy, and that is likely to impair the effectiveness of collective bargaining, lawyers say. A coolness among negotiators probably will replace any showing of undue friendliness so as to avoid any implication of collusion in bargaining.

Furthermore, companies appear to be restricted even more sharply than unions in that they may not be permitted to agree among themselves as to what kind of deal they would accept, unless they were bound into a formal bargaining unit. The consequence is likely to be a growing tendency for employers to band together in such units, lawyers say.

Unions, on the other hand, are free to decide unilaterally that they will insist on industrywide wage standards and can announce that policy to the world. Union attorneys are counseling their clients to express such desires through formal board resolutions and union conventions, spelling out reasons in the greatest detail. These resolutions are believed to rebut later charges of conspiracy.

Because big industry and labor may suffer equally, they are expected to join forces in an effort to get help from Congress to counter the court action.

COMPULSORY ARBITRATION: CAREFUL CONSIDERATION NEEDED [5]

I am sure that any public opinion poll would demonstrate that the public favors compulsory arbitration and a ban on strikes. Yet, most people who are familiar with collective bargaining are opposed to the settlement of labor disputes by banning strikes and compelling arbitration.

[5] From "Compulsory Labor Arbitration and the National Welfare," by Benjamin Wyle, attorney, Luxemburg & Wyle. *Arbitration Journal*. 19:98-102. '64. Reprinted by permission.

The more sophisticated in labor relations know that the weaker disputant, being more fearful of a strike, will avoid a negotiated settlement, hoping he will obtain a more reasonable "deal" through compulsory arbitration. Experience has taught management and labor that arbitrators normally proceed from the last position of the parties and that once a point is abandoned in negotiations, it can never be regained in arbitration. Neither party can therefore be expected to make a bona-fide effort to reach agreement for fear that any offer or compromise proposal will weaken his position in arbitration.

Thus, genuine collective bargaining with its give-and-take cannot survive alongside of a system of compulsory arbitration. Conditions of employment will be fixed not by the parties involved but by an agent of the Government under a system of imposed arbitration. Once wages and working conditions are settled through Government fiat, the Government will also be determining profits and possibly prices, changing our economic system completely.

Senator Robert A. Taft expressed it cogently during the course of the debate in the Senate on the 1947 legislative proposals to amend the National Labor Relations Act, when he said: "But if we impose compulsory arbitration, or if we give the Government power to fix wages at which men must work . . . I do not see how in the end we can escape a collective economy.

It is for this reason that we find agreement between representatives of organized labor and management on this issue. The United States Chamber of Commerce and the NAM [National Association of Manufacturers] join with the AFL-CIO in opposition to mandatory arbitration.

But, it may be pointed out, the proposal is not the universal application of compulsory arbitration, but arbitration limited to strikes which affect the national health and safety. Surely, the argument goes, our society cannot tolerate a policemen's strike, a hospital strike or a railroad strike. The difficulty with this contention is that once we set out on this strike substitute course, it is not easy to draw the line at just what point it is prudent to stop.

The 1959 steel strike incited threats of compulsory arbitration for that industry by the President. Governor Nelson A. Rockefeller advocated compulsory arbitration whenever the President finds that the "national welfare" is endangered and he sponsored the law providing for compulsory arbitration of labor disputes in our hospitals.

Now that compulsory arbitration has been invoked to settle the dispute on our railroads [see "The Use of 'Informed Neutrals,' " in Section III, above], legislative proposals are being considered in Congress requiring arbitration in lieu of strikes in the maritime industry and in the aerospace field.

The Taft-Hartley injunction, available in cases of strikes endangering the public health or safety, has been invoked in a coal mine strike, the meat-packing industry, the long-line telephone strike, atomic plant strikes, the steel strike, longshoremen strikes, a copper mine strike and in the maritime industry.

A number of states have statutes on their books outlawing strikes and compelling arbitration in public utilities. Kansas forbade strikes and lockouts in industries "affected with a public interest." This law was declared unconstitutional when the statute was invoked to force arbitration in a dispute in the food industry.

We can appreciate the considerations which led these states to enact these laws as we shudder at the thought of a crippled city without light, power or transportation. Yet, . . . [A. H.] Raskin of the New York *Times,* one of the most knowledgeable of labor observers, reports:

Utility strikes, once feared as the ultimate in community peril, now occasion only minor concern because the supplying of electricity and gas is so automatic a process that the supervisory force can handle all normal demand with little difficulty. Telephone strikes are in much the same category.

Professor Benjamin Aaron of the University of California, and a public member of the compulsory arbitration board in the railroad work rules dispute, observed that:

There is still no consensus as to when a dispute truly imperils the national health or safety. If purely economic criteria are applied, few cases would meet the test; but the line between emergency and inconvenience is frequently hard to draw, and public resentment against strikes in key industries, regardless of their effect on national health and safety, is a political force which cannot be ignored.

How many can honestly say that they have found themselves in danger because of a strike? Still, public agitation continues for laws immobilizing strike action.

Secretary of Labor W. Willard Wirtz noted . . . that "public tolerance for strikes is diminishing rapidly." What can be the basis for this growing antipathy to economic self-help through strike action? Is it due to rapidly rising strike activity?

The United States Department of Labor strike figures for 1963 show that the per cent of working time lost through strikes (excluding the depression years) has declined for the fourth consecutive year, to a sustained low level not matched during peacetime.

Is it developing because of concern over manpower and production losses due to strikes? The total number of strikers out one day or more in 1963 was a little over one million. Yet, between five and six million persons have been unemployed in recent years with no demonstrable concern on the part of the public over this loss of productive power.

Nor can this opposition be caused by concern over the hardships, privations and losses suffered by the participants in a strike. . . . The Flight Engineers . . . [were engaged] in a strike . . . [for] well over a year. . . . Because the planes are flying, no one seems to be interested. Picture the agitation and activity of the various Government agencies if these strikes had succeeded in grounding the planes by the withdrawal of their labor.

There are thousands of other workers on strike for many months, even years, throughout the country today. They may be hungry, cold and completely without resources, but no one clamors for Government intervention to end these strikes. No one is particularly interested in bailing out these unfortunates. No one is concerned over the fact that free collective bargaining has failed in these cases.

When Secretary Wirtz talks about the rising intolerance of the public to strikes, he is speaking about strikes which are strong, effective and successful in stopping or substantially curtailing the production of a commodity or the performance of a service which the public wants. Workers on strike against enterprises whose production or services are not missed, and workers on strike against enterprises which continue to operate, can march the picket line forever without the slightest public interest.

One never speaks about substituting another method of adjusting differences in the unsuccessful strike situation because such a strike does not affect the public health, the public welfare, the public safety, the public interest, or the public convenience. But the strike which deprives or just threatens to deprive the nation, or even a local community, of a particular commodity or service causes outcries of crisis. Where the strikers have not succeeded in stopping or substantially curtailing production to the point where the public is inconvenienced, there is no public clamor for compulsory arbitration and the union will ultimately be compelled to accept a settlement on management's terms.

Thus, the public takes the unfair position that a strong union should be compelled to accept terms of employment fixed as fair by a Government agent, but a weak union is forced to accept the employment terms fixed as fair by the employer. In no case where the union is strong would it be permitted to win employment terms which it regards as fair if the advocates of compulsory arbitration have their way.

I oppose compulsory arbitration for the same reason that I oppose a government-controlled economy. I oppose compulsory arbitration even in industries affecting the national health and safety. This proposal would not limit compulsory arbitration but would extend it virtually everywhere as the substitute for strike action. A strike affecting the so-called national health and safety would rarely cause a genuine emergency. I am confident that the labor organizations involved in any strike would demonstrate their responsibility by continuing essential operations where a complete cessation of labor would really endanger the public. I am aware, of course, that there is no assurance that the unions would do so under such circumstances. It is preferable to run the risk and even endure a strike than to alter our free enterprise system to resolve a temporary emergency situation.

However, if we are to have compulsory arbitration or use it as a tool in particular strike situations, I favor a statute which carefully circumscribes the affected industries and makes arbitration compulsory in all cases in these industries, before a walkout occurs. What I strongly object to, as manifestly unfair and inequitable, is special action by the chief executive or legislature on either the Federal or lower level imposing arbitration in a successful strike situation, usually because of public clamor built up by newspaper agitation, while the strike which is unsuccessful is ignored! Laws should make judgments; judgments should not make laws.

Action should not be taken on . . . [a case-by-case] basis depending upon how many strikers go out, how many replacements are available, and how long the strikers can hold out. Relief to the public, and thus to the employer, should not await a demonstration on the part of the strikers as to how strong they are and how successfully they can conduct a strike before the Government acts.

If we are not prepared to compel arbitration in every dispute before a walkout in well-defined and clearly established industries, then there is no justification for bailing out particular employers by imposing arbitration and banning a strike in the situation where the strike is solid and production has stopped.

If we are prepared to resort to compulsory arbitration and terminate real collective bargaining, we cannot permit the practice to be discretionary and political. If we must have compulsory arbitration coupled with a strike ban in certain areas of our economic activities, it should be carefully and soberly considered and determined in an atmosphere of calm objectivity and then uniformly applied in the interests of fairness and justice. We must not let a transitory mass clamor force radical and permanent changes upon our social, political and economic structure under the exigencies of the moment.

V.   LABOR UNIONS IN TODAY'S WORLD

EDITOR'S INTRODUCTION

With a few notable exceptions, American labor unions generally stick close to routine business—the representation of their members, encounters with management, and maintenance of their own internal power structure. But the currents of world and national affairs cannot be entirely resisted or ignored. This section deals with labor's participation in affairs outside its own orbit.

Most timely, of course, is the question of the effect on labor unions of the drama and activity of the civil rights movement. Professor Ray Marshall examines the background of union racial policy, while G. Robert Blakey looks at the Civil Rights Act of 1964 as it relates to unions. Unions play their part, too, in American world leadership, as is recounted in the summary from *Senior Scholastic.*

The story of labor's role in national and local political activity is more in the past tense than a current account. In the late 1930's and early 1940's, under the stimulation of rapid growth fostered by the New Deal, many labor unions apparently were able to direct and "deliver" the votes of their members. Partly for the reasons outlined in Section II above, the unity of the labor vote, if it ever existed, is not widely vaunted today. But big unions still undertake strenuous political activity in behalf of their "friends," as is detailed in the article from *U. S. News & World Report.*

RACIAL POLICIES [1]

Unions have the power to influence economic opportunities for minority groups through their control of apprenticeship training, referral systems, hiring, seniority systems (which control advance-

[1] From "Union Structure and Public Policy: The Control of Union Racial Practices," by Ray Marshall, professor of economics, University of Texas. *Political Science Quarterly.* 78:444-58. S. '63. Reprinted with permission from the *Political Science Quarterly.*

ment and transfer in unionized plants), and other practices which affect wages, hours, working conditions, and employment opportunities. While few union leaders could successfully deny that unions have caused and perpetuated existing patterns of racial discrimination, these patterns are not produced entirely by unions, but also by cultural patterns in the Negro community, employer hiring practices, inadequate education and training of Negroes, and intractable historical employment patterns. Moreover, it must also be recognized that unions have been responsible for some measures which increase the economic opportunities for Negroes, such as: insisting on seniority in promotion, transfer, and layoff, which gives Negroes contractual protection they would not have in the absence of unions (though Negroes are much more likely to be laid off during recessions than whites, it is frequently because their recent commitment to the industrial work force gives them less seniority; there is evidence that Negroes have been able to retain their proportions in industries and companies which are unionized and where Negroes have a long history of employment); working to abolish wage discrimination through collective bargaining and through such agencies as the War Labor Board; including nondiscrimination clauses in contracts with employers; promoting internal education programs designed to reduce discrimination against minority groups; and actively supporting the FEP [Fair Employment Practices] laws which cover over 90 per cent of the nonwhite population outside the South—the AFL-CIO, like its predecessors, the CIO and the AFL is on record in favor of a Federal FEPC.

Nevertheless, it is also true that unions, like other institutions in our society, have exaggerated their equalitarian racial policies for public relations purposes and engage in a variety of practices which limit economic opportunities for minority groups.

An important precondition to changing union racial practices is raising the priority of the problem in the organization's operational scale; we assume, of course, that union racial policies do not change unless there are some pressures for change. One of the reasons labor unions declare against discrimination, while permitting it to continue, is that equalitarian racial practices take lower priority than other objectives facing the union and its leaders. However, when other basic motives (like the achievement of political goals, getting reelected, building strike unity, or organizing a bloc of unorganized workers) are threatened by the continuation of discrimination, unions can be expected to take action against the discriminatory practices. One objective of organizations like the Negro American Labor Council and the National Association for the Advancement of Colored People has been to raise the priority of antidiscrimination objectives through publicity, outside pressures, the promotion of antidiscrimination laws, and other tactics. . . .

It is widely assumed . . . that unions will respond to moral pressures brought to bear on them through publicity (public hearings, recommendations of fact-finding boards, public statements by prominent officials, and so forth). According to our conceptual framework, however, moral pressure is more effective against the AFL-CIO and intermediate federations than against national or local organizations. The Federation's vulnerability to charges of immoral conduct is due partly to the fact that its functions are different from those of national and local organizations. The Federation is mainly a public relations organization; it is the keeper of the labor movement's conscience and seeks to influence legislation and perform other functions in the interest of organized labor. In order to accomplish these objectives, the AFL-CIO must appeal to nonlabor groups, including Negroes, and hence must be concerned with its public moral image. Moreover, the Federation is the most conspicuous part of the labor movement and there is a direct relationship between conspicuousness and vulnerability to moral pressures.

If this is true, and if the AFL-CIO is really sincere in its public declarations, why then does it not vigorously enforce its policies against offending affiliates? In order to answer this question we must understand the extent to which local and national unions are vulnerable to the kinds of power that the Federation has over them. Since the AFL-CIO is composed largely of autonomous national unions, the Federation's main power over an affiliate is moral suasion and its ability to resolve jurisdictional disputes between the nationals. While there is some evidence that national union leaders attempt to keep in the good graces of Federation officers in order to be the beneficiaries of any political favors the latter might be able to bestow, or secure any help AFL-CIO officials might give in jurisdictional dispute cases, these factors would appear to be of only marginal significance in the internal decision-making processes of most national unions.

It might be argued, however, that while the AFL-CIO expelled unions for corruption and the CIO expelled nine unions for being Communist-dominated, the Federation has refused to expel unions in order to enforce its equalitarian racial policies. Does this mean that the AFL-CIO is insincere about its racial position? Not necessarily. It does perhaps mean that in structuring its objectives the Federation places other goals, such as internal cohesion, ahead of enforcing its racial policies. However, there are other differences between the civil rights problem and the Communist and corruption problems. First, the public and Congress have been much less critical of union racial practices than of Communist and racketeer infiltration. Second, racial discrimination is practiced mainly by the membership and at the local level, whereas Communists and racketeers have been in leadership positions. Since national union leaders have generally expressed a willingness to comply with the Federation's racial policy, AFL-CIO officers have argued that their expulsion would be unwise because there is less likelihood that discrimination would be removed if these unions were expelled than if they remained within the Federation.

The record seems to show that while some national unions are more vulnerable to moral pressure than others, national unions are generally more sensitive to economic or political pressures in the short run than they are to moral pressures. This is so because national unions are mainly collective bargaining organizations and thus are primarily motivated by economic rather than political objectives. This is also one of the reasons "moral restraint" by unions cannot be relied upon to implement national wage policies. However, if the union has broad social objectives, it will be more concerned with its moral image than if its objectives are purely economic. This is one reason industrial unions are more likely than craft organizations to adopt equalitarian racial policies. Factors likely to cause national organizations to adopt equalitarian policies include: (1) large blocs of Negro workers whom the union wants to organize; (2) large blocs of Negro members, who might be important in internal union politics; (3) large numbers of Negroes competing in the trade who are not in unions; (4) the adoption of equalitarian racial policies by a rival faction within the union or by a rival union, as was the case with Communist factions and Communist-led unions; (5) the need for public support, to achieve political objectives, for example; and (6) the loss or threatened loss of collective bargaining or union security advantages because of discriminatory practices. This was particularly important in causing railroad unions to drop their racial bars after the state FEP laws were passed and the Railway Labor Act was amended in 1951 to permit the union shop only where all workers in the bargaining units had equal access to union membership.

Within the union hierarchy, local unions have been the most impervious to moral pressures and remain the main loci of racial discrimination. This is particularly true of craft unions in the building trades and on the railroads, where many locals bar Negroes from membership and discriminate against them in job opportunities, usually through informal means. Discrimination can be accomplished in a variety of ways, including: agreements not to sponsor Negroes for membership; refusal to admit Negroes into apprenticeship programs; refusal to accept applications from Negroes or simply ignoring those applications; general "understandings" to vote against Negroes if they are proposed for membership (for example, three members of a Railroad Trainmen or Railway Clerks' lodge may bar an applicant for membership); refusal of journeyman status to Negroes through examinations which either are not given to whites or are rigged so that colored workers cannot pass them; and by exerting political pressure on governmental licensing agencies to see to it that Negroes fail the tests.

Local unions have a variety of motives for discriminating against Negroes and other minorities. Our conceptual framework would lead us to expect that local unions continue discrimination partly because they have narrow economic objectives and are rarely interested in appealing to third parties for support. Indeed, many craft locals have monopoly and nepotic motives for excluding all applicants for membership other than relatives, in which case Negroes are discriminated against along with all others not in the favored group.

It is, however, difficult to generalize about the unions which bar Negroes from membership. They are not restricted to any particular geographical area, because there are actually stronger bars against Negroes in some locals of the same unions in the non-South than in their counterparts in the South, particularly in trades like the bricklayers', hod-carriers', common laborers', bartenders', waiters', and service employees' where Negroes have a long tradition in the South and are excluded in northern or western locals.

While some craft unions have egalitarian racial policies and some industrial union locals have refused to admit Negroes to membership, as a general rule the unions which practice exclusion are craft organizations. . . .

Because of the egalitarian trend in race relations, older unions, other things being equal, seem more likely to exclude minorities than newer unions; some unions were originally fraternal organizations at a time when it was not considered proper to have fraternal relations with Negroes; in many cases employers determine hiring policies and therefore decide whether Negroes are to be hired; whites are particularly likely to attempt to exclude Negroes from certain high-status jobs like airline pilots, stock wranglers, locomotive engineers, and white-collar and supervisory jobs; and, in some cases, local unions exclude Negroes because of internal political considerations which give racists the balance of power. These are the factors which must be overcome in changing union racial practices, and it is obvious that their multiplicity makes its unlikely that any single strategy or approach will succeed in solving this problem. The intransigence of local union racial practices produced by the foregoing factors can be better demonstrated by . . . [an example].

One of the most celebrated cases of racial discrimination by a local union occurred in Cleveland, Ohio, where Local 38 of the International Brotherhood of Electrical Workers (IBEW) defied efforts by Negro electricians to get into the union over a period of forty years, despite widespread publicity and moral condemnation. Local 38's power, like that of many craft locals, was based on its control of the supply of skilled workers. Indeed, an electrical contractor had great difficulty operating in Cleveland without Local 38's approval, an arrangement which was apparently quite acceptable to those contractors already approved by the union. Local 38's constitution required electrical contractors to be "certified" by the local in order to hire union electricians, and in order to be certified a contractor was required to serve two years as a journeyman—which normally meant he must have been a member of the union for two years. Craft unions are also strengthened by the fact that union members normally will not work with nonunion men. Since Negroes were barred from Local 38 and could not work on union jobs, they could not get certified by the union. Negroes could operate as contractors, however, if they passed a city licensing examination permitting them to vouch for the work of their electricians; union electricians did not have to pass the city examination in order to vouch for the work of their employees. But since they could not hire union electricians, colored contractors were restricted to nonunion work—usually in Negro neighborhoods. Moreover, there was apparently an "understanding" in Cleveland that a white electrician could not work for a colored contractor or a Negro electrician for a white contractor.

Negroes in Cleveland started agitating in 1917 to break Local 38's restrictions on their economic opportunities. In 1947 Negro electricians formed a club to bring action before various labor and governmental organizations to obtain relief. The club solicited the aid of international union officers, including IBEW President Dan Tracy and Vice President (now President) Gordon Freeman. These early efforts ended in failure, however, when a business agent who was disposed to help the Negro electricians drowned in Lake Erie and Dan Tracy, who had promised to do what he could to get Negroes admitted to the union, retired as President of the IBEW. ese failures caused Negroes to turn to legal action as a means of changing the union's practices.

In 1955 charges were filed against Local 38 before Cleveland's Community Relations Board, which found the local guilty of racial discrimination; but, in spite of widespread adverse publicity and the efforts of Mayor Anthony Celebrezze, the union steadfastly refused to admit a Negro to membership. After the union ignored the CRB's ruling, as well as vigorous public criticism which focused national attention on the union's practices, the case was referred to the AFL-CIO Civil Rights Department and the President's Committee on Government Contracts. This case went to the formal hearing stage of the AFL-CIO civil rights machinery after conciliatory efforts by IBEW President Freeman, AFL-CIO Civil Rights Committee Chairman James B. Carey, and AFL-CIO President George Meany failed to get the local to relent. Finally, Local 38 admitted three Negroes to membership on the last day of June 1957, after President Meany told the local to admit the Negroes by July 1 or lose its charter. The local showed its continued defiance, however, by refusing to admit the man who filed the complaint with the Community Relations Board. . . .

In conclusion, the evidence suggests that union policies will be changed only when the priority of the issue is raised within the organization by various pressures. Pressures for change might come from within through internal union politics or pressure on local unions by national organizations or the AFL-CIO, or it might come from outside agencies or the government. In order to affect organizational policy, however, these pressures must be of the right kind to influence the type of union whose policies are under attack.

The evidence also suggests that unions probably will not be able to solve their racial problems without outside pressures, because of the foregoing intra-union power considerations and the low priority unions normally assign racial policies. This realization was undoubtedly behind AFL-CIO President Meany's request for a Federal FEPC to help the labor movement solve this problem in its own ranks.

This does not mean, however, that legislation alone can solve the problem of equal employment opportunities for Negroes. The evidence does suggest, though, that legislation can establish a framework that will make it easier to enforce equalitarian policies. Within this framework, implementation will require the cooperation, and sometimes the conflict, of a variety of organizations using appropriate power and strategy.

DISCRIMINATION AND THE LAW [2]

On July 3 [1964] President Johnson signed the most comprehensive civil rights legislation enacted in the twentieth century . . . [the Civil Rights Act of 1964]. . . . The act deals with, among other things, discrimination in public accommodations, voting, federally assisted programs, and, most importantly (in Title VII), employment and union membership.

On August 4 [1964] labor gave its official reaction to the newly enacted statute. Meeting in Chicago, the twenty-nine-member executive council of the AFL-CIO, not unexpectedly, pledged labor's full support to the new act. At the Chicago meeting, the council adopted a multi-point program designed to assist in implementing it by instituting an educational program among union members, starting community committees to work for desegregation of various facilities, bargaining for fair employment clauses in contracts, seeking to make sure that unorganized employers comply with the act, lobbying in Congress for adequate enforcement appropriations, and observing the operation of the act so that developing inadequacies may be brought to Congress' attention. . . .

[2] From "Discrimination, Unions and Title VII," by G. Robert Blakey, assistant professor of law, University of Notre Dame. *America.* 111:210-12. Ag. 29, '64. Reprinted with permission from *America,* The National Catholic Weekly Review, 106 W. 56th Street, New York, N.Y. 10019.

The significance of Title VII to the Negro and other minority groups in our society—and of labor's support of its antidiscrimination policy—can hardly be overestimated. Anyone possessed of even a superficial understanding of our modern industrial life long ago realized the need of collective bargaining. For America's minority groups, however, today's problem is not the right to form a union, but the right to join a union without discrimination.

Union membership has in many areas of our industrial life become a prerequisite to employment and thus to a measure of economic freedom. A distinction, of course, must be drawn between the craft union and the industrial union. Generally, the industrial union exercises little control over employment. Not so the craft union. Despite the prohibitions of the Taft-Hartley Act, many craft unions operate under a virtually closed shop, [in which union membership is required *before* an employee is hired]. Such shops are found most frequently, and have their most significant impact, in the building and construction trades. In these and similar areas, job control is, more often than not, a matter of union policy.

Even when not an economic necessity, union membership remains a valuable asset. Only through it can the worker achieve a voice in determining the policies to be promoted and adopted in his industry—policies that deeply affect his everyday life. And only through the union can the worker effectively prosecute his individual grievances against the company. To be sure, the nonmember may have access to the union grievance procedure, but it will ultimately be a union man who will speak for him. Exclusion from the union actually amounts to a sort of industrial disfranchisement. It has more meaningful implications to the individual than a denial of the right to vote or equal educational or housing opportunities. Politics still has only an indirect impact on the average citizen's life, and without a degree of economic freedom, education breeds only frustration and open occupancy is meaningless.

Few unions, of course, want to restrict membership. They both want and need members. Most unions, such as the Steelworkers, not only freely admit members without discrimination, but actually state in their constitution that all workers, regardless of race, color, creed or national origin, are eligible for membership. Indeed, the constitution of the AFL-CIO contains such a provision. The fact remains, however, that some unions follow discriminatory policies. Traditionally, most of the Railway Brotherhoods have explicitly restricted membership to "white males" or members of the "Caucasian race." Only . . . [in 1963] the Brotherhood of Locomotive Firemen and Enginemen belatedly removed the "white only" clause in their constitution. Officially, discrimination in trade unions is, in the words of George Meany, president of the AFL-CIO, "a bootleg product, sneaked in by the back door and nowhere condoned." And yet it exists. In many cases it is impossible to become a member of a union unless you are a relative of a member or belong to the same racial or ethnic group as the present members. Locals in the building trades often consist entirely of Italian-Americans. The lily-white admission practices of Local 28 of the Sheet Metal Workers in New York, recently the subject of an anti-discrimination order by the State Human Rights Commission, are an example in another trade.

A further example is Local No. 2 of the Plumbers (embarrassingly enough, Meany's home local) in New York City. According to report, the hiring of three Puerto Ricans and one Negro was enough to bring on a walkout by thirty-five plumbers on the Terminal Market project in the Bronx. Local No. 2 officials explained the dispute in terms that emphasized the nonunion status of the men. One of the plumbers on the job was more blunt: "Animals don't mix; why should people have to?" Another observed: "God created me white. Is it any fault of mine they're created another color?" The walkout was not settled until Mayor Robert Wagner, Secretary of Labor Willard Wirtz and Meany himself intervened. Ironically, it was then settled only when the men failed the union's qualifying test, which apparently was fairly administered according to spokesmen for the NAACP, who observed the test.

The sometimes subtle discriminatory practices found in the North are often more objectionable than the overt discrimination of the South. . . . The apprentice program in some unions, too, may serve as a vehicle of discrimination; it is often impossible for certain groups to attain the required degree of "proficiency" to be admitted to journeymanship. Companies and unions sometimes work together. Isaac Borges, age forty-three . . . and a plumber for twenty-three years in New York and in Puerto Rico, and one of the individuals involved in the Local No. 2 dispute, tells a familiar tale: "When I went to the union to apply for membership, they said: 'Well, first you have to go and get a job in a union shop and then come back.' So I went to a union shop and I was told: 'First you have to be a member of the union, so get your membership.' So—what can you do?". . .

Realizing the inadequacies of the traditional approach, a number of states have passed statutes making it illegal for a union to discriminate on the basis of race, color, religious creed or national origin. Twenty-five states presently have some sort of fair-practices legislation. A few courts also have adopted a more realistic view. The California Supreme Court is one example. In 1958, in *Thorman v. the International Alliance of Theatrical Stage Employees,* it directed the admission of an arbitrarily excluded applicant. But these statutes or cases have efficacy only on a statewide basis, and they are most often found in the industrial North, where the problem of racial and other discrimination is present but does not loom large. Indeed, roughly 60 per cent of American Negroes live in states with no anti-discrimination legislation, and these are precisely those who need it most. (It must be added, of course, that the Negroes in the largely unorganized South suffer as much from the unorganized but bigoted employer as from the racist union.) . . .

The . . . [Civil Rights Act] has been subjected to severe and often misleading criticisms. Senator Joseph Clark of Pennsylvania has aptly termed them "fantastic." Critics . . . have said it would abolish union seniority and set up racial "quotas" to achieve some sort of racial "balance."

Title VII, in fact, outlaws just such a policy. Policies like "preferential hiring" advocated by Negro spokesmen like Dr. James M. Nabrit, president of Howard University, and James Farmer, national director of CORE (also criticized by men like Roy Wilkins of the NAACP) stand clearly condemned. Under the provisions of Title VII, discrimination by unions affecting commerce *for or against* anyone on the grounds of race, religion, sex or national origin is explicitly made illegal. (Here it should be parenthetically emphasized that Title VII will also have a significant impact on the largely unorganized white-collar worker; it applies equally to unions and employers.) Title VII is designed to encourage judging on the basis of ability. Professionally developed ability tests, administered in good faith, for example, and explicitly approved. Title VII does not set up any system of reverse discrimination.

Like the bill itself, Title VII, however, is not a panacea; the millennium will not arrive now that it has been passed. The enactment of Title VII cannot with a stroke of the pen end discrimination in our industrial life. One commission in Washington, as the New York *Times* noted editorially, cannot effectively check the admission practices of every local union or employer. The greatest effect of the statute, in all probability, will derive from its mere passage.

Unquestionably, the great majority of union leaders will obey the law. The adoption of the Chicago program may be taken as evidence of their attitude. Unfortunately, however, the declaration leaves a far more significant question unanswered: What will be the feeling of the rank and file? For it will be their feeling that will be decisive. That there is anti-Negro sentiment among even the most enlightened unions is not to be doubted. David McDonald, [former] president of the Steelworkers, for example, is reported to have told the President at a White House dinner of widespread anti-Negro sentiment in his union. . . . The problem facing union leaders everywhere, on the race question, is not unlike that facing America's religious leaders. There is a real gap between professed principle and actual practice. Here creative leadership is surely called for.

While not the final answer—that lies in men's hearts—Title VII nevertheless makes an honest attempt to strike at the vicious circle of poverty and ignorance, which is the crux of discrimination. People cannot be expected to become educated unless they have an opportunity to use their education, and the poor today without education will surely be poor tomorrow. Given effective and sensible administration—and most importantly, reasonable acceptance by the rank and file—Title VII will go about as far as law can go in helping us to realize in our industrial life the ideals of our democratic society. We can only hope, therefore, that union people everywhere will—along with Representative Charles Longstreet Weltner, the courageous Congressman from Georgia who changed his vote on final passage in the House— "accept the verdict of the nation."

U.S. LABOR ABROAD [8]

To thousands of workers in Kenya, the United States is represented not by a "diplomat in striped pants," not by a businessman interested in investments, but by an outgoing former garment worker from New York City. Mrs. Maida Springer, the unofficial diplomat, has been in Africa . . . helping to train Kenyan workers in the skills of making clothing.

Mrs. Springer represents something new in the U.S. labor movement. She is one of a dedicated corps of U.S. unionists who work to "reach the people" through trade union movements in other countries. The variety of their tasks is enormous, ranging from cloak-and-dagger undercover work in countries where unions are restricted by the government, to attending endless chicken-dinner banquets in countries where unions have government approval.

But in most of the emerging countries of Asia, Africa, and Latin America—where the labor movement may also be just emerging—the U.S. labor representative usually performs two basic tasks. One is to provide local unions with the know-how

[8] From "U.S. Labor on the Move." *Senior Scholastic.* 86:11+. Mr. 11, '65. Reprinted by permission from *Senior Scholastic,* © 1965 by Scholastic Magazines, Inc.

of the "developed" labor movement back in the United States. This may include advice on how to organize and form a union, or on collective bargaining techniques. The other task is to be a representative of the United States to people who may never have known an American personally before.

Mrs. Springer went out to Kenya . . . to open a garment training school in the capital city of Nairobi. She was armed with a modest grant of money from the International Ladies' Garment Workers' Union. Her purpose was to train unskilled workers in the art of making clothing so Kenya could develop its own garment industry.

Result: the hum of sewing machines and the smell of steam irons on wool have been brought to Nairobi. So many Kenyans want to learn needlework skills that the school has doubled its facilities in the past two years—and is still faced with a long waiting list of eager applicants.

"The eagerness of these students to learn is something to be seen," Mrs. Springer says. "Some of them spend up to five days on a backcountry bus to get to Nairobi."

The Kenya experiment had the benefit from the beginning of an experienced and friendly local labor movement. That is not always the case in other countries. Sometimes a labor representative must first break through a wall of mistrust and misunderstanding about the United States that has at its center the old leftist stereotype of a top-hatted capitalist oppressing downtrodden workers.

In such cases the United States unionist in shirtsleeves can play a crucial role in helping to change the whole image of the United States. He may be one of the few Americans a foreign worker ever meets. The impression he makes is likely to be lasting.

Once such initial obstacles are hurdled, a U.S. labor "ambassador" can settle down to the job at hand. He may teach classes in unionism, offer advice in contract negotiations, lend money in emergencies, or even help select foreign unionists to visit the United States. But at every turn his job requires tact—the ability to advise, not patronize.

"The best way to describe the job is 'guide but never instruct,' " says Curtis Hogan, a thirty-nine-year-old Denverite assigned to work with foreign oil unions by the U.S. based International Federation of Petroleum Workers.

If there is one area of the world where U.S. unionists have to put their tact to maximum use it is Latin America. Here the local union movement is highly developed. In Mexico alone, there are more than two million union members. But, anti-United States feeling often runs so high in the left-leaning labor movements that it frequently thwarts the help U.S. unions could and do extend.

Yet the picture isn't totally black. One of U.S. labor's proudest accomplishments "south of the border" is a $60 million program of low-cost housing for Latin American workers. The first completed development opened its doors last January in Mexico City. Named the John F. Kennedy Houses, it provides garden apartments at modest rentals to more than three thousand workers and their families.

Why all this concern with foreign labor? One answer is that unionists believe they have an obligation to help one another. But mixed with this idealism is a good measure of self-interest. U.S. labor leaders frankly acknowledge that by helping foreign labor, they *are* helping themselves. They count on the ability of strengthened foreign unions to narrow the gap between overseas and U.S. labor costs. Increased wages for foreign workers (who earn less than U.S. workers) will enable U.S. industries to compete more successfully with foreign products. And the U.S. unions hope their members will share in any resulting benefits.

Comments one United Auto Workers official whose union has helped organize workers in Western Europe, Japan, India, Turkey, and Brazil: "We have achieved a high degree of cooperation in the past few years. . . . Of course we are a far cry from the day when workers all over the world will have the same wages or hours. But we are narrowing the gap."

Another compelling reason for labor's worldwide programs deals more with politics than economics. The workingman throughout the world stands at the center of the "struggle for men's minds" being waged between communism and democracy. The U.S. labor "ambassador" is a natural for countering distorted views of America. He is living and breathing proof that the United States contains many millions of devoted and "unexploited" workers. His message to the foreign worker is simple: "We are all workers. So let's work together." And because he is a worker himself, he often succeeds where other Americans fail.

LABOR'S POLITICAL POWER [4]

The full force of union labor's power and money was turned loose . . . [in 1964] to help Democrats win election to Federal and state offices all over the country.

President Johnson, who has not always received labor support, was backed to the hilt by labor's national and state political organizations.

Strong efforts were devoted to increasing the number of "liberal" Democrats in Congress and state legislatures. In the process, probably more than $2.5 million of worker contributions was spent to achieve these goals.

Even larger sums, it was estimated, were made available from union treasuries to finance "educational" activities, such as registering voters and getting out the vote on Election Day.

Manpower also was provided for the Democratic campaign on a big scale. Thousands of paid union organizers and volunteer members participated.

Some 50 million copies of campaign leaflets were distributed by the AFL-CIO alone, plus 10 million copies of voting records of members of Congress. Many of the leaflets attacked the record and views of Senator Barry Goldwater.

Over all, the political campaign was spearheaded by the AFL-CIO's Committee on Political Education, better known as COPE, but the big international unions and their thousands of locals added financial and organizing aid.

[4] From "What Unions Did to Help the Democrats." *U. S. News & World Report.* 57:102-4. N. 9, '64. Reprinted from *U. S. News & World Report,* published at Washington.

All in all, it was labor's biggest effort yet in a political campaign. . . .

In working for a Congress and state legislatures that will support labor-backed bills, the unions supported a Republican here and there. But in the main the union efforts were in behalf of Democratic candidates.

A nationwide survey by members of the staff of *U. S. News & World Report* disclosed the scope and details of the unions' political undertakings.

The union efforts began . . . with a drive to get workers and their wives registered to vote. The AFL-CIO, nationally, spent about $600,000 of union funds on this registration drive.

Additional local-union funds were spent in the major cities to get members registered. Thousands of volunteers and paid staffers visited homes, phoned members, distributed leaflets at plant gates or mailed "literature" to homes.

Card files were set up by many local unions, listing members' addresses. These served as a master list for checking on registrations and on who voted, or failed to vote, on Election Day.

Unions arranged to provide cars to take people to the polls, and baby-sitters to release mothers to vote.

In New York City, for example, five hundred local unions were asked to assign crews for the registration and vote drive. Twenty-one district offices were set up. Some 5,000 volunteers helped. About 2 million leaflets were distributed.

Similar activity was reported across the nation. In Los Angeles County, California, COPE said more than 3 million pieces of "literature" were passed out.

At some of the 27 offices COPE established in Los Angeles, as many as 500 volunteers worked full time.

Texas unions also went all out to get members to the polls, with about 400 volunteers aiding in the drive.

The effort of Michigan unions, with some 65,000 members, was reported to exceed all such past efforts.

Illinois unions recruited at least 3,500 members for Election Day chores in Chicago alone.

Much of this effort was aimed at electing more "friendly" members to Congress. Much of the work was centered on 90 "marginal" districts where members of the House were chosen by narrow majorities in 1962.

To elect more "friends," COPE asked each of the 13 million members of the AFL-CIO to contribute at least a dollar to its "voluntary" fund. By law, only voluntary contributions by the members can be used directly in Federal campaigns.

A preliminary report filed with Congress showed that COPE had spent $885,497 through October 23 [1964]. That was well above the total the labor group reported for the 1960 campaign—$761,468. . . .

Still, COPE's spending is only a small part of the total labor effort.

In the 1960 presidential campaign, according to *Congressional Quarterly,* 60 labor committees reported expenditures of $2.5 million. . . . [In the 1962 off-year election] when there was no presidential campaign, 33 committees reported expenditures of $2.3 million.

Many of the big AFL-CIO unions again have been raising, outside COPE's effort, their own "voluntary funds for campaign purposes.

The 1962 report showed that the Steelworkers Union spent $186,645; the United Auto Workers, $178,570; the Ladies' Garment Workers, $149,775, and the Machinists, $100,574.

Before the 1964 campaign had ended, preliminary reports showed that several unions had spent more than their 1962 totals. The Steelworkers, for example, reported $226,000 spent in 1964; . . . the Garment Workers $156,000.

Unestimated sums also were spent on state and local elections by individual labor groups. The figures do not cover so-called "educational" expenditures, which Federal law allows to be paid out of union treasuries.

Little of the money went to Republicans, this magazine's survey showed.

In Michigan, James R. Hoffa, president of the Teamsters' Union, endorsed Republican Governor George Romney, while AFL-CIO unions lined up behind Democrats in state and Federal races. Mr. Hoffa also opposed Senator Goldwater, without specifically endorsing President Johnson.

The AFL-CIO backed three New York City Republicans for reelection to the United States House: Seymour Halpern, John V. Lindsay and Paul A. Fino.

Labor split on former Attorney General Robert F. Kennedy's move to unseat Republican Senator Kenneth B. Keating. Mr. Kennedy was endorsed by New York State COPE, but some fifty AFL-CIO locals and most rail unions supported Mr. Keating.

Mr. Hoffa and the state Teamsters' council also supported Senator Keating, while New York City Teamsters endorsed Mr. Kennedy. . . .

Altogether, COPE endorsed 31 Democratic candidates for the U.S. Senate, and no Republicans.

VI.   THE OUTLOOK FOR LABOR

EDITOR'S INTRODUCTION

Thirty years after the National Labor Relations Act (the Wagner Act), where does the trade union movement stand today in American society? This section offers a variety of views, some friendly, some critical. They reach no common conclusion, but offer food for thought for the student of unionism. If there is one inference to be drawn from the opinions expressed in this section, it is that the labor movement requires imagination, inventiveness, and determination if it is to continue to be a major force in American society.

The first selection, an outline of its own goals by the AFL-CIO, is followed by constructive criticism from the Committee for Economic Development.

Professor Benjamin M. Selekman takes an unusual approach to labor's conservatism. J. H. Foegen outlines the pros and cons of union membership in an article which should be of particular interest to readers who are faced with the decision of joining or staying out of a union.

Herbert Harris and the editor of this volume suggest that there are, indeed, unfinished tasks for labor unions in their underlying philosophy and objectives. Finally, Professor Philip Taft, one of the nation's most widely respected labor historians, finds little cause for alarm in labor's present status. From all this the reader, it is hoped, will draw his own conclusions.

THE LABOR MOVEMENT'S GOALS [1]

The labor movement's basic purpose is to achieve a better life for its members. A union that fails in this purpose has failed utterly. This is as true . . . [today] as it was in 1792, when the

[1] From "What the Unions Really Want," an article in *The Hands That Build America*, special supplement to the New York *Times*. Sec. XI, p 3. N. 17, '63. Reprinted by permission.

nation's first local union set up for collective bargaining was formed by the Philadelphia shoemakers.

But the scope of this basic purpose, and the avenues for achieving it, are vastly different today. Unions are no longer scattered and beleaguered little bands, struggling for survival and subsistence wages against the combined hostility of employers and the courts. Nor, as was the case as recently as a quarter-century ago, is the battle for bargaining rights and for basic contract terms so desperate as to be all-consuming. Labor's goals have broadened, and so, therefore, has its approach to them.

Today's union member is keenly aware that he and his union cannot make progress at the expense of the community, or even when the rest of the community is standing still. "What's good for America is good for the AFL-CIO" is not just an expression of labor's patriotism. Rather it is a statement of the practical realities.

This realization was not born with the AFL-CIO merger. It had been the prevailing attitude of both AFL and CIO, and of nearly all their affiliated unions for the previous decade.

Today the overwhelming preponderance of AFL-CIO policy statements—the expression of labor's objectives—have to do with the general good, in which union members will share only as a part of the American people as a whole. And a like proportion of the AFL-CIO's legislative and political efforts are devoted to those causes.

On some matters, such as international affairs, the broad view has a far longer history. To cite only a few examples:

As early as 1896 the AFL convention adopted a resolution, submitted by Samuel Gompers and ten others, expressing "hearty sympathy . . . to the men of Cuba" and calling upon the United States to "recognize the belligerent rights of the Cuban revolutionists."

In 1914, directly after the start of the war in Europe, a Gompers resolution authorized the AFL Executive Council to call an international trade union conference at the same time and place as the "general Peace Congress which will no doubt be held at the end of the war." This was done and from it emerged the International Labor Organization, the sole League of Nations agency which still survives as part of the United Nations.

Some twenty years later, even while engrossed in the great organizing drives of the period, the AFL (and shortly thereafter, the CIO as well) worked diligently to assist the refugees from Nazi terror. As the war ended, AFL and CIO experts followed close on the heels of the armed forces to locate the surviving trade union-ists—most of them in concentration camps—and help rebuild free labor movements from their shattered remnants. Except for the Marshall Plan itself, no other single activity was more important in averting a Communist takeover from Norway to Italy.

Merger has unified and strengthened the labor movement's role in helping to create free societies throughout the world. Yet these overseas programs, which claim nearly 25 per cent of the AFL-CIO's income, bring no direct return to union members, but in-directly benefit workers here and everywhere by advancing the cause of human liberty.

Perhaps the closest parallel on the domestic scene has been the continuing effort first to adopt and then to improve and broaden the Fair Labor Standards Act, which sets minimum wages and maximum hours for workers covered by its terms. To the unin-formed this might seem to be a self-serving endeavor by an orga-nization of workers. On the contrary, only a tiny fraction of the 13.5 million members of AFL-CIO unions are at or even near the legal wage floor, now $1.25 an hour.

Labor fights for a higher minimum wage, and for the inclusion of all wage-earners under its protection, for two fundamental rea-sons. The first is compassion; no American should do honest toil for wages too low to provide subsistence. The second is social and economic; if large numbers of American workers, although em-ployed, earn less than subsistence wages, their buying-power is in-adequate and the nation suffers in many ways. Neither reason involves a direct return to unions or union members.

Civil rights presents another parallel. In some parts of the country a union might gain a distinct organizing and bargaining advantage by following a "white only" policy in a biased com-munity. Admittedly, in earlier years a few union leaders succumbed to the temptation. Considering the way in which employers have used racial issues to fight unions, the wonder is that the great majority resisted. Today, the public interest, the cause of social justice, is prevailing locally as it has long prevailed nationally in the labor movement.

And over all this time, even when local shortcomings were more frequent, AFL and CIO leaders constantly pressed Congress for civil rights legislation—in particular, a fair employment practices law that would apply equally to unions and employers. Meanwhile at the collective bargaining table, unions called upon employers to write equal opportunity clauses into negotiated contracts. Here again, the issue was—and is—citizenship, not selfish gain. The AFL-CIO proudly stands in the forefront of the struggle for equal rights on every front.

Public education has been a primary concern of unions from the days of the Philadelphia shoemakers, cited earlier. But at the turn of the nineteenth century, wage earners wanted free public schools because they offered the only chance for the "children of the poor"—their own children—to learn to read and write. That first aim was long ago achieved, yet labor's fight for better education is waged as vigorously as ever.

The AFL-CIO is still concerned with the "children of the poor." Although relatively few sons and daughters of union members can be so described, there are still too many "children of the poor" in America. The AFL-CIO wants better schools for these children and for all children. It wants full educational opportunities for all—opportunities with no ceiling except the ability of the student. The AFL-CIO wants a broader educational system, too, covering those of all aptitudes, so that every youngster has a full and fair chance to prepare himself for the years ahead.

Social security—the whole area of public responsibility toward the aged, the disabled, the unemployed—is another instance. True, most of the sufferers were once wage earners and many were and are union members. But thanks to their union contracts, union members have protection against disaster, ranging from pensions to extra jobless benefits, not available to others. Even so, the AFL-

CIO has fought successfully for broad improvements in the safeguards covering all citizens, union or nonunion, rich or poor.

The point is this:

The labor movement for many years past, AFL and CIO alike, before and since merger, has by inclination and by circumstance become in fact the "people's lobby"—not a special pleader for 13.5 million Americans, but rather a voice for the 80 or 100 million who have no other, and beyond that, a voice for the advancement of America and of democracy everywhere.

The AFL-CIO claims no credit and seeks no kudos for filling that role. It is rather a matter of enlightened self-interest, undertaken in the certain knowledge that the well-being of union members depends upon the well-being of America and the survival of freedom in the world.

UNIONISM AND NATIONAL POLICY[2]

Unionism affects the national interest in many ways. It affects the economic performance of the nation—the rate of economic growth, the level of employment and unemployment, the stability of prices, and the distribution of income. It also has a fundamental influence upon the character of our society—on the freedom that individuals enjoy, on the equity of the relations among individuals and among groups, and on the role of government in relation to private institutions and individuals. There are wide differences among unions in their powers, structures, and policies; to generalize about American unions, therefore, is dangerous. Nevertheless, consideration of public policy toward organizations of labor must rest upon a judgment of the influences that unionism now exerts.

1. A basic characteristic of the American society is that we do not like to see people pushed around. As one aspect of this, we do not want workers to be subjected to arbitrary and indifferent treatment by employers with no defense except the threat to quit, a threat too costly to carry out in most cases. Unions have played a

[2] From *Union Powers and Union Functions: Toward a Better Balance*, by the Research and Policy Committee of the Committee for Economic Development. 711 Fifth Ave. New York 10022. '64. p 12-19. Reprinted by permission.

large part directly and indirectly in making and applying equitable rules governing on-the-job relationships.

To perform this function unions required a certain degree of power. Workers needed enough power relative to their employer to induce him, if necessary, to change his personal practices. The value to the employees of many of the changes made was often overlooked by the employer. To bring about these changes, however, did not require unions to have the power that many of them now have. It did not require a union to have sufficient power in relation to the whole industry to impose large cost increases on the industry and its customers.

2. That groups of people should organize to present their desires to the government and to work for adoption of government policies they favor is both legitimate and necessary in a democracy. For many interests of many workers this function is performed by labor unions.

It is not necessary that the political interests of workers should be represented by organizations—i.e. labor unions—that also represent workers in collective bargaining. The other sectors of the economy, such as business and agriculture, are represented in the political process by associations that do not exercise collective bargaining power. In many other countries labor is politically represented by organizations which, while closely allied to unions, do not perform the economic functions of unions. The political representation of American labor by unions rather than by purely political organizations has disadvantages, including its tendency to give excessive weight to the interests of organized labor as compared with the interests of the large majority of American workers who are not union members. However, the system also has some advantages. It probably tends to focus attention of American labor on collective bargaining rather than on the effort to invoke the power of government to change conditions best left to private decision-making.

3. The freedom of individuals to associate with each other, for almost any purpose, is one of the basic American freedoms. We value this freedom for its own sake and as a bulwark of other freedoms. The freedom of workers to associate in labor unions is, in

general, guaranteed by present law and the union movement is an effective vehicle for the exercise of this freedom. Nevertheless there are troublesome exceptions to this general principle. For the individual worker the significant freedom may not be the right to join or form "a" union but to join the particular union that is legally designated to represent him or that controls access to the employment which he seeks. Many unions are able to deny this right to workers seeking membership or employment, and some have done so, in order to limit the supply of their particular variety of labor skill, in order to discriminate against certain groups, or for other reasons.

Private association is a freedom, and private associations are legally protected because they are an expression of the voluntary choice of individuals. The freedom not to join a private association is equally precious and deserving of protection. This principle has substantial recognition in labor law. Nevertheless, in the . . . [thirty-one] states where this is legal, unions have been able to use their power to obtain contracts requiring that all employees covered by the contract become union members. Employment may thus be denied to an individual if he does not join the union. [See "Right-to-Work Background," in Section IV, above.]

4. A major accomplishment of American labor policy is the degree to which it has kept government out of the determination of specific employment conditions. Government has undertaken to assure the ability of the private parties, singly or collectively, to deal with each other freely and without interference. The underlying philosophy has been that the government should not otherwise influence the decisions that are reached, and that the public interest in these decisions will be best served if they are made by the private parties directly involved. This philosophy in turn rests upon the belief that the power of both parties to collective bargaining will be limited by competitive forces which prevent their using their powers to the detriment of the wider public.

Nevertheless this principle has not been followed with complete consistency. There seems to be danger of increasing government intervention to affect the consequences of collective bargaining. This results in part from failure to draw a sharp line between government's proper role in assuring that collective bargaining can go on and government's interference with the substance of bargaining. But the danger results more seriously from the hard choice that arises if either or both of the private parties has excessive power, so that their freely-reached agreements cannot be assumed to serve the public interest.

5. Probably the most visible consequence of unionism to many Americans is the occasional dramatic nationwide or citywide strike of a critical industry. Strikes have been a source of inconvenience to almost everyone at some time and of hardship to many, and some firms have been forced out of business by them. But in relation to the size of the American economy, losses from strikes have been comparatively small.

6. The stronger unions have been able to raise the incomes of their employed members, absolutely and relative to the incomes of other workers. In doing so they have been able to increase the percentage share of the nation's output received by their employed members and thus to reduce the percentage share received by the rest of the population. We do not believe that it is in the general interest for any group to have as much power as some unions do to force a redistribution of income in their favor by collectively withholding their productive services or threatening to do so.

To raise the incomes of their members is, of course, one of the main objectives of unions. There is no reason to doubt that where unions are very strong, covering a whole industry or craft and substantially free of competition, they have succeeded in this objective.

The conclusion that strong unions have been able to gain for their employed members a larger share of the nation's output and thereby reduce the share received by other workers is not always obvious. For example, it might seem that all workers gain when strong unions gain because the winning of a wage increase by one of the stronger unions usually causes an increase in wages paid to other workers in the same company or in the same area. However, this is only one of the forces set in motion when one of the stronger unions wins a big wage increase. The big rise in wages or other labor costs won by a strong union for its members tends to limit employment in the industry covered by the union by raising its costs and forcing it to raise its prices if it can. The rise in prices restricts sales and the rise in labor costs intensifies the effort by that industry to save labor. Workers who might have been employed in the industry will have to seek work elsewhere and this will both retard wage increases elsewhere and probably leave some workers unemployed.

At the same time, the spreading effect of the big wage increase won by the stronger union will force up prices not only in the industry which it covers but also in other industries which are more or less forced to follow with wage increases. These higher prices will be paid by all workers, as consumers, and this will offset a large part of the gain in money income received by other workers and especially those whose wage increases were smallest.

This whole process is superimposed on the rise of real wage rates as real output per worker rises, which has been going on for a long time in the American economy—long before labor unions were important. As a result the wages of all workers rise, despite the increase in the share taken by employed members of the strong unions. The effect of the activity of strong unions has been to get their members a larger share, and to leave other people a smaller share, of the income gains resulting from the general increase in output per worker.

7. The preceding discussion has related to the effects of union activity on the distribution of the *real* national income. That discussion did not deal with the effects of union activity on the average level of prices.

It seems probable that union power contributes to a tendency for money wage rates and fringe benefit costs in general to rise more rapidly than productivity with the result that production costs on the average rise. In this situation the country would have a difficult choice between inflation and excessive unemployment, the most probable outcome being some of each. Fear of this possibility has led to increased government concern with the results of the collective bargaining process and increased government intervention in that process. . . .

We offer the following recommendations:

1. Every worker should have the right to decide freely to belong or not to belong to a union.

2. Racial or other discriminatory barriers to union membership, apprenticeship or employment should be eliminated. The equal right of all qualified workers to join the union in their trade or industry should be recognized by law. The right of any worker to belong to the union that represents him should not be denied except for nonpayment of dues or similar good cause.

3. United States courts should be authorized to issue a restraining order or injunction against unions in cases involving strikes in violation of a labor agreement, as they are now authorized to compel an employer to accept arbitration of disputes arising under agreements.

4. The right of employers, singly or collectively, to use the lockout in the bargaining process should not be diluted by the National Labor Relations Board (NLRB) or the courts. This right should be clarified in the law if necessary to avoid dilution. The employer's right to use the lockout is the counterpart of the union's right to strike.

5. There is need for legislation in most states aimed at limiting the use of union resources for political purposes.

6. The intent of Congress to outlaw pressure by a union against a party with whom it has no dispute (secondary boycott) should be carried out, and the law should be clarified if reasonable interpretation of the present language proves incapable of preventing evasions.

7. Laws against violence and the threat of violence, which tend to coerce through fear, should be respected and enforced in labor disputes, by Federal, state, and local authorities.

8. The present provisions in the Taft-Hartley Act for government action in national emergency disputes should be retained. The recent tendency toward increasing government intervention in the settlement of labor disputes, through "fact-finding" or the participation of high public officials or otherwise, except through mediation, should be halted.

9. Determination of the form and content of collective bargaining should be left to the parties. The present legal requirement to bargain "in good faith" should not be left as a vague demand for good conduct that will lead and has in fact led to uncertainty, confusion, excessive government intervention, and a morass of bureaucratic legislation—all detrimental to free collective bargaining.

The effect of this provision of law has been not to assure bargaining in good faith but to involve the NLRB in determining both how bargaining should be conducted and the substance of the bargain. In lieu of this provision, if there are any actions by either party that should be required or prohibited they should be specified in law. Deletion of the present legal requirement would not allow either party to escape bargaining, because bargaining results from the economic necessity of the parties to reach an agreement in order to continue production and employment.

10. Unfair labor practice cases should be handled in a more judicial way. The NLRB, which now handles them, should be given more of the attributes of a court, or jurisdiction over such cases should be transferred to a court especially designated for them.

LABOR'S BASIC CONSERVATISM[3]

Just as business is inherently characterized by constant change, so labor is characterized by a built-in, natural conservatism. It takes time for the laborer to acquire a skill and to establish roots. He is bound by ties of family, friends, and neighborhood, and by working companions in his shop or office. Moreover, to live normally the laborer needs certainty and predictability in his life. Thus, except for major crises of famine, war, and revolution, labor is never as mobile as capital, plants, or machinery. The man on the job has always mistrusted a rapid rate of change—long before unions were organized.

[3] From "Conservative Labor/Radical Business," by Benjamin M. Selekman, Kirstein Professor of Labor Relations Emeritus, Harvard Business School. *Harvard Business Review*. 40:80-90. Mr.-Ap. '62. Reprinted by permission.

This basic conservatism of the average man is obscured by trade union tactics. Indeed, to the everyday observer it looks as if these organizations are radical, if not revolutionary. The reason is that:

They agitate and organize workers to protest against working conditions.

They demand a voice in determining these conditions.

And, if refused, they resort to using the ultimate form of economic power, the strike—closing down a plant and throwing a picket line around it.

In certain circumstances a union may even resort to raw power, that is, to violence on the picket line. The recurrent demands and counter-demands involved in negotiating union contracts—particularly in basic industries like steel, automobiles and shipping—almost always make newspaper headlines. Then union leaders deliver militant speeches over radio and television, with the threat of a strike menacing from the background. Negotiations to renew steel contracts, for example, have with few exceptions ended up with nationwide strikes.

Intervention by government officials, and the White House in particular, adds to the atmosphere of emergency in labor relations. Strikes are newsworthy, but the peaceful negotiations, which far outnumber the militant ones, receive scant attention. Thus, a climate of recurring crisis seems to permeate the nation. Because unions initiate labor's demands and declare the strikes, thus disrupting the peace, it is natural that they should be regarded as radical. "When will all this end?" is the usual, impatient query. . . .

If [however] we stop to realize that the original labor "agitators" only sought to change the sunrise-to-sunset working day to twelve hours, then to ten hours, and finally to eight hours, we can sense the moderation of their proposals. In fact, as late as the 1880's, the great reform sought was the eight-hour day, and this was not realized before the twentieth century. Similarly with wages: throughout the nineteenth and well into the early twentieth century, agitation was directed toward a living—actually a subsistence—wage. Later, the concepts of health and decency were added. It was not until the 1940's that a rising standard of living was also accepted as a desirable criterion for wage determination.

Again, it took over a century for states to establish rigorous safety standards for workers and to provide indemnity against accidents to life and limb. New York State passed the first workmen's compensation law in 1910, but it was declared invalid. It remained for Wisconsin to put the first law into actual operation in 1911. For the first time in history, responsibility was placed on management to indemnify, through insured funds, those injured or the survivors of those killed. Prior to this legislation, the burden rested upon the employee to prove that he and/or his fellow workers were not guilty of contributory negligence.

Also, Social Security was not realized until recently. Legislation to provide payments to the aged and unemployed was not enacted in most European countries until the early years of the twentieth century and in this country not until the 1930's.

Surely, the label "revolutionary" or "radical" does not fit labor leaders and reformers. Nevertheless, over the years they were so indicted. These measures were seen by businessmen as a threat to their freedom to introduce technical innovation and to reduce costs, and, generally as an intrusion of outsiders in their affairs. Moreover, government intervention was generally frowned on by businessmen. And on the whole these attitudes were shared by the majority of the middle class. To the latter, the occasional minister, teacher, or politician who became a reformer was considered an "agitator" who was "betraying" his class.

These attitudes should not seem surprising to us today. The technological revolution itself was, in a fundamental sense, like a glacier, much of it invisible, that moved relentlessly forward, transforming the face of industry and the community. But it did not make news. In contrast, agitation for shorter hours, for a living wage, for safety and protective devices, and for collective bargaining did make headlines, especially when agitation was reinforced by mass meetings and strikes. And, when the single taxers, the socialists, or occasionally even the anarchists, associated themselves with labor, especially when riots and violence ensued—for instance, the Homestead steel strike, the Pullman railway strikes, and the Haymarket riots—the epithets "radical" and "dangerous" naturally became associated with the labor movement.

However, it was labor's demand for union recognition and for collective bargaining that aroused the greatest opposition from business. Trade union organizers were adjudged trespassers and not infrequently jailed or expelled physically from industrial communities. Indeed, it was not until early in the twentieth century that unions were accorded full recognition in Britain as legitimate institutions. In the United States, while occasional laws and court decisions gave some recognition to the role of unions, it took the Wagner Act, passed in 1935 and finally upheld as constitutional in 1937, to endow unions with full legal sanction.

Since the 1930's collective bargaining has developed rapidly as the administrative instrument whereby labor and management could negotiate their respective rights and obligations within the new technological framework. Thus, a social mechanism was provided which, together with legislation, compensated the laborer socially for the intrinsic, dynamic nature of management to innovate through science, technology, and organizational methods. To be sure, neither legislation nor collective bargaining has proved to be the perfect answer to the problem of reconciling constant change with human needs. Both corporations and unions are now under constant surveillance by the government against possible abuses of the immense power granted them; and in recent years laws have been enacted which regulate unions just as a generation earlier regulatory laws were imposed on corporations.

But all this is historical. What about contemporary labor institutions and their leaders? How conservative are they *really*?

Today, readers who have reached middle age only have to recall a chapter from their own times to illustrate the conservative trend of labor. When the CIO sprang up during the depression years of the 1930's, with its tactics of mass picketing and sit-down strikes, it looked to many—in and out of industry—like a dangerous, radical movement.

But a quarter of a century later traditional collective bargaining over wages, working conditions, and social benefits has become the rule, almost without exception, in automobiles, rubber, coal, steel, and other industries which are relatively new to unionism. The number of serious strikes, moreover, has diminished dramatically in recent years. Even in steel, where both parties have thus far been unable to conclude their negotiations most of the time without a showdown, strikes have been conducted relatively peacefully, in sharp contrast to the violence of the Little Steel strike of 1937.

Indeed, considering the conservative drift of the CIO, its merger with the AFL in 1955 was to be expected. Neither the CIO nor the AFL wanted to change fundamentally the nature of American industry and its management. Instead, these groups both sought to pool their strength to eliminate wasteful jurisdictional competition and to obtain the traditional bread-and-butter gains in terms of wages and working conditions which have been close to the hearts of American wage earners since the days of Samuel Gompers. The only fundamental difference in the leadership over time has been the espousal since the 1930's of social legislation for men as well as for women and children.

The radicalism entertained by some of the early leaders of the CIO found very little support as the movement grew in numbers and influence. In fact, Communist sympathizers who joined the organizing drives during the 1930's, and gained leadership in some unions, were actually expelled in 1949. Thus, the merged AFL-CIO constitutes one of the major bulwarks against infiltration by the major revolutionary (or reactionary) force still in existence—worldwide communism.

Nor has the labor movement presented a radical threat on the political front. To be sure, both the CIO and the AFL threw their weight behind Roosevelt and Truman and, no doubt, played a major role in their election. But in 1946 the late Senator Taft was able to win a senatorial seat from Ohio for the second time, on a strictly conservative platform which presaged the Taft-Hartley Act, despite a massive attempt by the unions to rally the labor vote against him. . . .

A brief sketch of two labor leaders who are prominent in the public eye—John L. Lewis and Walter P. Reuther—highlights the essentially conservative character of labor.

Lewis would doubtless be considered the most militant labor leader of our times. For forty years the president of the United Mine Workers, Lewis was also the architect and leader of the CIO in its most aggressive period—from its founding in 1935 until 1942 when he broke with his colleagues in the CIO, and with Roosevelt. Yet his militancy was not directed toward a revolutionary political goal envisaged by labor. In fact, he has been a lifelong Republican, with the exception of the first two terms of Roosevelt.

Lewis fought mainly to establish collective bargaining in coal as well as in other heavy industries. He succeeded, by dint of many strikes and frequent violence, in winning for bituminous coal industrywide bargaining, the highest wages, the best working conditions, and a welfare fund for the retired, sick, and injured.

But his fundamental conservatism came to the surface when he faced up to the technical and economic implications of his victories. So that bituminous coal could meet the costs of labor and capital improvements, and still survive in competition with oil and gas, Lewis became an ardent advocate of mechanizing production, even though this meant that his union's membership was to be reduced to a fraction of what it had been at its peak. Indeed, the operators of the mines, once his implacable adversaries, now consider him a statesman who made a major contribution toward saving their industry.

And what about [Auto Workers' President] Reuther? Of all contemporary labor leaders, he would be considered the most radical. But he too espouses no revolutionary doctrine like nationalization of the auto industry. Whatever his youthful socialist leanings may have been, Reuther has long since abandoned the Utopian dream that collective ownership means any fundamental change in human welfare. Actually, such a step transfers control to a centralized bureaucracy, a situation which he saw all too clearly as undesirable during his year in Russia.

Nevertheless, Reuther might be considered radical in the same sense as the modern manager—that is, as an innovator. He would like to make collective bargaining an adequate mechanism for the scientific age—to stimulate full employment, raise standards of living, lower consumer costs, and nourish the economic and social vitality of the nation—so that we can successfully meet the challenge of Soviet communism for world domination.

In pressing to convert collective bargaining into such an instrument, he frightens management by seeming to invade its function. His proposals—an opportunity to examine books on wages, costs, profits, and prices, to share bonuses and profits with employees and customers, and to put everyone on a salary basis—are in a sense unorthodox. Reuther has no doubt been aggressive in pushing for benefits which will increasingly make labor a fixed cost of business enterprise. Thus, he was the first labor leader to obtain a $100 a month pension (including Social Security payments) in heavy industry in an agreement concluded with the Ford Motor Company in 1949. Again, in 1955, he obtained supplementary unemployment benefits to bring inadequate state unemployment compensation to a decent level—60 per cent to 65 per cent of take-home pay for a qualified worker. But as a practical matter of finance, he agreed to limit total company liability for this purpose to 5 per cent of the payroll. . . .

Surely this conception of collective bargaining does not justify labeling Reuther as a radical in the political sense. If we are to keep our economic and social life in some sort of equilibrium, we must find ways of maintaining social progress at a rate which is somewhat apace with technological advance. Perhaps, Reuther may still prove to be one of the real conservatives of our times, if he, together with management in the automobile industry, succeeds in formulating a workable mechanism for avoiding the pitfalls that have so far beset our undoubted success. It is his duty as a labor leader to keep trying—to keep articulating the human aspect of material progress.

Significantly, neither legislative nor administrative policies have changed the characteristic role of management and labor. And they have not halted the continuity of what one can now see as historical evolution. Recent years have witnessed, at one and the same time, the explosive growth of science and technology, the rapid development of management as a profession, and the emergence of the strongest labor movement in our history. . . .

Faced with . . . [the] drastic changes [introduced by automation], it is not unnatural for workers to be disturbed, for their unions to continue to agitate for specific protective measures both by industry and by government. But are they likely to urge *revolutionary* measures or the *reformist* type consistent with historical tradition?

Can management, together with labor and government, find ways to nourish reformist measures? Or will the ongoing scientific explosion not only aggravate blue-collar restlessness but at the same time also create a new redundant white-collar "proletariat"?

In particular, will computers spawn a new type of alienated man—a declassed white-collar member of an executive staff who is no longer needed to fulfill a task which he had always regarded as so important that it fed his self-esteem? If so, will he remain conservative? Or will he turn to demagogues who can articulate *his* expropriation?

WHY JOIN A UNION? [4]

Union membership is a subject well able to rile the emotions. For many people, there is no objective view possible, no middle ground; you're either for unions or "agin 'em" and that's that. . . .

Different approaches to this question of whether union membership is a gain or a loss can of course be taken. . . . What are the pros and cons of such membership? . . .

One of the major issues is that of wage gain versus dues loss. Strictly speaking, workers often view their dues payments as the purchase price of some service, a service not entirely dissimilar from that bought from lawyers, doctors, and even barbers. Naturally, they want to know if they are getting their money's worth. While many old-time unionists looked at unionism as something close to a crusade, their present-day kin are more likely to think of it in terms of a dollars-and-cents proposition.

[4] From "Union Membership: Gain or Loss?" by J. H. Foegen, associate professor of business, Winona (Minnesota) State College. *Personnel Administration.* 26:30-5. Ja.-F. '63. Reprinted by permission.

This viewpoint can be seen clearly in the experience of unions in past depressions, when membership figures had a tendency to fall. When no wage and benefit gains were immediately forthcoming, and especially when dues money was more urgently needed to put bread on the table, union membership was often seen as a "luxury" that could for the moment be ill-afforded. Even if a worker continued to pay his dues during recessions, there was little likelihood that he would realize any wage gain therefrom.

Another aspect of this issue can be seen in the controversy that is commonly aroused whenever a dues increase is proposed. Together with the contract-renewal situation, this is one of the two times when attendance at union meetings is not a problem. A dues increase is often a major political issue in a union's internal affairs, and is often strongly opposed. It is not clear just how close a relationship exists between a dues increase and accelerated wage and benefit gains, and many workers do not see any long-run benefits that might be forthcoming. The dues increase is seen simply as an increased out-of-pocket expenditure. Nevertheless, in some way, perhaps unconsciously or intuitively, the wage gain versus dues loss issue is of concern to anyone thinking of joining or being urged to join a union.

A second major issue is the risk of potential involvement in strikes that is taken by joining a union. In other words, the issue is the possible loss of wages suffered during a strike versus the gain in wages resulting from a strike that is successfully pursued. This is both similar to, and different from, the first issue considered. While both situations involve the question of financial gain or loss, the previous issue considered the normal, nonstrike situation, while here the abnormal one of a strike is being discussed.

If a worker is called out on strike, he is obviously going to lose the wages he would have earned had he worked. However, if as a result of striking, the union gets a wage increase, and especially if it wins an increase larger than what it would have gotten without striking, then the worker gets that much more for each hour worked, once he returns to the job.

Some workers, and many people generally, however, think that strikes are economically foolish. That is, how long will it take to make up the increase? For example, if a worker were making $3.00 per hour before the strike, and if he were working a regular, eight-hour day, he would gross $24 per day. If as a result of a strike his wages would go up by 10 cents per hour, for every day he was on strike he would have to work 30 days at the extra 10 cents per hour to make up the wages lost while on strike. To some people, this just doesn't make sense. [On the other hand, unions point out that a successful strike at *one* location may gain identical benefits at many other locations without a strike.—Ed.] The other alternative, of course, is not to go on strike, and to accept whatever the employer offers. This is often not too agreeable either.

In addition to lost wages, a strike can also involve extra assessments while working in order to build up a strike fund. This, it is readily seen, is closely related to the dues question, since both dues and assessments mean money out-of-the-pocket for the worker. Of course, if a strike *should* result sometime in the future, the worker would presumably benefit. If the strike fund is built up only by and for the use of the local union in the plant wherein the worker-contributor works, then he will be relatively certain that he will ultimately benefit from it. Because many locals are small, however, and because greater over-all efficiency in the handling and use of money is realized that way, strike funds are usually controlled and administered centrally by the international union. This could mean that, even though a given employee paid into a strike fund, if his local didn't go on strike, his money might be used to support his fellow-unionists in other plants who did. While this might be for the over-all good of the union, it is open to question how many workers would see it this way. The whole problem of assessments and benefits is a part of the larger one facing potential union members: strike losses versus possible wage gains.

A third major question is that of financial and job security versus psychological insecurity. On the one hand, a worker who joins a union is protected from being summarily dismissed, from having his pay reduced for no good reason, and from being shunted without cause to a lower-paid or more distasteful job. He is protected in his job by rather rigid procedural systems, bargained from the employer for his benefit. Most important of these are the seniority system and the grievance procedure. Under these two, he has respectively the assurance that his years of service mean something, and that if he has a legitimate complaint, over working conditions for example, he will get a proper hearing.

On the other hand though, by joining the union the worker appropriates to himself the psychological insecurity of never knowing when there will be a strike. Just when he thinks he has a little "nest-egg" built up, it can be rather quickly dissipated. Furthermore, the struggle between union and management for the employee's loyalty must also be faced. While this may be practically absent in a few happy situations, or as in many cases, undertaken rather subtly and using the "soft-sell," nevertheless it is always present to some degree, and the tensions and conflict engendered thereby often do not encourage a wholesome atmosphere in the work place. Admittedly, some . . . will be less sensitive to this than others, but its presence cannot be denied.

It can be argued also that the financial and job security resulting from joining a union contributes to the psychological security of the worker as well, and that that *security* overbalances the *insecurity* derived from joining the union. . . .

While it is not necessary that individuality be submerged by joining a union, the history of unionism has always stressed the need for and effectiveness of group effort. Present-day practices, too, such as production restrictions and across-the-board wage increases, tend to stress equality and standardization at the expense of the individual. So the relative degrees of individuality or conformity in a person's make-up will here be a factor in his deciding for or against union membership.

Finally, although it is more of an institutional factor than anything the individual can do much about, mention might just be made of the power factor again. To the extent that workers join unions, and to the extent that unions actively encourage their joining, the union grows more powerful. Power is based on the number of members, their votes, and their dues. As a union gains more members, and gains more power politically, it increasingly runs the risk—as shown by the circumstances surrounding passage of the Taft-Hartley and Landrum-Griffin Laws —of becoming the focus of restrictive legislation. Simply by becoming larger, the union is calling attention to its power. And while this might be good for the union leader's ego, it is not necessarily good for the union or for its members. . . .

For the individual employee, the question "Union Membership: Gain or Loss?" is much like that of whether or not to get married. Elements of security and the lack of it can be found in each situation; there is assumed to be a long-run gain obtained from "membership" versus a current "dues loss"; it is possible that by "joining" marital status, a worker may place himself under more control by his "union" than before; marriage can entail a sense of support and belonging as well as a potential loss of individuality. Each question is no less subjective than the other; each is almost equally vital.

WHY LABOR LOST THE INTELLECTUALS [5]

The American labor movement is sleepwalking along the corridors of history. At every step it is failing to adapt effectively to the innovations which science and technology daily impose upon our ways of work. Lacking boldness in social invention, it clings on the whole to precepts which run the gamut from static to archaic.

Typical are its responses to automation. Labor spokesmen keep pressing for the shorter work week. But this dubious palliative tends to raise labor costs and thus makes the new robotism more attractive than ever to management. Then to console the displaced worker who can rarely find anything else to do, union negotiators concentrate on larger lump sums in severance pay. This emphasis, in effect, turns the labor movement into a mortician preoccupied with arrangements for his own funeral.

[5] From an article by Herbert Harris, author, journalist, and editor. *Harper's Magazine.* 228:79-80+. Je. '64. Copyright © 1964, by Harper's Magazine, Inc. Reprinted by permission of the author.

In no small degree this state of affairs derives from the fact that the labor movement has been losing its minds. Ever since World War II, it has been estranging the people who produce, distribute, and conspicuously consume ideas. Intellectuals have been increasingly disengaged as labor activists and disenchanted as sympathizers. Many of them no longer regard the labor movement as protector of the underdog, pioneer of social advance, keeper of the egalitarian conscience. Merely to ask whether the labor movement has "failed" the intellectuals, or the other way round, is to start a donnybrook at any national union headquarters or university conference on industrial relations. The point may be moot and is still obscured by feelings of mutual guilt.

But there is no doubt that the cleavage between labor and the intellectuals accounts, more than anything else, for the present crisis in the labor movement, the erosion of its vitality and its membership rolls, and its prickly defensiveness toward even the friendliest critics. . . .

Conservative intellectuals, of course, have always been hostile toward the labor movement. During the entire nineteenth century they scolded it for getting born and trying to stay alive. And they have since kept whacking it for its refusal to comply with their misinterpretations of Adam Smith. But their animosity has been less important than the aid and amity of liberal and/or radical intellectuals. They have traditionally helped the labor movement to define and articulate its aspirations. They have also—at various times—explained, needled, split, glorified, and white-washed it. Their number has included middle-class and patrician reformers as well as self-taught workingmen. . . .

It was not until the 1940's that the mystique of the worker began to evaporate. The intellectuals discovered by means of personal contact that he was pretty much like everybody else; that, indeed, the son of toil they had romanticized at a distance could be anti-Catholic, anti-Semitic, a white supremacist, a rancorous xenophobe; that his favorite reading was the sports page, comic books, and detective magazines, and that this diet did not endow him with a profound grasp of national and international issues.

They discovered also that the CIO and AFL (they did not merge until 1955) were concentrating on business or market unionism, intent on taking care of their own, and downgrading social or national-interest unionism.

Critical reports and articles began to appear as labor's intellectual friends found, for example, that union "democracy" was not always of the New England town-meeting variety and that the corruptions of commercialism were infecting unions. [For other views of the "new democracy," see "Rising Membership Independence," in section II, above.] Perhaps they were naïve. But above all, these intellectuals did not want the labor movement to become merely the mirror of a society in which everybody sells out to everybody else. Workers, they believed, should use some of their new ease and leisure to pursue things of the mind and spirit. . . .

Why has the latter-day labor movement been largely impervious to the critiques and recommendations of intellectuals? The answer lies in the character of the typical labor leader, his background, his style, the way he sees his job. He is a blend of political boss, evangelist, military chieftain, and salesman. Above all, he is a self-made man. He is the Siamese twin of the versatile entrepreneur who has built the business from scratch, is reluctant to delegate authority, and yearns for the old days when he could call everybody in the shop by his first name. Moreover, the labor leader has had to claw his way up in a bruising competition that makes even the high-tension cabals of the executive suite seem genteel. He is manipulative and practical in all his dealings and it is in accord with these criteria that he measures the extent to which the intellectuals are useful to him.

Among the latter are the staff economist who prepares a presentation to justify a wage increase; the lawyer who argues the union case before labor-relations boards and commissions, and in the courts; the industrial engineer who figures out how the union can benefit from a new time study for production norms; the publicist who puts together a speech or congressional testimony; the actuary familiar with the intricacies of pension funds.

All these assist the labor leader to crystallize, express, dress up what he wants to do. (The Michigan professor, Harold L. Wilenski, who a decade ago conducted the only full-scale sociological survey of union intellectuals, thinks that their overriding function is that of "verbalizers.") The labor leader thinks it is up to him to create and coordinate policy while the experts implement it, rather than do much to formulate it. He regards such aides as his men just as he regards the union as an extension of his psyche. Even though he may respect the abilities and attainments of intellectuals, his attitude remains ambivalent, especially toward the university scholar, the foundation researcher, the writer turned social critic who concerns himself with union affairs. Labor leaders usually refer to the member of this genus as "pedantic," "an ivory tower guy," or as "out in left field, hell, further, out in space," or as a "pipe-smoking long-hair" (labor leaders cherish their cigars only more than their barbers).

Labor leaders are not impressed by the intellectual's inclination toward objective inquiry; they have felt too long beleaguered for that. They are even less impressed by his individualistic propensity to dissent from the prevailing values and mores of "the system." For the labor leader is gregarious, one of the boys, regards himself as chief of a tribe for whom he gets what he can out of the system which he accepts more than it accepts him.

Within the labor movement there is still a tiny handful of intellectuals who play a key role in formulating and initiating union policy. One of this small, select category is Gus Tyler, assistant president of the ILGWU and an author and editor who directs the staff-training, educational, and political departments of the union and collaborates in high-level strategy with its president, David Dubinsky. At AFL-CIO headquarters, Lane Kirkland exerts a similar influence as special assistant to President George Meany. So, too, does Jack Conway, the cerebral administrator for Walter Reuther, president of the AFL-CIO Industrial Union Department and of the United Auto Workers. Equally effective in the Teamsters until recently was the impressively informed Harold Gibbons, who broke with James Riddle Hoffa when the latter refused to send a message of condolence to the family of the late President Kennedy.

In recent years, two other intellectuals have become union presidents—Ralph Helstein, a lawyer who now heads the Packinghouse Workers, and David Livingston, president of District 65 of the Retail, Wholesale, and Department Store Union.

But this dwindling remnant can scarcely begin to meet the labor movement's need for brain-power at a time when leadership in our society is being everywhere transferred to people with intellectual training and capability. The labor leader who in most cases has only a high-school education is not unaware that the intellectual may one day threaten his own ascendancy. This fear explains his insistence that intellectuals be kept in their place and his lack of pronounced grief when they depart. He can then more comfortably rely on the old concepts and techniques of which he is master and which hasten labor's decline. . . .

Trade unions and corporations, as systems for the accumulation of power, are not only economic organizations. They are also private governments. Their relations with each other and with the public government, under national economic planning, must be seriously pondered and spelled out. This is no pastime for some rainy Sunday afternoon, as Mr. Reuther is the first to perceive. And this is only one among many reasons impelling him to establish a "new working alliance" between intellectuals and labor leaders. If he and others of like mind cannot get this kind of cooperation started soon within the higher reaches of the labor movement, the 1960's may prove to be the Gettysburg of its Confederacy.

BASIC FALLACIES OF UNION PHILOSOPHY [6]

[There] are three concepts that organized labor has succeeded in persuading management to accept—or that, at all events, management appears to have willingly accepted without considering their ultimate consequences. These concepts are:

[6] From "Union Philosophy: The Basic Fallacies," by Herbert L. Marx, Jr., assistant director, personnel relations, General Cable Corporation. *Personnel.* 36:31-7. S.-O. '59. Published by the American Management Association. Reprinted by permission.

1. That all workers assigned to identical or roughly similar tasks must receive the same pay—regardless of the attitude, effort, or initiative which the individual worker brings to his job.

2. That the desirable work level for all unionized employees is the minimum acceptable standard, rather than maximum effort and accomplishment.

3. That above all else, the seniority principle must prevail.

Each of these concepts is both fallacious and dangerous, and the continued refusal by either side to recognize or acknowledge this fact bids fair to lead our economy into serious trouble, sooner perhaps than we dare to think. Let us take a closer look at what they imply.

The Single-Rate Theory

One of the most destructive of union influences is the unremitting pressure on management to regard all industrial workers as having identical capabilities, aptitudes, characters, and ambitions. While this pressure may perhaps be relaxed at both the highest and the lowest levels of skills, it almost invariably applies to employees assigned to the same or similar tasks in the general run of production work.

It must be admitted that management itself has been partly responsible for this blanketing of highly disparate talents in one smothered group. Over the years, industrial engineers and others have developed exceedingly intricate techniques of assembly, aimed at task simplification and the so-called "one best way." A production line is so methodized, for example, that a woman with average finger dexterity can sit and braze wires all day. From this it is but a jump to the conclusion that *all* women, with certain minimum qualifications, can perform this task equally well. Thus, we arrive at a "standard" performance as something to be admired in itself, instead of being used as a springboard from which higher quantity and quality of work can be attained by the individual employee.

Such conclusions fit snugly into the union philosophy of "equal pay for equal work." In itself, an admirable principle, indeed; but labor has distorted it beyond recognition to mean, "Because we are all assigned to the same work (no matter how well or poorly we do it), you must give us equal pay"—a principle that offers no reward for the exceptionally good workers, no penalty or goad for the less proficient.

Yet even in the most elaborately engineered operation, one worker can be and often is more productive, more efficient, more quality-conscious than the majority of his fellows—even on the same task. Most labor contracts, however, provide for single rates for large groups of tasks; attempts to reward merit by additional pay are either forbidden or, at best, subject to negotiation with the union. This failure to reward the efficient, loyal, and ingenious employee has two cumulative effects: (1) For lack of incentive, the more proficient worker eventually takes refuge in a desultory, "what's the use?" attitude; and (2) the general level of performance is geared to the lowest acceptable pace and the minimum quality standard. . . .

Admittedly, it will be no simple task for American unionism to find a means of bargaining collectively for its members, retaining some sort of cohesion within its ranks as an economic necessity, yet at the same time enabling management to reward the individual employee in proportion to his initiative, ability, and good, old-fashioned work attitude. In the process, management, too, will have to abandon some of its own pet theories about "standard performance." But there is no reason why, once both management and labor have recognized that the single-rate theory inevitably breeds lowered industrial efficiency, with all its concomitant implications in the face of today's worldwide competition, some solution should not be found. Nor need it entail the abandonment of the wage "floor" for acceptable work. All that is required is a willingness on the part of labor to accept the doctrine that exceptional performance shall earn a higher reward and, on the part of management, a readiness to share the fruits of better effort with the employees responsible for it.

The Philosophy of Minimum Effort

Equally undermining of the individual worker's capacity for growth and greater responsibility is the second concept, whereby the unionized employee is encouraged to do only the minimum required of him, rather than the maximum of which he is capable. Indeed, in many unions, any attempt on the part of the rank-and-file worker to reach his natural and trainable peak must be avoided on pain of union discipline. Consider the futility of this principle were it to be applied, for example, to the performer in the field of art or entertainment, even when working on a fixed or contract "wage." What solo violinist would dare perform to a minimum standard? Does the television comedian gear his program to the lowest acceptable level of audience laughter?

Yet, working solely to an acceptable minimum is precisely the attitude adopted by vast numbers of industrial workers. While this attitude may not be openly encouraged by the union, it undeniably thrives most abundantly within a unionized situation. Again the contrast between union and nonunion employees is pertinent. Does any nonunion employee ever forget that his job tenure and hope of advancement depend on his consistent performance to the best of his ability?

"A fair day's wage for a fair day's work" is another slogan commonly heard in union circles. But this phrase, too, has been warped and now means: "Do no more than the standard quantity of work for a day's pay, or suffer the consequences of disfavor by your fellow workers and the union."

The philosophy of minimum effort received its impetus from the depression-born limitations on production, when the worker foresaw (or thought he could foresee) an end to his job whenever finished goods started to pile up. But . . . economic history . . . has shown all too clearly that only by getting a fuller measure of honest work can a company lower its costs, meet and beat competition and, ultimately, create the wider market for its goods that means more, not fewer jobs.

Much effort has been expended by management to bring these simple economic truths home to the individual employee. But how often, at the bargaining table, have demands for higher wages based on "increased productivity" been countered by demands for the abandonment of restrictions—whether actual or implied—on individual output? It is only very recently that a stiffening in management's attitude toward labor's monotonous reiteration of "more" has become apparent. It is to be hoped that as the demand for increased efficiency presses even more sharply on the American economy, unions too will come to see that the most significant gains in productivity follow from the greater effort and positive attitude of the individual worker.

The Ten Commandments of Seniority

If they had their way, unions would make seniority the ten commandments of the labor-management agreement. Here is a principle that, when strictly applied, makes the recognition of individual ability and ambition a joke and scientific job placement a shambles. The results are misuse, abuse, and underuse of employee potential and capabilities, and a general sluggishness of the workforce.

Yet in actual fact, the union, as a power group in itself, does not benefit directly by this insistence on seniority, nor does the union have any preferential interest in its longer-service members. The older employee rarely pays higher dues, and there is a better than even chance that he is a malcontent or a nonparticipant in union affairs. For that matter, unions completely ignore the seniority principle when it comes to selecting their own officers, negotiators, and organizers. The man who is chosen president of a local union is the one who swings—and usually deserves—the most votes. Paid staff representatives are selected on the basis of their particular talents and training for the job.

Yet, give a union the power to set contract terms unilaterally for, say several thousand workers in a complex chemical plant, and management will be told that seniority—absolute, if possible, or with minimum deviations, if necessary—in upgrading, layoffs, recall, and so on, is the single most important provision. Why? The reason is simply that seniority provides a measuring tape which can be used on each and every union member in an identical manner. The seniority principle makes it safe for a union to operate without falling apart into factions whenever an intraunion conflict arises.

Seniority can settle, to the union's satisfaction, virtually every intra-union dispute over labor-management contract provisions. Several employees are eager for a higher-rated job. Who should get it? The union steward's unvarying answer: The senior man (with an aside to the junior losers, "Be patient, some day you will be the senior man yourself"). The workforce must be reduced. Who goes? For the union no problem exists: Toss out the last ones hired.

Yet, this makes no industrial sense whatsoever. While management doubtless has some moral obligation to favor the fifteen-year-employee over one with a single year of service, what possible scientific justification is there for showing automatic preference to the eleven-year man over the ten-year man? On an industrial task which can be mastered in a week, a month, or even a year, what real purpose is served by considering an employee's years of service beyond his initial training and development period?

For management, the rules of seniority are the most secure handcuffs ever devised to hamper efficient production. They act equally as a brake on individual efforts to excel. "What's the good," the younger worker reflects, "if I cannot be rewarded by a better position now, even if the boss wishes to give it to me?" Conversely, the worker with long seniority can relax in the comfortable knowledge that better opportunities are his for the asking, provided only that he meets certain minimum requirements. . . .

Each of the three concepts discussed here hinges on the problem of freeing the union member to demonstrate his full talents and give of his best efforts. In essence, this is a challenge to labor rather than to management. Unions must realize that better wages and working conditions can result in the long run only through the greater efficiency of their members. Sooner or later, industry will have to rediscover the inescapable truth that economic security rests on individual peak performance. If this change in attitude is effected solely by management effort and example, unions may well lose their fundamental purpose.

If the unions themselves accept the challenge, however, they will be able to take at least partial credit for reversing the present deadly trend toward inefficiency. But at the present time, it would seem that they still have to learn that further benefits for their members can be forthcoming only if there is a return to greater respect for work itself and a greater understanding of the part played by each employee in contributing to the company's profitability and continued existence.

NO CAUSE FOR ALARM [7]

In its long history, organized labor has withstood open and concealed attacks of varying intensity. It has had to overcome differences which led to a division in the ranks lasting for twenty years. It has had to find formulas for overcoming work-assignment disputes affecting thousands and to repel at the same time attempts to undermine or weaken its legal position. All things considered, the labor movement, while far from perfect, has yet done quite well, if judged by the standards normally applied to other American institutions. . . .

In the past, the conclusion that labor faced a crisis was usually tied to internal discord, employer opposition, or hostile legislation. Consequently, the fears and warnings could be tested, at least to some extent. Those who believe that organized labor is facing a crisis at present have shied away from the necessity of attaching their views to some concrete episode or development and have failed to point to specific situations, events, or relationships which are causing the crisis. If one might be permitted to interpret the substance of the criticisms, the crisis in the labor movement is the result of a series of deficiencies and failures, all of which combine to create the present danger. The main ones mentioned, and therefore the ones I will discuss, are the failures of the labor movement to grow in membership particularly be-

[7] From "Is There a Crisis in the Labor Movement? No," by Philip Taft, professor of economics, Brown University, and author of many authoritative studies on the American labor movement. *Annals of the American Academy of Political and Social Science.* 350:10-15. N. '63. Reprinted by permission.

cause of the increasing number of white-collar employees, the role of automation, and excessive labor demands. . . .

Occupational Composition

If one assumes that the trend in the occupational composition of the labor force, revealed by the 1960 census, would not be reversed but would instead be accentuated, the labor movement would, in the opinion of these observers, gradually suffer an erosion of membership and eventually be reduced to much smaller size and influence. This argument is far from conclusive and implicitly assumes propensities and psychological attitudes which have not been proven. In fact, actual experience has shown these assumptions to be baseless, and not a scintilla of evidence has been presented to justify these conclusions. Moreover, no one has come forth with a plan for organizing these workers which is different from the traditional one. Nor has anyone asked whether the unorganized white-collar workers are different from those who already belong to unions.

Professional workers. In the United States, workers of the highest skills have been members of organized labor, some for almost fifty years. Screen writers, airline pilots, theatrical, night club, and circus performers, teachers and writers, movie photographers, directors and other technical personnel employed in various branches of the entertainment industries have maintained effective unions for several decades. Members of some of these unions are among the highest paid people in the world, and the average annual earnings of the members of the Air Line Pilots Association would certainly compare with those of most other occupations. What is interesting about the organizations of the above workers is that their policies reveal them as almost "ideal" labor organizations in Max Weber's sense. What was the appeal of Actors Equity during the 1919 strike? What is the appeal of the American Federation of Television and Radio Artists, or the union of the men in the pilots' cockpits who carry enormous responsibilities? Or of the American Newspaper Guild? Any examination of their problems or policies shows that it has noth-

ing to do with the color of the collar worn. The basis of trade
unionism is not skill or even whether the workplace is the factory
or office but whether a job allows for the existence of anomalies,
favoritism, or unequal bargaining which a labor organization can
rectify. A union, unless it wishes to transform itself into something else, can only base its existence upon the need for a job-
protecting institution. Where the work or relationship to the employer is sufficiently homogeneous as to make united action necessary or desirable, the basis for a union organization exists.
Whether these possibilities are realized depends upon a variety
of circumstances which differ in industries, in geographical areas,
and even in time. But when artists and writers, who are likely
to be individuals of strong character and personal initiative, find
the trade union necessary or at least desirable for their own advancement, it would appear that the attempt to divide the response to unionization on the basis of collar color is contradicted
by experience. One might also note that the newspapermen—
who were, before the formation of the Guild, supposed to lead a
life of carefree excitement and to be prone to undergraduate
pranks and inclined to be oblivious of anything but the story, as
were the heroes of *Front Page*—formed an effective union by the
traditional methods of organized labor.

The labor movement does face some serious problems from
the changes in the occupational composition of the labor force,
but it is certainly far from a crisis. In some industries, part-time
work has increased, especially among married women. Multiple
job-holding in families may also make the task of the organizer
more difficult. The secondary worker may not have the same
stake in the job nor feel the need for union protection as in-
tensely. Nevertheless, these changes are not sufficiently great to
present an overriding problem to the organizations of labor.

Sales workers. Increases in sales workers presumably offer
another insuperable problem to the labor movement. Some com-
mentators qualify the warning by calling for a new approach. It
would appear, however, that the unions which recruit these workers have had reasonable success in organizing. The Retail Clerks
union has over 300,000 in its ranks, and, even though this number

is not a major part of the workers in these occupations, it demon-
strates that they are not inevitably unresponsive to the traditional
appeal of the trade unions. Other unions—the Meat Cutters and
Butcher Workmen and the Retail, Wholesale and Department
Store Union—have also recruited thousands of sales workers.
Changes which are taking place in retail distribution may, in
fact, make organization more attractive. Growth of larger units,
the discount store, and self-service create problems of employment, seniority, and work division which only unions can handle.

Clerical employees. Clerical employees in finance, insurance,
and elsewhere have also increased, and, although these workers
have traditionally shown a lower propensity for organizing,
changes now taking place may actually increase the attractive-
ness of labor organizations. Large investment in office equipment
is drastically changing the content of jobs, but it is also effecting
changes in the employment relationship. Use of computers, data-
processing devices, and other highly mechanized office equipment
may encourage significant changes in the work patterns in these
organizations. Office employees in banks and insurance companies were often, in the past, able to escape some part of the
unemployment which is a concomitant of fluctuations in demand.
An employer with an idle or partially idle computer may be more
careful about allowing workers who cannot be fully occupied on
the payroll. Thus, white-collar workers are likely to be exposed
to the same economic vicissitudes as the blue-collar employee.
The factors that make for unionization in the manual trades—
irregularity of employment, "arbitrary" layoffs of individuals—
are more likely to appear than heretofore.

Government employment. Growth of government employment has taken place largely in the white-collar group, and some
critics point to the failure of the trade-union movement to make
much of an impression in this growing area of employment as
another symptom of the crisis. There are a number of changes
which indicate that this group may become more hospitable to the
traditional appeal of the union. At one time, the government
worker enjoyed a variety of fringe benefits shared by few in private
employment. These advantages have been narrowed, if not elimi-

nated. At least in state and local governments, the employee may face increasing difficulties in maintaining his relative wage position. Inadequate revenue sources and a refusal to tax may mean, in the future, lagging salaries and fringe benefits, usually regarded as favorable conditions for unionization campaigns.

In denying that the shift to white-collar employment has created a crisis in the labor movement, one need not insist that large numbers of these workers will soon find their way into the unions. Such a view would be far too sanguine of the immediate organizational possibilities in these sectors of the economy. The view advanced is that failure to gain large numbers in the short run would pose no threat to organized labor.

Automation

Some writers have also focused attention upon the effect of automation upon the labor force and have stressed the failure of organized labor to devise a policy to meet this problem. It is obviously not possible to devise a policy that would be equally fair, reasonable, and effective for all industries. The effect of automation upon wages and employment cannot be determined in a broad sense. Much depends upon whether an industry is expanding or contracting and the rapidity with which change is being introduced.

There is, however, no unanimity on the way this aspect of the crisis manifests itself: some perceive the crisis in labor's failure to solve the unemployment problems which sometimes follow the introduction of automated machinery; others insist that the crisis shows itself in labor's obdurate insistence upon the maintenance of obsolete rules. . . . Two observations on this question appear to be in order. One, automation, like any other kind of technological change, is largely a function of management. Also, the reaction of labor is a traditional one. In fact, the number of times that unions recently have accepted important technical changes without protest would, to some extent, indicate a new attitude. As for the broader issue, there is too little evidence on this question to attempt to devise a theory of crisis or, for that matter, any other. If there is a crisis, it is a crisis for society as a whole and not of the labor movement. It is the firm which controls employment. Fundamentally, no employer is obligated, even under union agreements, to provide a specific amount of work. The labor movement does not control the pace nor rate of technical change, and whatever crisis there exists is certainly not of its making. Moreover, no one has yet suggested the kind of solution organized labor might propose. The fact is that, without an organized labor movement, there would not even be a problem of automation, let alone a crisis. Changes would be introduced, workers would be displaced, and unemployment would be, in some instances, created, but it would be regarded as only part of the inexorable working of economic law.

Extreme Demands

The critics who follow the time-honored practice of using every stick to beat the dog have also pointed to serious interruptions in economic activity brought on by extreme demands by relatively few workers. The . . . strikes [in 1963] on the East Coast and Gulf Coast waterfronts as well as in the New York newspaper industry are the examples used to illustrate this aspect of the crisis. Whatever validity a criticism of the behavior of labor may have, obviously the strikes by themselves are a demonstration of militancy and vigor rather than crisis and decline. This type of an observation implies no justification of the aims of the walkouts themselves; they may have been imprudent and incapable of accomplishing the objectives sought. In fact, they may actually have harmed the workers and the industry. These matters require a different type of examination, but they can by no stretch of the imagination be regarded as signs of decadence and dissolution.

The above do not exhaust the symptoms. In fact, there are vast numbers of possible explanations, some stressing the inadequacy of labor's political program and others labor's failure to devise a detailed long-run plan for the future. It seems to me worth repeating that the American labor movement with all its defects and limitations fights harder, better, and more successfully for its members than any in the world.

BIBLIOGRAPHY

An asterisk (*) preceding a reference indicates that the article or a part of it has been reprinted in this volume.

BIBLIOGRAPHIES

American Federation of Labor-Congress of Industrial Organizations. Industrial Union Department. Guidebook for union organizers. AFL-CIO. 815 16th St. N.W. Washington, D.C. 20006. '61.

Princeton University. Industrial Relations Section. Outstanding books on industrial relations. The University. Princeton, N.J. Published annually.

United States. Department of Labor. Compulsory arbitration, selected references, 1951-1965. mimeo. Department of Labor Library. Washington, D.C. '65.

University of Illinois. Institute of Labor and Industrial Relations. Check-list of recent books. mimeo. The Institute. Urbana. '63.

University of Illinois. Institute of Labor and Industrial Relations. Check-list of recent non-book material. mimeo. The Institute. Urbana. '64.

BOOKS, PAMPHLETS, AND DOCUMENTS

Barbash, Jack. Labor's grass roots; a study of the local union. Harper. New York. '61.

Beal, E. F. and Wickersham, E. B. Practice of collective bargaining. Richard D. Irwin. Homewood, Ill. '63.

*Blood, J. W. ed. Personnel job in a changing world. (AMA Management Reports no 80) American Management Association. 135 W. 50th St. New York 10020. '64.
  Reprinted in this book: Year-round bargaining. R. H. Larry. p 101-5.

Brooks, T. R. Toil and trouble; a history of American labor. Dial. New York. '64.

Chamber of Commerce of the United States. Productivity and wage settlements. The Chamber. 1615 H St. N.W. Washington, D.C. 20006. '61.

Chamberlain, N. W. and Kuhn, J. W. Collective bargaining. 2d ed. McGraw. New York. '65.

Christensen, T. G. S. ed. Proceedings of New York University seventeenth annual conference on labor. Bureau of National Affairs. 1231 24th St. N.W. Washington, D.C. 20037. '65.

Cole, G. H. and others, eds. Labor's story as reported by the American labor press. Community Publishers. Glen Cove, N.Y. '61.

*Committee for Economic Development. Union powers and union functions: toward a better balance. The Committee. 711 Fifth Ave. New York 10022. '64.

Estey, M. S. and others, eds. Regulating union government. Harper. New York. '64.

Feather, Victor. Essence of trade unionism; a background book. Dufour. Chester Springs, Pa. '63.

Ford, Henry, II. Bargaining and economic growth; address before American Society of Corporate Secretaries, Coronado, California, June 22 1964. Ford Motor Company. Dearborn, Mich. '64.

Herling, John. Labor unions in America. (America Today Series no 6). Robert B. Luce. Washington, D.C. '64.

Jacobs, Paul. State of the unions. Atheneum. New York. '63.

Kerr, Clark. Labor and management in industrial society. Doubleday. New York. '64.

McDonald, Donald. Corporation and the union; interview with J. Irwin Miller and Walter P. Reuther. Center for the Study of Democratic Institutions. Box 4068. Santa Barbara, Calif. 93103. '62.

Madison, C. A. American labor leaders: personalities and forces in the labor movement. 2d ed. Ungar. New York. '62.

Peterson, Florence. American labor unions: what they are and how they work. 2d ed. Harper. New York. '63.

Selekman, B. M. and others. Problems in labor relations. 3d ed. McGraw. New York. '64.

Shostak, A. B. America's forgotten labor organization (survey of the role of the single-firm independent union in American industry). Industrial Relations Section, Department of Economics and Sociology. Princeton University. Princeton, N.J. '62.

*Somers, G. G. ed. Proceedings of the seventeenth annual meeting, Industrial Relations Research Association, Chicago, December 28-29, 1964. The Association. University of Wisconsin. Madison. '65.

    Reprinted in this book: Sources for future growth and decline in American trade unions. Joel Seidman. p98-103.

Sultan, P. E. Disenchanted unionist. Harper. New York. '63.

Taft, Philip. Organized labor in American history. Harper. New York. '64.

*United States. Department of Labor. Brief history of the American
labor movement. (Bureau of Labor Statistics. Bulletin no 1000)
Supt. of Docs. Washington, D.C. 20402. '64.

United States. Department of Labor. Directory of national and in-
ternational labor unions in the United States, 1963. (Bureau of
Labor Statistics Bulletin no 1395) Supt. of Docs. Washington,
D.C. 20402. '64.

United States. President's Advisory Committee on Labor-Management Policy. Free and responsible collective bargaining and
industrial peace; report to the President, May 1, 1962. Supt. of
Docs. Washington, D.C. 20402. '62.

Widick, B. J. Labor today: the triumphs and failures of unionism
in the United States. Houghton. Boston. '64.

Wirtz, W. W. Labor and the public interest. Harper. New York. '64.

PERIODICALS

AFL-CIO American Federationist. 70:15-17. Ag. '63. Industrial
peacemakers. W. E. Simkin.

*AFL-CIO American Federationist. 70:18-21. N. '63. New directions
in bargaining.

America. 107:1244-5. D. 15, '62. Is the agency shop legal? B. L.
Masse.

*America. 111:210-12. Ag. 29, '64. Discrimination, unions and Title
VII. G. R. Blakey.

Annals of the American Academy of Political and Social Science.
344:44-54. N. '62. Liberals, conservatives and labor. R. C.
Cortner.

*Annals of the American Academy of Political and Social Science.
350:1-147. N. '63. Crisis in the American trade union movement. Solomon Barkin and A. A. Blum, eds.
    Reprinted in this book: Is there a crisis in the labor movement? No. Philip
Taft. p 10-15.

Annals of the American Academy of Political and Social Science.
353:40-51. My. '64. Organized labor and the city boss. L. L.
Friedland.

*Arbitration Journal. 19:98-102. '64. Compulsory labor arbitration
and the national welfare. Benjamin Wyle.

Atlantic Monthly. 207:55-60. Ap. '61. Squeeze on the unions. A. H.
Raskin.
    Same abridged: Reader's Digest. 79:81-5. Jl. '61.

Atlantic Monthly. 209:87-95. Ap. '62. Unions and their wealth.
A. H. Raskin.

Atlantic Monthly. 211:37-44. Ap. '63. Labor's welfare state: the New York electrical workers. A. H. Raskin.

Atlantic Monthly. 211:53-8. My. '63. John L. Lewis and the Mine Workers. A. H. Raskin.

Atlantic Monthly. 212:85-90+. O. '63. Walter Reuther's great big union. A. H. Raskin.

Atlantic Monthly. 214:34-7. Jl. '64. What's ahead for labor? N. W. Chamberlain.

Barron's. 43:8+. Ap. 8, '63. Compulsory unionism has thrived only with the help of government. M. R. Lefkoe.

Business Management Record (National Industrial Conference Board). p 35-41. My. '63. Union profile: the Technical Engineers.

Business Management Record (National Industrial Conference Board). sup 3-12. My. '63. Strike policy and compulsory arbitration: round-table discussion.

Business Management Record (National Industrial Conference Board). p 45-52. Je. '63. Congress and restrictive labor legislation. R. A. Bedolis.

Business Week. p 90-1. Ja. 6, '62. Antitrust laws for unions, too.

Business Week. p 73-4. Je. 15, '63 UAW's own court sums up: review board.

Business Week. p 43-4. Ag. 24, '63. How to stop strikes before they start.

*Business Week. p 43-4+. My. 9, '64. "Informed neutrals" score a triumph; special mediators to reinforce collective bargaining.

Business Week. p 50+. Jl. 25, '64. Testing labor's "ultimate weapon" (the boycott).

Business Week. p 36+. Ag. 8, '64. New giant in union funds; merger of ILGWU pension funds.

*Business Week. p 43-4. O. 10, '64. Strike wanes as a weapon.

Business Week. p 24-6. F. 20, '65. State of the unionists: griping but living well.

California Law Review. 52:95-114. Mr. '64. State right-to-work laws and federal labor policy. J. R. Grodin and D. B. Beeson.

California Management Review. 4:4-12. Spring '62. Labor's power in American society. Irving Bernstein.

California Management Review. 6:37-40. Summer '64. Has collective bargaining degenerated? J. H. Foegen.

*Columbia University Forum. 5:18-23. Spring '62. Nice kind of union democracy. Ivar Berg.

Commentary. 36:18-25. Jl. '63. Obsolescent unions. A. H. Raskin.

*Commonweal. 78:11-12. Mr. 29, '63. Breakthrough at Kaiser: automation and unemployment. L. T. King.

*Commonweal. 80:391-4. Je. 19, '64. Decline of labor: unions within unions. Sidney Lens.

Conference Board Record. 1:22-31. My. '64. Human-relations committee—a breakthrough in collective bargaining? M. L. Denise and others.

Conference Board Record. 1:40-2. Ag. '64. Aftermath of a strike— a "no strike strike agreement." R. A. Bedolis.

Conference Board Record. 1:28-33. D. '64. UMW and the antitrust law. R. A. Bedolis.

Congressional Digest. 40:225-33. O. '61. Anti-trust action against labor unions?

County Officer. 28:320-1+. Ag. '63. Coming role of unionism in local government.

Dun's Review and Modern Industry. 79:46-8. Ap. '62. Supreme court of labor. G. T. Baker.

Dun's Review and Modern Industry. 83:47+. Ja. '64. Labor's controversial $6 billion. Thomas O'Hanlon.

Dun's Review and Modern Industry. 83:59-62. Mr. '64. Should the U. S. have a labor court? T. R. Brooks.

Dun's Review and Modern Industry. 84:65-6. Jl. '64. Kaiser's long-range sharing plan. T. R. Brooks.

*Dun's Review and Modern Industry. 85:34-5+. Mr. '65. Labor: the rank-and-file revolt. T. R. Brooks.

Dun's Review and Modern Industry. 86:59-60+. Je. '65. Role of the federal mediator. T. R. Brooks.

Dun's Review and Modern Industry. 86:45-8. Ag. '65. Labor's hardening arteries. T. R. Brooks.

Factory Management and Maintenance. 123:96-7. Mr. '65. Should "right-to-work" laws be repealed? M. J. Shapp and Howard Jensen.

Fordham Law Review. 30:759-76. Ap. '62. Antitrust laws and labor.

Fortune. 64:80+. Ag. '61. Court on worker's rights.

Fortune. 65:199-200. F. '62. Greatest unresolved problem (organizing).

Fortune. 66:152-4+. N. '62. House the janitors built; Marina City, Chicago. Gilbert Cross.

Fortune. 66:153+. N. '62. Labor's capitalists.

Fortune. 67:108-113+. My. '63. Labor unions are worth the price. Max Ways.

Fortune. 68:164-6+. N. '63. NLRB's new rough line. M. R. Lefkoe.

Fortune. 69:100-3+. Je. '64. Is labor's wage push more bark than bite? E. K. Faltermayer.

*Harper's Magazine. 228:79-80+. Je. '64. Why labor lost the intellectuals. Herbert Harris.

Harper's Magazine. 229:43-9. O. '64. Riddle of the labor vote. Herbert Harris.

Harvard Business Review. 38:88-96. Mr. '60. Taming wildcat strikes. G. L. Magnum.

Harvard Business Review. 39:63-9. N. '61. Collective bargaining—ritual or reality? A. A. Blum.

Harvard Business Review. 40:41-52. Ja. '62. New union frontier: white-collar workers. E. M. Kassalow.

*Harvard Business Review. 40:80-90. Mr. '62. Conservative labor/radical business. B. M. Selekman.

Harvard Business Review. 40:49-57. My. '62. Salaries for all workers. P. G. Kaponya.

Harvard Business Review. 41:82-96. Ja. '63. Federal fetters for featherbedders. L. K. Randall.

Harvard Business Review. 41:86-97. S. '63. Case for Boulwarism. H. R. Northrup.

Harvard Business Review. 42:84-98. My. '64. Transportation's labor crisis. E. B. Shils.

Harvard Business Review. 42:6-8+. Jl. '64. Labor at the crossroads (review of recent books on labor). A. A. Blum.

Harvard Business Review. 42:66-70. S. '64. Brighter future for collective bargaining. E. R. Livernash.

Harvard Law Review. 76:807-18. F. '63. "Boulwarism": legality and effect.

Holiday. 33:78-9+. F. '63. Department of Labor. J. D. Weaver.

Industrial and Labor Relations Review. 15:323-49. Ap. '62. Dual government in unions: tool for analysis. A. H. Cook.

Industrial and Labor Relations Review. 16:381-404. Ap. '63. Craft-industrial issue revisited: a study of union government. A. R. Weber.

Industrial and Labor Relations Review. 17:20-38. O. '63. Origins of business unionism. Philip Taft.

Industrial and Labor Relations Review. 17:179-202. Ja. '64. Unions and the Negro community. R. Marshall.

Industrial and Labor Relations Review. 18:3-19. O. '64. Collective action by public school teachers. W. A. Wildman.

Industrial and Labor Relations Review. 18:60-72. O. '64. Declining utility of the strike. J. L. Stern.

Industrial and Labor Relations Review. 18:73-80. O. '64. Non-stoppage strikes: a new approach. S. R. Sosnich.

Industrial and Labor Relations Review. 18:81-91. O. '64. Compulsory arbitration; some perspectives. O. W. Phelps.

Industrial Relations. 1:47-71. F. '62. Union member's "bill of rights": first two years. Benjamin Aaron.

Industrial Relations. 4:27-41. F. '65. Small community's impact on labor relations. Milton Derber.

Industrial Relations. 4:51-68. F. '65. American labor lore: its meanings and uses. Archie Green.

Kentucky Law Journal. 52:817-36. '64. Labor arbitration process, 1943-1963. R. W. Fleming.

Labor Law Journal. 14:166-77. F. '63. New labor relations policies and remedies suggested by different industrial settings. Solomon Barkin.

*Labor Law Journal. 14:834-8. O. '63. Aerospace bargaining: collective bargaining does work. W. E. Simkin.

Labor Law Journal. 14:935-50. N. '63. National union in federal labor legislation. H. J. Lahne.

Labor Law Journal. 15:177-87. Mr. '64. What's to be done for labor? trade unionists' answer. Solomon Barkin and A. A. Blum.

*Labor Law Journal 15:468-73. Jl. '64. Process of unionization in the South; address delivered at the 1964 spring meeting of the Industrial Relations Research Association, Gatlinburg, Tennessee. Tony Zivalich.

Labor Law Journal. 15:499-518. Ag. '64. Collective bargaining—the new trend. R. P. McLoughlin.

Labor Law Journal. 15:770-86. D. '64. Battle of Hillsdale—Essex Wire strike emergency. R. G. Howlett.

Labor Law Journal. 15:787-94. D. '64. Collective bargaining for public school teachers. M. H. Moskow.

Labor Law Journal. 15:795-801. D. '64. Real significance of collective bargaining for teachers. F. A. Padke.

Labor Law Journal. 16:100-10. F. '65. Unionism again at a crossroads. G. W. Hardbeck.

Look. 26:69-74. S. 11, '62. Is labor on the skids? T. B. Morgan.

Look. 27:84+. Ap. 23, '63. Way out of our strike dilemma. Max Lerner.

Management Review. 53:4-15. My. '64. What's ahead in collective bargaining? William Karpinsky.

Monthly Labor Review.
> Published by the Bureau of Labor Statistics. Contains surveys, excerpts of addresses, and news summaries.

Nation. 192:211-14. Mr. 11, '61. Is labor turning protectionist? J. A. Loftus.

Nation. 193:375-7. N. 11, '61. Unions and the anti-trust laws. William Gomberg.

Nation. 194:56-61. Ja. 20, '62. Future of collective bargaining. William Gomberg.

Nation. 195:86-9. S. 1, '62. Labor's ebbing strength. George Kirstein.

Nation. 197:107-9 S. 7, '63. Labor tries a comeback. Harry Bernstein.

Nation. 197:389-90. D. 7, '63. Labor ducks the future. B. J. Widick.

*Nation. 198:651-3. Je. 29, '64. Union or guild? organizing the teachers. Stanley Elam.

Nation's Business. 51:34-5+. S. '63. Eggheads are leaving unions.

Nation's Business. 51:36-7+. N. '63. Union's political machine builds more strength: Committee on Political Education.

Nation's Business. 52:38-9+. Jl. '64. Meet tomorrow's union leaders.

Nation's Business. 52:36-7+. D. '64. What unions want in 1965.

Nation's Business. 53:31-3+. Mr. '65. Dangers in more forced unionism; interview with Sylvester Petro.

New Leader. 47:10-12. O. 12, '64. Labor law and the Negro. W. B. Gould.

New Republic. 146:12-15. My. 21, '62. Future of collective bargaining. H. H. Wellington.

*New York Times. Sec. XI, p 1-44. N. 17, '63. Hands that build America; special supplement prepared by the American Federation of Labor-Congress of Industrial Organizations.
> Reprinted in this book: What the unions really want. p 3.

New York Times. p 1+. Ap. 27, '64. Railroad settlement: triumph for mediation. J. D. Pomfret.

*New York Times. p 47. D. 27, '64. Born of strife 50 years ago, Amalgamated union prospers. Foster Hailey.

New York Times. Sec. II, p 6. Ja. 17, '65. Room at the top in labor. A. H. Raskin.

*New York Times. p 39. Ap. 8, '65. Labor and its leaders. J. D. Pomfret.

New York Times. p 14. Ap. 24, '65. Steel contract ritual. J. D. Pomfret.

New York Times. Sec. IV, p 5. My. 2, '65. Right-to-work laws again provoke debate. J. D. Pomfret.

New York Times. p 22. My. 19, '65. Text of President Johnson's message to Congress on labor matters (right-to-work law).

*New York Times. p 14. S. 6, '65. Labor's unsolved problems.

New York Times Magazine. p 30+. D. 9, '62. Marital troubles in labor's house. A. H. Raskin.

New York Times Magazine. p 20-1+. N. 3, '63. Approach to automation: the Kaiser plan. A. H. Raskin.

New York Times Magazine. p 26+. N. 17, '63. New look at arbitration. Lawrence Stessin.

New York University Law Review. 37:362-410. My. '62. Individual rights in collective agreements and arbitration. C. W. Summers.

Notre Dame Lawyer. 37:172-93. D. '61. Politics and labor unions. E. J. Fillenwarth.

*Personnel. 36:31-7. S. '59. Union philosophy; the basic fallacies. H. L. Marx, Jr.

Personnel. 40:27-34. My. '63. What expanded bargaining means in practice. T. C. Kammholz.

Personnel. 42:34-42. Mr. '65. Emerging concepts in labor relations. M. E. Stone.

*Personnel Administration. 26:5-62. Ja. '63. Union-management relations. S. H. Torff and others.
        Reprinted in this book: Union membership: gain or loss? J. H. Foegen. p 30-5.

Personnel Journal. 41:222-5. My. '62. Duality in unionism. J. H. Foegen.

Personnel Journal. 42:437-9. O. '63. Compulsory arbitration: solution or anathema. W. D. Torrence.

Personnel Journal. 42:549-59+. D. '63. Right-to-work legislation: examination of related issues and effects. R. L. Hilgert and J. D. Young.

Personnel Journal. 43:88-93. F. '64. White-collar unions and the law. H. N. Rude.

Personnel Journal. 43:179-84. Ap. '64. Labor relations policy for 1964. T. W. Kheel.

Personnel Journal. 43:246-51. My. '64. Strikes: the private stake and the public interest. G. P. Shultz.

Personnel Journal. 44:72-5+. F. '65. Attitudes in compulsory arbitration. Philip Harris.

*Political Science Quarterly. 78:444-58. S. '63. Union structure and public policy: the control of union racial practices. Ray Marshall.

Railway Age. 157:34-41+. Jl. 27, '64. FEC story: survival without unions?

Reader's Digest. 81:97-101. D. '62. These labor abuses must be curbed. J. L. McClellan.

Reader's Digest. 83:125-9. Ag. '63. You can't steal a union anymore. Lester Velie.

Reader's Digest. 84:92-6. Mr. '64. Stakes in the struggle against Hoffa. Lester Velie.

Recreation. 55:17+. Ja. '62. Role of labor in organized community recreation.

Reporter. 30:22-4. Mr. 26, '64. Is Hoffa finished? A. H. Raskin.

Reporter. 30:24-6. My. 21, '64. Meaning of the rail settlement. A. H. Raskin.

Reporter. 31:23-8. S. 10, '64. Civil rights: the law and the unions. A. H. Raskin.

*Reporter. 32:23-5. Ja. 14, '65. "Right to work": a hard one for LBJ. Leonard Baker.

Reporter. 32:27-30. Ja. 28, '65. Rumbles from the rank and file. A. H. Raskin.

*Rutgers Law Review. 18:279-303. Winter '64. Internal relations between unions and their members: United States report. Benjamin Aaron.

*Rutgers Law Review. 18:304-42. Winter '64. UAW Public review board report. D. Y. Klein.

*St. Louis Post-Dispatch. p 1 C+. Je. 27, '65. Antitrust laws and the unions. J. C. Millstone.

Saturday Evening Post. 235:75-9. D. 8, '62. Has success spoiled big labor? H. H. Martin.

Saturday Evening Post. 237:84-9. F. 22, '64. Railroad that defies the unions. Trevor Armbrister.

Saturday Review. 46:21-5+. Mr. 30, '63. Labor's crisis of public confidence. A. H. Raskin.

Saturday Review. 46:20-2+. N. 16, '63. Big strike a thing of the past? A. H. Raskin.

Saturday Review. 46:63-4. D. 14, '63. Unions need public acceptance, too. L. L. L. Golden.

Senior Scholastic. 82:4-6+. F. 27, '63. Labor at the crossroads.

*Senior Scholastic. 86:11+. Mr. 11, '65. U.S. labor on the move.

Steel. 154:43-4. Je. 8, '64. Human relations committee bargaining pushed by U.S. mediators.

Tennessee Law Review. 31:218-29. Winter '64. Agency shop as a union security device. L. R. Hagood.

Time. 84:57. N. 20, '64. Common thread of trouble; defiance of union leadership.

U. S. News & World Report. 52:44-5. F. 19, '62. Next goal: union membership for all federal workers.

U. S. News & World Report. 52:80+. My. 14, '62. Union power; a monopoly that should be curbed? symposium.

U.S. News & World Report. 53:93-5. O. 22, '62. After an eight-and-a-half-year strike: who won and who lost; Kohler company strike.

U. S. News & World Report. 54:96-9. Ja. 21, '63. Where labor unions get their power. J. M. Swigert.

U. S. News & World Report. 54:98-9. Ja. 28, '63. Answer to strikes? Senator Goldwater's formula: statement. Barry Goldwater.

U. S. News & World Report. 56:78-81. Mr. 23, '64. Fewer strikes ahead in U. S.? (interview with W. E. Simkin).

U. S. News & World Report. 56:76-7. My. 4, '64. Who won what in the rail dispute; how a five-year-old fight was settled in 13 days.

*U. S. News & World Report. 56:91-3. My. 18, '64. When a big union gets into big business; banks and insurance business of Amalgamated Clothing Workers of America.

U. S. News & World Report. 56:89-90. Je. 15, '64. When strikes hit plants; employers' newest answer.

*U. S. News & World Report. 57:102-4. N. 9, '64. What unions did to help the Democrats.

U. S. News & World Report. 57:35-6. N. 30, '64. Why strikes are on the rise.

U. S. News & World Report. 57:73-4. D. 28, '64. Where employers are losing more ground to unions.

U. S. News & World Report. 58:64-5. Ja. 4, '65. Big year for unions, too? here's what they hope to get.

U. S. News & World Report. 58:66. Ja. 4, '65. Effects of pay raises in autos: an employer gives his views.

*University of Detroit Law Journal. 40:179-88. D. '62. Union member as a person. Barry Goldwater.

University of Florida Law Review. 16:103-19. Summer '63. Antitrust laws and union power. W. E. Blyler.

Vital Speeches of the Day. 28:434-9. My. 1, '62. Role of labor unions; address, March 29, 1962. G. W. Taylor.

Vital Speeches of the Day. 28:712-14. S. 15, '62. Labor-management relations; address, August 8, 1962. Barry Goldwater.

Vital Speeches of the Day. 30:189-92. Ja. 1, '64. Labor-management relations: role of labor; address, December 5, 1963. D. J. McDonald.

*Wall Street Journal. p 1+. My. 20, '64. Working "strikers." K. G. Slocum.

Wall Street Journal. p 1+. Jl. 20, '64. Bargaining alliances: unions press efforts to cooperate in their contract negotiations. J. A. Grimes.

Wall Street Journal. p 1+. Ja. 11, '65. Steel pact preview? Alan Wood, USW agreement. J. F. Lawrence.

*Wall Street Journal. p 1+. Mr. 1, '65. Death of a union? Railroad firemen's unit struggles on against threat of extinction. J. R. Macdonald.

Washington Report (Chamber of Commerce of the United States). 4:Special supplement. F. 19, '65. Your stake in Taft Hartley's 14(b).

Yale Law Journal. 73:14-73. N. '63. Collective bargaining and competition: the application of antitrust standards to union activities. R. K. Winter, Jr.

Warwick Studies in Industrial Relations

Workplace and Union

Studies were also conducted by

Brian Clifford
Howard Cohen
Joe England
Robert Fryer
Colin Gordon
John McIlroy
Sheila McKechnie
David Prentis
Robert Price
Christopher Ryan

Workplace and Union

A study of local relationships in fourteen unions

Ian Boraston
Hugh Clegg
Malcom Rimmer

*Industrial Relations Research Unit
of the Social Science Research Council
University of Warwick*

HEINEMANN EDUCATIONAL BOOKS
LONDON

Heinemann Educational Books Ltd

LONDON   EDINBURGH   MELBOURNE   AUCKLAND   TORONTO
HONG KONG   SINGAPORE   KUALA LUMPUR
IBADAN   NAIROBI   JOHANNESBURG
LUSAKA   NEW DELHI

ISBN O 435 850903

First published 1975

Published by
Heinemann Educational Books Ltd
48 Charles Street, London W1X 8AH

Set in 10pt Linotype Baskerville and
Printed in Great Britain by
Northumberland Press Limited, Gateshead

Editors' Foreword

Warwick University's first undergraduates were admitted in 1965. The teaching of industrial relations began a year later, and in 1967 a one-year graduate course leading to an M.A. in Industrial Relations was introduced. At about the same time a grant from the Clarkson Trustees allowed a beginning to be made on a research project concerned with several aspects of industrial relations in selected Coventry plants.

In 1970 the Social Science Research Council established three Research Units, one of them being the Industrial Relations Research Unit at Warwick. The Unit took over the Coventry project and developed others, including studies of union growth, union organisation, occupational labour markets, coloured immigrants in industry, ideologies of 'fairness' in industrial relations and the effects of the Industrial Relations Act.

This monograph series is intended to form the main vehicle for the publication of the results of the Unit's projects, of the research carried out by staff teaching industrial relations in the University, and, where it merits publication, of the work of graduate students. Some of these results will, of course, be published as articles, and some in the end may constitute full-scale volumes. But the monograph is the most apt form for much of our work. Industrial relations research is concerned with assembling and analysing evidence much of which cannot be succinctly summarised in tables and graphs, so that an adequate presentation of findings can easily take too much space for an article. On the other hand, even with a major project which will in the end lead to one or more books, there is often an advan-

tage in publishing interim results as monographs. This is particularly true where the project deals, as do several of the industrial relations studies at Warwick, with problems of current interest for which employers, trade unionists and governments are anxiously seeking solutions.

This study is the first to be planned, conducted and completed within the Industrial Relations Research Unit. The first four titles in the series were all associated with the Unit and written by members of the Unit, but the research had been planned and begun before the Unit was established. The original research programme of the Unit included a major project in the Organisational Behaviour of Trade Unions, which started with an investigation of the relationships between workplace organisations and unions outside the plant in Britain. The research was carried out by members of the Unit's staff and graduate students working under their supervision. This monograph is the outcome. Other stages of the project are now in hand, including a study which concentrates on relationships within the plant, an examination of higher levels of organisation in Britain, and international comparisons.

George Bain
Hugh Clegg

Contents

I

Introduction

The Problem

Although British industrial relations have been more extensively investigated over the last ten years than ever before,
the investigators have paid little attention to trade union
organisation. Their interest has been concentrated on
collective bargaining and associated topics such as productivity bargaining, incomes policy, wage drift, pay systems
and the like. The Trades Union Congress complained with
some justice of the Royal (Donovan) Commission on Trade
Unions and Employers' Associations that, despite their title
and their terms of reference, they had become primarily a
Royal Commission on collective bargaining.[1]

But it is impossible to understand the rise of domestic
bargaining and its current working without considering
trade union organisation. The shop stewards who negotiate
in the plant are trade union representatives, linked with
their unions. Studies of domestic bargaining have shown
that in many instances they act with considerable independence, so that in those instances the links must be relatively loose. But that does not tell us what the links are, nor
how they work. It does not tell us how they vary from union
to union and from plant to plant, nor why. What, then,
are the links between trade unions and their workplace
organisations?

If the surveys of the Donovan Commission and others
have established that shop stewards are primarily workplace

[1] Trades Union Congress, *Annual Report*, 1968, p. 409.

bargainers, often acting independently, they have also shown that 'first-line' full-time officers generally bear some responsibility for supervising shop stewards, and that negotiating with employers at the place of work is for most of them the largest single item in their job.[2] To what extent, then, and how do full-time officers work with shop stewards? And how does the workplace bargaining of the officers relate to the workplace bargaining of the stewards?

The full-time officer may be the most important link between the union and its workplace organisations, but he is not the only link. The branch, the branch committee and the branch secretary (where he is not the full-time officer) may all have a part to play, and it can be an important part. Where they exist, district committees may be charged with responsibility for union activity in the workplace. How, then, do all these elements in local union organisation fit together?

These were some of the questions in the minds of the members of the Social Science Research Council's Industrial Relations Research Unit at Warwick when planning a major project in the organisational behaviour of trade unions. Consequently the first stage of the project was an investigation into relationships between trade union organisation in the workplace and local trade union organisation outside, including, where appropriate, first-line full-time officers, branches and district committees.

The Methods of Investigation

The investigation consisted of a series of case studies. The most obvious alternative would have been a sample survey of full-time officers, branch secretaries and shop stewards

---

[2] Government Social Survey, *Workplace Industrial Relations*, p. 55, and H. A. Clegg, A. J. Killick and Rex Adams, *Trade Union Officers*, 1961, p. 44. These findings were generally confirmed by a survey conducted by the Industrial Relations Research Unit for the Trades Union Congress in 1970 (Trades Union Congress, *Training Full-Time Officers*, 1972).

designed to supplement the information provided by earlier surveys. But those earlier surveys had demonstrated the limits of a sample survey of individuals as a means to understanding the working of trade unions. They had revealed a great deal about the characteristics and jobs of full-time officers, branch secretaries and shop stewards, but relatively little about how their jobs relate to each other and fit into trade union organisation as a whole. It might have been possible to devise questionnaires to reveal rather more about the working of trade union organisation, provided we had known what questions to ask. But for that we should have had to be more knowledgeable about local union organisation than we were, and the only way to become more knowledgeable, as far as we could see, was to conduct case studies.

Most of the case studies were conducted by members of the Unit's research staff, but some were carried out as dissertation projects by students on the M.A. Industrial Relations course at Warwick, to fulfil part of the requirements for the degree. These students were supervised by members of the Unit's staff.

The case studies were chosen to give a fair coverage of major and middle-sized unions. More than one study was conducted in each of the three largest unions: the Transport and General Workers' Union, the Amalgamated Union of Engineering Workers, and the General and Municipal Workers' Union. The remaining studies were chosen to give a variety of types of union and industry: the National Union of Public Employees, the Union of Shop Distributive and Allied Workers, the Electrical Electronic Telecommunications and Plumbing Union, the National Union of Mineworkers, the National Union of Railwaymen, the Civil and Public Services Association (the only white collar union to be included), the National Graphical Association, the National Union of Tailors and Garment Workers, the Amalgamated Union of Building Trade Workers (prior to its absorption into the Union of Construction and Allied

Trades and Technicians), the National Union of Boot and Shoe Operatives (prior to the formation of the National Union of Footwear, Leather and Allied Trades) and the National Union of Hosiery and Knitwear Workers.

Studies began with an approach to the union's head office. A suitable local area or areas were selected and contact was then made with the local full-time officer—district secretary, district organiser or full-time branch secretary. Most of the studies therefore started with a review of the work of the local full-time officer through interviews with him, reading his records (including district committee or branch records) and accompanying him on his rounds. Then, with his agreement, several workplace organisations were selected for particular attention, and investigated mainly by interviewing shop stewards, but also using records where these were available and, in some instances, interviewing managers.

There were variations on this procedure. In some instances two or more local full-time officers worked together as a team and the investigator could not sensibly confine his attention to one of them. In others the full-time officers worked from a regional office or from headquarters in London, so that the study started with a local 'lay' officer. In one or two studies it seemed appropriate to confine the investigation to a single plant.

In selecting areas for study we attempted to attain a reasonable geographical spread. Accordingly, there were studies in Scotland, Wales, the North, the South and the Midlands. However, the South was under-represented, and, because of the location of the Unit, the Midlands were over-represented. Otherwise we were guided by the unions. It was evident that union head offices were unlikely to pick areas where they believed their organisation was defective, and that this would introduce a bias into the sample. But we did not think this a serious shortcoming, because each case study was certain to add to our knowledge and we had no particular concern to investigate trade union pathology.

While the case studies were in hand we were also engaged in conducting surveys of branch organisation and of the workload and functions of full-time officers in the General and Municipal Workers' Union, and some of the results of these surveys have been used to supplement the two case studies conducted in that union.

Because of our initial ignorance, there seemed to be no point in trying to draw up a careful plan for the conduct of each case study. Investigators were encouraged to use their initiative, find out what they could, and come back to talk over their provisional findings. As the work progressed investigators benefited from earlier studies; and about half way through the project a paper was written to indicate the kind of background material which would be helpful in each report, and the main questions which should be posed. But this could be no more than a rough guide to the investigators because of the widely different circumstances from one case to the next.

The Analysis of Results

It might have been preferable to start with a clear set of hypotheses to be tested. The case studies could then have been designed to test them as rigorously as possible. But as they were not available, we had to wait for ideas to develop out of the studies as they went along, and especially from the collation and comparison of results after they were completed.

One idea in our minds at the beginning was that the relationship between the workplace organisation and the union outside the plant was likely to be affected by agreements between the union and employers at a higher level, such as a company agreement or an industry agreement. For although the project originated in a criticism of earlier studies for concentrating too narrowly on collective bargaining, the case studies were also investigations into collective bargaining. Collective bargaining is the central activity of workplace organisations. The difference is that our studies were not concerned with collective bargaining as such, but with the relationship between the various elements of union organisation in the conduct of workplace bargaining. We supposed that workplace organisations were likely to be closely controlled by the union outside the plant where there were 'tight' industry or company agreements, and loosely controlled where there were no such agreements or where they were 'loose', leaving wide scope for domestic bargaining. These terms should be defined. A tight agreement covers a wide range of issues, specifies in some detail what is to be done on each of them, is made with the intention that its provisions are standards to be observed rather than minimum requirements which may be exceeded, and is supported by arrangements to make sure that the intention is realised. By contrast a 'loose' agreement covers few issues, is phrased in general terms, and (whether explicitly or implicitly) prescribes minimum requirements only. Such an agreement opens the door to domestic bargaining to fill in the gaps or to go beyond the minimum requirements, and we assumed that it would encourage a workplace organisation to be independent of the union outside, whereas a tight agreement would lead to dependence on the union outside. Where the plant was subject to an external agreement which fell between the extremes of tightness and looseness, we supposed that the relationship between the workplace and the union was likely to be neither wholly dependent nor wholly independent, but classifiable as 'co-operative'.

It did not take us long to discover that this notion was incorrect. The nature of the external agreement was indeed of great importance in determining the scope for bargaining at the plant, but there was no clear positive association between the scope for workplace bargaining and the degree of independence shown by the workplace organisation. We found instances where there was wide scope for workplace bargaining and the workplace organisation depended heavily on a full-time officer to conduct most or all of it, and other instances in which the scope for plant bargaining was narrowly limited by a tight external agreement but there was nevertheless a workplace organisation of some strength, exhibiting considerable independence in handling those matters which were left to it. Once we had appreciated this point, we had two headings under which to classify the workplaces we studied: firstly, according to the degree of the workplace organisation's dependence on the full-time officer in the conduct of workplace bargaining, and secondly, according to the scope for workplace bargaining; and we had to look for explanations of the position of each workplace organisation under both headings.

Before turning to explanations, however, there were other elements in the relationship between workplace organisations and unions outside the plant for us to consider. It was unusual for the link with the full-time officer to be the only link between the two. There were also the branches, in many instances district committees, and in some of them industrial conferences. And there were several instances in which the link with the full-time officer was not the most important link, for his functions had been partly or wholly taken over by a 'lay' union officer. All these elements had to be brought into the assessment of the degree of workplace dependence on the union.

In searching for explanations of the degree of workplace dependence, we began with the impact on workplace organisation of union policies concerning relationships with the plant, and of union structure outside the plant. Since these aspects of union behaviour did not appear to offer an adequate explanation of the variations which we discovered from one plant to another, we turned to the resources available to the workplace organisation within the plant, and to the factors which might influence these resources, such as the size of the workplace organisation, and the unity, trade union experience and status of its members. But this brought us back to the unions, for they have some influence on the resources available within the plant, and to

management which can supply resources direct to the workplace organisation; and to the relationship between the
union and the management whose joint style of bargaining
can encourage or impede self-reliance on the part of the
workplace organisation.

It would be incorrect to say that we *discovered* the explanation for variations in the scope of workplace bargaining in the tightness or looseness of external agreements
at company and industry level, for the link between the
two is a matter of definition. A tight external agreement
is an agreement which leaves relatively little to workplace
negotiation. Where an external agreement leaves wide scope
for workplace bargaining, that agreement is loose. But we
still had to explain why some external agreements are
tight and others loose. We found the answer in managerial
structure. Tight agreements are found where management
is centralised. But it was also necessary to consider
the influence of unions on the degree of control
exercised by these external agreements over the scope for
workplace bargaining; and we had to have a second look
at the interrelationship, if any, between the dependence of
workplace organisations and the scope for workplace bargaining.

However, the analysis began to take shape only when we
had the results of our case studies available, and could apply
it to them and alter it to suit their findings. The next seven
chapters set out these findings and also attempt to indicate
the significance of each of them for the general argument
which is taken up again in Chapters 9 and 10.

Before turning to the individual studies, the authors and
the Industrial Relations Research Unit as a whole must
record their thanks to the many trade union members, lay
officers and full-time officers—and in a number of instances
also to managers—who generously helped with the carrying
out of the research. A particular debt of gratitude is due
to those trade union officers who read drafts of the relevant
chapters, making many helpful suggestions and correcting

many errors. Several of them urgently requested us to draw special attention to one point. Since the case studies were carried out over varying periods during the years 1970–3, they describe union organisation in each district, area, branch or region as it appeared to the observer concerned at the time of the particular study. They do not represent the current situation. We have drawn attention to some of the major subsequent changes, such as amalgamations between unions and the termination of the disputes procedure for manual workers in engineering. But to bring the studies fully up to date would have required a further round of fieldwork; and in any case our objective was not to provide up to date descriptions of trade union organisation, but to assemble the material for an analysis which we hope will stand for some time.

2

The Engineers

The Union

The Amalgamated Union of Engineering Workers is the outcome of an amalgamation of four unions in which one of the four, the Amalgamated Engineering Union, dwarfed the other three put together. The four unions retain considerable autonomy as 'sections' within the amalgamated union operating under their former constitutions as regards their internal affairs. The engineering section—the only one of the four with which this study is concerned—works under the constitution of the Amalgamated Engineering Union (formed in 1920), and this in turn was largely copied from the rules of the Amalgamated Society of Engineers (formed in 1851).

The Amalgamated Society of Engineers was a union of skilled craftsmen. In its early years it members relied on their control over the supply of skilled labour to achieve results. If employers wanted skilled workers, they would have to employ them on terms acceptable to the union branch, and an elaborate system of friendly benefits supported the unemployed, the sick and the old, thereby helping to reduce competition for jobs. At this stage the main institutions within the union were the branch, which controlled the admission of members and administered benefits in its locality, and the head office which administered the funds and supervised the branches.

In time, branches within an area began to develop common standards concerning acceptable terms of employment, and to bargain about these terms with local associations of engineering employers. As a result there emerged a new institution, the district, governed by a district committee of representatives elected from the branches in the area. The district was recognised by the rules, and by the end of the nineteenth century it had accumulated wide powers to regulate wages, hours of work and conditions of employment within its territory, and to enforce its decisions by disciplining the members. The district secretary carried out a number of administrative tasks for the district committee and for the union's headquarters, but in dealings with employers he acted only under instructions from his committee. Shortly before the first world war the union recognised that the workload in the largest districts required provision for full-time secretaries.

The war hastened two processes which had important consequences for the work of the districts. By the time of the armistice the engineering industry was negotiating industry-wide agreements on pay and hours of work which led to the atrophy of separate distinct agreements on these issues, although the constitutional powers of the district committees remained as before. By contrast workshop bargaining flourished over such matters as piecework and the substitution of less-skilled workers for craftsmen, enhancing the authority of the shop stewards. The shop stewards were already recognised as the district committee's agents in the factories. An agreement with the employers' federation now gave them authority to deal with workshop issues, and the union rules were amended to grant them direct representation on the district committees.

Since that time there have been no important constitutional changes affecting the powers of the branch, the district, the district secretary and the shop stewards, but there have been great changes in the composition of the membership. Between the wars the union began to admit all grades of male engineering workers, and, during the second world war, membership was opened to women as

well. Today only a quarter of the members belong to the
skilled sections of the union (although some craftsmen join
the other sections with their lower rates of contribution).
Craftsmen still dominate the committees and major offices
of the union, but in most of the engineering factories in
which it operates, the union is no longer a craft union.

THE SOUTH MARLSHIRE DISTRICT

The size of the union's districts varies widely, from a few
hundred members up to thirty thousand. The South Marlshire district had about seven thousand members in 1970.
Four thousand of these worked in eight large engineering
firms. The rest were scattered over a large number of small
engineering firms and a considerable number of undertakings in other industries and services (for instance,
bakeries, bus undertakings, cement works, power stations,
steel works) which employ skilled engineers on maintenance.

The district covered several towns and the surrounding
countryside, and some of the factories were relatively isolated family concerns. The traditions of the area do not
include a reputation for industrial militancy, and one trade
unionist described it as a graveyard of trade unionism. However, there had been a substantial growth of membership
over the previous ten years, and this was attributed to the
development of shop steward organisation, especially in the
larger undertakings. Over that period the number of shop
stewards in the district had doubled to about 150, all but
thirty of them in the eight large firms.

The District Committee

The district committee had twelve members in addition to
the secretary. Nine of these were elected by the eighteen
branches, paired for the purpose. Two shop stewards' representatives were elected by the December quarterly meeting
of the shop stewards in the district, one of them a woman

elected as women's representative.[3] The district president is elected by a vote of the whole district every three years.

Most of the members held a minor office in their branches, but only one was a branch secretary. All of them were shop stewards, except for the branch secretary, and several of them were convenors of stewards, or senior shop stewards. No less than four of them worked in the largest engineering undertaking in the district, and another three worked in three of the remaining seven large engineering undertakings. One of these was the president, who was convenor of stewards at his plant. It was noticeable that where a large firm dominated one or other of a pair of branches, the branch representative on the district committee more often than not came from that firm, and the pairing of branches appeared to be arranged to increase the opportunity for the large firms to have representatives on the committee.

One member of the committee had served continuously for twenty years, but otherwise the longest period of service was six years, and most of them were relative newcomers.

The committee met fortnightly in the evening at 19.30. Usually the meeting finished at 21.00 after which some of the members moved to a pub. with the district secretary for a further talk. The business followed a routine. Proceedings opened with the approval of the minutes and expenses of previous meetings by the national executive committee; letters from the national executive on settlements for industrial injury and similar cases affecting members in the district; notification of industry-wide agreements; and instructions from the national executive concerning, for example, refusal to handle goods of firms affected by strikes, or relations with other unions. Most of these items were formal. Approval of expenses can be withheld to discipline district committees, but this had not occurred in South Marlshire. Most of the national agreements related to maintenance craftsmen employed in industries outside engineering. Relatively few of these industries are to be found in

---

[3] There were about 500 women members in the district.

South Marlshire and fewer still were represented on the committee.

The next issue was the notification of shop steward elections and resignations, and the issue of credentials to newly-elected stewards. There were no instances of refusing credentials in South Marlshire. Since new stewards require credentials and there is no equivalent compulsion on retiring stewards to notify the committee, the number of elections which were reported greatly exceeded the resignations and the list of stewards was therefore inflated.

The major remaining items were correspondence from the branches, from shop stewards and from employers, and the district secretary's report. All of them dealt almost exclusively with plant business—the progress of negotiations, agreements, redundancies, dismissals, strikes. These appear to be the items on which the committee might exercise its authority, for example by instructing the secretary and the shop stewards on the conduct of negotiations, by reviewing and approving draft agreements, and by taking emergency action where required. In fact the opportunities were rarely seized. The committee was not usually notified of issues settled by the stewards, and even if its members were informed there was little that they could do about an arrangement which had already been concluded to the satisfaction of the management and the stewards. Where outside advice or assistance was needed, the secretary was called in. He was meticulous in reporting his dealings with firms to the committee, and his reports normally occupied half the time of the committee, but he reported as an expert who knew the details of the business and had a long experience of negotiating behind him. Morever, the test of any settlement which he negotiated with the management of a local firm was its acceptability to the workers in the plant, rather than the approval of the committee. Consequently the committee did not exercise much control. Most managers did not appear to be aware of its existence.

There was at least one exception, however. The firm

which employed the district president introduced a bonus scheme in 1969. The management held that this had been approved by the district secretary and president (as convenor) but the members employed there, and their stewards, asserted that it had not been agreed. They decided not to work the bonus. The firm gave notice that they would discipline those who refused. There was a walk-out of the members affected by the scheme. The district committee called an emergency meeting from which the secretary was absent due to illness. It took the form of an inquiry with witnesses called in to give evidence on the dispute. After hearing them the committee decided to ask the national executive to give official approval to the strike. A compromise proposal from the firm was reported to the next fortnightly meeting, which agreed upon a return to work before the national executive had taken a decision. At the same meeting, the committee fined a member who had failed to join the strike.

One other function of the committee is to administer the district's share of the union's political fund and to sponsor candidates in elections. This did not occupy much of the committee's time, but was clearly of importance to the one member of the committee who showed an active desire to be elected to a local authority. He had been sponsored by the union and given grants towards his election expenses.

The other members of the committee showed by their replies to questions that the main advantage which they derived from membership of the committee was assistance in their job as shop steward or convenor. In particular they mentioned that it was helpful to discuss their domestic problems with other members of the committee. This was especially true when they were called upon to handle unfamiliar issues such as a redundancy, a productivity agreement or a strike. In addition, they found it helped them in their own negotiations to know about agreements and levels of pay elsewhere in the district. It was above all the convenors who emphasised these advantages of committee membership, and they acknowledged that the benefits were derived as much from the informal sessions after the meetings as from the committee meetings themselves. The quarterly meetings of the stewards, on the other hand, were not used for exchanging information. They heard a general report from the district secretary, followed by questions and debate mainly on general topics.

The District Secretary

The district secretary was first elected about ten years before this study was conducted, on the retirement of his predecessor. At that time he had been a member of the committee for some fifteen years, as shop stewards' representative, as a branch representative, and finally as president. Full-time officers of the union have to submit to re-election at the end of their first three years of office, and thereafter every five years. He was returned unopposed in the first instance, and had not been opposed in subsequent elections. There was no evidence of factional activity within the district, and he, along with all the members of the committee, would have been classified as on the right in terms of union politics.

The secretary's working time was roughly divided between: paperwork and administration, which took about 20 per cent of his time; negotiations and other dealings with plants which, together with travelling, took up about half his time; and a miscellaneous group of activities, including attending meetings and conferences, dealing with individual problems and queries, and serving on public bodies and as a magistrate, which occupied the remainder. As with most other trade union officers, many of his evenings were occupied with union work. On Friday evenings, for example, he attended branch meetings in rotation.

The branches are directly responsible to headquarters for the issue of cards, the collection of dues and the payment of benefits to members. So long as a branch was competently administered the district secretary had no call to intervene. Headquarters instructed him to step in when a branch had failed to make its quarterly returns, or where a branch was closed down, or where a branch secretary's books did not appear to be in order. Alternatively a branch might ask for his help, for instance in a dispute with its 'pair' over the election of their district representative. But the most noteworthy occasions for his intervention arose when plant issues were debated at a branch meeting. This did not happen often, and when it did occur it was usually in a branch dominated by a single firm. It could be a crucial stage in the handling of the issue. In one instance the branch meeting seemed to be the best place to discuss a major redundancy, and in another the issue was the advisability of a small group of workers coming out on unofficial strike to draw attention to their grievance.

The district secretary kept a detailed list of his visits to plants. During 1968 and 1969 he made 176 plant visits. Since 55 per cent of these visits were to the eight large plants which covered rather less than 60 per cent of the district's membership, there is no indication that large plants or small plants, in general, occupied a disproportionate share of his attention. But there were marked differences between firms in each category. Between them, two of the large firms accounted for 49 visits, and two others for only five, whereas two small firms accounted for twenty-two visits. Finally, it was evident that many small firms received no visits for several years on end, if ever.

There were also several employers' associations whose members employed engineering maintenance workers and which therefore had dealings with the union through the district secretary. But they did not occupy a great deal of his time. In all, fourteen meetings were recorded over the two years. He came into contact with the local engineering employers association only when the official disputes procedure was invoked, and that rarely occurred in South Marlshire. This is one reason why the union's divisional

organiser, who is responsible for handling cases in procedure for a group of districts, was rarely seen there. But in
any case he preferred to concentrate on the other districts
in his division.

There was relatively little to distinguish the secretary's
dealings with federated firms from those with the engineering firms which were not federated. There had, it is true,
to be periodic negotiations with each non-federated firm
(along with the other unions concerned) to settle general
increases in pay for the manual workers in the plant,
whereas the federated firms applied the general increases
negotiated from time to time by their federation. But, as
it happened, most of the federated firms of any size had
productivity agreements or job evaluation schemes which
covered all their manual employees, and entailed the
negotiation of increases over and above those settled by the
association. Moreover, the district secretary was just as likely
to be called in to deal with a pay claim or grievance concerning a section or a grade in a non-federated firm as in a
federated one.

Small firms provided two reasons for the district secretary's
intervention which did not apply in larger'firms. The first
of these was the absence of anyone else authorised to
negotiate with management. The district's records showed
that there were ten firms with one steward apiece. The
secretary had visited only two of these over the two years,
paying a total of five visits. Over the same period he had
paid 31 visits to twelve firms of comparable size, but without
stewards. In very small firms (nearly all of them with less
than thirty employees) the secretary and the shop steward
seem therefore to be alternatives. The second reason for
his intervention is related to the first. The secretary was
called into one plant to assist the members to find a
candidate and to elect him shop steward, and in another
rather larger plant he reorganised representation by persuading three men to stand as candidates for three constit-
uencies where there had been a single steward before.

Before meeting the managers, the secretary usually arranged a formal briefing with the stewards, or, if there was no steward, with the workers. This was done in 132 of the 171 visits for which details are available. He took shop stewards or workers into the meeting on 102 out of the 171 visits. The records show that stewards almost invariably accompanied him in the larger firms, and most of the unaccompanied meetings were in small firms. He reported back on the negotiations to the stewards, or to a shop stewards' committee, or to the members, on only 75 visits.

This figure is deceptively small, for three reasons. In many instances no agreement was reached, except to arrange a further meeting, so there was nothing on which to consult the members or the stewards. Secondly, there was no particular reason for consultation where the secretary had been fully briefed and had obtained from management exactly what had been asked of him. Thirdly, where he had been accompanied by a group of stewards they might take the responsibility for accepting the outcome. Consequently it is probable that he reported back and sought authority for a settlement in the great majority of cases where such consultation was relevant. On several occasions stewards or members rejected a proposed settlement, and negotiations had to be resumed.

The District Secretary and the Shop Stewards

In order to explore the secretary's relations with the plants more closely, a special study of negotiations was made in four of the large engineering undertakings within the district, two of them federated and two not.

The second in terms of numbers of employees, a federated plant, had a well-established shop steward organisation with a works committee to handle domestic negotiations. All the district secretary's visits to the plant were in connection with the negotiation and application of a productivity agreement. The district secretary was involved in the negotiation of the agreement because the stewards had no experience of productivity bargaining. After the signature of the agreement he was brought in to deal with the objections of two groups of workers to operating the agreement. Firstly, the toolroom and its steward refused to be included in the agreement. Secondly, the pieceworkers complained that their earnings were not rising as fast as they had been promised, and came out on strike. The convenor and his colleagues could not handle these situations, and the district secretary was called in.

Most of the district secretary's visits to the largest of the four undertakings—a non-federated firm, also concerned the negotiation of a productivity agreement. However, in this case the negotiation of the agreement led to a considerable increase in activity and organisation among the shop stewards who had previously been granted few facilities. The agreement included a job evaluation scheme, which was administered by a joint grading sub-committee including several stewards, and was negotiated by a bargaining committee consisting of the district secretary and a full-time officer of the other union at the plant (the General and Municipal Workers), the convenors of the unions, and several stewards. This committee reported to a meeting of all the stewards after each negotiating session. Five other visits were not connected with the productivity agreement. They arose from the failure of the stewards to secure acceptable concessions on other issues, three of them disciplinary cases. It is relevant that the district secretary was called in only once during the following year when the productivity agreement and its consequences had been digested.

During 1968 and 1969 the district secretary had paid only five visits to the two smaller firms selected for special study, in both of which shop steward organisation was manifestly weaker than in either of the first two. But the number of visits increased in 1970. In the first, a family concern, several visits arose out of two strikes. In one of them, a spontaneous walk-out, neither the managers nor the convenor dared face the strikers, and the district secretary was called in to try to get the men 'back into procedure'. In the second, the convenor called him in at once and left the negotiations, involving a series of visits, almost entirely to him. The third occasion for intervention was a redundancy. The secretary could not get to the firm until after the redundant workers had left and could do no more than extract a promise of consultation in future.

The fourth firm, the smallest of the four, had only three stewards to represent 170 members. A productivity agreement was negotiated almost entirely between the district secretary and consultants employed by the firm. The stewards did not question the agreement, which appeared to be acceptable to the men, but when it came into operation the workers in one department struck because it was not yielding the earnings which they expected. Their steward proved totally ineffective and subsequently resigned. The two others remained at work. After a week of negotiations the district secretary persuaded the strikers to return to work. He then secured the election of three new stewards, gave them tuition on the operation of procedure, and arranged for them to attend a shop stewards' training course.

The experience of these four undertakings is a warning against classifying plants—or at least the larger plants—into those which receive frequent visits from the district secretary and those which are rarely visited. The second received sixteen visits in 1968 and 1969, but only a single visit in 1970. The third and fourth, with only five visits between them in 1968 and 1969, both made sharply increased demands on his time in 1970. The evidence is rather of fluctuation over time according to the issues arising in the plant and the reaction of the members to them.

It is possible to suggest reasons for expecting heavier demands from the plants with strong domestic organisation —because they generate more issues—and for expecting heavier demands from the weaker plants—because they are less able to handle issues for themselves. But the evidence justifies neither of these expectations. There was fluctuation in both types of plant. There was, however, a difference in the quality of the secretary's dealings with them. Where domestic organisation was strong he was called in to work with the stewards and to provide a service for the members. Where organisation was weak, he was called in to take charge of the situation.

It is also possible that the presence of a representative on the district committee might affect a plant's demands for his services, and for 1968 and 1969 the figures suggest that the plants with representatives on the committee made heavier demands. The four large firms represented on the committee, with 2,200 members, received 63 visits; whereas the remaining four large firms, with 1,600 members, received only 33 visits. But the evidence is not strong enough to support a firm conclusion.

Less shaky conclusions can be established concerning the shop stewards' reasons for asking the secretary to intervene in plant affairs. The largest single group of visits arose because the stewards were faced with a problem beyond their experience or competence. Productivity agreements and job evaluation schemes are the most common examples of this category, but there were also redundancies and, in several instances, the negotiation of 'check-off' agreements for the deduction of union dues from pay.

The second most numerous category consisted of those instances in which the stewards were willing to handle the issues but had reached the end of their domestic procedures without obtaining a satisfactory settlement. Then the only constitutional alternative to calling in the secretary was to drop the matter.

Two other categories were instances of conflict within the labour force, as when a group of workers refused to accept or to work to an agreement, and instances in which the management refused to deal with the stewards, for example on a matter of managerial prerogative or because they declined to negotiate until there was a return to work in an unofficial strike. These last two categories merged into each other since both commonly involved stoppages, but most strikes in the first category took place against the advice of the stewards, whereas strikes in the second category might be led by the stewards.

The four categories cover the shop stewards' reasons for summoning the district secretary, but the request for a visit may also come from a manager. In South Marlshire, however, this did not happen often. When it did, it was almost invariably for one of two reasons: either it was a courtesy invitation to inform him of, for example, a change in the organisation of the firm, or a managerial intention to make proposals for a job evaluation exercise; or there was an unofficial strike or overtime ban, or some other form of interference with normal production.

Finally, the district secretary was in a position to initiate visits for himself, if he chose, but it appears that he never did so. He always waited to be asked, and, if the stewards decided that they could manage on their own, he did not interfere. However, once he was called in, he might go beyond the immediate issue by, for example, initiating reform of bargaining procedures or shop steward organisation where he thought that weaknesses had been revealed. In his first years of full-time office he had made vigorous efforts to recruit to the union, with some success. Then he decided that he had reached the point of decreasing returns, and left recruitment entirely to the stewards and the branches.

THE LEACHESTER DISTRICT

Leachester is one of the country's major industrial cities, and engineering is its major industry. Consequently the membership of the engineering section of the Amalgamated Union of Engineering Workers, at over 30,000, was much larger than in South Marlshire and concentrated in a considerably smaller area.

There were far more large plants, and indeed the very notion of what constituted a large plant was different. Whereas in South Marlshire an engineering plant employing more than 150 members of the union was relatively large, in Leachester there were nearly fifty of these, fourteen of them with five hundred or more members of the union in employment. And one of them with nearly four thousand.

This did not make it the largest engineering plant in the district since other unions have members in all the fourteen large plants and many of the smaller plants. The largest single plant employed about nine thousand in all, just over a quarter of them being members of the Engineers.

In addition the union had members employed on maintenance in a wide range of other industries and public services, in most instances in relatively small groups.

A number of plants, both large and small, belonged to major national companies, and some of these companies had several plants within the district. However, at that time this tie was of little importance to the union members and officers within the district, since in most instances the plant managers dealt with them separately, and apparently with considerable independence; and on the union side contact between stewards employed in different plants of the same company was, with rare exceptions, not noticeably closer than with stewards in other plants.

The shop stewards' returns gave details for over a hundred plants, which employed about thirty thousand members in all, but it was evident that union members were employed in an unidentifiable number of other firms, most of them small. The fourteen plants with five hundred members or more accounted for half the members and a little more than four hundred stewards out of a district total of over a thousand.

About two-thirds of the plants, including all fourteen large plants, were federated to the local engineering employers' association, which played a very much more important part in the industrial relations of the district than did its counterpart in South Marlshire. Some of the remaining plants were non-engineering undertakings affiliated to their appropriate employers' organisations, and others were part of a public service or a nationalised industry, but most of them were non-federated engineering undertakings.

The Structure of the District Committee

Between them, the 54 branches within the district returned 25 representatives to the district committee. Because of the size of the district, the December quarterly meeting of shop stewards elected six shop stewards' representatives to the committee, along with the women's representative. With the district president, chosen by a vote of the whole district, the committee consisted of 33 members. Eight of the fourteen large plants were represented among them, and 22 members of the committee were employed in those eight plants. Since the total membership of the union in those eight plants numbered about 9,500, it follows that plants employing less than a third of the members provided two thirds of the district committee.

Seven members of the committee, all of them branch representatives, were not currently shop stewards. Four of them had previously been shop stewards, two of them having been defeated in an election and a third having been made redundant from the factory where he had been convenor until he left.

There were eleven convenors among the 26 members who were currently shop stewards, and one senior steward in a plant in which the union had minority membership. Five of them were branch representatives, and they held all six places elected by the shop stewards, and the presidency. Of the ten members who had more than five years' service on the committee in 1970, six were convenors. Thus there was a fair turnover in committee membership, and it seemed to be no great problem for a convenor who had lost his seat as a shop stewards' representative to regain it as a branch representative.

Where branch voting figures were recorded they were generally less than ten per cent. By contrast about four hundred stewards attended the December quarterly meeting, where the number of candidates seeking election as shop stewards' representatives usually exceeded thirty. Many of them harangued the meeting, emphasising the achievements of the shop stewards in their own plants. Convenors from large factories were accompanied by groups of colleagues prepared to cheer them and to vote for them.

Consequently there was a distinct hierarchy in the Leachester district committee which had no counterpart in South Marlshire. At the top came the convenors returned by the robust electoral process of the December quarterly meeting, followed by the remainder of the convenors. Members of both these groups had a position of considerable authority in their own plants, and most of them also had long experience of plant negotiations and some years of service on the committee. The remaining members of the committee trailed a good way behind with no rousing electoral victories, little experience, short service and no more than modest status in their own plants.

Another contrast with South Marlshire was the division between left and right factions, which played a considerable part in elections. The factions were fairly evenly split, although for some time the left had enjoyed a small majority on the district committee. Elections in which the votes of the branches were pooled, such as those for district secretary and president, and for divisional and national officers, were dominated by a few strongly partisan branches, since the turnout in other branches was very low. The partisan branches therefore tried to secure a relatively high poll by, for instance, opening their branches early, or arranging branch meetings on the factory site, or hiring mini-buses to bring voters to the poll.[4] The December quarterly meeting of the stewards was another opportunity for partisan activity, and had the added excitement that both factions mustered their support for the one meeting.

Branch elections for the district committee occasioned less excitement. The partisan branches could return their own candidates without much fuss, so long as branches of rival factions were not 'paired', and many branches were apathetic or neutral. Similarly most plants were remote from factional strife. Only fifteen plants could be identified as under the control of one faction or the other, nearly all of them large.

Some of these were dominated by one faction, whereas in others the opposition group also had a following. Since members employed in one plant may be scattered over several branches, the branch elections to the district committee provided an opportunity for the minority group within a plant to secure a place on the committee; and in fact several large plants were represented on the committee by members of both factions.

The Work of the District Committee

The committee normally met every week for two hours or more. There were 44 meetings in 1969, and the general purposes sub-committee met in several of the intervening weeks to deal with committee business.

Several aspects of its work were affected by the use made of the industry's disputes procedure (then still in force).[5] In South Marlshire the procedure was used very rarely. In Leachester there were 247 works and local conferences

---

[4] Since then the union's constitution has been altered to provide for the election of full-time officers by postal ballot.

[5] The procedure was terminated at the end of 1971. Since then, disputes reported to the district as not settled within the plant have usually been discussed at informal meetings attended by representatives of the employers' association and full-time union officers.

under the procedures during 1969 alone. Since the local employers' association was represented at all these conferences, their number helps to explain the importance of the association in Leachester's industrial relations. On the union side the conferences were handled by the divisional organiser and the assistant divisional organiser (except on the few occasions on which the district secretary substituted for one of them). Since their division included seven other districts, the organiser and his assistant were almost entirely occupied with the operation of the procedure. It was the prerogative of the committee to decide whether a dispute should go into procedure, and whether an issue unresolved at works conference should go on to local conference. If it was not settled at that stage, the dispute was handed over to the national executive and the national officers.

The final stage of the procedure—a central conference at York—provided one of the items of correspondence from the national executive with which the committee began its business. The executives notified the relevant district of all disputes handled at central conference, and as many as two or three of these might be reported to the Leachester committee at a single meeting.

Before that, however, came the approval of the district committee's minutes, and correspondence over disputes. From time to time a district decision was reversed, as when a shop steward's credentials, withdrawn by the district, were restored by the executive, or when, in the past, the executive had objected to district approval of strikes in breach of procedure. At the time of the study the executive appeared to accede, in the end, to every district request for dispute benefit to be paid. Some requests for dispute benefit were sent by the branches direct to the executive, and when that happened the executive asked the district for information on the dispute. The remainder of the dealings between the district and the executive related to administrative detail, or formal business such as the notification of industry-wide agreements.

Thereafter the proceedings of the Leachester committee diverged from South Marlshire, where correspondence was separated from the district secretary's report and this report was a detailed account of his dealings with employers over the previous fortnight. In Leachester the district secretary included correspondence (except from the executive) in his report, and said little or nothing about his doings except on matters where he needed the support of the district. Plant disputes which were in procedure were the subject of the district organiser's report.

Most of the correspondence was from shop stewards—141 out of 238 items of correspondence in the first four months of 1969. Of these 141 items, 107 came from convenors, reflecting a convention that it is the prerogative of convenors (where they exist) to deal with the committee. The channel for the dissatisfied steward—or member—is through the branch. About half the letters from the branches dealt with industrial matters and most of them drew the attention of the committee to dissatisfaction with the handling of an issue within the plant.

Over half of the items submitted by the stewards (73) reported failure to settle a matter in the plant with a view to going into procedure, and in these instances the committee required the countersignature of the convenor, if the letter was not from him. Fifteen items informed the committee that agreement had in fact been reached on an item previously reported as unresolved. Twenty-eight plant agreements were submitted for ratification. In addition seven strikes were reported; the committee's advice was sought on a variety of plant problems including demarcation and dismissals; and in two instances stewards wrote direct to inform the committee of differences with their convenors.

Plants differed considerably in their use of the committee. The largest, with nearly four thousand members and three members on the committee, wrote in four times during the four months; another, with 1,500 members and four members on the committee, wrote ten times; a third with 900 members and no representatives, wrote nine times; and a fourth, with less than two hundred members but two representatives on the committee, wrote five times. Since more than half the items were requests to go into procedure, there is a fairly close correlation between frequency of correspondence with the committee and the use of the procedure. Most plants which keep themselves out of procedure have little to do with the committee, whereas procedure-prone plants must deal with the committee.

Procedure

The union rule requiring the divisional organiser to attend all local conferences is interpreted as making him responsible for conducting works and local conferences. He has to report to the district committee, and, because of its importance, he nearly always reported to the Leachester committee in person. Thus the committee had full information on the cases going through procedure; but it does not follow that they exercised much authority over the conduct of cases.

The procedure would have been wholly clogged up if the divisional organiser had been required to report back each new offer from the employers, and each change of tactic which he adopted. Accordingly, he reported back the outcome of a conference. On the other hand, representatives of the plant concerned accompanied him to the conference, so he could confer with them during the proceedings. When the result was a settlement agreeable to the organiser, the stewards and the firm, the committee could do nothing but accept. When the result was a clear failure to agree, there was little that the committee could do but send the issue on to the next stage in procedure.

One or other of these two decisions was reached in 150 out of the 247 works and local conferences in 1969. The rest (apart from two in which no outcome was recorded) were retained for further discussion which gave the committee a chance to influence proceedings. Even then, however, they usually recorded that 'the question be continued' giving the organiser a free hand to carry on.

The committee's authority in relation to procedure was most evident in their decision to allow disputes to enter procedure in the first instance. The great majority went forward without demur, but the committee did not allow disputes about overtime to enter procedure where the overtime in question had been worked beyond the limit of the national agreement on overtime; and they tried to keep piecework disputes out of procedure. It is union policy to 'put the job on the floor' (i.e. to refuse to work the job) rather than record a failure to agree and then work on the employer's terms until the dispute is settled. This puts the onus to settle on the employer.

The District Secretary

The district secretary had served for three years at the time of this study, and was therefore less experienced than his colleague in South Marlshire. In addition, he belonged to the right-wing faction which was in a minority on the committee. Along with the greater use of procedure in Leachester, these factors could account for him having less influence over the committee and the conduct of negotiations in the plant than his South Marlshire colleague, but there were other reasons for the contrast.

Because of the size of the district the volume of administrative work was much greater than in South Marlshire, so that he spent more time in his office than did his colleague. One indication of this was the weekly report of the Leachester district secretary of 10–12 pages compared with 3–5 pages once a fortnight in South Marlshire. Instead of one day a week in South Marlshire, administration took about half the secretary's time in Leachester.

Even when he was available for negotiations, he was not

often called in by the large plants, or, for that matter, by most of the small plants. The convenors in the large plants were effectively full-time negotiators, at the head of powerful workplace organisations, and they preferred to manage for themselves. When they were forced to take issues outside their own plants, they went into procedure or referred them to the district committee dominated by their peers. They did not send for the district secretary. In some instances the influence of the convenors extended beyond their own plants. Some convenors of large plants took the shop steward organisations of smaller plants under their wings, giving them advice and encouragement, so that they too had no need of the district secretary.

Nevertheless the secretary's dealings were mainly with small plants, especially with non-federated plants in which the official procedure did not operate, and the divisional organiser therefore had no business. If union members reported that their employer did not recognise the union (and this could happen especially where new plants were opened up) he had to organise pressure for recognition. Where recognition was granted he negotiated a procedure with the employer, and under the procedure he would be called in when the stewards and the employer failed to reach agreement. Similarly it was the district secretary who was called in when no agreement could be reached domestically in private firms outside engineering, and in public services and the nationalised industries. In 1970 he was called into non-federated engineering firms and undertakings outside engineering on 160 occasions.

Some business also came his way from federated firms. Like his colleague in South Marlshire, he had become an expert in check-off agreements, which were complicated by the need to distribute the dues deducted from pay between several branches. He was therefore called in to negotiate check-off agreements. He had also benefited from the growth of formal domestic agreements on other issues in engineering.

Such agreements were rare until a few years ago. Formal dealings were through the official procedure. In the plant, managers and shop stewards dealt with each other informally by adding to the volume of 'custom and practice' in the plant, although one side or the other might write down what was done for future reference. Where there were formal agreements in the plant they rarely went beyond an arrangement for handling disputes and a few fragmentary decisions affecting particular issues in particular sections. Over the last few years, however, under the pressure of government policies and the influence of the Donovan Report, formal domestic procedures have multiplied and there has been a fashion for plant-wide pay agreements, either as productivity agreements or as measured daywork agreements (normally replacing piecework). These in turn have led to annual pay reviews. Such agreements require a formal signature on behalf of the union. They come within the scope of the divisional organiser only where the negotiations fail and the issue enters procedure. Otherwise the district secretary signs.

The South Marlshire agreements of this kind were negotiated by the district secretary. In Leachester the convenors in the large firms called their district secretary in only at the end of negotiations, to sign the agreements. But he was called in to negotiate where plant-wide agreements were under discussion in smaller federated firms with less experienced shop stewards. According to the district secretary this was the aspect of his work which gave him most satisfaction, and he had too little of it.

Occasionally the employers' association or a firm asked the secretary to persuade unofficial strikers back to work. On these occasions he began by investigating the issue, and sometimes told the firm that it had brought its troubles on itself, and must find its own solution. But usually Leachester firms, like South Marlshire firms, left the stewards to call in the district secretary. In contrast to South Marlshire, this meant that he was rarely invited to the large Leachester firms.

The Stewards and the District Committee

So long as they stayed out of procedure, then, the only check on the independence of the large workplace organisations was the district committee.

Plant business came to the attention of the district committee because plant agreements were submitted to them for approval, or because the convenor asked for their advice, or because one or more shop stewards or members had complained about the conduct of affairs in the plant. The committee gave serious attention to these items of business. Many of them were referred to their most important subcommittee, the shop stewards' sub-committee, which usually summoned the stewards concerned to discuss the matter. In dealing with agreements, the committee acted as a panel of experts searching the text for possible flaws and suggesting improvements. They also vetted agreements to see that they did not offend against principles upheld by the district committee. Being shop stewards themselves, they usually upheld the authority of the workplace organisation in the plant on matters of union discipline or dissension within the plant.

One of the committee's principles was that no one should work overtime beyond the maximum of thirty hours a month prescribed in the national agreement, except by permission of the district committee. Consequently a good deal of the relatively sparse correspondence from firms to the committee consisted of requests to relax the agreement in their favour, in most instances with the support of the stewards in the plant. The committee refused to approve productivity agreements leading to redundancy, although where a firm was closed there was little they could do except to seek the best possible redundancy terms. Where measured day-work was introduced they sought to ensure that 'control was not lost'. Under piecework the principle of 'mutuality' ensures that the price for a given job is negotiated with the worker or workers who are going to do the job, and thereafter the pace at which the work is done is largely their affair. Under measured daywork, pay is settled in a plant-wide agreement and work measurement is used to indicate the work to be done in a given period. Control is said to be lost if work standards are settled by management alone, and 'retained' if the standards are subject to negotiation. By 1970 the district's concern for control had led to a policy of rejecting all measured daywork agreements.

However, the committee and the shop stewards' sub-committee could not impose these principles throughout the district. They could act only where their attention was drawn to a draft agreement or to excessive overtime working, and they had no effective means of ensuring that their decisions were carried out.

A few examples illustrate the extent of the district committee's authority. In one of the largest plants, well-represented on the district committee, the stewards kept strict records of overtime and all requests for relaxation of the national agreement had to be referred to the convenor who sent them on to the district committee with his recommendations. Maintenance engineers were allowed to exceed the limit so long as they took time off during the working day to balance the excess. Control was probably effective among the skilled workers but production workers were divided between several unions, and the other unions had little regard for the agreement. There was therefore no means of ensuring control of overtime worked by members of the union on production.

Another plant, employing about four hundred members of the union, was dominated by a convenor who has held that post for many years. At one time he had been a member of the district committee, but at this time the plant had no representative there. Indeed the convenor was openly at odds with many of the current members. Within the plant he had no rivals among the unskilled labour force. He handled almost all issues personally, and referred nothing to the district. Rates were low, and earnings depended on high overtime. At times the average for some sections had risen to between fifty and sixty hours a month. The convenor, himself opposed to systematic overtime working, had warned the firm on several occasions, but had not referred the matter to the committee, and the committee had never intervened in the plant's affairs.

Another group of 250 skilled members, employed in a plant with over two thousand manual workers, had no representatives on the district committee and kept their affairs to themselves. Communication with the district committee was rare, but in 1969 they submitted for approval a grading agreement affecting the pay of all skilled men. The shop stewards' sub-committee recommended rejection because only the toolroom stewards had come to defend it, and the sub-committee feared that its effect might be to the disadvantage of the other skilled workers. Their report came before the next committee meeting which heard representations in support of the agreement from the remaining stewards and approved it.

The plant, which employed almost four thousand members, also kept its affairs to itself, except for reporting domestic 'failures to agree' so that the issues could go into procedure, and the occasions for that were rare. Average earnings in the plant were among the highest in the district, and it was generally regarded as an example to the others, so that no one outside was likely to question the stewards or their convenors too closely. In 1970, however, the management wished to introduce a measured daywork scheme. The scheme was to be applied section by section, and it had been devised so that it was acceptable to the sections which would operate it first. With them and their stewards in favour, it was not easy for the convenor to reject the scheme. On the other hand, such an important agreement had to be put before the district committee, who were at that time opposed to all measured daywork. Apparently he persuaded his colleagues on the committee that it was 'not really' a daywork agreement, but just 'another form of piecework'. The committee approved and the district secretary signed the agreement.

At a fifth firm there was a conflict between the nightshift and the main body of workers who thought the nightworkers left the machines in a bad state and relied on the effort of the dayworkers to maintain the factory bonus. In 1970 the firm began to cut back their operations, and the nightshift was made redundant. The nightworkers complained through their branch of victimisation. The stewards were summoned before the district committee and instructed to record a retrospective failure to agree over the dismissal of nightworkers, although this was no more than a gesture as they had already left for other jobs.

Another test of the district authority is strikes. Requests for official support came to the district, although claims for payment of dispute benefit could go straight to the executive. The committee considered the circumstances, among which breach of procedure was not necessarily regarded as the most important, and made a recommendation to the executive. But only a small fraction of the district's strikes came before the committee, and its records give no clue that certain plants were strike-prone and others were strike-free, although several strike-prone plants were represented there. The overwhelming majority of strikes were not reported to the committee, whether they were condoned by the stewards or 'unofficial-unofficial' strikes of small sections within the plant.

The reasons for referring issues to the committee remain to be explained. Some plant-wide agreements were so obviously important that they had to be sent for district approval. Others were in no danger of rejection and were sent to advertise the negotiating prowess of the stewards concerned. Some of them were rewarded by congratulatory messages. Still other references were to forestall criticism and to make sure that the stewards concerned were not summoned before the committee to rebut the complaint of a section within their plant.

But why were the stewards in some plants more concerned to avoid this risk than their colleagues elsewhere? Complaints came from groups whose special interests had been upset, such as nightshift workers or high-paid pieceworkers whose earnings had not been sustained under a daywork agreement, but all plants of any size had groups with their own interests, so this does not explain differences between plants. There was some evidence that factional conflict was a reason for going to the committee. The factions were fairly evenly divided in the first of the five plants, with the right in control. The convenor and his colleagues were extremely careful to obtain the approval of the committee for all their actions which might be subject to challenge. On the other hand, the plant with almost four thousand members was controlled by a left-wing convenor and group of stewards who were in firm control. They rarely bothered the committee.

But this was not the only reason for going to the committee. The stewards in the third of the five plants were surprised by the sharp intervention of the committee over their grading agreement. Henceforth they took trouble to refer doubtful issues to the committee. Once bitten ...

Conclusion

These two district studies have been set out at greater length than any of the succeeding case studies for three reasons. Firstly, the records of the district committee provided fuller written information than was available in any other union; secondly, several explanations offered in this chapter need not be repeated; thirdly, as will emerge, the district committees, especially the Leachester committee, played a larger part in relationships between workplace organisations and the union than any comparable body in another union, and their work had therefore to be described in some detail.

However, by themselves studies of two districts of a single union cannot yield conclusions about union organisation in general. Studies within a single union cannot provide information about the effect of differences in union structures and constitutions, and these two studies yield little information about the effect of different bargaining arrangements. Most of the plants which were examined came under the engineering procedure and the rest were non-federated. Workplace relations with the union did not seem to vary greatly between the two types of plant, but it might be expected that no significant difference would be found between plants governed by so loose an industry agreement as applies in engineering and plants unfettered by industry agreements. Their experience gives no indication of what might happen under a tighter industry agreement.

Nevertheless some impressions emerge which may be worth noting for comparison with the findings of the studies which follow. The degree to which workplace organisations relied on their district secretaries (or, in some instances in Leachester, on the district committee) appeared to be related to their size. Many small workplace organisations in South Marlshire managed for themselves, but those which called on the district secretary allowed him to take charge of the situation, whereas larger workplace organisations called him in to work with them on major negotiations or unfamiliar problems, or where they had done all they could on their own. Much the same behaviour was observed in Leachester workplace organisations of smaller size, but the largest workplace organisations there—considerably larger than any in South Marlshire—were almost entirely independent of the district secretary, calling him in to transact formal business only. This self-reliance might be the outcome of differences between the two districts: the atmosphere of a major city compared with that of a scattered district covering several towns; the relative inexperience

of the Leachester secretary; the size of his membership compared with his heavy load of administrative
duties; and his political differences with the majority
of his committee. But it could also be explained by
the strength which the largest Leachester workplace organisations have acquired because of the numbers they represent,
and the power which they confer on their convenors. If
so, an association between size and dependence may be
tentatively postulated for testing against the findings of
later studies.

The power of the major Leachester workplace organisations and their convenors may also explain the contrast
between the two district committees. Although the South
Marlshire committee dealt with one important dispute in
the absence of their secretary, normally they did little more
than approve his actions in plant negotiations, whereas the
Leachester committee cut a more important figure. They
advised workplace organisations on negotiations and draft
agreements, and some of the convenors took smaller workplace organisations under their wings. In all these respects
the committee were doing jobs performed by the district
secretary in South Marlshire, and which their own secretary
carried out elsewhere in Leachester. Beyond this, they tried
to impose general standards throughout the district in relation to overtime working, redundancy and measured daywork. In this respect their strength was also their weakness.
The committee's power derived not only from the union
rules but was also due to the presence on the committee of
representatives of many of the strongest and most independent workplace organisations in the district. There was little
they could do to impose their standards upon powerful
workplace organisations which chose to keep their affairs to
themselves.

3

The Transport and General Workers

The Union

The Transport and General Workers' Union is the largest in the country, with about 1.7 million members. Founded in 1921 by the amalgamation of a number of unions, mainly in transport, the union has absorbed many others since then, notably the Workers' Union in 1929, which brought with it claims to represent large numbers of engineering workers, and the National Union of Vehicle Builders in 1973.

In contrast to the Engineers, full-time officers (apart from the general secretary) are appointed by the executive council which consists of lay members. For administrative purposes the union is divided into regions, each with its regional committee and regional secretary; industrial issues are handled by national trade group committees, each with its national trade group secretary. Traditionally, regional trade group secretaries dealt with industrial issues in the regions, subject to the national trade group, and to the regional secretary on administrative matters. However, there is provision for an alternative arrangement whereby a district committee can be established in a suitable area. Power is conferred on the district by the executive council and most districts have their own full-time district secretaries to handle matters which would normally be the business of the regional trade groups.

The traditional arrangement gave great authority to the national trade groups, and was especially appropriate at a time when industry-wide bargaining predominated in British industrial relations. But when Jack Jones, the present general secretary, took over in 1969 he had already formed the view that it was much less appropriate at a time when bargaining within the plant had taken on great importance. He had himself held office as district secretary in Coventry for a number of years, and his experience led him to believe that district organisation was better suited to current conditions. He therefore set himself energetically to multiplying the number of district committees in the union.

However, a district structure cannot fit the diverse membership of the Transport and General Workers as neatly as it does the members of the Engineers, over threequarters of whom are to be found in engineering plants of one sort or another. This is particularly true in sections of the union which are still covered by fairly tight industry-wide agreements with relatively little scope for bargaining at the plant, such as the road passenger transport industry. Consequently this section continues to operate the trade group system both within the regions and nationally, leaving the rapidly-extending district organisation to deal, in the main, with the membership in the whole range of manufacturing industry, such as metals, engineering, chemicals, food manufacture, and, in some instances, commercial road transport, docks, construction and local authority and hospital services as well.

This experiment permits a particularly interesting comparison between the Transport and General Workers and the Engineers, for it is possible to examine not only the effect of two strongly contrasting structures, but also the consequence of reconstructing the Transport and General Workers on a pattern more like that of the Engineers.

Three districts were studied: the Leachester district, which covered a larger area than the Engineers' district there; the East Sandshire district which covered a group of towns of roughly similar size to those in South Marlshire, but scattered over a considerably larger geographical area; and the relatively small Steel Valley district.

LEACHESTER

A district committee was first established by the union in Leachester on an 'unofficial' basis in 1966, with the regional trade groups retaining their formal authority. It covered the engineering branches, which provide the bulk of the union's membership there, and consisted of branch delegates meeting quarterly and electing an executive committee to transact business in the interval. A regional officer acted as secretary.

Originally the main functions of the committee were recruitment, securing co-operation between branches, and the collection and distribution of information. Members pooled information about ill-organised and unorganised plants, and discussed what might be done about them, but action was left to the stewards and the branches. A card was designed for shop stewards to fill in details of pay systems and earnings in their plants, akin to the quarterly returns of the Engineers. Gradually other functions were acquired. Shop stewards and full-time officers were encouraged to report plant agreements to the committee. At first these were merely received, but subsequently the executive began to comment on them, and to try to move towards a general policy on productivity agreements and schemes of measured daywork.

At the end of 1969, soon after Jack Jones became general secretary, this unofficial committee was disbanded and a new district was constituted under the rules. It comprised nearly fifty thousand members in metals, engineering, car manufacture, chemicals and rubber. Each branch within the district had the right to elect representatives in proportion to membership (one representative for five hundred members, with a maximum of four representatives to a branch), giving 72 representatives for 48 branches. These representatives, most of them shop stewards, met quarterly. They elected from their number an executive committee of fourteen, roughly divided among the industrial sections according to their membership. Nearly all fourteen were convenors or senior stewards, most of them with long records of union activity. The informal hierarchy of the Engineers' district committee was thus formally recognised by the Transport and General Workers.

A district secretary and four other full-time officers were engaged in the work of the district, although two of them also had duties outside it. All five were required to report to the district committee and its executive.

In addition to the functions previously carried out informally by the old committee, the new committee assisted members in dispute, and vetted agreements. All branches and shop stewards were required to seek and obtain ratification of agreements from the district committee. A conference of branch secretaries and shop stewards was called to inform them of the authority now vested in the district committee.

By now the organisation of the Transport and General Workers in Leachester was on a very different footing from before 1966. The most influential lay members of the union in the city now met together regularly and officially. They considerably outnumbered the city's representatives on the old regional trade group committees and they were more closely linked to the branches and the plants. They had the constitutional right to submit resolutions on any aspect of union policy or activity to the appropriate authority of the union, and in Leachester they could formulate their own policies (within the scope allowed by national and regional decisions) and co-ordinate action in the branches and the plants. The full-time officers had to report to the district committee. Since there are no standard arrangements for district committees, the constitution of the

Leachester committee had been designed to meet local needs after careful study within the region.

One outcome was the release of a great deal of energy and enthusiasm, not only among the lay members of the committee, but also among the full-time officers. Most of these were young men who had chafed under the old arrangements and were convinced supporters of the 'grass roots' philosophy of the new general secretary. They now felt that they had been released to run their union as a trade union should be run. Among other things the new attitude showed itself in a keenness on the part of full-time officers and lay members for shop steward training. The training of stewards was discussed at almost every meeting of the committee, and in addition to the union's existing courses, new residential and day-release courses were arranged through a nearby university and at technical colleges.

Nevertheless the committee's powers fell short of those possessed by the Engineers' district committee. The branches retained a direct link with the regional committee which remained responsible for administrative matters. Shop stewards had access to the committee only through their branches. The committee lacked the express powers in relation to disputes and collective bargaining issues which the Engineers' rules grant to their district committees. The full-time officers were not elected by the members in the district, as is the Engineers' district secretary. They were appointed by the executive. And besides their responsibilities to the committee they were subordinated to the regional secretary and the regional committee.

Meeting only once a quarter, the committee were in no position to review all the settlements negotiated throughout Leachester. The time which the intervening monthly meetings of the executive could give to vetting plant agreements was also meagre in comparison with the volume of settlements. The committee therefore agreed to leave 'normal' negotiations and unwritten agreements aside in order to

concentrate on procedure agreements, productivity agreements, measured daywork, job evaluation, and plant-wide
pay adjustments. They laid down four principles to guide
plant negotiators. Three of them were similar to those
ordained by the Engineers' district committee. All productivity agreements were to be opposed if they had led to a
reduction in employment; the principle of 'mutuality' was
to be upheld in all negotiations over pay systems and the
organisation of work; and the substitution of measured
daywork for piecework was not to be permitted. The fourth
principle would not have commended itself to the
Engineers, dominated as they are by their skilled membership. This was a preference for flat rate increases instead of
percentage increases in general pay adjustments. The full-
time officers vetted agreements, reporting to the committee
those which made major advances and those which did not
match up to the criteria, or about which they had doubts
for other reasons. From time to time the committee sent a
provisional agreement back to a plant with a note of its
shortcomings. But what effect this action had could be
discovered only by looking into what happened within the
plants. Four were chosen for study.

The first was a small galvanising plant with between
thirty and forty employees, nearly all of them Indians or
Pakistanis. The senior steward was a Pakistani. Although
the union had had members there since 1960, effective
organisation dated from 1966. Earnings were high, but in
1971 the workers became dissatisfied because of the large
increases in pay elsewhere reported almost daily in the
newspapers. The steward contacted the full-time officer
responsible for the plant, who arranged a visit. After a
short discussion with the senior steward, the two of them
met the manager for a protracted negotiating session. The
manager was prepared to grant an increase provided that he
could adjust the tonnages as part of the deal. The officer
refused to negotiate details of a piecework scheme on the
grounds that neither he nor any other full-time officer could

possibly know enough about such a scheme, but he pressed the stewards into accepting the proposals for a trial period of a month.

A nightshift had recently been recruited from outside the plant because the dayworkers refused to work nights. But, owing to the high earnings of the nightworkers, the day-workers now wanted rotation of shifts. The officer refused to submit a claim for rotation, because the dayworkers, he said, had rejected the opportunity when nightwork was offered to them. However, he suggested to the manager that rotation might be introduced later on.

The new pay system was thrown out at the end of the trial period. On this occasion the full-time officer wrote to the manager suggesting that he negotiate a revised agreement with the stewards. This was done. Bonus earnings were adjusted upwards to the satisfaction of the stewards, and the revised agreement was sent to the district office.

There was no mention of the district committee at any time. The shop stewards, who spoke little English and did not attend branch meetings, were unaware of the committee's existence. When he visited the plant, the full-time officer was careful to secure the agreement of the stewards for each move that he made, and to explain each stage in the negotiations at length, but he dominated the occasion. Along with the manager, he shaped the proposal; it was he who suggested a trial period when the stewards feared that their members would reject the scheme; and he persuaded the stewards to drop the proposal for rotation of shifts. His desire to see the stewards develop more independence was evident in the arrangements for revising the agreement, but the senior steward continued to 'phone the district office for guidance on all but the most trivial issues.

The second plant produced special metals. The manual labour force numbered about 250. About fifty skilled workers belonged to the appropriate unions, but in 1968 only half of the two hundred employees eligible to join the Transport and General Workers were in the union, and there were no arrangements to co-ordinate the work of their shop stewards. At this stage the management opened negotiations on a complex productivity deal which involved new joint committees, new procedures, a new pay structure, work measurement and changes in work methods. The manager responsible for the deal insisted on calling in the full-time officer then responsible for the plant, but he rarely attended negotiating meetings. He was an older officer, ignorant of the technical details of the proposals and hostile to their principles.

A new officer began to take over from him as the negotiations reached their final stage. It was evident that the stewards favoured the proposals, and the new officer undertook to pilot them, through the district committee provided that they were shown to be what the members wanted. A mass meeting addressed by both officers ended in confusion, but subsequently the proposals secured a 90 per cent vote in a secret ballot and the agreement was signed early in 1969. The application of the agreement was accompanied by a successful drive for complete unionisation, with the support of the personnel manager, and a reconstruction of the shop stewards' organisation inspired by the new officer.

Thereafter he was called in only once by the shop stewards until a general increase in pay was negotiated at the beginning of 1971 along with a number of revisions in the scheme. A few months later he was again summoned to deal with a redundancy. A fall in demand had led to a proposal from the firm that 64 workers should be declared redundant. This occurred before a crisis in another plant caused the district committee to insist that full-time officers should be brought into redundancy negotiations from the outset. The stewards were able to cut the number down to forty before the officer was called in, and he could do no more than secure improvements in redundancy pay for those who were to go.

The third plant was one of the largest in Leachester with nearly seven thousand manual employees spread over a number of unions. The Transport and General Workers was one of the three major unions there, with about 1,200 members, thirty stewards and a convenor who gave all his time to the job. Weekly meetings of the stewards at the plant were dominated by the convenor, who persistently refused requests from subsections to have their own stewards on the grounds that one steward for each complete section provided a more effective and administratively convenient organisation.

In 1970 the firm was developing plans for measured daywork, intending to introduce them section by section. The rates of pay suggested by the firm were attractive to the men, and backed by a threat that new work would be sent to other plants unless measured daywork was accepted. In these circumstances the convenor concluded that it was impossible to resist the proposals, for a mass meeting might vote for them over the heads of both the union and the stewards, and he would lose control. It was the tradition of the plant to keep the full-time officer out, and the convenor did not make an exception on this occasion, merely informing the officer of what was happening; nor did he inform the district committee. In the end the officer himself brought the proposals to the notice of the district committee's executive, of which the convenor was a member, and the convenor defended himself on the grounds that negotiations were preliminary talks with no need for the committee's intervention at this stage.

The fourth plant employed about two thousand manual workers in 1970, some six hundred of them members of the Transport and General Workers. Nearly threequarters of this six hundred were indirect workers on time rates. During 1969 a productivity deal was being negotiated with a committee representing the stewards of all the unions in the plant. Negotiations ran into trouble because of inter-union rivalry and personality clashes, and because the Transport and General Workers' stewards felt that the proposals gave too little to their members on time rates.

These problems were analysed and debated at a series of meetings between the stewards and the full-time officers at the district office. The officers wanted the stewards to continue to work with the other unions, but in the end the stewards withdrew from the joint negotiations, and, after a one-week strike, secured a further increase for all indirect workers.

This was followed in 1970 by measured daywork, and next year a job evaluation scheme out of which the indirect workers claimed to have done well. The introduction of the scheme was accompanied by a reconstruction of the Transport and General shop stewards' organisation in which their numbers were reduced from 35 to 22. The senior steward asserted that this reorganisation owed nothing to the full-time officer, although the latter said that it followed his advice.

In 1971 came a large-scale redundancy involving seven hundred workers in all, three hundred of them belonging to the Transport and General Workers. This was accepted contrary to the principles subsequently adopted by the district committee. The stop stewards did not consult the district committee, and they would have nothing to do with the company combined committee. They concentrated on securing better terms for those who had to go, and on a campaign to persuade stewards at other factories to waive their normal demarcation lines and recruitment procedures to enable the redundant workers to obtain jobs. They reported that they received a lot of co-operation from other plants.

The experience of these four plants cannot accurately represent the large number of undertakings organised by the union in Leachester, but as far as it goes it indicates similarities and differences between the Transport and General Workers and the Engineers in that city. In both unions the full-time officer's authority was at its greatest in the small plants, where he was given considerable freedom to conduct negotiations as he thought fit, and was able to persuade the stewards to follow his lead and to agree to what he has done. Even in rather larger plants his intervention was important where the shop stewards lacked confidence and effective organisation; but as they gained confidence and their organisation improved they acted more independently.

The authority of the full-time officers was at its weakest in the large plants with strong shop steward organisation, and self-reliant convenors or senior stewards. From time to time the convenor of the third and largest plant approached his full-time officer with a request to go 'into procedure'; but this was intended to put pressure on the managers, who were reluctant to use procedure; and in most instances the outcome was an improved offer in domestic negotiations. The additional increase for indirect workers at the fourth firm was sent to central conference, as were several issues arising under the job evaluation scheme. But the full-time officer there was hesitant to use procedure, and it seems reasonable to accept the stewards' assertion that procedure was used at their insistence. They sent representatives to central conference to keep an eye on the conduct of their cases. It should be noted that they did not lose their independence as the size of their workplace organisation dwindled.

Nevertheless the full-time officers probably exerted more influence than either the Engineers' district secretary or their divisional organiser. Their numbers allowed them more time for plant business. For example, they spent a great deal of time on the affairs of the fourth plant, despite its size, and if the stewards usually went their own way in the end, it was only after full discussion. They had more control over information than the Engineers' district secretary, since neither the quarterly meetings of the committee nor the monthly meetings of the executive provided such an opportunity for gleaning information about negotiations in other plants as did the Engineers' weekly committee meetings. Consequently shop stewards and convenors were more dependent on information from the full-time officers. Finally, the full-time officers could report plant agreements to the district committee as a means of influencing the stewards in the plant.

It would be a mistake, however, to attach much importance to this sanction, because the committee lacked effective authority to intervene in the plants. Proposed agreements acceptable to the members and the stewards in a plant went through whether the committee approved them or not, and whether or not they offended against the principles laid down by the committee to guide domestic negotiations.

There was little evidence of left-wing and right-wing factions at work within the district. But there was a division of opinion about the work of the committee. Except at the first plant (where the committee's doings were unknown) the leading stewards at the plants under study—and many of their colleagues elsewhere—advocated most frequent meetings of the committee lasting for a whole day to allow a full exchange of information and ideas with stewards at other plants. As things stood, they rejected district supervision of plant agreements since they considered that the district committee did not possess the knowledge to intervene effectively in plant negotiations. But they said that they would have accepted district policies if they had really been binding on everyone. On the other hand the full-time officers, with the support of other leading stewards, held that the existing committee was an important extension of democracy, and criticised the proposal for frequent one-day committee meetings as too expensive and unlikely to assist the conduct of business. But even the critics acknowledge that the district organisation and the campaign to bring the union closer to the stewards and to the members had been effective in supporting the stewards in the smaller plants and building up weak shop stewards' organisations until they could stand on their own feet. This was a job which could not have been done without the committee and the full-time officers with their new policies.

EAST SANDSHIRE

In East Sandshire the consequences of reform were even more evident than in Leachester. The membership—twenty thousand—was less than half that of the Leachester district, but spread over a far greater area. By road it was ninety miles from one end of the district to the other. There were 46 branches, fifteen more than when the district was established. Even before that a reconstruction of the branches had begun. There had previously been large composite branches in the main towns. These had included workers in a number of plants scattered over several industries and services, and some of them had full-time branch secretaries appointed by the union to run their affairs. The reconstruction divided the branches on the basis of industry, with plant branches where possible, each having its own part-time secretary elected by the members. The full-time secretaries were promoted to district officers, freed from responsibility for branch administration, and given responsibility for organising and negotiations in one or more industries.

The transformation was hastened by the creation of the district committee in 1969. One of the five officers in the area became the district secretary, and the remaining four worked under his general supervision. The district was thus far more generously staffed than the Leachester district.

The committee itself was not of great importance. Many members held important positions as convenors or branch secretaries, or both, but the committee lacked authority. The district secretary's reports to the quarterly meetings dealt with increases in membership, the exploitation of opportunities for growth, the opening of new branches, check-off agreements and recognition agreements, which he regarded as the 'high-lights' of district affairs. There was an opportunity to discuss developments within the plants, but this committee had not been given authority to ratify agreements. On occasion the district secretary sought the committee's support for action which he had taken, for example in a dispute, in order to issue a statement to the press. Finally, the district committee from time to time sent on a resolution about some national issue to the appropriate national trade group. Four plant studies were undertaken, the first of them in the local docks, where there had been a radical change in relationships. Up to 1969 a full-time branch secretary had been the sole negotiator for more than a thousand dockers and ancillary workers. As in most other ports, there had been no shop stewards so long as dockers were employed on a casual basis, and both he and the local manager were hostile to the recommendation of the Devlin Committee that a shop steward system should be instituted along with permanent employment. But there were signs of trouble; for instance most of the dockers were badly in arrears with union dues. A failure to resolve a piecework dispute led to a prolonged unofficial stoppage during which an unofficial strike committee emerged as the leaders of the men. The new district secretary intervened, not so much to settle the strike as to deal with the underlying defects which it had revealed. He separated the ancillary workers off into their own branches, creating a new dockers' branch, with an elected part-time branch secretary, in which the strike committee emerged as the new branch committee. The same men were also chosen as shop stewards, for the manager had now no alternative but to recognise shop stewards under a procedure which gave them wide powers to negotiate on rates of pay, hours of work, overtime, piecework and manning scales, among other issues. The former branch secretary became a district officer with considerable responsibilities outside the docks and no authority to intervene there until the shop stewards came to the end of their procedure, or decided to invite him in. Subsequently the stewards negotiated a productivity agreement, following the recommendations of the Devlin Committee.

The second plant chosen for study was a plastics plant

employing predominantly male workers, with its own plant agreement. At the time of the study the union had over a thousand members and thirty stewards there, but this was a recent development. Until 1965 organisation had been poor and the membership apathetic. Negotiations had been conducted between the personnel manager and a regional trade group secretary who worked at regional headquarters. At that time a new and energetic shop steward succeeded in recruiting all the workers in his department into the union and began an agitation for a closed shop. The regional trade group secretary asked the firm to institute a check-off to assist union membership, but this was refused, the tradition of the firm being strongly paternalistic. By the end of 1967 the agitation had brought everyone except a few recalcitrants into the union. The firm refused to make them join and there was a strike. As in the docks, the existing leadership was swept away and replaced by a strike committee led by the shop steward who had started the agitation. Subsequently he was appointed convenor and later became branch secretary as well.

The strike lasted three weeks and ended with a check-off agreement. But the militant new leadership and the members wanted to use their new strength to secure more than this. During 1968 there were negotiations on a productivity agreement which was to introduce work-studied standards throughout the plant in return for considerable increases in pay. By this time the district secretary had taken over responsibility for the plant from the regional trade group secretary. Since the stewards lacked experience, he conducted the negotiations along with a committee of stewards.

The agreement included a procedure which gave the shop stewards and the convenor considerable authority to negotiate, with a final reference outside the plant to the district secretary. By the time the agreement was signed the stewards had gained in experience, and were able to handle the considerable number of disputes over the application of the agreement—which involved a number of short

sectional strikes—without calling in the district secretary
at all.

It was evident that the new convenor exercised great
influence. He was anxious to settle disputes within the plant,
and he was able to use the authority of the branch to support
the decisions of the shop stewards. On one occasion the
branch committee withdrew a shop steward's credentials
and fined several employees for failing to take part in a
strike. The firm also built up his authority by changing its
approach to industrial relations and appointing an industrial relations officer to take over shop floor negotiations
from the personnel manager. This new man shared the
convenor's desire to settle issues without reference to a
higher authority.

The third plant was a textile plant employing nearly
three thousand workers, with a majority of Asians and West
Indians in its spinning department. The union began to
recruit about 1960, soon after the present district secretary
became a full-time branch secretary, and by 1963 he had
achieved complete unionisation and a check-off agreement.
A separate branch was established for the plant, but for
the time being he remained secretary of this as well as of
his original branch.

Until 1967, rates of pay were negotiated nationally, with
work-studied payment-by-results schemes in the plants. In
that year, however, under the influence of government
policy, a new agreement provided for plant productivity
negotiations, and the plant managers took advantage of
this provision to negotiate productivity deals, department
by department. To facilitate these negotiations it was
arranged that the convenor should give his whole time to
them, and a new personnel officer was appointed to handle
the business on the company's side. Not long afterwards,
with the establishment of the new district, the present
district secretary was succeeded as branch secretary by an
elected part-time secretary who gave about half his working
week to union business. At the time of the study the union

had about 2,500 members, with the maintenance craftsmen belonging to their separate unions.

As a result of reorganisation within the company and the union, the great majority of issues were now settled within the plant. The district secretary maintained close personal contact with the convenor, but he was rarely called into the plant except on the rare occasions when a dispute went into the official national procedure. The main problem of industrial relations within the plant—recognised by both sides—was communication with the Asian and West Indian workers. In 1965 there had been a strike of Asian workers in protest against a bonus agreement negotiated by the branch secretary (the present district secretary), the convenor, and the departmental shop stewards, all but one of them white. After the men returned, the branch made changes designed to remedy the shortcomings which the strike had revealed. More Asian and West Indian stewards were elected. Union notices in several languages announced the outcome of each stage of negotiations. Frequent sectional meetings were held, and where appropriate the convenor and the plant negotiating committee attended to explain and discuss their actions. A number of stewards were trained in work study techniques to assist them in productivity negotiations. But tension remained, with periodic complaints from the Asians and West Indians that the convenor and his colleagues were too close to management, and some murmuring from white shop stewards that the Asians and West Indians were trying to take over the union within the plant.

The fourth plant belonged to the Atomic Energy Authority (as it then was), and employed rather more than two thousand workers at that time of the study. About three-quarters of these were in the Transport and General Workers' Union, and the remainder were skilled workers in their appropriate unions. The plant had been organised from the start, and many of the shop stewards had held office for many years. The convenor was first elected to his office in 1958.

The Authority negotiated through a National Joint Industrial Council with Local Joint Industrial Councils to deal with plant issues. Up to 1968 the national agreement exercised tight control over pay and conditions in the plant. Although the Authority had been planning a productivity agreement for some time, and had started negotiations in 1965, progress had been held up by the 1966 standstill and a reference to the National Board for Prices and Incomes. When the agreement was finally signed in 1968, rates of pay were still settled nationally, but with provision for phased wage increases to apply locally as work was reorganised to improve performance. Work study was applied and jobs reorganised by negotiation within the plant. In addition there was a new job evaluation and grading structure to be applied within the plant subject to the national agreement.

These changes brought a greatly increased volume of business to the Local Joint Industrial Council. Although the present district secretary had been employed at the plant before becoming full-time branch secretary, and had then run the branch for a number of years, by the time of the productivity agreement he had been replaced by an elected part-time secretary. The consequences of the productivity deal were handled almost entirely by the shop stewards. One of the rare occasions when the district secretary was called in occurred soon after the deal when there was a dispute because a non-unionist was put on a job which earned bonus. The stewards claimed that non-unionists should be excluded from such jobs.

One reason for self-reliance was that the shop stewards were better informed than the district officers about the national agreements which were negotiated by the national trade group secretary, since the convenor was a member of the national trade group committee. On the management side, the general manager took a close interest in industrial relations, and shared the stewards' preference for settling issues in the plant wherever possible.

At the time of the study it was too early to predict the kind of long-term relationship which might emerge in the end in East Sandshire between the shop stewards and the district officers who were then still handling the consequences of reorganisation, organising new plants, negotiating further productivity agreements and nursing new groups of stewards towards independence. Moreover, the district officers had close personal relations with the senior stewards in most of the plants. Many of the stewards had been groomed for leadership by the district officers and had worked with them in the negotiation of new agreements and procedures in the plants and in the reorganisation of their branches. The same relationships may not persist when new district officers succeed the present incumbents.

Perhaps the study permits rather more definite conclusions to be drawn about the relationship between union organisation in the plant and the reconstructed branches. In every instance the branch had become subordinate to the shop steward organisation in the plant. Branches met only once or twice a quarter. They were ill-attended and their business was mainly social and administrative. The inner core of shop stewards in the plant formed the branch committee and met more frequently to transact most of the branch business. To communicate with their members, they relied almost entirely upon sectional meetings, mass meetings and informal gatherings at work.

STEEL VALLEY

More settled relationships could be observed in Steel Valley where a district had been established under the rules long before the reorganisation initiated by Jack Jones, and where a new district secretary had taken over shortly before the study began.

The district included 22 branches. Seven of them, ranging

in size from just under two hundred to just over seven hundred, organised steel workers, who constituted more than two-fifths of the district's 5,800 members, and the remaining fifteen covered workers in a wide variety of other industries. Only twelve of the branches had bothered to choose representatives to sit on the district committee, and they included all seven steel branches. In addition most of the remaining five members were relatively poor attenders so that the committee was dominated by the steel industry. However, by long tradition trade union branches in the steel industry exercise an exceptional degree of autonomy, so that the district committee was almost entirely precluded from intervening in the affairs of those branches with whose business its members were conversant.

One feature of industrial relations in steel is the system of promotion from labourer through jobs of higher skill and responsibility to the senior posts available for manual workers. Each promotion brings a higher rate of pay, and, since differentials in steel are wider than in many other industries, the senior posts are highly prized. Consequently a great deal depends on the operation of the promotion system which, by tradition, is controlled by the union branches. Since promotion is by seniority it might appear that there is little to argue about, but in fact there are frequent disagreements. The rules of seniority differ from branch to branch. For example, the date from which seniority is counted may be the date of joining the union, or the date of joining the firm, or the date of starting in a particular department or section within it. Moreover, the rules may restrict seniority to a single section, or permit interchange between two sections in the same department; and these are only some of the possible variations. Given these differences in rules and the technical changes which may involve closing or running down some sections and departments, and expanding others or opening up new sections and departments, the frequency of disagreements on promotion can readily be understood, and the importance attached to them by the men whose future earnings will be determined by the outcome.

Based on their control over promotion, the autonomy of the steel branches is reinforced by the existence of separate branches for each major department of a steel works, and the tradition of separate negotiations for each department, whereby pay and conditions of work were either settled by a national agreement affecting that stage of the steelmaking process throughout the country or negotiated within the individual departments in the plants.

Despite this autonomy, the steel branches had need of the district to settle appeals against their rulings on promotion. From time to time an aggrieved member declined to accept the verdict of the branch, and the district would then appoint a sub-committee to hear and settle the appeal. There were also disputes between branches, mainly arising out of reorganisation of work within the plant. One instance in Steel Valley was the removal of the packing of a product from the department of its manufacture to another area of the plant. This move took the work over the boundary between two branches, and they disputed whether the members of the first branch should follow the work to its new location or the second branch should take over the job which was now within its territory. Prospects of seniority would be considerably affected by a decision one way or the other. On this occasion the dispute was referred to the national negotiating machinery for that section of the industry which set up its own sub-committee to hear the spokesmen of the two branches and issue a verdict.

Although autonomy was a common feature of all the steel branches in their relation to the rest of the union, there were considerable differences between them in the way they ran their internal affairs. One branch with over seven hundred members, known as the 'Sundries' branch, organised small pockets of members not covered by the departmental branches, and also the employees of sub-contractors who had, by agreement, to be union members before they could start work in the plant. Consequently the branch lacked cohesion. Meetings were rare and poorly attended. There were frequent negotiations about the pay of individuals or small groups conducted by the branch secretary alone. In effect he was the branch, and was held in high regard both by the management and by his members.

It is common for the secretaries of steel branches to give all their time to union business, as he did, but another branch in the same plant with nearly seven hundred members had avoided this practice by delegating the business of the several sections in the branch to sectional committees. Decisions of these committees required ratification by the branch committee or the branch meeting. The branch officers had also limited the authority of the committee by restricting its business to promotion and to branch expenditure. All other business had to go before the branch meeting. It was their intention to encourage attendance, and they seemed to have succeeded. Although there were wide fluctuations in attendance, one meeting to discuss the branch's attitude to a pay claim brought three hundred members together, about half the total membership.

By branch rule the district secretary attended only by invitation, and he was excluded from this meeting. The branch officers took the view that neither he nor the district committee understood their business. Nevertheless their representative was a regular attender at district committee meetings.

The managers of the plant were anxious to break down branch autonomy because they hoped to end competitive departmental bargaining by means of a plant-wide pay structure. For some years there had been a joint works committee of all the unions in the plant including the craft unions organising maintenance workers and the main steel union, the British Iron Steel and Kindred Trades Association. The committee's main function was to discuss the future of the plant within the nationalised steel industry. More recently a joint committee of the Transport and

General Workers' branches had been set up. But neither body had much authority.

Consequently, although the quarterly meetings of the district committee heard reports dealing with steel issues, most of them were not matters in which they had power to intervene. There was also general union business, for example information on the Industrial Relations Bill as it stood at that time, and a report from the district representative on meetings of the regional committee. The district secretary's report paid considerable attention to settlements obtained on behalf of members involved in accidents, and also outlined the progress of negotiations in plants outside the steel industry.

One of these plants was an electronic engineering works employing about three hundred workers, all but twenty of them women. Although the plant had been established in 1963, and the majority of the employees must have been the wives or daughters of trade unionists, the union was not recognised there until 1970. After two earlier attempts at unionisation within the plant had failed, four girls approached the district secretary that year. They decided to launch a recruiting campaign while the owner was on holiday. On his return he threatened one of the four girls with dismissal. The other girls downed tools and the owner was forced to concede recognition.

A personnel officer was appointed, and on the union side a branch was established for the workers in the plant, with a chairman, a secretary and six shop stewards to handle the business. Branch meetings were well attended because they were held only when there were major grievances or demands to discuss. Nevertheless the branch relied on the district secretary in all its dealings with the management. The new personnel manager showed a strong preference for settling matters with him, and the branch officers lacked the confidence and experience to insist upon serious negotiations with them. Trade union training might have helped them, but the available courses had been arranged to suit male trade unionists who could attend evening classes or travel from home. The branch officers rejected a suggestion that they should give up a week of their summer holidays to attend a course. At the time of the study the district secretary was still handling every issue within the plant, including complaints about toilet facilities.

A very different state of affairs existed in the branch at the local rubber factory with well over a thousand employees, nine hundred of them members of the union. All four leading branch officers had considerable trade union experience in coalmining or steel before their present employment, and the practice of the branch had been to deal with its own affairs from the start. In 1968, however, the district secretary was forced to intervene because of a crisis in industrial relations in the plant.

Two issues were in dispute. The works manager had announced a redundancy and his intention to select those who were to go, thus disregarding the customary rule, 'last in, first out'. At the same time the application of a complex job evaluation scheme had run into increasing difficulties. The resolution of these problems entailed going over the head of the local management to the senior managers of the group, a move which led up to the replacement of the works manager.

Meanwhile another issue had come to a head. A productivity agreement was under discussion. Considerable savings were anticipated from the reorganisation of the jobs of the process workers, and the works manager insisted that these must pay both for their wage increases and for those of the ancillary workers. The branch view was that the savings should all go to the process workers and that a separate increase should be negotiated for the ancillary workers. The district secretary was called in but the works manager would not discuss the dispute with him. The union had to appeal to group management on this issue as well, and a meeting attended by group personnel officers sanctioned a separate increase for the ancillary workers.

All this turmoil led to a reconstruction of industrial relations in the plant. The branch secretary was given a sinecure to enable him to devote all the time he needed to union business. A personnel officer was appointed with a special responsibility for securing good industrial relations. The plant procedure was formalised, with explicit recognition for shop stewards, a joint works committee, and a disputes procedure which brought in the district secretary as the final stage. In contrast to the electronics plant, joint arrangements were made for a course for shop stewards, which ran successfully.

Once these new arrangements began to operate, the district secretary dropped out of the plant's affairs, and the stewards took control once more. The crisis had demanded his intervention, and he had played a considerable part in the reconstruction of industrial relations, but they felt that he lacked both the knowledge and the time to play an effective part in the normal business of negotiation. Although they regarded the use of the final stage of procedure as a very serious step, he might be able to afford them no more than a few minutes to brief him before he met the manager. In such circumstances they did not believe that he could do full justice to their case, and they therefore preferred to settle before the final stage was reached. They had even less regard for the district committee, which they contrasted with the shop stewards' combine committee covering all the plants within the company. They regarded pay and conditions in the company's plants elsewhere as far more relevant to them than pay and conditions elsewhere in Steel Valley, and they could learn about these at quarterly combine meetings. Moreover the combine committee circulated information about redundancies and other developments within the company, and co-ordinated action on pay claims and occasionally also on disputes. Under the new general secretary this committee had been recognised to the extent of sending a full-time officer to its meetings.

Conclusions

If the evidence from Leachester supports the association between size and dependence of workplace organisations, the evidence from the two other districts, while not inconsistent with it, adds modifications. The experiences of the Steel Valley electronics plant and the plastics plant in East Sandshire suggest that until a workplace organisation has developed its resources to the full it is likely to be less independent than it might otherwise be. Secondly, the experience of the Steel Valley rubber plant indicates that a workplace organisation which normally prefers to manage its own affairs may nevertheless be forced to call in a full-time officer in a crisis. Thirdly, the steel plants demonstrate that the independence of a workplace organisation may be buttressed by the recognition of its authority over such an important issue as promotion. Finally, East Sandshire docks, and perhaps also the plastics plant there, seem to show that a workplace organisation which is capable of running its own affairs may stay in a subordinate position for years if both union and managers co-operate to keep it there.

This leads on to the effect of union structure and policy on the relationship between workplace organisations and unions. In Leachester this relationship seemed to be substantially the same as in the Engineers, despite the different structures of the unions and the differing composition of their membership. This was true both before and after the reforms associated with Jack Jones, which do not seem to have made a great difference in the larger plants there. On the other hand, radical changes in East Sandshire were associated with the new philosophy even if some of them were introduced before the district committee was established. Since shop floor eruptions and new managerial policies played their part in these changes, it is impossible to assess the precise influence of the new philosophy, but it was substantial.

The East Sandshire district committee itself, however,

had not acquired much importance. The Leachester committee attempted far more, but they were not able to exercise much control over workplace organisations. The Steel Valley committee had a much longer history than either of these, but their achievements were equally modest.

Most of the Transport and General Workers' plants were non-federated or covered by relatively loose industry agreements, including steel and rubber as well as engineering. But there were a few plants governed by tighter agreements, such as the atomic energy plant and the East Sandshire textile plant—although both agreements had been modified to allow for productivity bargaining—which can offer a first hint as to the effect of tight central agreements on the relationship between workplace organisation and unions. For what they are worth, they suggest that the effect is slight. Both workplace organisations had developed a high degree of independence within the scope allowed them by their agreements, and made no more calls on their full-time officers than workplace organisations elsewhere operating under looser agreements.

4

The General and
Municipal Workers

The Union

The constitution of the General and Municipal Workers
Union emphasises regional organisation. The general council and the national executive (which is a sub-committee of
the general council) are both elected on a regional basis.
All ten regional secretaries sit on the general council—and
five of them on the national executive. In addition the four
largest regions each have two lay representatives on the
general council, and the remaining six regions have one
each. Five of these lay representatives sit on the national
executive. There are no districts within the regions,
although in some regions there are sub-offices, manned by
regional officers, to cover areas remote from the regional
headquarters.

The importance of the regions is also evident at the
union's annual congress—its supreme authority—which consists of regionally-elected delegations. The regional and
national officers, however, being primarily concerned with
negotiations and other industrial issues, are given responsibility for one or more industries; and over the last few
years the union has modified its methods of formulating
industrial policy by introducing advisory industrial conferences, within the regions and nationally, for representatives of particular industries to meet with the officers
responsible for their industry to discuss bargaining strategy

and the problems of the industry.

Although the great majority of the union's branch secretaries are part-timers, a number of its largest branches
are administered by whole-time branch secretaries who are
technically lay members, entitled to be elected to the general
council and national executive. However, in 1965 the union
discontinued the appointment of whole-time branch
secretaries, substituting a new grade of branch administrative officers, who are employees of the Union under the
direction of the regional secretary.

MELFIELD BRANCH

Because of the union's structure, it was not possible to
examine relationships within a district. Instead, two large
general branches were studied, one of them, Melfield, with
a branch administrative officer.

The Melfield branch covered a sizeable town, some
distance from the regional headquarters, and the surrounding countryside up to a distance, at the furthest, of about
twenty miles from the branch office. Although its 3,500
members included local authority employees and workers
in nationalised industries, about four-fifths of them worked
in manufacturing industry, mainly in engineering but also
in several other industries. Branch meetings, attended by
about fifty members, were held quarterly. The branch committee met once a month to deal with correspondence from
the regional officers, circulars setting out agreements affecting members of the branch, industrial injury claims, and any
business from the plants which members of the committee
chose to raise. As might be expected, these items concerned
the plants represented on the committee, whose ten members included four of the three hundred local authority
employees in the branch, and three representatives from the
largest plant covered by the branch, which employed about
450 members of the union. Consequently the great majority
of the plants were not represented on the committee and

their affairs were not discussed there. Plant questions could also be raised at branch meetings, but branch attendance showed a similar distribution, with most plants unrepresented there even by their shop stewards, so that branch discussions dealt with the business of those plants whose affairs were also aired at the branch committee.

The branch officer's heavy administrative load took precedence over other responsibilities, but he was also drawn into plant business. Generally he waited for an approach from the plants. Several plants lacked shop stewards. Consequently the members who worked there brought their grievances to him at the branch office and he visited the plant to deal with them. At other plants the steward or convenor would report to him the issues that could not be settled at the plant, but in most instances he would pass these on to the regional officer responsible for the relevant industry, although he might attend the plant with the regional officer when he came to Melfield. Plants which did not summon the branch administrative officer did not see him.

Contacts between regional officers and shop stewards were examined in three plants: the largest, a ceramics plant which was the plant with three members on the branch committee, the convenor and two stewards; a chemicals plant employing four hundred members of the union, whose convenor was on the branch committee; and an engineering plant employing two hundred members with no representation on the branch committee.

The regional officer responsible for the ceramics plant lived in Melfield and had a special responsibility for keeping an eye on the branch. He attended all branch meetings and branch committee meetings. He was also a fairly frequent visitor to the plant which was prone to stoppages, having a decayed piecework system of payment which was the cause of many anomalies in the earnings of the workers. In his view the management of the plant was as ready to deal with him as with the stewards, whereas the regional officers who dealt with the other two plants took the view that their managers preferred to deal with shop stewards. A survey of a sample of members showed that over half at the ceramics plant thought their full-time officer decided what action should be taken on a complaint or claim within the plant, whereas 80 per cent at the chemicals plant said that the decisions were taken by the shop stewards and at the engineering plant almost 80 per cent said that they were taken by the members themselves. At the first plant a majority of the members said that they saw a lot of their regional officer, whereas at the chemicals plant none of the respondents had ever seen theirs. In addition to his avail-ability, the frequent attendance of the regional officer at the first plant may have been due to its unhappy financial situation which predisposed managers to resist the many sectional pay claims thrown up by the piecework system at least to the stage at which he was called in.

By contrast, at the chemicals plant all issues were settled within the plant including two productivity deals which have been negotiated in recent years. When these agreements had been finalised, the regional officer visited the plant to sign them on behalf of the union. The engineering plant received more visits from its regional officer, perhaps because it was also a pieceworking plant with frequent pay disputes, some of which led to stoppages. Just before the study, the branch committee fined six members there for refusing to come out in a strike provoked by a management instruction to staff employees to take over the jobs of a section which had downed tools in a pay dispute. The men would not go back to work until the offenders were punished. The intervention of the regional officer was also elicited by the extreme inde-pendence of the polishers. Within a period of twelve months they had twice forced their shop steward to resign, and were often at odds with the convenor who was the youngest steward in the plant, pushed into the office because none of his colleagues would accept nomination.

Nevertheless, all three convenors had considerable

influence in their plants, and handled most of the union business within them. They averaged about fifteen hours a week each on union business whereas the other stewards put in three or less. It was evident that the convenors took over complaints and disputes at an early stage, and that they were far better informed than their colleagues. There were no shop stewards' committees, or regular meetings of the stewards in the plants. However, all three convenors took the view that on any important issue they had to consult their members and carry out their wishes. This was as true in the ceramics plant, despite the prominence of the regional officer there, as in the other two. 'Sectional' meetings of the members there were held to decide plant issues, and in negotiations on a general pay claim, conducted during the study, the members rejected an offer which had the backing of both the regional officer and the stewards.

HAMBRIDGE BRANCH

Hambridge is a town about the same size as Melfield, but in a different region. The union's membership in Hambridge was less than half that in Melfield, and concentrated in the public services. Almost a quarter of the 1,350 branch members worked for the local authority, and nearly half the remainder worked in electricity supply, gas, water and the health service or for the county council, so that almost two-thirds of the membership was employed in public services. Most of the rest of the members worked for a brewery in Hambridge or a textile plant in a village outside the town.

The branch secretary was a part-timer, but he managed nevertheless to devote a good deal of attention and great enthusiasm to branch affairs, keeping 'open house' in his front room for branch members on almost every night when he was not at a union meeting. Although the branch chairman was also a figure of some importance, the secretary dominated branch affairs. When asked about the branch committee, he said that it consisted of the branch officers together with the shop stewards, but that it met rarely, if ever. There was no record of a meeting and no list of shop stewards. The secretary carried their names and addresses in his head.

Branch meetings were held fortnightly, and attendance varied between twenty and fifty in a room which could not accommodate many more than fifty. Most of those attending were shop stewards. A survey of the 29 shop stewards in the branch indicated that almost all the local authority shop stewards said that they had been to nearly every branch meeting held over the previous twelve months, compared with an average of rather less than half the meetings for the other stewards.

An analysis of items discussed at branch meetings showed that two-thirds of them were industrial issues affecting a group of members in the branch. Half of these industrial issues concerned local authority employees who constituted less than a quarter of the branch, whereas electricity supply workers, almost one-fifth of the membership of the branch, accounted for about 4 per cent of the issues.

The branch secretary also held sectional meetings for the members in the various plants and services to discuss their own affairs. At the time of the study, sectional meetings were being held fortnightly for the textile plant, and some five or six meetings a year were held for gasworkers, electricity supply workers and the brewery employees. Sectional meetings were also held occasionally for employees in particular local authority departments, and, as the analysis of branch business reveals, the branch meetings came near to being sectional meetings for local authority employees as a whole. The sectional meetings were held in the evening at the Hambridge Labour Club. Generally attendances seemed to run to about twenty with most of the relevant shop stewards present.

The textile mill employed about nine hundred workers. Its traditions were hostile to trade unionism, and the union

secured recognition only in 1968 when its membership there
stood at nearly two hundred. The original agreement merely
authorised shop stewards to raise grievances, and did not
constitute a pay agreement or an undertaking to negotiate.
The following autumn the company announced an increase
in pay after discussion with the regional officer in which he
said the amount would not be acceptable to the employees.
The union staged a brief strike which won almost complete
support, and the company consented to reopen negotiations
which led to agreement on a considerably higher advance
in wages. Thereafter membership in the plant increased to
almost five hundred.

The regional officer took the lead in all these negotiations
and in other dealings with the plant managers. He attended
nearly all the sectional meetings arranged for the members
in the plant. This was the only forum for discussing the
business of the plant apart from the branch meeting, and
the survey showed the textile shop stewards were less frequent attenders at branch meetings than their colleagues in
other plants. Little reliance could be placed on the convenor. He was a demoted supervisor who appeared to have
more loyalty to the company than to the union. There were
signs that membership would fall away again unless the
weakness of shop floor organisation could be remedied.
Within six months of the strike the total had started to
decline.

The local authority was a closed shop in respect of the
grades organised by the union. Matters other than wages
were discussed on a Local Joint Consultative Committee
with five workers' representatives, three of them shop stewards. They believed that it was an efficient body because it
was able to take up grievances with the heads of departments. Pay questions, even those concerning plus rates for
particular jobs, were matters for the regional joint council
and the national joint council where they were handled by
the regional officers.

It was, however, possible to negotiate work-studied incentive schemes provided that these were approved by the joint councils. One such scheme was agreed for the refuse department in 1968 after two years of discussion and preparation. Prior to that the section had been a constant source of trouble, with the men often failing to clear the bins within the week, high labour turnover and a need to employ seasonal workers. Their regional officer was called in frequently, and in 1966 he persuaded the section—about sixty men—to give work study a trial. Consultants were employed to devise and apply a scheme of measured daywork which was to yield each worker 25 per cent above his basic rate provided the weekly task was fulfilled. Approval from the national joint council took some months to secure, but eventually the scheme was applied and worked to the satisfaction of the authority and the men.

During the negotiations the regional officer dealt with the consultants and discussed proposals with the men, virtually carrying out the functions of the shop steward, and keeping the branch informed of progress; but at the time of the study he had not visited the refuse section for more than twelve months. Discussions with the work study team and the negotiation of changes in job content and of times for clearing bins on new premises were conducted by the shop steward, who was a regular attender at the branch meeting and showed by his conduct there that the section now felt themselves fully capable of running their own affairs.

SURVEY RESULTS

Not long after these two case studies were completed the Warwick Industrial Relations Research Unit undertook two surveys within the union. The first was a study of communication in a national sample of nineteen large and middle-sized branches; and the second was a study of the workloads of regional officers and branch administrative officers throughout the union. Since many of their findings are not relevant here, there is no need for a detailed account of the scope and method of the surveys, but several points are pertinent.

The survey of regional officers showed that the two main calls on their time were service on district, regional and national negotiating bodies (mainly joint industrial councils) and demands for attention from the plants. Demands from the plants were growing in volume and could not all be met. Most of the officers admitted poor contacts with some of the members for whom they were responsible, especially in remote areas and small plants.

About half the branch secretaries in the branch survey complained that they saw too little of their regional officers. Some of the branch secretaries in the survey were senior stewards as well, but most of them were not. About a third of the senior stewards in these remaining branches also complained that they saw too little of their regional officers, but, surprisingly, most of these senior stewards came from branches whose branch secretary had not complained of lack of attention from the regional officer. The explanation for this apparently puzzling result seems to be in the considerable part which several secretaries of general branches played in plant negotiations. Those senior stewards who could not manage for themselves nevertheless had no need for a regional officer if they could call in an experienced branch secretary to assist them. But if they could not rely on their branch secretaries for help in negotiations they wanted the regional officer and complained if he did not come. On the other hand, branch secretaries who confined themselves to administration had relatively little need for their regional officers, whereas their colleagues who took part in plant negotiations were much more likely to want to consult them.

It seems to follow that so far as the workplace organisations were concerned, the branch secretary could be a substitute for the regional officer. It must also be noted that not all the branch secretaries who negotiated were branch administrative officers. Some branch administrative officers gave considerable time to plant negotiations; others took a relatively small part in plant negotiations (like the Melfield officer); and others none at all. For their part, several of the part-time district secretaries gave a generous share of their time to plant negotiations. It is evident that their employers—most of them public authorities—must have allowed them time off for the purpose, but the survey does not indicate how this was arranged.

One more finding deserves attention. The analysis of the branch survey tried to measure the state of workplace organisation by whether the shop stewards were elected or merely took the job on because no one else would do it, whether they had small or large groups of members to look after, whether they had regular meetings of their members and how much time they gave to union business. The state of branch organisation was measured by average attendance at branch meetings, by shop steward attendance at branch meetings, by the readiness of the stewards to raise plant issues at branch meetings and by the participation of shop stewards in the work of branch committees. On the whole, high scores for plant organisation were associated with high scores for branch organisation; and where one was weak, so was the other. But there was also a marked difference between public and private employment. In most branches which members worked exclusively or predominantly in private industry (like Melfield) the score for plant organisation was relatively high and the score for branch organisation relatively low. In branches catering entirely or mainly for public employees (like Hambridge) plant organisation scored relatively badly and branch organisation relatively well.

Conclusion

These studies of the General and Municipal Workers yield evidence of the effect of union structure on relations between workplace organisations and their unions. Because they were stationed at regional headquarters and had substantial responsibilities for negotiations outside the plant, regional officers had difficulty in maintaining contact, especially with remote branches and small plants. Some branch secretaries and branch administrative officers undertook plant negotiations and therefore served as substitutes for the regional officers within their branches, but others did not.

The consequence at Melfield was that the branch administrative officer attended to small plants with dependent workplace organisations. If he had not done the job, it probably would not have been done. Of the three larger workplace organisations which were examined there, two were self-reliant and the other co-operated closely with the regional officer responsible for its affairs. The obvious explanation for this difference is that he was readily available because he lived in the town and had special responsibility for the branch, whereas the regional officers who covered the other two plants did not find it so easy to get to Melfield. This reasoning suggests a general conclusion that workplace organisations which have just about sufficient resources to sustain independence (the membership here varied from two hundred to four hundred and fifty) may nevertheless be content to maintain a closely co-operative relationship with a full-time officer if one is available; and will be pushed into self-reliance if they cannot easily get hold of a full-time officer.

The largest workplace organisation in either branch was the Hambridge textile plant, which was very dependent on the regional officer and the branch secretary, both of whom gave a good deal of time to its affairs. However, the plant was far from fully organised, so that it may be regarded as another instance of the general rule that a workplace organisation which has not developed its full potential is unlikely to be as independent as it otherwise might be. This workplace organisation was far off its full potential.

Hambridge also provides another example of a workplace organisation of public employees. By themselves the Hambridge refuse collectors can hardly support generalisations about the difference between public and private employment, but their experience has some interest. Under the tight local government agreement, before it was modified to suit their needs, they were a tiresome section in the eyes of the authority and of their regional officer, and they often called him in to handle disputes. Their measured daywork agreement was negotiated entirely by the regional officer. But once it was installed, the shop steward was able to deal with all the issues that arose under it. The adjustment of the agreement to allow limited scope for workplace action appeared to make it possible for their workplace organisation to show greater self-reliance.

5

The Electricians

The Union

The Electrical, Electronic Telecommunication and Plumbing Union is the product of a relatively recent merger which has not yet brought the complete integration of the plumbing section with the rest of the union. This chapter does not deal with the plumbing section.

With about 400,000 members, the union is no more than half the size of the smallest of the three unions examined so far, but it shares with them the task of organising trade unionists in almost every industry in the country, for there are very few industries which do not employ maintenance electricians. It has much in common with the Engineers. Beginning as a union of skilled male craftsmen, it opened its doors to less skilled male workers and to women, as did the Engineers, and its industrial distribution is akin to that of the Engineers, with large concentrations of members in one or two industries, and the rest scattered in small groups in almost every industry. But there are also important contrasts with the Engineers.

Founded at the end of the nineteenth century, the Electricians were never so committed to the full range of craft principles as the Engineers. They were more ready to organise craftsman's mates, to permit and promote their upgrading to skilled jobs, to accept adult trainees generally, and to tolerate trade-testing. At one time the constitution provided for area committees which had some of the functions of the Engineers' district committees, but they did not have the same powers or the same influence, and they were abolished some years ago in favour of industrial conferences on similar lines to those introduced more recently by the General and Municipal Workers. There are area conferences of shop stewards by industry, and advisory area industrial committees are appointed from their number. Partly as a result of these changes, the administration of the union is far more centralised than that of the Engineers. At one time the Electricians' full-time officers were subject to periodic elections like their colleagues in the Engineers, but they are now appointed by the executive. There is also an important difference in industrial distribution between the two unions. Perhaps threequarters of the Engineers are employed in engineering, and they usually constitute either the largest or the second largest group of trade unionists in engineering plants. More electricians are employed in engineering than in any other industry, and in a few electrical engineering plants theirs is the major union, but normally the union organises only the skilled electricians and their mates, who may constitute about five per cent of the workforce or less. In electrical contracting, the Electricians are the only union, but this is an industry of small firms. They are the major union on the distribution side of the electricity supply industry, but they take second or third place to other unions in most power stations. Consequently, in contrast to all three unions examined so far, the Electricians have few large concentrations of members in a single plant, and the majority of their members are scattered throughout industry and the public services in relatively small groups.

REDCASTLE AREA

At the time of the study the union had about 17,000 members in the Redcastle area, excluding the 5,000 members in the plumbing section. Some 7,000 were employed in engineering, perhaps 4,500 in electricity supply, and 2,000 in electrical contracting, with the rest scattered over about thirty other industries. The twenty-four branches, the most distant of them being about twenty-five miles from the centre of Redcastle, ranged in size from fifty to three thousand members. Some of them were general branches, others organised members in a number of plants from a single industry—engineering, electricity supply, electrical contracting, newspapers—and one or two were dominated by the employees of a single multi-plant engineering company. More than half the engineering members worked in eleven plants owned by four major companies.

There were two area officers. One of them concentrated mainly on engineering, and the other mainly on electricity supply. Each of them was also responsible for a list of other industries, and the two largest branches (with 5,000 members between them) were run by full-time branch officers who handled negotiations in addition to their administrative duties. One of them had the main responsibility for electrical contracting.

Periodic conferences of shop stewards were held in engineering, electricity supply and electrical contracting. Otherwise the member's contacts with his union were through his branch or the visits of a full-time officer to his place of work.

The study proceeded by examining the work of the union in several undertakings—an engineering plant, three power stations, two electrical contractors, a chemicals plant and a food manufacturing plant.

ENGINEERING

The engineering plant was one of the largest in the city with some 5,000 manual employees, of whom about two hundred were Electricians. The Engineers were by far the largest union in the plant, and held a majority of the seventeen seats on the works committee. But since each department elected its own representatives to the committee, the minority unions were assured of some weight there, and the Electricians' senior steward was a member. Managers thought that the minority unions resented the dominance of the Engineers, but the Electricians' shop stewards, of whom there were twelve, said that this was not so.

The works committee handled union affairs in the plant with very little interference from outside. Their records, which had been carefully kept for many years, provided a body of precedents which they guarded jealously. The main payment system was piecework with the timeworkers' earnings linked to those of the pieceworkers by a 'productivity' agreement, but earnings were not so high as in most Leachester plants, so that increases in the industry's minimum rates had more impact on pay packets than they did at Leachester. However, the settlement of industry rates did not entail any direct intervention in the plant, and the piecework system and the productivity agreement were negotiated by the works committee and administered by the shop stewards.

Redundancy was the main topic of interest at the time of the study. The Engineers' district committee had put a ban on overtime as a means of sharing work and reducing lay-offs, but the works committee was unsympathetic to the ban despite the dominance of the Engineers. The committee did not intervene when the ban was breached, and they considered requests from managers for overtime 'on their merits'. This avoided a possible source of conflict with the Electricians whose area industrial committee had decided against a ban on overtime. Although redundancy is an issue which many shop stewards elsewhere feel unable to manage on their own, all the redundancy negotiations had been conducted by the works committee without reference to full-time officers. There had been an attempt to join with shop stewards from other plants in the same company in setting up a combine committee, mainly to cope with redundancy, but joint meetings had not led to an effective organisation.

With the prior permission of the works committee, the Engineers' full-time officers visited the plant from time to time to deal with references under the engineering procedure, but there was no record of a visit by a full-time officer of the Electricians. Plant business was not discussed in the branches which the stewards seemed to value mainly as agents for dispensing union benefits. It was their general view that 'the works committee runs things here'. However it does not follow that there were no contacts with the Electricians' full-time officer. The stewards telephoned him for information about industry agreements, on which he was better briefed than works committee members. The stewards were also anxious to trace transfers of work from one plant to another, which might have a bearing on redundancy, and they relied on him to try to find out what had happened.

In addition one or more of the stewards normally attended the engineering shop stewards' conferences which were held roughly once a quarter. Average attendance was about fifty out of over 250 shop stewards in the area, most of them from the large plants. The conduct of business was in the hands of the full-time officer. When appropriate, the regional executive councillor reported on industry negotiations, and the area officer gave an account of his dealings with the plants in the area. From these it appeared that, although he often visited other large plants in the area, most of his time was taken up with the affairs of the many smaller plants.

The officers' reports were followed by lively debates. In the first half of 1972 these centred on the national strategy of the engineering unions. Having failed to reach agreement with the Engineering Employers' Federation on a number of claims for substantial improvements in pay and conditions, the unions were seeking to impose their demands by local action, plant by plant. The conferences debated the steps which the Engineers were taking locally and what action they themselves should take, and criticised the union's executive for their part of the industry negotiations. They instructed the executive to give full support to those who took local action.

These events showed that the works committee of the plant under examination were not entirely in control of their own affairs. The plant was selected for a strike to enforce the demands. Although opinion in the plant seemed to hold that the claims were too ambitious, the Engineers came out and the other unions stopped work in sympathy. The final settlement fell well short of the claim.

ELECTRICITY SUPPLY

Most of the electricians engaged in electricity supply are employed in distribution. The power stations employ maintenance electricians, but they are usually outnumbered by the maintenance engineers, and both groups together are outnumbered by the operators, a majority of whom belonged to the General and Municipal Workers at two of the power stations (A and C) which were examined, although the Transport and General Workers had a substantial membership at the third (B). Consequently the Electricians came third or fourth in numbers in each of the plants. The official works committees were elected by the employees and there was no guarantee that only shop stewards would be elected. At A station, for example, four of the works committee members were shop stewards, and three of the seven stewards, including the Electricians' steward, were not on the committee. Issues which cannot be resolved by the committee are referred to the District Joint Industrial Council, whose secretary in this part of the country was an officer of the General and Municipal Workers. It was he who usually visited a plant if a visit was needed, regardless of whose members were involved in the issue in dispute. Within the power stations there was an understanding that all the stewards would support any colleague on an issue, whether he belonged to the majority union or one of the minority unions. Consequently individual union boundaries and loyalties had little significance in the handling of power station business.

The main industrial relations issue at the power stations during 1971 and 1972 was the introduction of lead-in payments. Following the national work-to-rule in the industry towards the end of 1970, the Wilberforce court of inquiry recommended that these payments should be introduced for workers who had not yet had the opportunity to benefit from stepped incentive payments for achieving specified performance levels under an agreement signed three years earlier. To become eligible for lead-in payments, power station employees had to vote in favour of the scheme, and it was understood that the vote committed them to accept work study on the basis of standardised performances collated in a national data bank. Before the ballots were held, managers and trade union officers toured the plants in the region to explain the scheme. The union spokesman was the General and Municipal Workers' officer who was secretary of the workers' side of the district council. One of the main issues for discussion was the effect on employment, for the scheme would inevitably reduce manpower requirements, and the region was experiencing considerable unemployment.

Two stations (A and C) voted for the scheme and received their lead-in payments, followed by incentive payments. Events did not proceed quite so smoothly at B station where the Electricians' officer had told the meeting called to discuss lead-in payments that they could still object to the actual work study scheme even after voting for the lead-in payments. The workers there had opposed reductions in manpower requirements on previous occasions, and had not changed their minds. Accordingly, when the detailed scheme was submitted to the works committee they rejected it. This led to a visit of a working party of national union officers and officials of the Electricity Council, whose recommendations were followed by an agreed compromise on manning levels.

The shop stewards seemed to think that even those full-time officers who had misgivings about the scheme were obliged to support the introduction of lead-in payments once the industry agreement had been signed, and were therefore not in a position to offer their members disinterested advice. Moreover, they said, the standardisation of work study values restricted the scope for stewards to bargain about the power station scheme, and they also felt that it limited what their officers could do for them. Circumstances are usually different when work-studied incentives are introduced in an engineering plant. There the shop stewards are free to bargain about any element in the scheme which they choose to challenge, and if they call in their full-time officer, he can advise his members according to the circumstances as he finds them in the plant, without reference to external standards.

There was in existence an unofficial combine committee for shop stewards in electricity supply. The shop stewards at B and C stations had nothing to do with it, but their colleagues at A station participated in its work and found it useful, including the Electricians' steward. They said that its regular monthly meetings provided them with more up-to-date information than came through union channels, and gave them an opportunity to debate freely about such issues as lead-in payments and work study. Power station business was not debated at branch meetings and, although electricity supply conferences are generally the best attended of all the union's industrial conferences, these stewards had attended none.

ELECTRICAL CONTRACTING

In 1967 the agreements of the electrical contracting industry were taken over by a National Joint Industrial Board established by the union and the National Federation of

Electrical Contractors (as it then was). Besides their functions of negotiating agreements and settling disputes which they inherited from the old national joint council, the national and regional boards operated a scheme for grading employees as 'electricians', 'approved electricians' and 'technicians', promoted technical education, provided welfare benefits, and acted as an employment exchange. Up to 1972 incentive payments were not permitted. The Board's agreements yielded relatively high time rates and attempted to regulate every aspect of industrial relations on contracting sites. Any variation on site required specific sanction. Union membership was not a condition of employment.

Of the two firms examined, one had about forty employees, most of them working in pairs—an electrician and an apprentice—on small jobs. Although all the electricians appeared to have held a union card at one time —perhaps when working on a job where membership was enforced—only a minority were current members and there was no steward or workplace organisation. A full-time officer had visited the firm on one occasion when a dismissal was challenged. Otherwise the men regarded the board rather than the union as their protection. New agreements were notified through the board, not by the union, and applied rigorously by the firm. Some of the men had attended branch meetings, and some of them had been involved in site activities when working for other firms, but neither the branch nor site organisations elsewhere appeared to have any impact upon industrial relations in this firm.

The other firm was a national contractor employing about 175 technicians, electricians, apprentices and labourers in the Redcastle area. They were spread over several sites. About sixty currently worked on a major new construction job and another twenty were engaged on extensions to a major steel plant. Both groups had site representatives and union membership was universal. On the new construction site this was the rule imposed by the various trades engaged on the job, and the workplace organisation at the steel plant would not allow non-union labour to be engaged on work within their plant. Both sites had asked the board to sanction additional site rates without success.

The main issue settled on the sites was overtime. The board's rules condemn systematic overtime and authorise regional boards to regulate overtime (except in emergencies), but systematic unauthorised overtime of about ten hours a week was regarded as normal throughout the company. Because the electricians at the steel site who were 'site engaged' rather than 'shop engaged' (permanent employees of the company) would lose their jobs when the contract was completed, an overtime ban was imposed with the intention of creating more work for them, since the completion date assumed systematic overtime. Both sides were in breach of the board's rules, the company for relying on systematic overtime and the men for banning overtime, and neither side appealed to the board. The dispute had to be settled on the site. There was another conflict over lay-offs as the job ran down. The company wanted to dismiss the site-engaged electricians first, but the men objected. There was a strike, but the company had its way. Again there was no appeal to the full-time officer who seems to have had very little contact with either of the sites. On the other hand the internal workplace organisation at the steel plant had a considerable influence on the electricians working on the contract. The Electricians' senior steward in the plant planned the various moves to keep the site-engaged electricians in employment.

The impression created by these instances is that the right agreements of the Joint Industrial Board reduced the need for workplace activity in small firms, and sometimes contributed to workplace activity outside the official union procedure on large sites.

CHEMICALS

The chemicals plant, employing over six hundred manual workers, was part of a national company which operates a company agreement. Rates of pay were governed by a job evaluation scheme under which jobs were examined and assessed in each plant against nationally-determined grades.

The great majority of the employees were organised by the General and Municipal Workers, but the maintenance engineers and electricians—about forty in all—were in their own unions, and each of them had their own steward. There were fourteen electricians. The unions operated an informal closed shop.

The works committee and the sectional plant committees were mainly concerned with the production workers. Job evaluation was handled through the official machinery. If a question had arisen about the assessment of an electrician's job, their steward would have been involved, but as they were all in the highest grade there was no problem. Otherwise the maintenance stewards dealt with their own affairs informally in their own department. They negotiated an extra site stand-by bonus, in addition to the company rate for stand-by duties, travelling time allowances, payment for attendance at courses, and the distribution of overtime. There was a good deal of exchange of information with other plants, mainly over the telephone, about the 'little extras' which the company could be induced to concede. There were also occasional combine meetings, but the Electricians' steward felt that these could not do much except allow stewards to compare notes. Within the plant he often relied on the Engineers' steward for information, and the two worked closely together, although the electricians took their own stand if they disagreed with the engineers.

The only full-time officer to visit the plant was the General and Municipal Workers' regional officer. The Electricians' steward conceded that he might call in his full-time officer if his members were involved in a major dispute in the plant, but that had not happened. Relations within the plant seemed to be amicable and orderly.

FOOD MANUFACTURE

The food manufacturing plant employed about 650 manual workers. Over a hundred were in the maintenance section where the two main unions were the Engineers with 65 members and the Electricians with thirty. The plant had its own agreements with the unions, one for the process workers negotiated with the Transport and General Workers, and the other for the maintenance section negotiated with the full-time officers of the unions concerned. New employees were required to join the appropriate union.

The agreements were revised each year. The practice of the maintenance stewards was to discuss among themselves what they should ask for, and then call in the full-time officers to submit the claim, discussing with them not only the demands they were to submit but also the sticking points. The draft agreements were submitted to the members for ratification. In addition to these occasions the Electricians' full-time officer was called in three or four times a year to handle disputes through the final stage of the plant procedure agreement.

The maintenance stewards had also developed several practices which had a considerable effect on earnings. For the shift workers this was achieved through arrangements about shift cover and guaranteed earnings, and timeworkers were assured of $7\frac{1}{2}$ hours overtime a week. Usually the Electricians' stewards worked closely with the Engineers' stewards, but there was some jealousy because the engineers enjoyed a higher level of overtime due to the difficulty of carrying out mechanical maintenance in normal hours. Consequently when the engineers complied with a ban on overtime imposed by their district committee, the electricians refused to co-operate.

Despite this scope for workplace bargaining, it was evident that the stewards relied heavily upon their full-time officer. There seemed to be two reasons for this. The first was that, since theirs was a plant agreement, they would have to do everything for themselves, negotiating all their agreements and operating their own procedure through all its stages, if they did not want to rely on their full-time officer. The second was the severe disciplinary code in the plant. They felt that only the full-time officer could protect them if they were charged under the code. For both reasons they believed that there was a limit to what they could do for themselves, and beyond that they must rely on their full-time officer.

Conclusion

It would be rash to suppose that this case study gives a typical picture of relationships between full-time officers and workplace organisations in the union. It appeared, for example, that full-time officers played a larger part in other engineering plants than they did in the plant chosen for investigation, and that they have more business in electricity distribution than in power plants. But the study gives some indication of the relationships which may emerge between full-time officers and minority workplace organisations in the plant; and of the effects of tight industry and company agreements.

The engineering plant and the power stations seemed to show that a minority workplace organisation which might otherwise be too small to look after its own affairs may nevertheless be able to achieve independence from the full-time officer outside by relying on the resources of an inter-union organisation within the plant. In all these instances the inter-union organisation was fairly close-knit. The two electrical contracting site organisations might be considered to be examples of the same point, for both of them drew strength from other workplace organisations—from the workplace organisation inside the steel plant, and from the inter-union organisation of contractors' employees on the new construction site.

The workplace organisations in supply and contracting operated under tight industry agreements, and the chemicals workplace organisation was subject to a tight company agreement, but all of them were self-reliant within the scope allowed to them, and even went beyond the permitted scope. Some of this unofficial action may be explained by politics, for in some instances left-wing opposition within the union shows itself in a hostility to the official procedures, although this motivation was not evident to the observer. Leaving that aside, these four instances of small but independent workplace organisations, together with the workplace organisation in engineering, might appear to indicate a degree of independence among maintenance craftsmen which is unequalled elsewhere, but the food plant provides a contrary example. The maintenance stewards there could not manage without the support and co-operation of their full-time officers. The contrast argues that it is easier to operate independently within the scope of an industry or company agreement than to sustain the full weight of negotiating and administering an independent plant agreement.

It is impossible to say much about the availability of the full-time officers since the study did not include an analysis of their work. Taking account of the two full-time branch officers, they were not responsible for a larger number of members than the officers in the earlier studies; but their members were dispersed over a larger number of places of work, and this must have made it more difficult to maintain contact. However, no workplace organisation in the study complained that the officers did not come when they were wanted. Only the maintenance electricians in the food manufacturing plant showed much interest in using the services of their full-time officer, and they got them.

6

Craft Unionism

The Nature of Craft Unionism

Something has already been said about craft unionism in the second chapter. A craft relies upon control over entry into a trade through apprenticeship, and upon reserving certain jobs for apprenticed craftsmen. Thus their pay and conditions of work are protected and improved through control over the supply of labour for certain jobs.

This method can be effective without direct control over pay and conditions on the part of the union, for employers come to realise that they cannot expect to employ the number of skilled men which they require except on attractive terms. But craft unions have added direct regulation of these terms to their control over the supply of labour and the manning of jobs. In the first half of the nineteenth century this was commonly done by unilateral assertion of the rate of pay which a craftsman would expect to receive and the hours which he was prepared to work, with provision for penalising craftsmen who did not insist upon these terms. Subsequently these issues became subjects of collective bargaining between unions and employers' associations which laid down agreed terms intended to apply throughout the craft, or throughout a district.

Behind these agreements, however, the craft control of the supply of labour remained the main guarantee of acceptable settlements in negotiation with the employers. Strikes could also be used to put pressure on employers in the short run, but the long-run success of the craft, including its ability to wage successful strikes, depended upon its control of labour supply and jobs.

A workplace organisation may be an instrument of craft control within the plant, but it cannot operate its own system of craft controls. If it tried to do so while the supply of skilled labour was unregulated elsewhere, the employer would be able to evade control by recruiting from outside. Craft regulation therefore limits the independence of workplace organisation.

THE NATIONAL GRAPHICAL ASSOCIATION: CORBURY BRANCH

The National Graphical Association is the main craft union in the printing industry, formed through the amalgamation of separate London and provincial societies, and of societies representing separate crafts. Outside London the head office deals direct with the union branches. There are about two hundred branches in all, but the bulk of members are to be found in the thirty or so large branches with full-time branch secretaries, whose numbers the union is actively seeking to augment by the amalgamation of smaller branches.

The full-time branch secretaries outnumber the rest of the full-time officers by more than two to one. They provide several members of the national council of the union and of the executive committee which deals with the business between council meetings. They are employees of their branches, paid out of the proceeds of a branch subscription, which can under certain conditions be supplemented by a grant from central funds.

Branches have considerable autonomy. Communication with the plant is a monopoly of the branch. In contrast to most unions, branches can communicate direct with each other. Moreover, each branch has its own rule book to regulate the conduct of its business, subject to ratification by the council.

The printing industry is renowned for its long-standing

and highly-developed form of workplace organisation, known as the 'chapel'. By rule, there must be at least one chapel in every office recognised by the union, and where four or more members are employed in such an office they are required to draw up chapel rules to be approved by the branch and to be binding upon them.

At the time of the study the Corbury branch covered about a thousand members of the union in the city of Corbury and one or two nearby towns. More that two-thirds of the members worked in five firms employing between fifty and three hundred journeymen and apprentices, and the rest were scattered over about thirty small firms. Each of the two largest firms had three chapels to cover different departments—for example, the composing room, the machine room and the lithographic process. The rest had a single chapel each.

In addition to the full-time branch secretary, the branch committee consisted of a president, a vice-president, an assistant secretary and fourteen 'delegates'. Most of the delegates' seats were allotted to the larger firms, and, in the two largest, to separate chapels. The remainder were elected by and from smaller firms. Many, but not all, of the fourteen delegates were 'fathers' of their chapels, which is the industry's term for shop stewards.

The committee were the most important authority within the branch. They directed the work of the secretary and handled issues referred to the branch by the chapels. The branch meeting, with an average attendance of about forty, generally ratified the decisions of the committee, although it could be used as a court of appeal against a committee decision, and on one occasion recorded its disapproval of the committee's action.

Most of the issues which the chapels referred to the committee concerned the control of labour supply—recruitment, transfers between plants, demarcation with other printing unions, flexibility between trades within the union, training and retraining. Method study, shiftwork and overtime affects the supply of labour by varying the use made of the available supply, and the transfer of work to be done elsewhere alters the relationship between the supply of labour and the demand for labour. These items also figured in the committee's business.

Some branches act as employment agencies, but printing employers in Corbury were entitled to employ any card-holding member of the union provided that he had a clearance card from his branch secretary. The main problems over recruitment arose with the training of adults which the union permitted in certain instances where there was a shortage in particular trades. Adult trainees were carefully vetted by the branch committee. In 1966 the union signed a national agreement allowing the recruitment of adult trainee readers and keyboard operators. The branch committee approved thirteen trainees under the scheme and allotted them to firms. But one chapel refused to accept any trainees and, after discussion, the committee supported them. A second chapel objected after the event, and was able to secure enough signatures to call a special meeting of the branch which recorded its disapproval of the committee's action. The decision came too late to exclude the trainee already allotted to the second chapel, but they successfully resisted subsequent demands from their firm for trainees under the scheme.

For the most part flexibility was allowed between the different trades within the union so long as the chapel was in agreement. But if the chapel refused, that was the end of the matter even though a national agreement in 1967 purported to give managers greater scope in this respect. Similarly a request from a craftsman to retrain in another trade within the union was accepted with the approval of the chapel. A relaxation of demarcation with the Stereotypers, prior to their amalgamation with the union, was permitted at the discretion of the chapel, in order to avoid unemployment among stereotypers. But the chapel had to get a written assurance from the management that the decision would not be taken as a precedent.

In addition to the rates of pay specified in the national agreements, the five larger firms operated incentive payment schemes, and merit rates were commonly paid in the smaller firms. But there was remarkably little negotiation about these payments or about the 'house rates' which constitute an important element in printing pay packets in some other parts of the country. Incentive schemes required the approval of the chapel in the first instance, and chapel bonus representatives could intervene where the time of a job was disputed, but this seemed to be a rare event. One chapel whose members worked for the printing department of a major engineering works had secured a house bonus to match earnings elsewhere in the plant, and another had successfully argued for a house bonus as a result of a change in production methods.

The branch took no part in these negotiations, and the understanding seemed to be that, so long as the national agreements were observed, pay was a matter for the chapels. But the branch encouraged house negotiations on two issues—to secure average earnings for holiday pay and to achieve improvements on the national shift rates. Several chapels had succeeded on the first issue.

This low level of plant bargaining over pay cannot be explained by union weakness or by lack of negotiating skills and experience. The chapels were well-organised. The chapel fathers were accustomed to dealing with managers and insisting on the right of their chapels to discuss and veto proposals concerning labour utilisation. The tradition of the printing industry in Corbury was paternalistic, and this may have inhibited the development of plant bargaining on pay. For whatever reason, the general attitude to pay appeared to be that, with incentive schemes, merit payments and plenty of overtime available, the level of earnings in Corbury was acceptable.

The chapels were responsible for administering the craft rules on labour supply, and they showed considerable independence in doing so. They were allowed to relax the rules so long as the branch saw no danger to craft principles in what they did, but for the most part they showed their independence by refusing to relax the rules as far as head-quarters wished and the branch was prepared to allow. Head office, branch and chapels all accepted the importance of the framework of craft rules, and any disagreements were within that framework.

The members of the branch committee did not appear to report back to their chapels, but they took care to keep the committee and the branch secretary informed of events within their chapels. Chapel autonomy did not mean that chapels went their own way without the knowledge of the committee.

Administrative methods were cumbersome, and it took the branch secretary about three days a week to keep his books in order. A fourth day usually went on union meet-ings at head office. The fifth day he spent on visits to the firms in Corbury, not usually in order to negotiate with the managers, for there was little negotiation to be done; but in order to keep in touch with the firm and the chapel. Con-sequently both he and the branch committee were well informed.

THE NATIONAL GRAPHICAL ASSOCIATION: CAMHILL BRANCH

Camhill branch was about twice the size of the Corbury branch and covered a considerably larger area. But half of its strength was concentrated in two large plants, each of them employing about five hundred members.

Nine of the seats on the branch committee were allotted to the nine chapels with more than fifty members, and the rest were filled by a ballot of the remaining chapels. A full-time assistant secretary carried out most of the adminis-trative work of the branch, so that, although the branch secretary spent more time at head office than his Corbury colleague, he also had about three days a week to give to plant affairs.

This time was needed, for, in contrast to Corbury, there was a great deal of plant negotiation over pay. These negotiations were concerned with house rates, settled chapel by chapel except for one of the two major firms which had recently negotiated a plant-wide 'house agreement' covering five unions and cutting down a vast array of rates of pay to eight standard rates.

Negotiations were generally handled by the chapel fathers. In the two major firms the chapel fathers were allowed to give their whole time to union work, and were men of prestige and experience. Consequently they tried to settle business within the chapel. But they and their colleagues in smaller plants kept in close touch with the branch secretary. In contrast to the practice at Corbury, the Camhill chapel fathers never took their problems direct to the branch committee. They put them to the branch secretary, and it was his choice whether they went on the branch committee agenda or not.

Consequently the branch secretary was usually well-briefed concerning plant negotiations, and ready to act if he should be called in. When he did intervene in the affairs of one of the larger chapels, the request came more often than not from a manager who had reached deadlock with the chapel, and might be facing sanctions imposed by the chapel. Then the secretary would take up the negotiations in consultation with the chapel, and on one or two occasions held the chapel back on the grounds that it had gone too far.

Matters of labour supply were also taken up with the branch secretary, who settled most of them himself without reference to the committee. The branch concerned itself with labour supply mainly in relation to recruitment by the two major firms. The high level of their pay attracted large numbers of applicants. Consequently recruitment was restricted to members of the branch. They could put their names on a list kept by the branch for the purpose. As vacancies arose they were offered to the man at the top of the list.

All agreements had to be reported to the branch committee. This arrangement provided an important source of information for the chapel fathers on the committee, who gave this as the main advantage of membership. But other chapel fathers found the branch secretary readily available to give them information and advice.

The larger branches of the National Graphical Association are wealthy organisations, and a good deal of the committee's time went on financial business, including appeals for financial assistance. The committee also found time to debate general issues affecting the industry such as the consequences of technical change, reports of committees of inquiry and proposals for amalgamation; and these discussions could have greater effect than similar discussions at most trade union branch committees, for, as a member of the national council, the branch secretary shared in making the union's policy.

The high level of earnings in the two major firms dates back to the origin of plant negotiations over house rates. Their chapels started ahead of the rest, and kept their lead. Their example was followed by the smaller chapels within the branch, but, lacking the resources of the large chapels, they had to rely heavily upon the branch secretary to achieve results. Even at the time of the study it was evident that the chapels in the two major firms made disproportionately small demands on his time, and thereby allowed the smaller chapels to get a better service.

There is no equally satisfactory explanation for the original development of chapel bargaining over pay in the two major firms. One background factor is the high level of profitability which they enjoyed in the years after the war, and another is their need at that time to recruit labour from London where chapel bargaining was already flourishing.

THE BUILDING TRADE WORKERS

Prior to the formation of the Union of Construction and
Allied Trades and Technicians in 1971 as an amalgamation
of carpenters, painters, bricklayers and other related building trades, the Amalgamated Union of Building Trade
Workers organised bricklayers, masons and tilers. It was not
a pure craft union, for in 1952 it absorbed a union of
builders' labourers, but the labourers' section formed a
minority of the new union and the craft section maintained
its identity. Many craftsmen regarded the labourers' section
as a nuisance which absorbed a disproportionate share of
the union's resources.

Because of casual employment, the British building
unions have never been able to establish effective control
over the supply of skilled labour in the industry, except
occasionally on a local basis. A site may be closed to non-
members and the check-off is introduced on some large
sites, but when the job is finished the labour force is
dispersed and organisation has to build up again from
scratch. Consequently the industry is badly organised. In
recent years the unions have suffered further inroads from
'labour-only sub-contracting' and 'self-employment' whereby
employers have been able to avoid some of their insurance
obligations and workers have been able to dodge tax and
union membership, and to work outside the code of
negotiated agreements.

The Glassford district of the union was in an area of the
country in which organisation had remained relatively
strong, and the proportion of bricklayers within the union
was said to be relatively high. The district comprised fifteen
branches with about 2,500 members in all, about 550 of them
in the Axton craft branch. There were some separate
labourers' branches, but craftsmen's branches also accepted
labourers into membership.

District committees were formerly elected to supervise

the work of the branches, and had considerable authority over industrial relations within their areas, but their functions withered away with the growth of site bargaining in the post-war years, a development usually attributed to a national agreement in 1947 which permitted the introduction of incentive payment schemes. As a result, and for the sake of economy, the union authorised the replacement of district committees by branch conferences (of one delegate to a branch) to be held twice a year, and the reform was readily accepted in most districts, including Glassford. The main functions of the branch conferences were to receive circulars and correspondence, and to hear reports from the district organiser and the divisional secretary, whose division covered Glassford and four other districts.

The job of the district organiser was substantially different from that of any of the full-time union officers described so far. His main responsibility was for 'the organisation and membership within the district', and fulfilling this responsibility took most of his time. New sites had to be located and visited, non-members had to be persuaded into the union, and a member had to be appointed shop steward, if any of them was willing to take the job. Since most building jobs are relatively small and relatively short-lived, there was no end to the task. His second job was to 'give service to the members'. This entailed visiting the sites and trying to settle the men's grievances.

He first visited one site because he happened to meet the foreman socially and learned that work had started there. The four bricklayers were already in the union, but he was able to recruit the labourers. Three weeks later he went back to find the men complaining bitterly of low earnings under their incentive scheme, although no one had attempted to contact him or made an approach to the manager. His proposal of a 'spot' bonus of £1 a day in addition to the incentive scheme was accepted, but only after two of the bricklayers had left. He explained that the habitual reaction of the men to unsatisfactory conditions was to leave the job rather than to try to secure improvements by collective action.

At a factory construction site the main contractor had a check-off agreement negotiated with the divisional secretary, and employed sixteen bricklayers and sixteen labourers, all members of the union. The labourers' shop steward said that his only contact with the union was through the organiser. He received no communications and attended no meetings. His main task as steward was to handle queries about 'targets' under the incentive payment scheme. The calculation of targets for labourers was more straightforward than for bricklayers, and the bricklayers' shop steward had resigned some time earlier. In addition to his grumbles about the calculations, he complained that he received no reimbursement for his time, and the other bricklayers did not support him. No one was willing to take his place, so that queries had to be settled with management by the individual bricklayers or wait until the organiser was able to visit the site.

At a housing site employing fourteen bricklayers and sixteen labourers, most of the bricklayers were in the union, but not many labourers. Earnings were low under an incentive payment scheme which the men did not understand. The manager showed no inclination to alter the scheme, and for some time there was no volunteer to act as steward although the men agreed with the organiser that something should be done about it. This meant that the organiser had to pay periodic visits to the site to recruit new labour into the union. In the end he called a site meeting at which one bricklayer agreed to act as steward. A work-to-rule was imposed when the manager refused him any concessions. The company then offered a 10 per cent additional bonus, leaving the incentive scheme otherwise unchanged, and the men accepted against the advice of the organiser.

The branch secretary of the Axton craft branch reported an average attendance of about twelve members at the weekly branch meetings, in addition to those who dropped in to pay union dues and then left. Most of the work of the branch and the branch committee was administrative and financial. Book-keeping and paying benefit—mainly sick benefit—occupied much of the secretary's spare time. He did not deal with industrial issues at all, although the rules required industrial grievances and complaints to be channelled through the branch to the organiser. In fact most members contacted the organiser direct at his home or through the divisional office, or waited for him to visit their sites. When industrial business came to the branch secretary, he passed it straight on to the organiser without reference to the branch. The organiser thought that the branches ought to play a bigger part in the industrial work of the union, but the pressure of his job prevented him doing anything about it.

One other aspect of branch business was the vetting of applicants for craft membership by the branch committee. Labourers were enrolled on application, but craftsmen had to 'justify' themselves. The normal requirement was a tradesman's card, but the committee would also accept the testimony of the organiser as to the ability of the applicant.

Conclusion

The Corbury branch was a more closely integrated local union organisation than any of the others examined so far. The workplace organisations were all in close contact with the branch secretary, and their representatives worked with him through the branch and the branch committee. One reason for this was the relatively small number of members for whom the branch secretary was responsible in comparison with full-time officers in other unions. A second was the care taken to ensure that the larger chapels were represented on the branch committee. But the third and most important reason was that the main method by which all the elements in the branch pursued their objectives was different from those employed by the unions which have been examined so far. This method was craft regulation. Workplace bargaining over pay and conditions may supplement agreements made outside the plant, or it may undermine them. Either way the workplace organisation can bargain without outside intervention if it has the resources to do so, and has to rely on outside assistance only to the extent that it is not self-reliant. But the maintenance of craft rules requires the co-operation of workplace organisations with each other, with the local union organisation and with the national union in a common endeavour. In the terminology of the sociologists, the craft is a *culture* which is *internalised* by all the members of the craft including those who become full-time officers. They see things the same way. Consequently the generalisations derived from earlier studies—the association between size and dependence, and the effects of tight agreements and the availability of officers—have relatively little relevance to Corbury.

The Corbury craftsmen relied on craft controls to provide acceptable earnings. Their colleagues at Camhill had learned to supplement craft controls by bargaining over house rates in the plant, and workplace bargaining had come to take first place in their union activity. They had not abandoned craft controls—far from it—but the chapels relied on the branch secretary to supervise the application of the rules and concentrated their attention on workplace bargaining over pay. Since the availability of the full-time officer was not in question, and the agreement allowed ample scope for bargaining over house rates, the relationship between the officer and the chapels varied with size. The smaller chapels depended on him and the larger chapels handled most of their business for themselves. But even they kept him fully informed and co-operated closely with him in running the branch. This highly developed teamwork may be attributable, in part at least, to the culture of the craft.

The study of the Building Trade Workers showed a craft in decay, with incomplete control over labour supply and over jobs. By themselves the vestiges of the craft system were not sufficient to support an acceptable level of earnings, and there was site bargaining over incentive systems and bonus payments. But, whatever might be the case on major construction sites, the sites which were examined had not developed workplace organisations capable of handling domestic bargaining on their own. They relied on the district organiser, but he was not always available because of the large number of small sites he had to cover and because the union depended on him to recruit and retain members. The demands for his services were far greater than the demands for the services of full-time officers on electrical contracting sites because the high time rates of the electrical contracting industry provided relatively attractive earnings except on the largest sites.

If all trade unions were constructed on the Corbury model, the generalisations which apply to the relations between workplace organisations and their full-time officers would be very different from those that emerge from the previous chapters. However, there are two reasons for supposing that the behaviour observed at Corbury is exceptional, even in unions which organise craftsmen. The first is that the 'mystery' of the crafts is gradually being dispelled by treating their jobs in the same way as those of other workers. The electrical contracting agreement distinguishes the more skilled jobs from the less skilled by testing and grading, principles which can be applied to production workers as easily as to craftsmen; and many plant agreements have brought craftsmen into a common system of job evaluation. The second is that the craftsmen themselves are adopting methods of operation equally open to other workers by bargaining over pay in the plant, some of them from choice like the Camhill printers, others because they are driven to it like the Glassford bricklayers. They still expect a skill differential, and they still object if other workers are put on their job, but a worker does not have to be a craftsman to experience those reactions. No doubt there are other craft organisations which keep craft regulations intact while at the same time pursuing plant bargaining, as the Camhill printers did. But where that happens, the relations between workplace organisations and the union outside will to some extent be influenced by the same considerations as apply to workplace organisation elsewhere.

7

Other Unions in Private Industry

The studies included in Chapters 2–5 were undertaken in the country's three largest unions and the sixth largest; and their membership in manufacturing industry was predominantly in engineering. This chapter comprises four studies in unions smaller than those, and in manufacturing industries other than engineering: a district of the National Union of Tailors and Garment Workers (114,000 members),[6] two plant branches of the Union of Shop Distributive and Allied Workers (319,000 members),[6] a district of the National Hosiery and Knitwear Workers (64,000 members),[6] and a town branch of the National Union of Boot and Shoe Operatives (70,000 members),[7] before its transformation during 1971 into the National Union of Footwear, Leather and Allied Trades, due to a transfer of engagements from three other unions.

THE TAILORS AND GARMENT WORKERS

Almost half the labour force of the clothing industry is employed in plants employing less than a hundred workers. In this respect, the West Sandshire area was untypical. The No. 2 branch of the National Union of Tailors and Garment Workers there, it is true, covered sixteen plants, none

---

[6] These membership figures are for 1971, the year in which the studies were undertaken.

[7] This is the 1970 figure, for that was the year of the study.

of them employing as many as a hundred members of the union, and amounting to about eight hundred members in all. But the No. 1 branch, with 2,500 members, covered three separate plants of one of the major firms in the industry, and the No. 3 branch consisted of over five hundred members employed in a fourth plant of the same firm, together with nearly a hundred more who worked for three small firms. Women constituted about two-thirds of the manual labour force in the four larger plants, and about 90 per cent in the small plants.

The organisation of the district has been streamlined to a point where the branches had almost disappeared, and business was conducted either within the plant or between the shop stewards and the area officer. There was no district committee, although a divisional consultative council had recently been established. Attempts to stimulate branch activity had met with little success in No. 2 and No. 3 branches, and No. 1 branch met only twice a year although the rules required quarterly meetings. Only No. 1 branch had a branch committee, which was a committee of shop stewards from the plants covered by the branch. The area officer was the branch secretary of all three branches, but administrative work took up little of his time, for he was served by a secretarial staff of three who enabled him to give most of his time to plant business.

It was his habit to visit each of the small plants, which he called the 'outside factories', once a fortnight. The visits followed a routine. He talked with the manager about the state of the trade, and collected from him a cheque for union dues—for almost all of the plants had check-off agreements. Then he talked to the steward, in most instances a woman, to deal with any outstanding problem such as piecework dispute or a claim for benefit, and to give encouragement. The steward was more closely under the influence of the manager than a steward in a large plant, and as the sole representative of the union, she had to take all the responsibility and all the criticism. He saw his task, therefore, as 'countering the boss psychology' and 'letting her know she has done the right thing'. Since there were no branch meetings and no branch committee, he was her only contact with the union. Nearly all the workers in these plants were on some form of piecework, so there were plenty of piecework disputes. Some of the stewards were adept at handling them, but most were not. It was the officer's decision whether he advised them how to handle a problem, or intervened directly.

Each of the large plants had a head steward who gave all or almost all of his or her time to union business—three were men and one was a woman. Piecework was regarded as a domestic matter for each of the plants. In three of them there was a thriving business of 'horse-trading' to push actual prices above the work-studied times. In the fourth, the results of work study were challenged only where a machinist could not maintain her previous level of earnings, and average earnings in this plant were lower than in the other three.

The four head stewards asserted that they were able to settle all but a tiny fraction of these and other domestic issues within the plant. But the area officer visited each plant once a week to keep in touch, and occasionally a domestic issue was referred to him under the company procedure which provided for him to handle unresolved plant disputes. One example is a dispute originating with the cutters at one of the plants. These men are the aristocracy of the industry who negotiate a 'log', or task, and cease work when it is finished. At this plant it was their habit to return to work after Friday lunch-break only when the pubs had closed. On their return one Friday they were locked out. In retaliation the head steward submitted a list of outstanding issues and demanded immediate action upon them. The manager refused to negotiate and the area officer was brought in to smooth things down. More commonly head stewards threatened reference to the area officer in order to induce a plant manager to be more amenable.

Some issues were regarded as company matters to be dealt with by a negotiating committee, set up in 1964 and consisting of six representatives of the No. 1 branch committee with two shop stewards from the fourth large plant and the area officer. The four head stewards were permanent members, with the other four lay members selected according to the matter under discussion. Prior to 1964, all improvements on the minimum provision of the industry agreement had been settled separately within the plants, leading to a good deal of leapfrogging. In 1964 the company persuaded the union that a change was needed. In 1968 the committee negotiated the company procedure agreement which was in force at the time of the study and in 1970 they negotiated a productivity agreement designed to put an end to overtime, and to provide guaranteed wages for those on time-rates, such as the cutters, pressers, canteen staff and labourers.

The negotiating committee limited the freedom of the plant organisation. This was most evident in one of the three plants covered by the No. 1 branch. This plant had objected to the reorganisation which had led to its inclusion in the branch; and the head steward was critical of the area officer because he was 'not tough enough in dealing with management'; and of the union hierarchy in general because 'they know nothing about what is happening on the shop floor'. The committee also restricted departmental independence. An agreement in 1970 gave a proportionately larger increase in pay to women as a move in the direction of equal pay. The cutters struck in all four plants, and, although they secured some concessions, they were forced to return to work without restoring their former differential.

The existence of the negotiating committee reinforced the authority of the area officer. Since the plant representatives often took parochial attitudes and the negotiating committee had to reach a common view on company issues, he often had the opportunity to give a lead. But he was in a weak position on matters over which the plant representatives were united. This weakness was clearly visible in the working of the No. 1 branch committee which was 'the governing body of the branch', so that the area officer in his role of branch secretary was its servant. The committee consisted of five shop stewards from each of the three plants, chosen on a departmental basis. They voted on any agreements reached by the negotiating committee, and listened to reports from the three head stewards who might seek the committee's support on domestic issues. In 1971 one of them reported that the company industrial relations officer had gone back on a verbal undertaking to a section in his plant and the committee required the area officer, much against his better judgement, to write to the managing director demanding the dismissal of the industrial relations officer. In the end the controversy was settled without such drastic action. For the most part, however, relations between the stewards and the area officer were friendly and co-operative.

THE SHOP DISTRIBUTIVE AND ALLIED WORKERS

Although the largest section of the Union of Shop Distributive and Allied Workers' members is employed in retailing (mainly in co-operative shops) the union has a considerable membership in a wide range of manufacturing industry. At the first of the two plants under study, which manufactured soap and detergents, all manual employees other than maintenance craftsmen were members of the union to a total of about 1,700, half of them women. Up to 1968 the workers had relied upon overtime to yield an acceptable level of earnings, and work practices were adjusted to sustain the volume of overtime. In that year a productivity agreement attempted to put an end to systematic overtime and to raise productivity by revising work practices in return for a substantial increase in basic rates above the minima prescribed in the industry agreement. Thereafter annual increases in the basic rates were fixed under a job evaluation scheme supervised by a joint wages structure committee. There was a thriving business in requests for revision of job rates, with appeals settled by an appeals board of two managers and two shop stewards. Working practices were kept under review by departmental committees under the supervision of a plant co-ordinating committee. Officially the departmental committees were consultative bodies. It was their function to help the company to achieve greater efficiency which constituted an important factor in the annual pay negotiations. In practice some of them aired and even settled grievances over shifts, overtime, discipline and other non-wage issues.

There were 35 shop stewards in all, and fifteen of them, including the branch secretary and chairman, constituted the branch committee which ran the union in the factory. Although all negotiating items were submitted to the branch, branch meetings were of much less importance than committee meetings. Attendance was low, with an average of about forty, and it was the committee's practice to determine a common line to be followed on all matters of any importance on the branch agenda. In its turn the committee was dominated by the branch secretary, who had held the post for eleven years and was a man of character and considerable debating skills. He was allowed to give most of his time to union business, and led in all negotiations with the company.

Nevertheless there were signs of conflict within the plant. In the twelve months prior to the study three sections had asked for their stewards to be deposed. It is significant that the complainants did not attend a branch meeting to make their protest, but wrote a letter to the branch secretary who read it out to a branch meeting in their absence and then visited the relevant section to deal with the complaint, in two instances arranging for a new steward to take over. But the main source of conflict was a process which the workers believed to be a hazard to health, with some justification in the number of workers who withdrew from the

process on health grounds. Although the company maintained that there was no danger to health so long as proper
precautions were taken, discontent in the department led
to the negotiation of a special allowance for those associated
with the process. This was not the end of the matter.
Following further transfers out of the section concerned, the
branch committee negotiated an increase in the allowance
and a fall-back arrangement to sustain the earnings of those
who withdrew. Even so they were not able to secure
acceptance from all the sections affected until they had
obtained further guarantees from the company. Meanwhile
there were problems in determining precisely the workers
who came into contact with the process, and the allowance
began to spread. The stewards concerned began to hold
separate meetings to discuss the problem, against the wish
of the branch secretary.

The full-time area officer responsible for the branch had
been a frequent visitor to the plant before 1968, but the
occasion of the productivity negotiations was used to put
into practice a union policy of withdrawing as far as possible from plant negotiations in order to permit full-time
officers to concentrate on other work. There is a high turnover of membership in the private retail trade, and, as in
the Amalgamated Union of Building Trade Workers, the
full-time officers were required to give much of their time to
recruiting.

Thereafter the area officer put his signature to the annual
pay settlements and other important agreements, but took
no part in negotiations except on one occasion when he
sought and secured a revision of a clause in the agreement
requiring new employees to join the union, and on another
when there was a difference of opinion as to whether an
annual pay increase applied to juvenile workers. But he
kept in close touch with the branch secretary, and, at his
invitation, attended the crucial meeting on the increased
allowance and fall-back guarantee for those working on
the allegedly dangerous process. He did not speak, but his

presence lent support to the branch committee's proposal.

The branch secretary was a member of the union's divisional committee, but his work there seemed to have little bearing on the business of the branch. The union supplements its divisional organisation by trade conferences of representatives from individual industries, and in this instance there was also a periodic meeting of representatives from other plants of the same company within the division. These meetings were welcomed as a means of keeping the branch secretary and his colleagues informed about developments elsewhere, but they did not lead to joint action.

The second plant, in a different part of the country, was in the food industry. At the time of the study it employed just over two hundred members of the union including almost all the manual and clerical employees in the plant. Recognition had been secured in 1963, and the area officer who negotiated the agreement was still responsible for the branch.

Subsequently a company agreement had established a procedure and a pay structure for this and the several other plants owned by the same firm. This agreement laid down standard rates of pay and conditions of employment. Many of the workers were paid under incentive schemes, but there was little opportunity to challenge the times which were settled by work study. Consequently the four stewards in the plant were limited to raising grievances and matters of interpretation under the agreement.

Nevertheless the stewards depended on their area officer to a surprising extent. The branch insisted that grievances must be brought to branch meetings for discussion on the line of action to be followed. The minutes contained several reprimands of members who had complained direct to their supervisors. If the branch considered that a complaint was justified they would authorise an approach to a manager by the steward, or quite commonly by the area officer who was frequently present at branch meetings, where attendance seemed to fluctuate between twenty and forty. He was, for instance, asked to raise with management a question as to how many employees in one department could be on holiday at a time, and to deal with an alleged slight to one of the stewards from a supervisor.

The area officer was a frequent visitor to the depot, coming and going as he pleased, talking to the stewards, or dropping in to chat with the manager. He saw himself as 'the joint manager of the plant', and claimed that he was pushing the branch towards greater self-reliance, although there was no evidence of this in his behaviour.

The company agreement was negotiated by a national officer of the union after consultation with the relevant area officers. But informal meetings of delegates from the relevant branches at the union's annual conference led to the establishment of an inter-depot liaison committee of two stewards from each plant. This committee was recognised by the union and provided a means of collating branch opinion on the claims which the national officer should submit. In 1970 some of the plants rejected the settlement which he had negotiated. He then submitted an improved offer to a special meeting of shop stewards and officers which recommended acceptance. The branches covered by the inter-depot liaison committee took no part in the union's trade conference for their industry.

The remarkable features of this plant were the central position of the branch meeting in the handling of grievances, and the dependence of branch and stewards on the area officer although nearly all the business they handled was of a relatively minor character, and at least two of the stewards were experienced and seemed capable of handling almost all the issues which arose.

THE HOSIERY AND KNITWEAR WORKERS

The National Union of Hosiery and Knitwear Workers is divided into twelve districts, and the district which was the subject of the study covered nearly seven thousand

members serviced by two full-time officers—a district secretary and an assistant district secretary, both appointed by
the executive. The members were employed in 75 plants,
the great majority of them within a four mile radius of
the district office. Fifty-four of the plants employed less than
a hundred members, and only two of them more than
three hundred, but each of these employed more than
six hundred.

The knitting of hosiery is a machine operation performed by men who are comparatively well-paid, and men
are also employed on ancillary jobs. The making-up, finishing and packing stages in the section of the industry which
predominated in this district were hand operations, carried
on in separate departments by women who constituted the
majority of the labour force. Within each department each
employee worked on his or her own, and earnings were
dependent on individual effort. These arrangements diminished the incentive to collective action.

Up to 1964 an industry agreement on piece rates provided
some guidance for the plants, although there was a good deal
of bargaining in the plants as well. In that year, at the
instance of the employers, individual firms were empowered
'to negotiate factory agreements alternative to existing
sectional or factory agreements with their employees and
representatives of their organisations, if any.' This agreement both increased the volume of domestic bargaining
and removed the price-lists which had previously served as
a guide to domestic bargaining. Most plants in the district
made no use of work study, and negotiations in the plant
were aptly described as 'Persian market' haggling so far as
the women were concerned. But the performance of knitting
machines can be timed, so that the knitters' piece rates were
more firmly based and there was less room for 'tight' and
'loose' rates. The knitters' disputes often concerned workloads.

The industry was highly competitive, with comparatively
low profit margins. Each firm constantly sought for some

new style which would attract a larger share of the market and enable it to make a short-run killing. Competition and low profits impelled managers to seek savings in labour costs. As the earnings of women workers rose with continued practice on a new style, managers proposed to 'dock' their rates. The women objected; the full-time officer was called in; a compromise 'dock' was agreed; the women worked harder to restore their earnings; and the manager decided to ask for a further 'dock'. With their more stable earnings, the knitters were less subject to docking, but not immune.

The industry agreement provided for shop or factory committees, but only one shop committee in the district existed under the rule. In addition there were informal committees of knitters in several plants. There were a number of collectors, some of whom acted as shop representatives, as did some former collectors in firms which had check-off agreements. In other plants spokesmen 'emerged', or the managers 'sent for' workers who, they felt, could speak on behalf of their fellow-workers. Workshop organisation was therefore rudimentary, but stronger among men than among the women.

The district formed a close-knit community. Managers and knitters might well have been to school together, and knew each others' background and personal circumstances. They attended the same chapels and drank in the same pubs. It seemed to the observer that the knitters became uneasy whenever they had a dispute with their managers. They called in the full-time officers, not only because of their superior skill and experience, but also as external conciliators who could smooth away disturbing friction. Thus, despite their superior workshop organisation and their status as the aristocrats of the labour force, the knitters did not set the women an example of independent action.

For their part, the women were much more likely than the men to be aggrieved by proposals to dock their piece rates. They did not share the knitters' close social relations with the managers, so they felt no need to restrain their feeling that they were being badly treated. They also called in the full-time officer, but not to act as a conciliator. They wanted him to prevent reductions, and they were not always happy when he proposed a compromise, as he often did, even though they accepted it.

Thus the men saw the full-time officers' task as 'keeping a happy relationship between workers and employer, then his job's done'; and they were satisfied with the results. The women were more critical, and some of them felt that the officers 'did not push management hard enough'. One of the managers said of the two officers that 'they understand our point of view ... They act as arbitrators between shop floor and management.'

There were no branches within the district except for two small groups of specialists who had come into the union by amalgamation. Of the sixteen members of the district committee, thirteen were men, eight of them knitters. Much of the committee's time was taken up with reports—from the specialist branches, from the Trades Council, from sub-committees, organisation reports from the assistant district secretary dealing mainly with the installation of check-off arrangements, and the reports from the executive given by the district's executive member who was the dominant figure in the committee. At the appropriate stage in the year, the committee discussed resolutions to be presented to the union's annual conference, and these came almost entirely from the executive member and the district secretary. If negotiations were on hand with the local employers' association the district secretary reported the decisions of the delegation which had met them and, after discussion, these were invariably approved. The secretary had 'made it a policy' not to discuss routine plant negotiations on the district committee. Consequently the full-time officers generally had a free hand in negotiations so far as the committee was concerned.

It seems that up to 1970 there had not been an election for the committee because the number of nominees did not exceed the number of places. Sometimes the committee ran below strength. If a member resigned, his place was filled by co-option. But in 1970 the nominees outnumbered the places so there had to be an election, which was conducted by postal ballot.

All the male committee members who were questioned about this unprecedented interest in union affairs explained it by the threat of a strike that year in the industry negotiations over a pay increase and a new shift system. This was the first time in the union's history that it had threatened a national stoppage. The women, on the other hand, all referred to the District Wage Structure Agreement for Females which was negotiated and applied during the year.

This agreement divided the making-up, finishing and packing operations into five groups with 'wage values' for each group, ranging in 1970 from £14.50 to £15.00 for group 5 up to £20.50 to £21.00 for group 1. The intention was that piece rates should yield earnings within the range for each grade over a forty-hour week throughout the district. On the introduction of the agreement, piece rates were to be adjusted up or down to achieve this aim.

The agreement was originally suggested by the employers, but the district secretary subsequently gave the proposal his wholehearted support. There had been attempts since 1955 to achieve an industry agreement on wage values but they had failed. He thought a district agreement could lead the way. The district committee received brief reports on the negotiations, and, dominated as they were by high-paid men, consented to recommend the draft agreement to the members. Meetings were held in three centres to allow the members to discuss the agreement and to vote. The arguments in favour of the proposal were that it would provide a floor for earnings, prevent constant docking and bring order into a chaotic pay structure against a background of falling market prices. From the employers' point of view, it would check wage drift. The result of the meetings was nevertheless inconclusive.

The officers noticed that some members had attended more than one of the meetings, which had been held on different evenings. The district committee therefore sanctioned a second vote by secret ballot at three meetings to be held on the same evening. As one committee member recalled: 'It was a terrific struggle to get it through the meetings. But we all knew that if we didn't get agreement there would be terrific piece rate cuts the next year. That's the way we had to sell it to the girls.' This time the vote was 146 to 132 in favour, on an agreement which would affect three thousand women. This narrow margin gave the district secretary a bargaining counter to secure upward adjustment of the values and a guarantee that thereafter adjustments to rates should not be made 'except where necessitated by changes in method, style, material or machine'. In the event the agreement had a significant stabilising effect on piece rates.

District agreements required the approval of the union executive. Approval was given mainly on the grounds that this was what the workers had shown by a majority vote that they wanted. Then came the problems of application.

The prolonged process of negotiation and approval, extending over three years of rapid inflation, meant that earnings had moved ahead of the agreed values, and many workers were due to suffer considerable reductions, with 'docks' of up to 40 per cent for some warehouse workers. Although these were to be applied in stages over a period of twelve months, in many plants the women refused to accept them in full. The two officers had to visit the plants and try to persuade their members to accept compromise settlements.

The remarkable feature revealed by this study is the domination of the district, and of district and plant negotiations, by the full-time officers in conditions which might have seemed very well suited to independent bargaining by shop stewards. Plant bargaining over piece rates and workloads were not limited by an industry agreement, nor, in most instances, fettered by work study. Nevertheless the officers were in control, and were called in to handle negotiations at an early stage, even in the larger plants, on the principle that 'we pay them to do the talking'. Signs of revolt emerged only when considerable sections of the members were subjected to wage-cuts in a period of rapid inflation.

THE BOOT AND SHOE OPERATIVES

The main purpose of including a brief account of a study of the National Union of Boot and Shoe Operatives is to show that many of the features of the hosiery district are to be found in other unions. The unit under study was a town branch, not a district, but the membership, at six thousand, was much the same with about equal numbers of men and women. There were three full-time officers, not two, and they were elected by branch ballot, not appointed by the executive. There were branch meetings, but average attendance fluctuated between twenty and twenty-five. At the 1970 election for the branch committee there were only eight candidates for eight places, four of them from the largest firm in the town.

The average size of plant was larger than in the hosiery district. There were 27 firms, ten of them employing less than two hundred union members, and the largest of them with a workforce of well over a thousand. Perhaps because of this, workshop representation was better organised. Shop stewards are known as shop presidents, and there were 104 shop presidents registered with the branch. The rules also provide for shop committees, and, although until recently there had been few of these, at the time of the study the branch was encouraging their formation to provide support for the presidents and to encourage interest in the union.

The duties of the shop presidents include the collection of union contributions, and ensuring the observation of union rules and agreements. Payment by results is traditional in the industry. There was an industry 'Agreement on Incentives based upon Time Study' with prescribed values for converting times into earnings, but in this branch the agreement had been applied only in the largest firms. Otherwise workers were paid on shop statements of piece prices or on contract wages—additional day rates above the industry minimum settled with the managers for specific jobs. These arrangements might have been expected to provide generous opportunities for domestic bargaining. But it was the constitutional duty of each member, including the shop president, 'to see that he is being paid the proper rate of pay, whether on day work or on piece work. Failing to secure proper rates he must report the real position to the branch officer, who will advise him as to the course which should be pursued in this matter.' Consequently, although some shop presidents negotiated with managers, the branch officers were usually brought into plant or departmental disputes at an early stage. If the shop presidents did not send for them, the managers did, or they reported disputes to their association, which automatically referred them to the branch officers. The tradition of the industry was to rely on the full-time union officers to service their members.

The boot and shoe industry is famous for its conciliation and arbitration procedures backed by monetary penalties for strikes and lockouts in breach of procedure, and there was a Conciliation and Arbitration Board in the town. Where the branch officer could not settle a plant or departmental dispute with the plant manager, it was referred to a sub-committee of three from each side, then to the full board, and finally to an umpire. But the branch officers had a strong preference for settling at plant level. The sub-committee stage had been used only 'once or twice' in the previous six years. They argued that the board was dominated by the more backward firms and it was in their members' interest for them to come to terms with the managers.

The board was nevertheless used to negotiate local agreements and in December 1970 such an agreement was rushed through to deal with the consequences of the work-to-rule in the electricity supply industry. During the negotiations the branch officers called a meeting of shop presidents to let them know what was happening, and probably as a show of force.

Meetings of shop presidents were also called to discuss national agreements. This enabled them to let off steam by criticising the settlements, but its main purpose was to inform them of the contents of an agreement for whose application they would henceforth be responsible.

In the past the arrangement had been for branch presidents to be responsible for industrial work, with the secretaries confined to administration and the vice-presidents in a subordinate position. Tensions had developed which had allowed the branch committee to exercise some influence. But the three men in the office at the time of the study were all involved in industrial work as a team. Consequently they were able to dominate the branch committee. Nevertheless the committee could not be ignored. They did not tolerate systematic overtime working. Firms which wanted to work overtime had to secure the committee's consent, and an average working week for the town of 40.1 hours at that time showed that permission was not granted lightly.

In the absence of the frantic competition of the hosiery industry in its search for new styles, and with larger plants, industrial relations in the boot and shoe branch presented a rather more orderly appearance than in the hosiery district. But the realities of power were much the same.

Conclusion

The main characteristics of relationships between workplace and union revealed by the studies in clothing, soap and food manufacture are already familiar. Workplace organisations in the larger plants showed a good deal of independence and the smaller workplace organisations relied heavily on full-time officers. It is true that the food plant's stewards seemed unnecessarily dependent, given their experience and the relatively minor issues they were called on to handle, but that could easily be explained by the special position of their full-time officer. He originally organised the plant; he took pride in it as a showpiece of good industrial relations; and he enjoyed the role he had built for himself there. The full-time officer in the clothing district gave unusually full attention to the small plants in his care; but he had the time to do so. In addition, the experience of the large clothing plants and the food plant indicates that a company agreement limits the scope of workplace bargaining by reducing the number of issues which can be settled in the plant.

The lessons of the two other studies are more novel. Although shop presidents in the larger footwear plants did a little more for themselves than their colleagues elsewhere, there was a remarkable reliance on the full-time officers throughout the hosiery district and the footwear branch, whatever the size of the plant. Some of the influences at work have been set out: the organisation of work which inhibited collective action; the close social relations between the knitters and their managers; the compact nature of the areas; the part played by the managers and the employers' associations in sustaining the influence of the full-time officers; and the dominating position of these officers in the hosiery district committee and the footwear branch. But it is a subject which must have more attention in the final chapters.

8

Public Employment

This chapter reports the findings of four studies of unions which organise public employees—men and women working for the government, local authorities, public services and nationalised industries. The first deals with one of the smaller areas of the National Union of Mineworkers; the second with two large branches of the National Union of Railwaymen; the third covers two regions of the Civil and Public Services Association; and the fourth reviews four branches of the National Union of Public Employees.

THE MINEWORKERS

At one time the pay structure and methods of domestic bargaining in coalmining had much in common with those in engineering. Industry agreements on pay settled minimum rates, leaving ample scope for domestic bargaining in the collieries. Faceworkers and many other underground workers were on piecework, with piece rates settled by haggling. There was also a great deal of bargaining by small groups and individuals over 'allowances' for circumstances in which they were unable to make their normal piecework earnings through one or more of the hundreds of obstacles which may obstruct production at the coalface. The difference was that there was only one union for all manual workers at the colliery, and the great majority of collieries had their own branches, so that much of this domestic bargaining was conducted by branch officers and not by shop stewards.

With nationalisation in 1947, colliery managers became subject to Area and Divisional control in their bargaining over pay, but a greater change came in 1955 with the National Daywage Agreement which fitted the timeworkers into nine grades, four for underground workers and five for surface workers. The standard rates for these grades were henceforth settled in national negotiations between the union and the National Coal Board.

Meanwhile work at the face was rapidly being mechanised. By 1966 well over 90 per cent of faceworkers worked with powerloading machines, and the National Powerloading Agreement of that year transferred them to day rates negotiated nationally between the union and the board. Because of differences in the previous levels of piecework earnings, there were differences between the day rates from one area to another, but these differences were themselves subject to national negotiation, and it was the intention that they should be gradually phased out.

The Scarshire area of the union had about three thousand members at the time of the study, employed in six collieries and organised in eight branches, for one colliery had two branches and there was a branch for transport workers. There were also nearly a thousand clerical, supervisory and craft members of the union in the area, but they belonged to separate branches organised in the clerical section of the union and its power group.

Each branch had its committee consisting of the president, delegate, secretary and six members. In contrast to many other areas of the union, the Scarshire delegates not only represented their branches on the area council, but also acted as branch negotiators. The board allowed them all, except the transport delegate, to give their whole time to the job, paid as faceworkers, although one of them preferred to work underground. Each of them was expected to take up grievances with the appropriate level of management whenever he decided it was necessary.

To an extent the other members of the branch committee

might have been regarded as ordinary stewards with the delegate as convenor, but these other members were not necessarily chosen to represent the various grades of miner and 'districts' in the pit, so that the delegate was sole representative for some groups, and he was the only member of the branch with overall, up-to-date knowledge of conditions throughout the colliery.

His position was enhanced by his membership of the colliery consultative committee, the safety committee and the productivity committee, all of which added to his information; and above all by his membership of the area council, which was the members' link with the national union. This link became far more important once the miners' pay was settled nationally, since information about national affairs came to the area through its secretary's reports from the national executive to the area council.

Before 1966 the delegate's time was mainly occupied with pay disputes. He negotiated piece rates and allowances, and handled 'dozens' of complaints each week about the make-up of individual pay packets. An area powerloading agreement in 1962 added to his responsibilities. Without putting an end to piecework, it brought a great deal of domestic bargaining over work norms and levels of manning on the powerloading machines. But the national agreement of 1966 provided for these matters to be decided by work study, and took them outside the scope of the industry's procedure agreement. Consequently, after a year or so in which the agreement was introduced and the initial problems ironed out, the main element in the delegate's work almost disappeared. Standard rates of pay also put an end to most of the queries about the make-up of pay packets.

The delegate continued to agree work terms with management, but this became something of a routine. He argued the case of men who wanted to be regraded to a higher rate of pay, or moved to another job or shift; dealt with disciplinary cases; investigated accidents; checked on safety, dust and lighting; advised the injured and the sick on their

entitlements; and helped his members with domestic problems—housing, debts, divorce and so on. But all this allowed
him to go about his business in a leisurely fashion between
meeting the night shift going off and the morning shift
coming on at 0600 hrs and the change from morning to
afternoon shift at 1300 hrs—and some of the delegates did
not invariably attend the first changeover. He was often to
be found where there was a chance of a cup of tea
and a chat.

The delegate's job had thus become largely administrative
—not administering the branch, for that was the secretary's
job, but helping to administer the colliery by co-operating
in the organisation of work, in safety matters and over
problems as they arose. Close relations with colliery management were made easier by the local origins of the colliery
managers who had worked their way up, were indistinguish-
able from the men in their manners and accent, and took a
personal interest in their men.

Four of the colliery delegates thought that the powerloading agreement had taken the interest out of the job.
'It's a full-time job doing nothing', said one. But the three
others thought differently, including the one who chose to
work underground. His two colleagues felt that there was
now more time to deal with individuals, and that:
'You can talk to the men without money being brought into
it.'

The job of the full-time area secretary had also been
affected by the 1966 agreement. Before that he was frequently
called into piecework negotiations, and the 1962 area powerloading agreement brought him a large harvest of problems
from the pits. After 1966 his main work, like that of the
delegates, was individual cases, most of all claims for compensation for injury or disease in which he dealt with the
individuals concerned and with the solicitor. In addition
he had his correspondence, and the minutes of the various
area meetings; and a good deal of his time went in national
union business. But much of the individual case load was

handled by his assistant, leaving him the opportunity to chat with the colliery delegates when they dropped into his office as they frequently did. For although he was rarely seen in the collieries after the 1966 agreement came into force, he kept himself informed on what was happening there. The delegates were anxious to 'keep him in touch'; partly because the colliery managers also knew him well and often rang him up over pit problems.

The area council consisted of the delegates, a part-time president and vice-president and three trustees. The council met for a full day once every month, and once a year there was an area conference attended by all the members of the branch committees. After dealing with correspondence, the main business of most council meetings was to listen to reports, above all to reports from the national executive and from the branches. These, along with much of the other business, were handled by the area secretary who was the area's representative on the executive. Many important items were discussed by a finance committee (consisting of the officers and the trustees) before they came to the council; and the custom was that committee members were bound by the committee's decision when these were reported to the council. Similarly the area conference debated resolutions already passed by the council.

Given these arrangements, it is not surprising that the council was dominated by the area secretary, and his forceful personality added to his authority. The minutes revealed that his control had been less secure before the 1966 agreement, for colliery piece rate disputes then came before the council. Delegates with an intimate knowledge of pit customs and conditions were more ready to confront him over such issues than over administrative matters and the negotiation and application of national agreements. The functions of council became, in the words of one delegate, 'airing one's views and the views of the membership' and 'a means of communication from national level to pit'. All the delegates said that their membership of the council assisted them in their work at their collieries. 'Men come and ask all the questions under the sun and I've got first-hand information for them.'

The Scarshire area of the union therefore presents a text-book case of the effects of tight industry-wide agreements. The colliery delegate's part in wage bargaining was narrowly limited. His function was changed to make him more a part of the colliery administration. His status came to depend more upon his membership of the area council, and this made him more dependent on the area secretary. The area secretary also ceased to be predominantly a bargainer, but he gained in authority as a member of the national executive, which monopolised negotiations and dealt with important disputes.

Some of these effects may have been more marked in Scarshire than in other areas of the union because of the traditional characteristics of the area. It has always been less strike-prone than most other mining districts, and has long boasted a reputation for hard work and high productivity. Consequently the shift from 'protest unionism' to 'administrative unionism'[8] may have gone further in Scarshire than elsewhere, but the direction of change, and the impact of the powerloading agreement were not confined to Scarshire

THE RAILWAYMEN

To some extent the structure of collective bargaining on the railways has been changing in the opposite direction to that of coalmining. Since the first world war railwaymen have been paid nationally-negotiated rates, and additional emoluments such as mileage rates have also been settled in industry-wide negotiations. But ten years or so after the second world war the railways began to introduce incentive payments for some groups of staff—permanent way men, for example, and parcels staff—under locally devised

[8] G. B. Baldwin, *Beyond Nationalisation*, 1955, p. 51.

schemes. The Pay and Efficiency Agreement, signed in 1968, reduced the number of grades in order to increase flexibility between jobs.

The procedure agreement on the railways has some unusual features. Except at national level, it is sectionalised. In the regions there are five separate sectional councils dealing with, for example, traffic staff, footplate staff and permanent way, signal and telecommunication staff. Where more than fifty members are employed in a given station or depot there is provision for a local departmental committee of not more than four elected representatives of the staff and four managers. Where the staff number less than fifty they are entitled to elect up to two local representatives. There is a separate procedure for the workshops, whose local representatives and committee refer unresolved disputes direct to national level.

The local departmental committees generally meet once a month, but they can also be called together fairly quickly. The sectional councils meet only by arrangement, once a quarter, so that they are not suited for handling urgent business.

Highridge and Lowborough are two considerable cities about fifty miles apart, each at the time of the study having a branch of the National Union of Railwaymen with rather less than 1,500 members. The Highridge branch covered ten stations, depots, workshops and hotels; Lowborough branch covered twelve. They came within the responsibility of separate full-time district officers, the first of whom dealt with rather more than 10,000 members and the second with rather less.

The main business of many of the local departmental committees and representatives was provided by bonus schemes, but there was also the arrangement of work, manning, rotas, working conditions and safety. The committees covering large groups of staff generally handled their business for themselves, the guards being especially independent. But the representatives of smaller groups of

staff were in need of assistance and guidance. Having no
convenor or steward to whom they could turn, most of them
went to their branch secretary, although he had no status
under the procedure. One or two representatives preferred
to go direct to their district officer but in most instances he
was regarded as a second resort.

The branch secretary was an authority on national agreements and local practices, and he was also called in as a
conciliator welcomed by the manager and the representatives to help them with their problems. The district officer,
on the other hand, was often used as a threat to press
management into action on an urgent issue. This was most
evident at the Highridge parcels depot where the men had
lost confidence in their local departmental committee
because they felt the managers were not prepared to negotiate. When they had a problem they usually stopped work
briefly, or used some other form of industrial action, and
sent for the district officer. This was one section which went
direct to the district officer. Another was the workshop in
Lowborough whose representative went to him with any
problem that also involved one of the other unions in the
workshop. The representative of another Lowborough section who went straight to the district officer was an
experienced negotiator who felt that if he could not settle
a problem, the branch secretary would not be able to do
so either.

The hotel representatives were especially dependent on
the branch secretaries. The hotels did not come within the
scope of the closed shop agreement between the Railways
Board and the unions. Both branches were still concerned
with building up hotel organisation, and at Highridge
there was still a long way to go. Consequently the representatives lacked confidence and experience, and branch intervention was necessary to see that they were given reasonable
facilities by the hotel managers.

There was, however, a considerable difference between
the two branches and their secretaries. The Lowborough

secretary's job at the city's main station allowed him considerable scope to handle union business in the course of the day, and he was available at home for part of every evening. The Highridge secretary was less accessible at work and at home, and dealt with most business over the telephone. Local representatives in his branch were encouraged to be independent, and his members in the hotels had suffered as a consequence until the assistant branch secretary accepted responsibility for them.

The difference between the secretaries was one of the reasons for a difference in the type of business at branch meetings. The Lowborough branch spent most of its time on the business raised by local representatives who used branch meetings to sound out proposed courses of action on their problems. The branch records were full of decisions to refer issues to the district officer, or back to the local departmental committees, or instructing the branch secretary to deal with a matter. There was much less of this at Highridge where discussions on industrial matters more commonly dealt with national issues, and led up to resolutions condemning the national executive or demanding that they submit further claims to the Railways Board. In addition the Highridge branch debated many political resolutions over which the members polarised for and against the Communist Party. Both branches were worried about attendance, which could fall as low as six, although each of them averaged about twenty; but when there were elections at the Highridge branch both factions attempted to pack the meetings. When contentious subjects were discussed at Lowborough, expression of opinion usually led up to a resolution to 'agree to note'.

The sectional council's staple business lay in appeals on grading. This has always been one of the readiest means for a railwayman to increase his pay, and, although ultimately the Pay and Efficiency Agreement should reduce disputes over grading along with the number of grades, this had not happened by 1971 when the study was made. On the contrary, regrading under the agreement had added to the volume of appeals. Claims for regrading were not too urgent to wait for the leisurely procedures of the councils.

There was a separate procedure for railwaymen 'charged with misconduct, neglect of duty or other breach of discipline' who normally asked to be accompanied by their district officer. These hearings took up a significant part of the officers' time, and they were also involved in all fatal accident enquiries. Otherwise they had no formal position in the procedure, but they were summoned wherever there was industrial action, and the smaller branches called on them frequently. Most sections at Lowborough and Highridge preferred to do without them, because 'there were less likely to be hard feelings if we settled the matter ourselves' and because they felt that the district officers were 'out of touch'. Both branch secretaries favoured keeping the district officers out of local negotiations as much as possible, and there seemed to be some personal feelings between the secretaries and the officers.

All this must not be allowed to obscure the part of national negotiations in determining the bulk of the pay packet of most railwaymen. The most important industrial issue in either of the two branches for several years had been an unofficial strike of guards at Highridge and elsewhere in protest against merging the grades of guard and ticket-inspector, and against the abolition of certain long runs which brought high mileage payments. The district officer had the difficult task of persuading the guards to resume work without the authority to negotiate anything on their behalf. The outcome was a good deal of ill-feeling and a letter from the branch to headquarters voicing their lack of confidence in the officer.

The interest of this study does not lie merely in the volume of domestic negotiations over a range of issues, including pay, in a nationalised industry with relatively tight agreements; nor in the ability of the larger departmental committees to handle their negotiations for themselves. It lies also in the relatively limited role of the district officers in the two branches; and particularly in the assumption by the branch secretaries, without any authority under the union rules or the agreements, of much of the work that is elsewhere carried out by full-time officers. It seemed that smaller branches relied more heavily on the district officers, but in these two large branches it was the branch secretaries (or their assistants) who usually provided advice and information to the workplace negotiators, and usually supported, or took over from, the representatives of smaller or relatively ill-organised groups. Nevertheless the branch secretaries could not be classified along with convenors or colliery delegates, for they did not operate within the place of work or the local committees (except their own). They came in from outside.

THE CIVIL SERVICE

A similar use of lay officers, but more thoroughly institutionalised, was found in the Civil and Public Services Association.

This union organises the clerical assistants, clerical officers and related grades of the civil service, and similar grades in the Post Office. The total membership is about 200,000, some 65–70 per cent of them women. There are in all only fourteen full-time officers in the union, all stationed at the London headquarters. Most of their time is spent dealing with government departments there, so the union has no option but to rely heavily on lay officers in the regions.

This dependence is supported by the generous provision of 'facility time' for lay officers by government departments, particularly for the staff side secretaries of regional and local Whitley committees. Most regional staff side secretaries are accorded full-time facilities, as are their local colleagues in large offices. Consequently the most apt description for them, contradictory though it may appear, is 'full-time lay officers' of the union. Up and down the country there are hundreds of these officers, who therefore outnumber the full-time officers of the union many times.

Since the union's members are to be found in every government department, their pay is negotiated through the machinery of the National Whitley Council along with pensions, recruitment, training, London weighting and dispersal policies. Departmental Whitley Councils deal with matters within the competence of their own Ministers—organisation of work, promotion procedures, discipline, transfers, accommodation—with the interpretation of national agreements, and with matters in dispute in their local and regional Whitley committees. These committees in their turn deal mainly with matters within the scope of regional and local managers, although they may also be used to air grievances about general departmental matters.

The department which was the subject of study employed about 40,000 members of the union. They had the services of only one full-time officer, the section secretary, supported by three assistant section secretaries and a section chairman, all of them full-time lay officers. Of the 26 members of the section executive, only one is not a full-time lay officer.

The study covered two regions within the department. No. 1 region was the largest in terms of members and the most compact in size, covering about 10,000 members who staffed a vast 'clerical factory' with a growing volume of automatic data processing. The region operated as a single branch. Most of the members worked in large rooms, each with its union representative. The rooms were located in blocks, each with up to twenty rooms, and these in turn had their union agents. The branch executive committee of 45 included nine branch officers, and 24 block agents. There were six full-time lay officers—two regional staff side officers,[9] and the chairman, secretary, deputy secretary and organiser of the region. The facilities of these regional union officers

_____

[9] Although other unions were represented on the staff side, the association was the major union and filled most of the offices.

(who were elected at the annual general meeting of the branch) had been secured under a special arrangement following the introduction of the check-off, as compensation for loss of facility time for collectors.

No. 2 region covered some 35 local offices of the department, the largest of them employing a staff of 350. They were grouped in area branches with their own meetings and branch committees. Each branch committee sent a representative to the regional committee, whose secretary, as regional staff side secretary, was the only full-time lay officer in the region.

The Whitley committees were not of much importance in themselves, for they rarely met, and the No. 1 region committee had some difficulty in spinning out their one meeting of the year long enough for coffee to be served. Their importance lay in the authority which they conferred on their officers to handle informally the business which, formally, should have been settled by the committees. Consequently the staff side officers conducted almost all their business by interviews with the appropriate senior officers. The issues which they handled varied enormously, from dismissals to holiday rostering, but probably most of their time was spent on the organisation of work, the allocation of jobs and overtime, and handling individual cases on behalf of their members, such as an appeal against dismissal by a clerical officer who had been judged to be below standard after an extended probationary period; or securing an afternoon off for examination candidates who had to take an exam in the morning.

There had also been major issues, such as the negotiations over a proposed redundancy of six hundred temporary clerical assistants in No. 1 region—eventually cut down to less than two hundred. But the conclusion to be drawn is that the full-time lay officers were doing a job which would elsewhere be divided between shop stewards and full-time officers. Block agents in No. 1 region are entitled to represent their members, but few of them did so. Twenty-one of the

24 were interviewed, and only three of these said that they took up their members' grievances with the manager before passing them on to the union office.

Things were a little different in No. 2 region. The full-time lay officer could not usually be on the spot as quickly as his colleagues in No. 1 region. The region covered a large area, and he had no car so that he had to justify his expenses to an establishment officer on the basis of his staff side duties. Most of the local offices had their own Whitley committees. His job therefore resembled that of a full-time officer servicing shop stewards. There were differences between the committees in the demands they made on him. Generally those in the larger offices handled most of their business themselves, and it was the smaller offices which made most calls on his time. In addition, because of his difficulty in visiting the more remote offices, their committees tended to look after themselves.

The dominant position of the full-time lay officers was assisted by the age structure of the union. Despite the numbers of women in the union, union offices went mainly to the men, but the post of clerical officer was no longer regarded as a career for a man. Most clerical officers of any ability and ambition were promoted to executive posts in their twenties or early thirties, with consequent transfer to the Society of Civil Servants. The union depended upon senior clerical officers left from a previous generation, and experienced high turnover among its younger office-holders. It is significant that all the three block agents in No. 1 region who claimed that they handled grievances were older men. The records show branch attendances of 250–500 in the immediate post-war years, when total membership was less than three thousand, the majority of them men; and there were bitter factional struggles. Subsequently it became rare for attendance at quarterly branch meetings to reach much more than the quorum of fifty. Since the branch committee decided their line beforehand, and voted together, the branch had very little chance of taking effective decisions.

In many respects the function of these full-time lay staff side officers was akin to that of the Scarshire colliery delegates. They formed part of the administrative machine, helping the department to function effectively. However, there were differences. On the one hand, they were less in touch with their individual members than were the colliery delegates, because of the numbers for which they were responsible, and the way in which their work was done, closeted with managers. On the other hand, from time to time they found themselves in conflict situations. In recent years the machine grade girls had been the most militant group in No. 1 region. At one stage six hundred of them walked out in protest against a delay in a central pay settlement for machine grades, although they left the subsequent negotiations entirely to their officers, and only seventy of them attended the special branch meeting which they had asked for in order to discuss the matter. Following a subsequent central agreement dealing with the standards required to qualify for proficiency payments, a local arrangement was made to vary standards in favour of the staff. Within a year over 60 per cent of the machine operators there were receiving the payment, against a national target of 30 per cent. This concession was in part due to the girls' show of militancy and in part to the local labour market.

From time to time the full-time lay officers in region No. 1 were pushed into more vigorous action than they themselves would have chosen over an issue which aroused strong feeling among their members. One such issue was the standard of their office accommodation which was generally admitted to leave a good deal to be desired, and the slow progress of rebuilding. After a series of protests over several years, in 1972 the officers proposed to the branch committee that the departmental staff side should be asked to take the matter up. The committee decided that this was not enough and instructed them to ask the departmental staff side to send a deputation to see for themselves. Neither the officers nor the local official side were keen on this move which was a little too much like having their dirty linen washed in public, but the visit was followed by strong pressure from the local official side on the department to get something done. This incident recalls the use of the full-time trade union officer as a 'bogeyman' in negotiations between branch secretaries and local managers on the railways; and it was not an isolated incident. Local managers in both regions wanted to settle problems without reference to Whitehall, and a threat to call in the section secretary was often enough to secure further concessions from them.

Meeting only once a quarter, and with many issues settled in the branches, the No. 2 regional committee had to allow greater scope to their secretary. However, members of the committee often accompanied him in discussions with regional managers, and had the opportunity to exercise some influence there; and issues often went straight to the committee, whereas in region No. 1 the full-time lay officers would already have discussed them as a group. The introduction of a scheme of 'management by objectives', for example, was the occasion of a vigorous debate on the No. 2 regional committee which determined the lines on which the secretary was to act.

THE PUBLIC EMPLOYEES

The National Union of Public Employees has its main strength among wage-earners employed in local government and the hospitals. Over the last four decades it has been one of the two fastest-growing British unions. In 1934 its membership was about 13,000. At that time the main union in the fields of its operation was the General and Municipal Workers Union. In 1972 its membership exceeded 400,000, comfortably passing the General and Municipal Workers in both local government and hospitals. With 60 per cent of its members women, it had the largest female membership of any British union.

This growth was assisted by an emphasis upon recruitment as a major item in the officer's job. Traditionally the officer has also played a large part in handling workplace grievances. The collector might pick up complaints as he went his rounds collecting the dues, but he normally reported them to the branch secretary or chairman who in turn generally passed them on to the full-time officer. The collector was not recognised as a negotiator. Indeed, local authority and hospital officers generally regarded their manual employees as occupying a far more clear-cut position of subordination than is general in manufacturing industry, so that it was less disturbing to both managers and workers to leave grievances to be handled by the full-time officer who could approach the local government officer as an equal; and the demeanour of the union officer usually fitted in with these attitudes. In addition, with tight industry agreements, most grievances were individual, concerning grading, promotion, discipline or accidents. They were handled by accumulating a set of 'case papers' which might have to go through the appeals procedures to regional and national level. In the preparation of these papers the officer was the expert, and he had the backing of the necessary secretarial services.

Following Report No. 29 of the National Board for Prices and Incomes,[10] however, there has been a continuing development of local incentive schemes and productivity agreements in local government, followed by the hospitals. In 1971, in an attempt to hasten progress, industry agreements provided for local negotiation of 'lead-in' payments where the workers were prepared to take part in such a scheme, but the authority was not yet in a position to introduce it.

The schemes entailed collective action by groups of local

[10] *Pay and Conditions of Manual Workers in Local Authorities, the National Health Service, Gas and Water Supply*, Cmnd 3230, March, 1967.

government and hospital employees. Moreover, their installation and maintenance created additional work which the
full-time officers could not easily handle. At the same time
there was a growing emphasis on promoting democratic participation at all levels of the union. Shop stewards were
given recognition to act on behalf of their members by the
local authorities' national joint council in 1969 and by the
hospitals two years later. In 1970 the executive committee
made general provision for the selection of shop stewards
who were to be under the control of the branches.

The union is split into divisions, each in the charge of
a divisional officer who directs the work of a number of
area officers. Four branches were studied in the city of Redcastle, all of them under the care of the one area officer.
Theirs is the most rapidly growing division in the union,
and the divisional officer puts special emphasis on recruitment.

The most immediately striking feature of the area officer's
work was the volume of his correspondence. He received
correspondence from head office concerning the accounts of
the branches for which he was responsible, and from
national officers seeking and giving information. Many local
and individual problems came to him through the mail,
from branch secretaries or chairmen, from individual members, and more recently from shop stewards; problems were
also raised directly with him in letters from local government or hospital managers. Furthermore the normal method
of initiating dealings with managers was an exchange of
letters. He estimated that he wrote between eighty and a
hundred letters a week. In addition, members, stewards and
branch officers got in touch with him by phone, at branch
meetings, and in the pub afterwards.

The Redcastle school meal supervisors had their own
branch, between sixty and seventy strong, but they had no
shop stewards and no regular meetings. Meetings were
arranged by the full-time officer, and notices were sent out by
him when he thought fit or when pressed by the branch

secretary and chairman. He handled all dealings with the authority through the Assistant Education Officer (Catering), and there was on the files a letter of protest to the Chief Education Officer for allowing an issue to be handled by discussion between a catering superintendent and the branch secretary.

The main issue for negotiation over the period of the study was the question of downgrading of supervisors due to a decline in the numbers of children taking school meals, in accordance with a national agreement which linked grades to the number of meals served. There was little that the officer could do for the members affected except to ensure that they would have the first chance of upgrading when numbers rose again. But the members were naturally upset, and felt that their grievances did not receive prompt attention or forceful support. The branch officers wrote to the national officer and to the divisional officer, without effect except to offend the area officer who commented that he was becoming 'fed up with a branch that is totally dependent on me and yet keeps going over my head'.

The branch illustrates one common feature of local authority trade unionism—the wide dispersal of many members both at work and at home. In this instance they were scattered throughout a major city, and there was no scope for developing effective branch or workplace organisation.

There were several contrasts between the officer's relationship with this branch and that with his largest hospital branch, which grew from a thousand to almost 1,500 members over the period of study. The branch covered nine hospitals. Its branch secretary was a member of several higher committees of the union (and chairman of some of them). He expected the full-time officer to attend every monthly branch meeting. When the officer failed to appear, the branch secretary upbraided him in front of the next meeting.

From time to time the officer was also summoned to sectional meetings of the members in one or other of the hospitals, or to a meeting with a hospital officer arranged by the branch secretary, sometimes without notice of the purpose of the meeting. Nevertheless he attended.

The branch secretary, chairman and ten other representatives acted as shop stewards, between them covering all nine hospitals. Shop stewards had first received local recognition in 1967, before the national agreement, and without any incentive schemes and lead-in payments. The stewards met irregularly between branch meetings, and the branch secretary tried to insist that all issues which the stewards did not settle for themselves should be passed on to him.

Several of these characteristics of the branch secretary's behaviour seemed to indicate that he dominated the area officer, but this relationship did not carry over into dealings with managers. When he met managers the officer always tried to arrange for the branch secretary to be there, but he took the lead and turned to the branch secretary only for detailed information.

Most grievances came to the officer at branch meetings or by letter from the branch secretary, who usually wrote to him twice a week. Very few of them concerned the branch secretary's own hospital, and it may reasonably be assumed that he dealt with these himself, but grievances from other hospitals—rotas and shifts, promotions, ventilation, responsibility for lifting patients, failure to pay sick pay, rates of pay on transfer, tea breaks, accidents, dismissals and many others—were handed on to the area officer who prepared the case papers and wrote to the hospital. Most of them were dealt with entirely by correspondence, with copies to the branch secretary, but in dismissal cases the officer always met the manager with the member present. About fifty cases of all kinds were handled in this way in the course of a year.

Two major issues arose during this period. The first was a 'management survey' of one of the hospitals. There was no question of an incentive payment or lead-in payment, but the survey was expected to lead to considerable reorganisation of duties. The hospital informed the area officer who arranged a meeting with four shop stewards (including the branch secretary). The officer led the discussions, asking for an assurance that there would be no redundancy and that the union would be kept informed of the progress of the report. When the report appeared he went over it with the stewards and then arranged a meeting with the heads of the departments affected, where, accompanied by the stewards, he secured a number of amendments, and the report was cleared for action. The officer was in control throughout the whole affair, although he relied on the stewards for a number of detailed criticisms of the report.

The second major issue was a proposal for a lead-in payment at a second hospital group. In this instance the area officer took the lead by writing to the group, and asked his divisional officer to complain when he did not get a prompt response. He took the lead when he met the group secretary, although the branch secretary went with him. He then put proposals to meetings of the domestic and catering staff at the hospitals concerned. They were approved, except by the domestic staff at one hospital.

A keen advocate of the new policy of greater participation by the members, the area officer was critical of the branch for being too reliant upon him, and for handling too few issues for themselves; but he had not been able to pass over much of his work to the branch secretary and the shop stewards. However, the integrity of his intentions was demonstrated by his relations with the Redcastle school caretakers' branch. Previously this had been an independent local union, whose general secretary had handled all negotiations and cases with the education authority, and continued to do so on amalgamation with the Public Employees. When he fell ill, the area officer was instructed to take over as branch secretary, and he began by conducting the business in the same way as his predecessor. But the burden became too onerous, and, after a year of it, he persuaded one of the members to take over as branch secretary, and arranged for the election of shop stewards. He continued to attend branch meetings, but encouraged the stewards to meet on their own.

The next step was to pass over some responsibility for negotiations to them. He arranged a meeting with the education authority to discuss payment for caretakers while the schools were in use as polling stations, and then 'found' that he could not attend. The stewards said they could not manage without him, and the department assumed that the meeting would be postponed, but he insisted that they went ahead, and in the event the stewards secured a higher rate of pay than previously. 'They were as delighted as dogs with two tails', he said.

Two sections of the union's membership which have long been noted for their self-reliance are the refuse collectors and the ambulance drivers. They have more opportunity for meeting and talking at their depots than most local authority employees; and they are relatively highly paid, the refuse collectors because they were the first section of local authority employees to negotiate bonus schemes, and the ambulance drivers with overtime and shift pay as well as bonuses. The Redcastle ambulance branch was a good instance of this self-reliance. In 1956 it secured its own joint consultative committee with management, and an assurance that new starters would be 'strongly encouraged' to join the union. A shop steward was recognised in 1959, and at the time of the study the branch secretary was operating as a full-time representative—an unusual arrangement in local government—although his branch membership was less than two hundred, including pool chauffeurs and garage mechanics.

Issues such as shifts, rotas, uniforms and sick pay were handled domestically. The area officer had attended only two branch meetings in fifteen months, and did not go to consultative committee meetings. 'If they cannot get what they want in the branch,' he said, 'then there's no chance of getting it.' The branch secretary, who had attended work study courses, negotiated incentive bonus schemes for several groups hitherto not covered, including the pool chauffeurs, and the area officer intervened only to ratify them by letter. 'There was nothing more I could have done to them. They were excellent.'

The area officer nevertheless had a number of dealings with the branch. Some issues, such as a long-standing claim for a higher rate for mechanics, could not be settled by the branch secretary; he was asked to look into the fluctuating membership of the branch by head office and the divisional officer; the branch secretary asked him about developments in ambulance negotiations in other areas, and for copies of earlier correspondence relevant to current negotiations, as well as sending him draft agreements for approval; and he was always brought into dismissal cases. But his involvement was far lighter than in any of the other three branches. He put this down to the competence of the branch secretary, but the secretary was not discernibly more intelligent and able than the secretary of the hospitals branch. The difference lay in his willingness to negotiate with management, and the expectation of both his members and the managers that, wherever possible, he would settle matters without calling in the area officer. Since similar self-reliance is to be found among other groups of ambulance drivers, it seems reasonable to seek the explanation in the characteristics of their work and the way they are organised to carry it out; and in their professional approach to their jobs and their expectations from them.

Nothing has been said in this study about the various area committees and sectional committees in the division, because they had no effect at all on events within the plants or on handling of grievances and bargaining issues. They were mainly concerned with reports from the divisional officer dealing with such matters as recruitment, administration and national policies.

Conclusion

The main objective of the studies reported in this chapter was to discover whether the relationship between unions and workplace organisations in the public sector differed from those in the predominantly private undertakings which have been described in earlier chapters.

The most obvious contrast is between the tight agreements of the industries and services with which this chapter is concerned and the comparatively loose industry agreements which apply throughout the private undertakings covered in previous chapters, except for electrical contracting and the non-federated firms. Nevertheless, despite the tightness of the industry agreements, there remained a good many items for settlement by workplace bargaining, and workplace organisations played a considerable part in handling them.

At the same time there were some differences between the agreements in the scope allowed for workplace bargaining, and greater differences from one workplace to another in the way workplace bargaining was carried on. The railway, local government and health service agreements left scope for work-studied incentive and bonuses to be negotiated in the plant, whereas, apart from overtime, the civil service and coalmining agreements allowed for local bargaining over pay only through claims for grading. But under all five of them the organisation and allocation of work constituted staple items for workplace bargaining. In addition there were further instances of the now familiar contrast between those workplace organisations which dealt with business of this kind for themselves and those which relied more or less heavily on help from the union outside.

There was little difference between the collieries in this respect. The colliery delegates dealt with the managers themselves although they kept in touch with the area secretary of their union. The contrast was in the attitude of the delegates. Some of them considered that the powerloading agreement had taken the meat out of workplace bargaining; others took a different view. But since the collieries were of roughly equal size and all fully and effectively organised, the kind of factors which have so far been associated with differences in the degree of workplace dependence were not present. On the other hand, workplace dependence was related to size on the railways, with the hotels as the exceptions to be explained by the incomplete organisation of the hotel staffs; and a relationship between size and dependence was also observed in Region No. 2 in the civil service, and in Region No. 1 if it is classed as a single large workplace, for the executive of this vast branch guarded its independence jealously from intervention by the London headquarters of the union.

Variations in workplace dependence among the Public Employees, however, cannot be explained by reference to the size of workplace organisations. The most independent of them, the ambulancemen's branch, numbered less than two hundred. But another explanation is available which has already appeared several times in earlier chapters. Traditionally senior local government officers and full-time union officers have adopted a style of dealing with each other which was designed to minimise the participation of workplace organisation in the settlement of workplace issues. Over the last few years this style of bargaining has been questioned, and there have been moves to encourage greater self-reliance in the workplace, but it has been challenged over a much longer period by the two groups of local authority employees with the greatest resources for independent action in terms of unity and status—the dustmen and the ambulancemen. Consequently variations in workplace dependence among the Public Employees can be explained in terms of the traditional style of bargaining and the extent to which this has been challenged by the stronger workplace organisations, or modified by full-time union officers.

Another feature of union organisation in the public

sector which is not unique, but more noticeable there than elsewhere, is reliance on lay officers to do the work normally carried out by full-time officers. The two branch secretaries on the railways dealt with most of the issues which could not be resolved by local committees and representatives, and in the civil service all the union posts outside London, including regional posts, were held by lay officers. For assessing the dependence of workplace organisations it does not make much difference whether their dealings with the union are through a full-time officer or a lay officer (whether full-time or not), but it is possible that it makes a great deal of difference to regional and national union organisation. Regions and headquarters might be expected to exert greater influence over the work of full-time officers whose salaries are paid by the union and many of whom are appointed by the union, than over the work of lay officers. But since the case studies did not investigate these levels of union organisation, that remains a matter for speculation.

Similarly one of the consequences of the powerloading agreement bears primarily upon national union organisation. Following the agreement, it was evident that the miners were more dependent upon, and more concerned with, industry negotiations than before. This altered the focus of interest in area council meetings and made the colliery delegates more dependent on the area secretary who reported the decisions of the national executive to them. But this dependence had no obvious effect in the conduct of colliery business. It indicated the distribution of power in the national decision-making process, and that was outside the scope of the case studies.

9

Analysis

Workplace Organisations and Full-Time Officers

Chapter 1 suggested that the relationships between workplace organisations and full-time officers might be classified as dependent, co-operative or independent, and these words have been used from time to time to describe the relationships observed in the case studies. How useful are they as a starting-point for analysis?

They cannot be used as entirely distinct categories without doing violence to the material, for an element of co-operation was found in every case study. This is true even if the simplest definition of dependence and independence is adopted, namely: who deals with the managers? For the most self-reliant shop stewards, such as those in some of the large engineering plants at Leachester, had to call in full-time officers to sign major agreements. At the other extreme, full-time officers who carried the full load of dealing with management nevertheless sometimes took one or more of their members with them into negotiations. Consequently we have varying degrees of interdependence ranged along a continuum, approaching complete independence at one end and verging on complete dependence at the other.

In addition to that, the location of a workplace organisation along the continuum cannot depend entirely upon the answer to the question: who deals with management? There are no figures for the proportions of plant issues handled by workplace organisations on the one hand and by full-time officers on the other; and even if figures were available they might not settle the matter. For the decision must also depend on an assessment of the importance of the issues handled by each of them, and of the degree of influence exercised by the full-time officer over the workplace representatives. For example, the area officer at the Shop Distributive and Allied Workers' soap plant rarely intervened in negotiations, but his vetting of agreements negotiated in the plant was more than a formality as he showed by securing an amendment to one of the proposed settlements, and he attended a branch meeting to support the branch secretary when a crucial decision had to be taken there. Moreover, he gave the impression that he kept in close touch with affairs in the plant and with the branch secretary, so that he was in a position to exercise influence behind the scenes on other occasions. This may be contrasted with some of the major engineering plants in Leachester where the full-time officer's signature on agreements appeared to be a formality, and where he did not seem to be in such close touch with plant affairs or in a position to exercise much influence over the shop stewards' decisions. Consequently, although the soap plant must be located towards the independence end of the continuum, it was not as close to complete independence as some of the major Leachester engineering plants.

An even better example of the exercise of influence behind the scenes is to be found among the Scarshire miners. Their area secretary was rarely seen in the pits and left face-to-face dealings with the colliery managers to the colliery delegates. But he spoke to managers over the telephone and used the frequent visits of the delegates to his office and their attendance at area council meetings as a means of keeping in touch with pit affairs and guiding the delegates. His influence was evident throughout the area, and the Scarshire collieries must be placed nearer the dependence end of the continuum than the soap plant.

The workplace organisations in the four major clothing

plants in West Sandshire handled their own piecework negotiations in the plant, although their full-time officer visited each plant every week to keep himself informed. But there were also the company agreements covering the four plants in whose negotiation he played a larger part, not only because he was the spokesman in negotiations but also because he was able to guide the senior stewards in preliminary discussions so long as they were not already in accord as to the line to be followed. Consequently the location of these workplace organisations on the continuum depends upon their status as separate workplace organisations. They can be seen either as separate organisations operating in four individual plants, or as a single workplace organisation covering the four plants. If the former, their position on the continuum is nearer independence than if they are seen as a single organisation; but either way they probably come somewhere between the soap plant and the Scarshire collieries.

On the other hand, the shop stewards and branch secretary of the Public Employees' hospital branch at Redcastle should probably be classed as less independent than the Scarshire colliery delegates, for the area officer led in all negotiations with hospital managers and dealt with many issues which would have been left to the delegates in Scarshire. But the scrutiny of the area officer's work at branch meetings and the debates at briefing meetings before negotiations showed that the stewards and the branch secretary were a good deal less dependent than the hosiery workshop representatives.

These qualifications and complications do not destroy the value of the notion of a continuum between dependence and independence in classifying workplace organisations. The workplace organisations described in the case studies can be located along the continuum with a fair degree of certainty about the rank order. Most of the case studies covered several plants. In some of these, such as Leachester engineering, the plants are spread along the whole length of the continuum. In others, such as hosiery, all the plants are at much the same point.

If the cases may be taken as reasonably representative of British unions as a whole, then relationships at every point along the continuum are common in British trade unions. There are many examples of almost complete independence, many of almost complete dependence, and examples of different degrees of co-operation covering the whole range between them.

Changes over Time

Before seeking explanations for varying degrees of dependence and independence, there is another consideration which cannot be neglected. Had similar studies been undertaken a few years earlier, the rank order of the plants along the continuum would have been different, perhaps very different. For the existing studies record a number of important changes which had taken place not long before.

The outstanding example is East Sandshire where the dependent situation of the dockers and the workers in the plastics plant had been transformed by creating new workplace organisations and endowing them with wide authority. But there are other instances of reorganisation elsewhere. Authority had been transferred to the soap plant's workplace organisation and there had been an attempt to encourage the Redcastle school caretakers to handle some of their business for themselves. On a smaller scale, the refuse collectors' shop steward at Hambridge gained an agreed bargaining role, within which he could operate independently, as a result of a measured daywork agreement.

The Hambridge case is an example of fluctuation in dependence, upwards as well as downwards. The consequence of the new agreement was to leave the steward with a new independence, but the negotiation of the agreement entailed greater intervention by the full-time officer, and a temporary growth in the dependence of the refuse collectors on his authority and skill. Several other studies provide comparable examples. A breakdown of relations between workplace organisation and managers at the Steel Valley rubber plant brought greater intervention by the full-time officer, and this led to the negotiation of a new agreement which restored and extended the independence which the stewards had previously enjoyed. A crisis at one of the South Marlshire engineering plants prompted the district secretary to replace the stewards and reconstruct the workplace organisation, a sharp act of intervention which was nevertheless intended to establish a workplace organisation capable of standing on its own feet.

It follows that an explanation of the location of workplace organisations on the dependence-independence continuum will not pass muster unless it is also capable of accounting for shifts along the continuum.

External Lay Officers

Up to this point the subject of analysis has been the relationship between full-time officers and workplace organisations. But in some of the case studies the workplace organisations did not deal direct with a full-time union officer, or did not normally do so. Their first resort outside the plant was to a lay officer.

In the two branches of the National Union of Railwaymen this officer was the branch secretary. There is nothing exceptional in a branch secretary taking a leading part in negotiations. Many other studies provide examples of workplace branches whose branch secretary did so. They include most of the Transport and General Workers' branches, the Shop Distributive and Allied Workers' soap plant and the Redcastle ambulance drivers' branch. But the Railwaymen's branches cannot be classed with these plant-based branches. Both of the Railwaymen's branches covered a number of stations, depots, workshops and hotels, each with its own local departmental committee or representative. Their secretaries had no place in these workplace organisations. They were called in from outside when the workplace organisations were in need of help to settle their business. The formal authority of the branch secretaries was confined to their union posts, for they had no place in the recognised procedure for negotiation on the railways. It therefore seems reasonable to regard a local departmental committee which relied upon one of them as dependent, and a local departmental committee which managed without them as independent, unless it called in a full-time officer instead.

There were instances elsewhere in which the secretary of a general[11] branch acted as a link between the full-time officer and the workplaces. The Public Employees' hospital branch secretary, and the Hambridge branch secretary of the General and Municipal Workers both filled this role, and at Hambridge the branch secretary carried out a good deal of the work which might properly have been regarded as within the responsibility of the regional officers. But the Railwaymen's branch secretaries served as alternatives rather than as links. The local committees and representatives approached them instead of going to the full-time officers, and were given advice and assistance independently, without reference to the full-time officers.

Another example of lay officers substituting for a full-time officer comes from Leachester, where some of the Engineers' convenors in major plants took smaller workplace organisations under their wings, so that the smaller workplace organisations were dependent on them. In the Civil and Public Services Association, however, the regional lay officers did not substitute for full-time officers, for there were no full-time officers in the regions. In region No 2 the lay secretary was formally recognised as the next stage in procedure when the local committees could not settle an

---

[11] The term 'general' branch here refers to any branch covering two or more plants, although some unions reserve the term for a branch covering several industries, and call a branch covering several plants from one industry an 'industrial' branch.

issue, and these local committees were therefore more or less dependent upon him. But region No 1 was a single branch, covering a vast office complex. Consequently the room and block agents could be regarded as forming a single large workplace organisation along with the full-time lay officers who staffed the regional branch and the regional Whitley committee. Alternatively each block could be regarded as a separate workplace organisation with the regional and staff side officers as their external recourse. The choice has a profound effect upon the classification of the workplace organisation along the dependence-independence continuum. If region No 1 is seen as a group of workplace organisations, then they depended almost completely upon their full-time lay officers. But if region No 1 is regarded as a single workplace organisation, then, although its internal organisation was highly centralised, externally it showed a robust independence from the sectional secretary and committee in London—the next stage in the union's hierarchy—by settling almost all regional problems within the region. For the moment, the choice can be left open.

Branches and Districts

The studies therefore indicated three different roles for the lay branch secretary in relation to the full-time officer. In a plant-based branch, his job as branch secretary was subordinate to his position in the workplace organisation, and he dealt with the full-time officer primarily as a representative of the workplace. In most of the general branches he served as an administrative link between the workplace organisations and the full-time officer, but in some of them he partly or largely took over the job of the full-time officer. However, the branch secretary is not the branch. What part did branch committees and branch meetings play in relation to their workplace organisations and full-time officers?

Plant branches *were* workplace organisations. Their

committees consisted of shop stewards, and their meetings were meetings of union members in the plant. The only important difference between them and other workplace organisations which emerged from the case studies was the additional powers which accrued from the authority of the branch, particularly to impose disciplinary penalties upon branch members.

General branches might be expected to have a very different relationship with workplace organisations. When plant business is brought before their committees and meetings it is subject to the scrutiny of outsiders, who may be expected to take a wider view than the members of the workplace organisation. In fact, whereas some of the general branch meetings, like that of the Building Trade Workers, do not seem to have discussed plant affairs, most of those which debated branch business seem to have functioned more or less as workplace branches. Plant issues, for example, were not often brought to the attention of the Engineers' district secretary in South Marlshire at branch meetings, but when they were it was usually in a branch dominated by a single firm. In the General and Municipal Workers' branch at Hambridge there were sectional meetings for all the main sections of the branch apart from local authority employees, and the branch meetings themselves had come to be something close to sectional meetings for local authority employees. The only plant whose business was regularly discussed at the Melfield branch was the ceramics plant which was heavily over-represented on the branch committee and whose regional officer regularly attended its meetings.

However, it was not universally true that general branches tried to turn themselves into workplace meetings when plant business was under discussion. The Railwaymen and the Graphical Association behaved differently. Their branches regularly dealt with plant business in meetings at which the majority did not come from the plant under discussion. The explanation for the difference lies in the status of the branch secretaries. The two Graphical Association branch secretaries *were* full-time officers, and the secretaries of the two Railwaymen's branches commonly substituted for full-time officers. Other general branches had no standing unless they could constitute themselves into substitutes for plant meetings, for plant business was normally settled in the plant or passed on to a full-time officer. In these two unions, by contrast, unsettled plant business went to the branch secretary, and to the extent that he was willing to listen to the advice of his branch committee and branch meeting, they had a recognised authority in dealing with plant business. Confirmation of this interpretation can be found in one of the differences between the Highridge and Lowborough branches of the Railwaymen. Highridge branch meetings discussed plant business far less frequently than Lowborough branch meetings, and the case study indicated that this was because the Lowborough branch secretary intervened in plant affairs far more frequently than his colleague in Highridge.

There was another relevant factor at work in the Corbury branch of the National Graphical Association. The main concern of the branch was the maintenance of craft regulations. But craft regulations, in their pure form, are the business of the whole membership of a craft union. Whereas in other unions the worker in one plant is unlikely to take much interest in the details of an agreement signed at another plant, every member of a craft union which takes its craft seriously is equally interested in the enforcement of craft regulations throughout the trade. The branch is the local guardian of the craft, so that its committee and meetings have a recognised authority over the behaviour of the chapels in this respect. At Camhill, however, plant bargaining had come to take precedence over craft regulation in the work of the chapels. Their branch meetings did not give much time to craft matters which were left to the branch secretary and the committee.

What part did district committees play in plant negotiations? Several unions had no district committees or their equivalent. These included the National Graphical Association, the Electricians, the Boot and Shoe Operatives and (at least in West Sandshire) the Tailors and Garment Workers. The Railwaymen's district councils serve a different purpose; the Building Trade Workers had replaced their district committees by branch conferences; the area committees of the Public Employees did not deal with plant business. The regional committees of the General and Municipal Workers and the divisional committees of the Shop Distributive and Allied Workers covered such large areas, so many plants and so many union members that they could give very little attention to the affairs of any individual plant. It therefore seems appropriate to regard them as a higher stage in the hierarchy than district committees, and the equivalent of the Transport and General Workers' regional committees. This interpretation gains strength from the position of the regional secretaries and divisional officers who work with these committees in the two unions. They are the superiors of the regional officers (in the General and Municipal Workers) and the area officers (in the Shop Distributive and Allied Workers) who deal direct with the workplace organisations.

This leaves the district committees of the Engineers, the Transport and General Workers, the Hosiery Workers and the Scarshire miners, and the two regional committees of the Civil and Public Services Association. But the committee of No 1 region was also the branch executive committee, and might be regarded as a workplace committee. For the moment it can be set aside. The remaining committees all covered a number of plants, and all of them handled plant business, although the Transport and General Workers' district committees in East Sandshire and Steel Valley handled very little of it. In one respect the hosiery district committee was the most important of them all since it was responsible for a district agreement negotiated directly with the district employers' association, but in fact it was dominated by its district secretary as the Scarshire miners' area council was dominated by its secretary. Region No 2 of the Civil and Public Services Association was able to play a rather larger part in decision-making because the regional secretary was too busy to handle everything himself. Similarly the Engineers' district committee in South Marlshire cut a figure of some importance on one occasion when their secretary was absent through illness but otherwise they generally approved his actions after the event. All these committees played a subordinate part to the full-time officers (or full-time lay officers) with whom they were associated. The exception is the district committee of the Engineers in Leachester which had intervened in plant affairs with some success, and had done so in spite of the district secretary rather than with him. By contrast the Transport and General Workers' full-time officers in Leachester had taken a lead in the endeavour to secure some control over plant affairs for their district committee, but they had not achieved very much.

In addition there were the industrial or trade conferences in which the General and Municipal Workers, the Shop Distributive and Allied Workers and the Electricians brought together workplace representatives from plants in the same industry to discuss common problems, exchange information and debate issues coming up in industry negotiations. These conferences were held both regionally and nationally, but the case studies provided evidence about the effects of the regional conferences only, and showed that their impact was patchy. They were valued mainly for the opportunity to learn what was happening elsewhere, although the Redcastle engineering conference of the Electricians provided the occasion for a lively debate on the current national engineering negotiations which may have given the delegates the feeling that they were helping to influence national policy. Otherwise the conferences had no authority in negotiations, and this limited their importance.

Finally, there were conferences of delegates from plants in the one company. Some of these were official, like the conferences attended by the representatives of the Shop

Distributive and Allied Workers soap plant. These were welcomed as a means of gaining information about developments elsewhere, but they did not lead to joint action, because there were no company agreements. By contrast the food company's inter-depot liaison committee had made its weight felt in the negotiations which settled pay and conditions throughout the company's plants. There were also unofficial combine committees. Those encountered in the engineering studies did not seem to have great influence, but the stewards at the Steel Valley rubber plant and one of the generating stations regarded their combine committees as more fruitful sources of relevant information than any of the official union bodies, and the monthly meetings of the electricity supply combine made it possible for the information to be up-to-date. Combine committee meetings could also debate common problems, but they had no access to the official negotiation procedures or to managers. The rubber combine had called on its members to help in a redundancy dispute elsewhere by blacking the relevant plant's products, but took no part in the resolution of the crisis at the Steel Valley plant, which was the consequence of intervention by senior union officers and group managers.

Trade Union Policy and Structure

The main relationships between workplace organisations and their unions have now been outlined. In nearly every instance the most important relationship was with the full-time officer, or, less frequently, with a lay officer substituting for the full-time officer. Branches, districts, industrial conferences and the like almost always played a subordinate role, either as adjuncts of the workplace organisation, or as advisers and assistants to the full-time officers. It therefore makes sense to differentiate the relationships between workplace organisations and unions primarily according to the degree of dependence upon the full-time officer observed in the workplace organisation's handling of plant affairs. What explains the differences?

One hypothesis which finds some support in the case studies is that the unions choose for themselves the kind of relationships which they want to see between their full-time officers and their workplace organisations. The switch in the policies of the Transport and General Workers and the Shop Distributive and Allied Workers towards workplace independence had altered relationships between full-time officers and workplace organisations in East Sandshire and at the soap plant. The Transport and General Workers' new policy had led to the appointment of a new type of officer and to the encouragement of new attitudes among existing officers. By contrast the hosiery district officers went about their business so as to reinforce the dependence of workplace representatives upon them, and they appeared to have the support of their union headquarters in doing so.

However, the case studies also show that there are limits to the influence of union policies on the degree of workplace dependence. The Transport and General Workers' steel branches and many of their engineering workplace organisations in Leachester had established a high degree of independence long before the change in policy, and the attempt at Leachester to use the new policy to give the district committee some control over workplace organisations did not meet with much success. There appeared to be an almost equal degree of independence in some of the General and Municipal Workers' workplace organisations without an official policy of fostering workplace independence.

By itself, the announcement of a new policy cannot be expected to have much effect on workplace dependence, and even the encouragement of new attitudes may not make much difference unless they are translated into new structures. In East Sandshire the new policy of the Transport and General Workers was accompanied by a shift from general to workplace branches and the redeployment of full-time officers from branch to district duties, as well as the establishment of a district committee. Perhaps, therefore, the explanation for varying degrees of dependence should be found in differences in union structure, with union policies taking effect only to the extent that they lead to structural alterations. In particular union structure can have an effect on workplace dependence by varying the availability of the full-time officer to deal with workplace affairs.

The most obvious determinants of availability are the number of members for whom the full-time officer is responsible and the extent of his administrative duties. With thirty thousand members the Leachester district secretary of the Engineers could not conceivably have given close attention to the affairs of every plant within his district, even without the heavy burden of administrative work which occupied most of his time. On the other hand his colleague in South Marlshire with seven thousand members had a considerably lighter administrative load, and therefore more time for fewer plants. With about ten thousand members each, and very large geographical areas to cover, the full-time officers of the Railwaymen who were responsible for the Highridge and Lowborough branches could not give close attention to the affairs of every local departmental committee and representative within their districts. On the other hand, the Scarshire miners' area secretary, with three thousand members concentrated in six collieries in a relatively small area, had time both for his demanding duties on the national executive and for keeping in close touch with the colliery delegates and managers. The hosiery district had two full-time officers for seven thousand members. Between them they seemed to be able to cope with the heavy calls made on their time by the plants.

The General and Municipal Workers' regional officers, who have the main responsibility for dealing with plant affairs, are concentrated at regional headquarters. In Melfield the ceramics plant saw a great deal of its regional officer who lived in the town and had been given special responsibility for the branch, but the engineering and chemicals plants received few visits from their regional officers. Things might have been different if the full-time branch officer had seen it as his duty to intervene in their affairs. But he was encouraged to concentrate on his administrative duties, and his dealing with the plants was confined to handling grievances in small plants which lacked stewards, and to passing information between regional officers and shop stewards.

The availability of full-time officers therefore has an effect on workplace independence, but the studies also show that there are limits to this effect. In Leachester and South Marlshire it appeared that the insecure workplace organisations in many small engineering plants would have collapsed without the support that full-time officers were able to give them. Wherever the Tailors' and Garment Workers area officer in West Sandshire found a shop steward in a small clothing plant who could handle plant business, he encouraged her to do so, but most of the stewards were not capable of self-reliance. Similarly the full-time officers responsible for Steel Valley's electronic plant and Hambridge's textile plant would have liked to hand over greater responsibility to the workplace organisations there, but feared that the shop stewards were not capable of carrying the load. At the other extreme, there is not much evidence to suggest that the availability of a full-time officer is likely to persuade a workplace organisation which has already established its independence to enter into close co-operation with him. With half his 5,500 members in steel branches, the Steel Valley district secretary could have found more time for the affairs of those branches if they had asked for his help; but they preferred to keep him out.

There is even more convincing evidence that neither union structure nor union policy can provide a complete explanation for variation in the degree of independence. Several case studies found every variation from almost

complete independence to almost complete dependence in
the relationships between a single officer and the workplace
organisations within his responsibility. These include both
Leachester studies, Steel Valley, the Railwaymen and the
Public Employees. It is impossible to explain these variations by differences in policy or structure. Some other explanatory variable must be found.

Size and Resources

Many of the case studies suggested a relationship between
the size of workplace organisations and the degree of their
dependence on full-time officers. All the dependent organisations in the engineering industry were small, and there
was a contrast between the largest workplace organisations
in South Marlshire, none of them with more than a few
hundred members, which called their district secretary in
to help them with important negotiations and disputes, and
some of the largest workplace organisations in Leachester
with a thousand members or more, in which the Engineers'
district secretary and the Transport and General Workers'
full-time officers had little to do except to sign agreements
which they had not negotiated, or to deal with references
to procedure.

Corroboration comes from the West Sandshire clothing
industry where the workplace organisations in the four
large plants showed far more independence than those in
the small firms; from the Shop Distributive and Allied
Workers' two plants, with the large soap plant organisation
showing considerable independence and the small food plant
a high degree of dependence; and from the Civil and Public
Services Association, provided that region No 1 is classed
as a single workplace organisation.

A correlation, however frequently observed, does not
amount to an explanation unless it can be shown how the
one variable affects the other. Consequently a causal link
between size and independence has to be found if it is to

serve as an explanation; and it is not hard to find. Other things being equal, a large workplace organisation has greater resources at its disposal than a smaller workplace organisation. There is greater opportunity for shop stewards to acquire skill and experience in handling a variety of grievances and negotiations in a large plant than in a small plant. When he cannot handle an issue himself, the steward in a small plant has a choice between dropping it and calling in the full-time officer; but the steward in a large plant has a convenor or senior steward to whom he can turn, or a shop stewards' committee. There is therefore a greater likelihood of the issues being retained in the plant, allowing the convenor and committee members to acquire wide experience.

Convenors and committee members must give more time to union business than a single shop steward in the small plant. As this comes to be accepted by managers, some convenors are recognised as full-timers, or given sinecures. Their prestige is thereby enhanced, and they are able to plan and organise their work. Some of them are given offices and other facilities. All these resources bring them nearer to an equal footing with the managers with whom they negotiate, and with the full-time officer responsible for their plant.

The number of members in the plant affects the chances of leading stewards being elected to union committees outside the plant. Membership of these committees can give a steward information on pay and agreements elsewhere, and on new developments and current negotiations. This may give him an advantage over the managers with whom he negotiates and it further diminishes the distance between him and his full-time officer. Where a convenor rivals his full-time officer in skill and experience, in time and facilities, and in his knowledge of conditions elsewhere, there is little reason for him to call in the full-time officer except to perform those tasks which only a full-time officer is author-ised to carry out, such as giving formal ratification to an agreement, or taking a dispute into procedure.

So far no distinction has been drawn between the size of the plant and the size of the workplace organisation, although it is obvious that there may be small workplace organisations in large plants. As it happens, the case studies provide few examples. In the great majority of the plants chosen for study, the union concerned was the largest in the plant, and in one or two engineering plants in which either the Engineers' workplace organisation or that of the Transport and General Workers was under observation and was not the largest union, it was nevertheless a large workplace organisation. However, there was one important exception. In the Redcastle engineering plant, the chemicals plant and the power stations, the electricians constituted relatively small groups in a labour force dominated by one or more larger unions. In each of them the electricians had little contact with their full-time officers and showed a capacity to look after themselves. In these instances independence cannot be explained by the size of the workplace organisations.

Size, however, does not of itself give independence to workplace organisations. Large workplace organisations are more likely to be independent because their size helps them to acquire resources. Consequently the example of the Electricians does not upset the argument so long as it can be shown that these small workplace organisations in Redcastle had considerable resources at their disposal; and three of them had. The Electricians' stewards at the two power stations and at the engineering plant took their place in larger workplace organisations whose resources were at the disposal of all the stewards. At the fourth, the chemicals plant, their steward held himself apart from the production workers' stewards, although he co-operated closely with the Engineers' stewards whose members outnumbered his own. But since they had less than forty members between them, this instance must count as an exception to the rule unless they can be shown to have other resources at their disposal.

Numbers bring strength, but it does not follow that each individual counts the same as the next, or that one trade unionist is as good as another. The Hambridge textile plant provides an example. With almost five hundred out of nine hundred employees in membership, its workplace organisation had numbers. Most of them, however, were recent recruits with no trade union traditions. Even their senior steward was regarded as poor trade union material by his full-time officer. The managers had opposed the union for years, and even at this stage their recognition was reluctant and partial. It is not difficult to believe that this workplace organisation disposed of fewer resources than forty electrical and mechanical craftsmen, most of them probably having been trade unionists since their apprentice days, represented by two experienced stewards and working for a firm which had recognised unions for more than fifty years.

Consequently the cohesion, trade union experience and status of the labour force must be considered along with the numbers represented by the workplace organisation. Some such factor as this is needed to explain the considerable variation in dependence among groups of Railwaymen and Public Employees, for example between guards and railway hotel employees, or between hospital staffs and ambulance drivers. Many of the differences which have just been noted between Redcastle electricians and Hambridge textile workers applied equally between guards and hotel employees. The guards had venerable union traditions, experienced spokesmen and full recognition from management. The hotel employees had been organised more recently, their spokesman lacked experience and confidence, and managerial recognition was grudging and uncertain. Some of these differences also applied between the hospital staffs and ambulancemen in Redcastle. The ambulancemen had a longer history of trade unionism, a more experienced representative, and probably greater regard from their managers.

Systems of Collective Bargaining

The analysis so far has made substantial progress towards
an explanation of the degree of independence shown by a
workplace organisation in terms of its size, adjusted for the
cohesion, trade union experience and status of the labour
force. But it has totally ignored one crucially important
factor in workplace organisation. Up to this point the
relationship between workplace organisations and full-time
officers has been treated as though every workplace organisation had a similar job to do, and the only difference in the
way it was done from one workplace organisation to the
next was in the extent of intervention from the full-time
officers, and in some instances from branch secretaries,
branch meetings or district committees. In fact, however,
the studies revealed wide variations in the job to be done
because of the differences in the scope for workplace bargaining permitted by the relevant collective agreements.

Broadly considered, collective bargaining deals with
remuneration and jobs. Remuneration includes everything
that goes into the pay packet or the monthly salary cheque,
and also holiday pay, pensions, sick pay, redundancy pay
and so on. Jobs include the grading of posts and the
qualifications for the job; recruitment, training, promotion
and redundancy; the speed of work and the quality of work.
Even discipline is mainly concerned with permitted
behaviour on the job, and the penalties for falling short of
the required standards.

Historically, employers have been more willing to
negotiate with unions about remuneration than about jobs.
They have taken the view that, once the rate of pay was
settled, the job to be done was for the manager to determine.
Practically, it is easier to determine rates of pay in an
agreement, especially an industry agreement, than to regulate jobs. An agreement can specify the rate for the job and
the rate of overtime pay, but it cannot easily determine
the amount of overtime working required by the job. Since

in the past industry agreements have been prevalent in Britain, remuneration has been a subject for formal industry agreements whereas many aspects of the job have been dealt with by custom and practice arrangements at the plant. But in recent years the Donovan Commission, the National Board for Prices and Incomes and the Commission on Industrial Relations have emphasised the disadvantages of leaving work to be regulated by custom and practice arrangements in the plant; and productivity agreements and similar innovations have brought many aspects of the job within the scope of formal collective bargaining.

These new developments in collective bargaining had affected many of the industries and plants covered by the case studies, but not the civil service establishments covered by the Civil and Public Services Association. The Whitley system for the non-industrial civil service is probably the most highly centralised system of collective bargaining in Britain, if not in the world, and has always endeavoured to impose central control over every aspect of remuneration and also over every aspect of the job which is subject to trade union influence; but even this endeavour has not met with complete success. There are matters which must be handled locally, including not only individual cases of discipline and grading, but also collective issues susceptible to local negotiation such as redundancy and eligibility for proficiency payments. But the non-industrial civil service has probably gone as far as possible in limiting the issues available for workplace negotiation to the irreducible minimum.

The only other agreement which attempted to achieve nearly as much as this was the electrical contracting agreement; and it does so no longer. For since 1972 the agreement has made provision for incentive systems and for the payment of additional rates on large sites. As a result of the powerloading agreement, the rates of pay of the great majority of miners are settled by the industry agreement. But there is scope for workplace bargaining not only over the grading of jobs, but also over the task to be done at the face, and the size of the team to do it. The Atomic Energy Authority agreement of 1968 went further than this by negotiating stepped wage increases to be applied in the plants as they improved productivity with the application of work study schemes agreed in the workplace. The electricity supply agreements allowed a variety of workplace options by giving a choice of 'staggered hours', by permitting stepped incentive payments in return for improvements in performance measured against studies centralised and standardised in a national data bank, and by allowing 'lead-in' payments at plants where workers were willing to accept incentive schemes, but the schemes had not so far been prepared.

The railway agreements determined all aspects of pay for jobs, like those of the guard and the driver, which were standardised throughout the railway system, and permitted the negotiation of workplace incentives for other groups of railwaymen—in the workshops, on the permanent way, in parcels depots and so on. These incentive schemes allowed both the task and the payment to be settled in the workplace, giving more room for bargaining there than the schemes in atomic energy and electricity supply. The local authority and hospital agreements allowed incentive schemes to be negotiated within each authority for any group of manual workers, so long as they complied with requirements laid down nationally; and there was also provision for lead-in payment.

These agreements reveal a gradation from the extremely tight provision in the civil service through various stages of loosening, but all of them must be classified as at least 'moderately tight' in comparison with most industry agreements in private employment. All the agreements so far described are in the public services, except for electrical contracting. The agreements of the remaining publicly-owned industry encountered in these case studies—steel—should probably be classed as 'moderately loose' along with building and printing, with most of the rest of the private industry agreements, including chemicals, clothing, engineering, hosiery and rubber, classed as loose without qualification. The building agreement, for example, purports to set out standard payments except for additions allowed under site incentive schemes, but many of these incentive schemes are little more than 'spot bonuses' and other forms of additional payment are not uncommon. By comparison, so far as pay is concerned, the loose agreements provide little more than minimum requirements and periodic general or minimum increases, leaving the rest to the workplace.

There were also several company agreements in multi-plant companies, most of them non-federated. They too could be grouped into the moderately tight, including the food and chemicals companies, which left a relatively narrow margin for workplace negotiation; and the moderately loose, such as the clothing company, which left more room for workplace bargaining.

The Shape of Bargaining Systems

Given that the scope for workplace bargaining is controlled by the systems of collective bargaining within which workplace organisations operate, the next question to be asked is why these systems differ.

The clearest contrast observed in the case studies—and noted often enough elsewhere—is between the tight and fairly tight agreements of the public services (with the exception of steel) and the loose and fairly loose agreements elsewhere (with the exception of electrical contracting). Most public services are centralised undertakings, and, in addition, they operate under public scrutiny with standardised administrative arrangements and accounting procedures. Neither of these characteristics fits easily with a loose collective agreement, and both of them accord neatly with a tight agreement. For decades before nationalisation the coalmining industry worked under loose district or industry agreements with fragmented bargaining in the pits, but after nationalisation the Coal Board could not properly fulfil their responsibility for running the industry unless they could control wages costs centrally, and it was impossible to do that under the existing agreements. Consequently they negotiated a tight industry agreement for daywagemen in 1955, and followed this up with the power-loading agreement for faceworkers in 1966. If this interpretation is correct, then steel is not necessarily an exception to the rule, for its present agreements were inherited from the days of private ownership. Nationalisation may push the Steel Corporation towards a more centralised form of bargaining.

The limited relaxation of some of the centralised public service agreements, such as electricity supply and atomic energy, does not conflict with the general rule, for the intention of these two instances was to increase central control over wage costs. Managers came to realise that systematic overtime was being worked in their undertakings, and that jobs were being arranged so as to provide the overtime, quite outside their control. Accordingly both undertakings set about designing agreements which would allow local bargaining over the relationship between pay and jobs in ways that could be supervised from the centre.

There are two important contrasts in the structure of management between the public services and companies in private industry. Firstly, most private industries consist of a large number of independent firms each with its own administrative arrangements and accounting procedures, and usually in competition with each other, whereas most public services are run by a national board, or by regional boards. Secondly, private firms are not subject to the pressures of public accountability, so that a private multi-plant firm can permit wide variation in managerial methods from one plant to another, if it chooses to do so, whereas public services come under the scrutiny and centralising influence of government departments. These administrative differences provide an explanation for the loose industry agreements common in private industry, and the widespread practice in multi-plant companies of allowing considerable scope to individual plant managers to negotiate with the unions.

But private companies do not have uniformly decentralised administrative arrangements. On the contrary their freedom from the pressure of public ownership and public accountability permits a wide variation in methods of administration, and of collective bargaining. Most of the multi-plant companies in the case studies left collective bargaining to the plants, but a minority had negotiated company agreements, some of them moderately loose and others moderately tight. Here again there was a link between collective bargaining and managerial organisation, for the companies with relatively tight agreements stood out as having more centralised managerial methods. An example is the Redcastle chemicals plant, which may be contrasted with the soap plant whose managers had comparatively wide autonomy both in running their undertaking generally and in negotiating plant agreements.

The extent to which industry agreements control workplace bargaining in private undertakings is, of course, influenced by the cohesion of employers' associations and the authority which their members are prepared to delegate to them. In this respect, the case studies revealed a contrast between the tightly-knit and authoritative Electrical Contractors' Association and all the other employers' associations which were encountered. Consequently the shape of collective bargaining system—and the scope allowed for workplace bargaining—is affected not only by the internal administrative arrangements of the undertaking, and whether or not it is publicly owned and subject to public accountability, but also by the functions and powers which the managers are prepared to grant to their employers' association, if they have one.

The Scope for Workplace Bargaining and Dependence

The preceding pages have constructed a theory of the relationship between trade union organisation in the plant and union organisation outside. The main link between the two is the full-time officer, except in those instances where an external lay officer takes on some or all of the duties normally performed by a full-time officer. The extent to which the workplace organisation manages its business for itself or relies on the full-time officer (or external lay officer) depends on the resources which it can deploy within the plant, and although these include the cohesion, trade union experience and status of the labour force, the most general influence at work is the size of the workplace organisation. But the extent to which negotiable issues are settled within the plant or subject to agreements signed by the union outside the plant is determined by the tightness or looseness of the revelant industry or company agreement, if any; and this in turn is closely associated with the administrative structure of the undertaking, with public accountability where it applies, and with the cohesion and authority of employers' associations.

But is it a tenable theory? Does it not leave too many loose ends? Is it not massively oversimplified? To take one instance, is it reasonable to make a sharp distinction between the scope of workplace bargaining and the degree of dependence shown by workplace organisations in dealing with matters that fall within their scope? It might be expected that a wide scope would encourage independence and a narrow scope would stunt it, so that independence would flourish under loose agreements and in non-federated firms, and fail to grow or wither away under tight industry or company agreements.

That is not what the evidence showed. Workplace organisations in building, footwear and hosiery were highly dependent although their industry agreements allowed wide scope for workplace bargaining; and among plants covered by tight or relatively tight industry agreements, region No 1 (if it can be classified as workplace organisation) showed a high degree of independence, and so did the ambulance drivers, the atomic energy workplace organisation, electricity supply workers and several groups of railwaymen. It is true that the Scarshire study suggested that the colliery delegates had become more dependent on their area secretary since the powerloading agreement, which greatly reduced the scope for workplace bargaining. But the agreement did not cause him to intervene more frequently in colliery affairs; in fact he visited the pits less often than before. The effect of the agreement was to make faceworkers dependent on industry negotiations for their pay increases, so that colliery delegates became dependent on their area secretary's membership of the national executive to learn of the progress of negotiations and to try to exert an influence on them. There is no evidence to show that they relied more heavily upon him than before in dealing with the issues which were still handled in the pit.

On the contrary, it appears that a relatively narrow scope for workplace bargaining may assist workshop organisations to be self-reliant within the permitted limits. Redcastle ambulancemen can serve as an example. Their branch secretary negotiated incentive pay schemes and dealt with most of the issues which arose at the workplace. Their organisation is therefore classed as relatively independent. But he worked within the framework of a moderately tight agreement which placed most aspects of an ambulanceman's pay and job beyond the reach of workplace bargaining. It is plausible to suggest that he might not have been able to undertake the whole range of negotiation which would have been forced into the workplace if Redcastle Council had taken it upon themselves to negotiate a separate agreement with their own ambulancemen. He might then have been driven to rely heavily on his full-time officer. There were also a number of relatively small groups of workers on the railways who were able to look after their own affairs within the confines of a fairly tight industry agreement. The same line of reasoning could help to explain the independence of the Electricians and Engineers at the Redcastle chemicals plant, for they and their managers worked within the limits of a fairly tight company agreement. It is also relevant that the railway agreement and those of several other public services influence the extent of workplace bargaining within the permitted scope by spelling out a wide range of matters concerning the organisation of work which workplace bargainers are enjoined to handle, whereas most private industries merely leave workplace negotiators free to act or not as they please on matters not finally determined by the industry agreement.

Consequently it is not safe to assume that there is no association between the scope for workplace bargaining and the degree of dependence shown by the workplace organisation; but the case studies produced no instances of a wide scope for bargaining encouraging independence. The evidence of the studies is that a tight industry or company agreement may facilitate the exercise of independence by the workplace organisation within the limits allowed for workplace negotiation, and some of them positively encourage it.

Trade Union Influence on Union Organisation

Thus the relationship between the scope for workplace bargaining and the dependence of workplace organisations on full-time officers is not quite what might have been expected. But the theory set out at the beginning of the previous section contains a far bolder challenge to received opinion than that. It implies that trade unions have no influence over their relationship with their workplace organisations, this relationship being determined instead by the structure of managerial organisation. For, according to the theory, the size of workplace organisations is the chief influence on the dependence of workplace organisations upon their unions, and their size is governed by the size of the plants which, within the limits of technology, is a consequence of managerial decisions; and the division of negotiable issues between workplace organisations and higher levels of union authority is determined by the shape of industry and company agreements which follow the structure of managerial organisation.

Stated thus, the theory defies not only received opinion, but also some of the evidence of the studies. The availability of full-time officers affects the dependence of workplace organisations and dramatic transformations in the relationships between workplace organisations and unions in the East Sandshire docks and plastics plant, and in the soap plant, were associated with radical changes in union policy. How can the theory be reconciled with these events?

A vigorous drive for union membership had been a prelude to independence at the plastics plant, which had hitherto been badly organised, and there had also been signs of defective organisation in the docks branch, with most of the dockers in arrears with their dues. Other studies also revealed dependent workplace organisations in relatively large but poorly organised plants. Poor organisation enfeebles the resources available to a workplace organisation. But there was another common factor, also present at the soap plant. In all three instances the managers revised their approach to plant bargaining and tabled proposals for a productivity agreement. In the docks, change was forced on the manager by the union, but the union's task was made easier by the decision of the National Association of Port Employers two years earlier to accept the Devlin recommendations on introducing shop stewards and moving to port productivity agreements.

These examples therefore reveal two methods by which unions can encourage their workplace organisations towards independence. Firstly, they can help workplace organisations to build up their strength until they can assert their independence. Secondly, they can join with managers to institute a style of bargaining which promotes workplace independence. But if unions can encourage workplace independence, it follows that they can discourage it. They can strive to keep workplace organisations weak, and they can join with managers in sustaining a style of bargaining which inhibits workplace independence.

This twist of the argument is confirmed by the hosiery and footwear case studies. All the workplace organisations in hosiery were strikingly dependent on their full-time officers, and only one or two in footwear achieved a modestly co-operative relationship. Why? Partly because the union organisation outside the plant co-operated with managers in denying the workplace organisations the resources needed for independence, and in following a style of bargaining which gave them no opportunity to develop their resources. When an issue began to cause trouble, the manager sent for the full-time officer. The officer expected to be called in and to take charge of negotiations. And also because the workplace representatives lacked the experience and the desire to handle matters for themselves, they were happy to have their officer called in, or to send for him themselves. Workplace representation in hosiery was rudimentary and patchy; the footwear shop presidents occupied a more recognised role, but it was nevertheless modest and subordinate.

Co-operation between the hosiery managers and full-time officials kept the workplace organisations dependent. The district committee supported the right of the full-time officers to intervene in plant affairs at their will, as, apparently, did the national union. The managers also sustained it, claiming a reciprocal right to the attention of the full-time officer when they wanted it, and they were backed by the association. The practice went back beyond living memory, and may be rooted in a tradition of co-operation between managers and union officials dating from the industry's first Conciliation Board over a century ago.

This state of affairs may be contrasted with the practice of the engineering industry. The tradition of managers and their associations in engineering was to keep the unions and their full-time officers at arm's length. The first national engineering procedure agreement of 1898, dictated by the employers after a successful lockout, was phrased so as to keep the full-time officers out of negotiations on piecework, manning and the organisation of work; and to exclude them from all negotiations until the officials of the employers' association had also been called in. But as workplace organisations developed and gathered strength the managers could not avoid dealing with them. Grudgingly, therefore, the managers provided workplace organisations with the resources to buttress their power and their independence. Consequently managers had to allow the workplace organisation to call in the full-time officer if they wanted him, and to keep him out if they preferred to do that.

Similar contrasts can be found in the studies in public employment. The tradition in local government was for departmental chiefs and their assistants to deal with full-time union officers, who might be accepted as equals, rather than with labourers; and the union officers had been ready to oblige, at least until recently. On the other hand local railway managers were afraid that reference to a full-time union officer would entail bringing in their own supervisors. This they were anxious to avoid where they could, and they were therefore predisposed to deal with the branch secretaries over issues which could not be resolved with the local committees and secretaries.

Region No 1 presented a particularly interesting example of managerial preferences in dealing with union officers. The local managers were much exercised to avoid differences in the treatment of clerical staff between one block and another in their vast office complex, so they tried to ensure that even minor issues should be settled regionally, and close managerial control ensured that this was done. At the same time they endeavoured to keep to themselves any special interpretations of central agreements and any special

administrative arrangements introduced to meet local problems. Because they were anxious to keep London out of
their domestic affairs, they treated the regional lay full-
time officers as 'insiders', as if they had been senior stewards
in a large manufacturing plant. Consequently the managers
behaved as though the office complex was a single undertaking, internally cohesive and externally distinct from the
rest of the department. Their behaviour made it difficult
for block agents to exercise independent authority, and
allowed regional union officers to put pressure on managers
by threatening to refer an issue to London unless more
favourable consideration was given to their point of view.

Thus tradition and managerial structure both contribute
to managerial preferences in dealing with full-time officers
and workplace organisations. But a full explanation of these
preferences would require a far more thorough investigation
of managerial behaviour than was undertaken in the case
studies, and for the purpose of this chapter it is enough
that the influence of unions—and of managers—on the
dependence of workplace organisations has now been more
fully spelled out.

The dependence of workplace organisations, however, is
only half the story. The other half is the scope for workplace bargaining which has so far been explained entirely
by managerial structure. But is it credible that the unions
have no influence upon it? Does not this part of the theory
also require modification?

In most of the case studies there was no dispute over the
scope for workplace bargaining, and no record of such a
dispute. Engineering and hosiery accepted the wide scope
traditionally allowed to workplace bargaining. Building and
footwear did not seem to question the slightly more limited
room which their arrangements permitted for workplace
settlement. As a non-federated firm, the plastics plant in
East Sandshire was restricted to plant bargaining, and the
union could do nothing about it.

Other case studies revealed instances in which the unions

had accepted management proposals to vary the scope for workplace bargaining. The textile plant in East Sandshire is one instance, the atomic energy plant there a second, and the soap plant a third. Union agreement was required before the changes could be made, but the proposals came from management and the union readily consented.

There were other instances in which an extension in the scope of workplace bargaining was recommended by a public body. If a port is a workplace, as it was at the East Sandshire docks, then the change in the scope for port agreements followed from the Devlin recommendations. The proposals for local productivity agreements and incentive schemes in local government and hospitals originated with Report No 29 of the National Board for Prices and Incomes; and in both services the pressure for the application of the proposals came from the unions rather than the authorities.

However, in the two cases in which union influence was most evident the unions used it to limit the scope for workplace bargaining. The powerloading agreement in coalmining owes at least as much to the firm support of Will Paynter, then general secretary of the Mineworkers, and to his handling of his union, as it does to the Coal Board. In electrical contracting the employers have special reasons for preferring a tight industry agreement to the arrangements which prevail elsewhere in construction,[12] but it is difficult to believe that they would have been able to achieve and maintain their objective without the forthright support of the single union with which they deal, the Electricians.

Taken together, these instances indicate the extent of trade union influence on the level of bargaining in general, and on the scope for workplace bargaining in particular. If the managers propose a change the unions are often willing to go along, although they may drag their feet. The steel plant managers had met nothing but opposition from the unions to their suggestions for a move towards plant-

[12] These reasons are listed in the Commission on Industrial Relations' study, *Employers' Organisations and Industrial Relations*, 1972, p. 24.

wide bargaining. Beyond that, the unions may choose to push for a modification in the level of bargaining—an increase or a decrease in the scope for workplace bargaining—but they cannot accomplish the change without the consent of the managers, and unless it fits the structure of managerial organisation. A modest scope for workplace bargaining within the framework of a fairly tight industry agreement fits the structure of management in local government and in electricity supply. The national powerloading agreement suits the organisation of the nationalised coalmining industry far better than piecework. The support of a cohesive employers' association was even more essential to the tight electrical contracting agreement than the support of a single powerful union. The union could do very little if the employers decided to treat the provisions of the agreement as minimum requirements. Whether officially or unofficially, such a decision would lead to company or site bargaining for higher rates and better conditions. In the extreme case the employers could disband their association and the union would then have to bargain piecemeal or not at all.

It is not true, therefore, that unions have no influence on the scope for workplace bargaining. They can modify it, but they can do so only by agreement with the other side, and within the framework established by the structure of managerial organisation.

Conclusion

The argument can now be summarised by enumerating the influences on the relationship between union organisation in the workplace and the union outside.

The relationship is described under two headings: the dependence of the workplace organisation on the union organisation outside the plant in the conduct of workplace bargaining, and the scope for workplace bargaining. Although the workplace organisation may have links with various union bodies outside—for instance a branch, a district committee or an industrial conference—the studies indicated that they were commonly subordinated to the relationship between the workplace organisation and the full-time union officer, unless a lay officer took the place of the full-time officer. Consequently the dependence of the workplace organisation is treated as dependence on the full-time officer or on a lay officer who has taken his place.

The most general influence on dependence is the size of the workplace organisation. The larger the workplace organisation, the greater the resources at its disposal, and the more independent its behaviour. But size is not the only influence at work. The greater the unity within a workplace organisation, the trade union experience of its members and their status as employees, the larger will be the resources at its disposal, and the more it will tend to act on its own. Close association with a powerful workplace organisation in the same plant can also help a relatively small workplace organisation to act independently of its full-time officer.

It follows that a workplace organisation may not achieve the independence which its potential membership would seem to support because the potential members have not all joined the union, or because they have not formed the habit of united action, or because they lack trade union experience. Consequently the trade union outside can encourage or discourage workplace independence by promoting or hindering organisation, unity and experience. Managers can also encourage or discourage workplace independence. Many of the resources commonly enjoyed by independent workplace organisations—facilities for shop stewards' meetings and mass meetings, time off for shop stewards, sinecures for senior stewards or convenors, an office, a telephone—are concessions which managers can make or try to withhold. Besides that, union and management can co-operate in developing and sustaining a style of bargaining in the workplace which fosters independence, or they can adopt a style of bargaining designed to keep a workplace organisation in subjection. The availability of the full-time officer is for the union to determine, and, within limits, the lack of a full-time officer to whom its representatives can turn may push a workplace organisation towards independence, whereas the ready availability of a full-time officer may hold it back.

In a non-federated single-plant firm the scope for workplace bargaining is as wide as the participants choose to make it. Elsewhere it is limited by such agreements as its association or parent company have signed. Nearly all these external agreements are either at industry or company level and can be ranged from 'tight' to 'loose' according to the scope they give for workplace bargaining. Tight or relatively tight agreements are associated with centralised managerial structures, especially in the public services, and loose or fairly loose agreements with decentralised managerial structures. Trade unions can influence the scope for workplace bargaining only by agreement with the managers with whom they negotiate and only within the limits imposed by the structure of managerial organisation.

The scope for workplace bargaining can influence the dependence of the workplace organisation. Since bargaining within a narrow scope places less strain on the resources of a workplace organisation than bargaining over a wide range of issues, a narrow scope for workplace bargaining may permit a relatively small or relatively inexperienced workplace organisation to exercise greater independence than it could if it were faced with wider responsibilities.

I0

Implications

Chapter 1 opened with the observation that the extensive investigation of British industrial relations in recent years has been almost entirely directed at matters other than trade union organisation; and that the Donovan Commission, in particular, focussed their attention upon collective bargaining. But when they came to making recommendations, the Commission nevertheless included proposals for reforming union organisation, and a convenient means of indicating the significance of our findings for those whose job it is to devise policies and make recommendations is to examine these proposals on union organisation in the light of our findings.

The Commision's central proposition was that British companies should 'develop, together with trade unions representative of their employees, comprehensive and authoritative collective bargaining machinery ... at company and/or factory level'.[13] They predicted that many benefits would follow from these agreements, and, among them, that unions 'would be able to close the gap between head office and shop stewards, and between full-time officers and members, by concentrating on the negotiation of agreements at a level meaningful to them all'.[14] But they also wanted the unions to make a number of changes to facilitate the negotiation of the agreements and to help them to work smoothly. There was, for example, room for more mergers between unions; trade union boundaries and rights to repre-

[13] *Donovan Report*, p. 45.
[14] *Ibid.*, p. 51.

sentation should be tidied up; trade unions should set up official bodies to perform the functions of unofficial combine committees; they should seek facilities from employers for formal union meetings at the place of work; they should amplify and codify their rules relating to shop stewards; they should provide more training for full-time officers and shop stewards; and they should make more use of the check-off as a means of collecting union dues.[15] But 'the most important' change[16] was a prerequisite of the reform of plant and company bargaining. 'If the system of formal factory and company bargaining which we envisage is to come about there will be a need for far more frequent and regular contact between shop stewards and their officials.... All the evidence suggests ... that the reconstruction of industrial relations which we advocate will require a substantial addition to the number of full-time officers of trade unions.'[17]

There has been considerable reconstruction of British collective bargaining since the Donovan Report appeared. As several of the studies testify, many of the larger plants in manufacturing industry have introduced formal plant procedures and plant-wide pay structures (through productivity agreements, measured daywork, job evaluation and the like) although all this might have happened without the report. There has also been substantial progress in the introduction of incentive schemes and productivity payments requiring plant-level negotiations into such public services as electricity supply, local government and hospitals. But these developments have not been matched by trade union action along the lines recommended by the report. It is true that the check-off has been widely extended, and the Transport and General Workers and one or two other unions have given a measure of recognition to combine committees; there have also been mergers, although it is a

15 *Ibid.*, Chapter XII.
16 *Ibid.*, p. 188.
17 *Ibid.*, p. 189.

matter for debate whether these have simplified trade union structure or left it more complex; but growth in union training has been slow, most unions have not altered their rules on shop stewards, and rights to representation remain much as they were; above all there has been no substantial increase in the number of full-time union officers. No census has been conducted, but the ratio of officers to members has fallen in the Transport and General Workers' Union, and probably among the Engineers as well, while the General and Municipal Workers' ratio has remained much the same. There have been substantial additions to the numbers of full-time officers in several smaller unions, notably the Public Employees and some white collar unions, but no more than sufficient to keep pace with their rapidly rising membership, if that. There is no reason to believe that the overall ratio is higher than it was at the time the Donovan Report appeared, although the report argued that the reconstruction of industrial relations would require a substantial increase.

There is evidence of a shortage of full-time officers. Employers' associations and managers complain about their difficulties in getting hold of full-time officers. Branch secretaries, shop stewards and union members make the same complaint. Many full-time officers protest that they are overworked, and some that they are overwhelmed by demands for their attention from the plants. But the studies show that these demands are not constant and universal. On the contrary, they vary almost infinitely. There are some plants where nearly every problem and dispute is passed on to the full-time officer. Nothing is done unless he does it or gives detailed instructions to the shop stewards as to what they should do. At the other extreme there are plants at which no full-time officer is seen except by invitation of the stewards, and their invitation is rarely extended to him, although he may keep in touch with them by phone and at union meetings. In between come the many plants where the stewards handle most of the business, but keep in close contact with the full-time officer and call on him when they run into difficulties or to negotiate major issues. Evidently the first type of plant makes most calls on the full-time officer unless discouragement leads to apathy; and the second type makes least demand on him. But there is no reason to suppose that the existence of plant procedures and plant-wide pay structures make workplace organisations more dependent. On the contrary the case studies show several instances in which they assisted workplace organisations to be more self-reliant, reducing the demands on full-time officers in the long term, even though the negotiation of the new agreements initially made heavy claims on them.

This distinction between the immediate and the long-term effects of the reform of collective bargaining may help to explain why the members of the Donovan Commission thought as they did, for they buttressed their assertion of the need for more full-time officers by reference to the early experience of productivity bargaining. 'Already the experience of trade union officers responsible for major productivity agreements,' they wrote, 'has been that they take up a great deal of time, and that they sometimes involve frequent meetings with stewards and their members....'[18] It seems that they were concentrating on the immediate impact of reform, and neglecting the long-term effects.

There remains a puzzle, however. If the immediate impact is to increase the full-time officer's load, if there has been a rapid growth in the number of these agreements in recent years, and if the number of full-time officers has remained static, how have these officers been able to carry the burden? The case studies suggest an answer by showing that the negotiation of this type of agreement made heavy claims upon the full-time officer only in certain plants. In others the burden was carried by the shop stewards. This finding is confirmed by the Department of Employment's survey of eleven large undertakings, entitled *The Reform of Collective Bargaining at Plant and Company Level*, which

[18] *Ibid.*, p. 189.

reported that 'on the union side, the main burden at almost all stages of the move to plant bargaining fell upon chief lay officials' (senior stewards or convenors).[19] It is therefore reasonable to infer that reliance upon senior stewards to cope with many of the new agreements helped to keep the demands upon full-time officers within bounds.

If most of the long-term burden and much of the immediate burden of the reform of collective bargaining has been borne by senior stewards and other lay officers rather than by full-time officers, it would seem to follow that it has been possible for the ratio of full-time officers to members to remain roughly stable because there has been a substantial increase in the time given to industrial relations in the plant by shop stewards. The studies point to a fairly rapid and continuing growth in the number of convenors, senior stewards, lay branch secretaries and other lay union officers who are paid by employers to give most or all of their time to union business. The Donovan surveys suggested that there were something like 1,750 British trade unionists in this position in 1966, when it was estimated that there might be rather more than 3,000 full-time officers. In 1974 it is as good a guess as any that the full-time laymen may now outnumber the full-time officers.

All this must not be taken to suggest that there has not been an increasing demand from the plants for the services of full-time officers. In some instances the increase cannot be doubted. Where the scope for workplace bargaining has been increased in plants with dependent workplace organisations, the burden has to be carried by a full-time officer unless there is an external lay officer to take the load, and the studies suggest that far more often than not there is none. The introduction of incentive schemes into local government and hospitals provides an example where much of the burden of an extension of the scope for workplace bargaining has fallen on the full-time officers of the relevant unions. It need not always be so. The Hambridge study

[19] Published 1971, p. 84.

showed that a local authority shop steward could learn to maintain a work-studied incentive which had been negotiated by his full-time officer; and the study of the Public Employees described an ambulance steward who had learned to negotiate incentive schemes so admirably that he left nothing for his full-time officer to do but sign the agreements. This may be the pattern of the future, but for some time to come the spread of incentive payments is likely to increase the load on the full-time officers in these services.

Equally the evidence of the case studies must not be taken to imply that British unions do not need more full-time officers. Perhaps the greatest need is to be found in plants which have so far been little affected by the reform of collective bargaining—the relatively small plants, the ill-organised plants and the plants which for other reasons have failed to develop strong workplace organisations. Some of these plants are able to call on the help of a lay branch secretary or a convenor from a nearby plant, but the majority of them cannot have effective trade unionism without the attention and support of a full-time officer. The study of the Tailors and Garment Workers showed a full-time officer who was able to pay regular and fairly frequent visits to all the small plants in his charge, but this is not the general picture revealed by the studies, although the areas for study were selected by the unions themselves, and it was certainly not their intention to reveal themselves at their worst. Some of the studies mentioned plants with weak workplace organisations—or none at all—which rarely or never received a visit from a full-time officer. It may not be an exaggeration to say that there are millions of employees in Britain, both trade unionists and non-unionists, who cannot enjoy effective trade unionism unless more full-time officers are appointed to service them. But if that is the assignment given to additional full-time officers, they will be engaged in duties very different from those envisaged by the Donovan Commission for the officers whose appointment they advocated.

If the Donovan Commission were wrong in thinking that the negotiation and maintenance of plant procedures and pay structures required a substantial addition to the number of full-time officers, perhaps they were also wrong in predicting that these procedures and pay structures would 'close the gap between head office and shop stewards, and between full-time officers and members'. For the gap was to be closed by increased co-operation between the full-time officer and the workplace organisation in carrying through a task in which both of them were needed, and the evidence shows that in some instances the full-time officer is hardly needed at all, and in others the need for him arises in the negotiation of the agreement but not in its subsequent operation.

If true, this is an important conclusion. For some considerable time British governments, whether Conservative or Labour, most politicians, most managers and some trade union leaders have held that a major defect of British trade unions is their failure to exert sufficient control over their workplace organisations. For them 'closing the gap' implies increasing the control of the full-time officer over the workplace organisations with which he deals. If the application of the Donovan Commission's proposals is shown not to have this effect, then for them the Donovan Report must be a failure. But perhaps the evidence which reveals the shortcomings of the Donovan proposals can also be used to suggest other ways of closing the gap?

There is little a union can do to stop a self-reliant workplace organisation settling for itself, without reference to anyone else besides the plant management, those items of business which are left for decision in the plant. So long as the decision suits the workers and managers in the plant, full-time officers, district committees and national headquarters usually have little choice but to accept it. Consequently a union cannot easily withdraw independence from a workplace organisation which has already learned self-reliance. Admittedly some managers and full-time officers co-operate in a style of plant bargaining which prevents workplace organisations achieving independence, but it would be a far more onerous task to impose this style of bargaining on a workplace organisation that had achieved independence, and the studies record no instance where this had been done.

On the other hand, in co-operation with employers, unions can limit the business left for decision in the plant by means of a collective agreement at a higher level. In most public services and nationalised industries, and in a few private industries, the scope for workplace bargaining is fairly narrowly limited by relatively tight industry agreements; and there are also some company agreements in multi-plant companies which have a similar effect. Such agreements do not destroy the independence of the workplace organisation, but they limit the scope for its application and thus transfer authority to higher levels of union organisation.

It appears to follow that governments, managers and union leaders concerned to increase the authority of the higher levels of union organisation over plant industrial relations should concern themselves, not with the independence of workplace organisations, but with the scope for workplace bargaining. But is this realistic? The powerloading agreement may show what can be done in a public service, but can private industries be expected to negotiate and maintain a comparable centralisation of collective bargaining? Whatever their mistakes, the Donovan Commission convincingly demonstrated the close link between the decline in the regulatory effects of industry collective agreements in private employment and the increasing power of workplace organisations. Can that process be reversed? It seems improbable. Most employers' associations now lack the authority over their members which would be needed to negotiate and operate a tight industry agreement, and there is little prospect of their getting it back.

But some multi-plant companies negotiate and maintain tight company agreements. Most large plants now belong to multi-plant companies, and workplace independence is a characteristic of large plants. Consequently a general move to multi-plant company agreements could lead to a widespread and substantial reduction in the scope for workplace bargaining open to these workplace organisations. However, this method of centralising authority in the unions is not available just for the asking. The structure of collective bargaining is closely associated with the structure of management. A centralised company agreement requires centralised company personnel policies, and centralised managerial authority in labour matters. Consequently an alteration in the distribution of trade union authority along these lines depends upon managers at least as much as it does upon the unions.

Perhaps, therefore, if the Donovan Commission had been able to carry their analysis further, they would not have left it open to companies to decide whether 'to negotiate company agreements rather than allow each factory manager to negotiate separately'.[20] Instead they might have expressed a strong preference for company agreements, and argued that it is the duty of multi-plant companies to work towards company agreements, and to make whatever changes in the structure of managerial authority may be required to ensure that the agreements operate effectively. Had they modified their argument in this way, however, they might have been accused of inhibiting the development of industrial democracy. They professed that their 'proposals for the reform of collective bargaining ... will do more than could any other change to allow workers and their representatives to exercise a positive influence in the running of the undertakings in which they work'.[21] But if company agreements transfer authority to the higher levels of trade union organisation they thereby reduce the direct influence of

[20] *Donovan Report*, p. 41.
[21] *Ibid.*, p. 257.

workplace organisations over the running of the undertakings in which their members work; and thus restrict
industrial democracy.

However, as several of the studies showed, the issues are
not as simple and clear-cut as that. They indicated that
workplace organisations which lack the resources to sustain
independence over the whole range of possible issues for
workplace settlement, may nevertheless learn to be self-
reliant within the scope for workplace action allowed by
relatively tight company or industry agreements. Moreover,
such workplace organisations may be positively encouraged
to exercise an influence on the running of their undertakings by provisions in these company and industry agreements enjoining plant managers and workplace organisations to settle a range of matters specified in the agreement,
commonly including incentive payments and many issues
concerning the organisation of work. The most notable
example was the railways, where the system of local departmental committees spread participation in bargaining more
widely among relatively small workplace organisations than
appeared to be the case in other industries. This finding
tallies with the results of the Donovan surveys in which
samples of workplace representatives from six major unions
were presented with a list of 28 issues amenable to workplace bargaining and asked whether or not they dealt with
them. The Railwaymen's representatives replied that they
'discussed and settled as a regular practice' a far higher
proportion of the issues on the list than was claimed by
the shop stewards of any of the five other unions. Half the
Railwaymen replied that they regularly handled eleven or
more of the listed items, whereas the proportion regularly
handling this many issues in the other unions was 27 per
cent and in none of them did it rise as high as 30 per cent.[22]
It could therefore be inferred that the effect of relatively
tight company agreements on the influence of workplace

[22] Government Social Survey, *Workplace Industrial Relations*, 1968,
p. 29.

organisations in the running of their undertakings may be in two different directions. Whereas in comparison with loose industry agreements or unfettered plant bargaining they limit the scope for independent workplace organisations to bargain on their own, they may support and encourage less well-endowed workplace organisations to make full and effective use of the margin for workplace action which the agreement allows them.

This final chapter has been given the form of a critique of some of the proposals of the Donovan Report in order to bring out the implications of our findings for those whose job it is to devise policies and make recommendations. In brief, these implications are: that the rapid growth of formal plant procedures and plant pay structures has not created a greatly increased demand for the services of full-time union officers in the plant since workplace representatives have shouldered much of the burden, and in some instances most or all of it; that these new agreements have not 'closed the gap' between workplace and union; that, if a greater concentration of authority at higher levels of union organisation is thought to be desirable, it cannot be achieved by attempting to reduce self-reliant workplace organisations to dependence on their full-time officers in the conduct of workplace business, but it might be attained by company agreements limiting the scope for workplace bargaining; that, to be effective, such agreements would need to be accompanied by a centralisation of authority within the companies; and, finally, that even though agreements on these lines would limit the scope for workplace industrial democracy in plants with self-reliant workplace organisations, they might encourage and support a greater degree of workplace industrial democracy than at present exists where workplace organisations are weak.

Traditional studies of trade unions concentrated on their formal structure – branches, districts, regions and head offices. More recently the emphasis has been on shop stewards and workplace organisations. But little information has been available about the links between union and workplace. This book aims to fill the gap.

Twenty case studies in fourteen unions reveal the wide range of relationships between trade unions and their workplace organisations. District committees and branches are important links in some unions, but in most of them the key figure is the full-time officer. In some plants workplace negotiations are handled almost entirely by workplace representatives, whereas in others the full-time officer is called in on almost every issue; and there are instances of almost every possible variation between these extremes. Moreover, the whole range of variations can be found within a single union.

These findings demand an explanation. Two features of the relationship between workplace and union are selected for analysis: the degree of dependence of the workplace organisation upon the union, and the scope for workplace bargaining. Among the influences on dependence the most important is shown to be the size of the workplace organisation, although the style of dealings between managers and full-time officers can also